BENEATH THE SCARS

MASTERS OF THE SHADOWLANDS
BOOK 13

CHERISE SINCLAIR

VanScoy Publishing Group

Beneath the Scars
Copyright © 2018 by Cherise Sinclair
ISBN: 978-1-947219-09-0
Published by VanScoy Publishing Group
Cover Artist: April Martinez

ACKNOWLEDGMENTS

So many hugs go to Bianca Sommerland, Monette Michaels, and Fiona Archer for being the best crit partners ever. Love you guys.

Thanks to Ruth Reid, Barb Jack, Lisa White, and Marian Shulman for beta reading the manuscript—and making me laugh at my bloopers and your comments. Y'all are *amazing*.

A big shout-out goes to Red Quill Editing's editors for their meticulous work in making this book the best it can be.

My Shadowkittens—oh, what can I say? Thanks to you all for demanding Master Holt's story and for all the inspiration, ideas, hot pictures, serious conversations, and laugh-out-loud fun. And hugs and kisses to Lisa Simo-Kinzer, the most tactful person I've ever met.

For Autumn: Master Z says *thank you* for the Cops 'n' Robbers theme.

A big hug—and much sympathy—to Leagh Christensen for trying to ride herd on a group of kittehs. You rock, girl!

Finally, if you've enjoyed the recent Shadowlands T-shirts, the credit goes to Niki Ellis for her brilliant designs. *Muah!*

TO MY READERS

The books I write are fiction, not reality, and as in most romantic fiction, the romance is compressed into a very, very short time period.

You, my darlings, live in the real world, and I want you to take a little more time in your relationships. Good Doms don't grow on trees, and there are some strange people out there. So while you're looking for that special Dom, please, be careful.

When you find him, realize he can't read your mind. Yes, frightening as it might be, you're going to have to open up and talk to him. And you listen to him, in return. Share your hopes and fears, what you want from him, what scares you spitless. Okay, he may try to push your boundaries a little—he's a Dom, after all—but you will have your safe word. You will have a safe word, am I clear? Use protection. Have a back-up person. Communicate.

Remember: safe, sane, and consensual.

Know that I'm hoping you find that special, loving person who will understand your needs and hold you close.

And while you're looking or even if you have already found your dearheart, come and hang out with the Masters of the Shadowlands.

Love,
Cherise

CHAPTER ONE

W hy was her kick-ass heroine drooling over the hero as if he was an ooey-gooey-chocolate chewy? Grumbling under her breath, Josephine Collier stepped out of her car. The half-written book was a teen fantasy—not a love story. Why couldn't her heroine understand that romances rarely turned into happy endings? *Honestly.*

Then again, teens were naïve. Not to mention stubborn.

Her soon-to-be-a-teenager son jumped out of the car.

Definitely stubborn.

"Groceries, honey," she reminded him as he turned toward the house, and his long-suffering sigh made her snicker. She ruffled his light brown hair. "My child, you sound as if Darth Vader has been torturing you with long needles."

"Mo-om."

Three years ago, he'd loved helping with each and every chore. Now...well, now he was eleven years old and ever so jaded with life.

Grinning, Josie picked up a sack and glanced next door at the one-story duplex where her great-aunt, Stella Avery, lived. Where would Josie and Carson be without the wonderful woman? In fact, she'd become so beloved that Josie and Carson called her *Oma*, German for grandmother.

The bright tropical sun on white stucco made Josie squint, but she could see the driveway on the right side was empty. Oma must be at her Friday afternoon bridge club—her first recreational outing after spraining her ankle three weeks ago. After "serving time" in the rehab hospital, her great-aunt was thrilled to resume her busy social life.

Josie trotted up the porch steps and into her rent-with-option-to-buy house. Although the bungalow was close to forty years old, she hadn't thought twice about signing the contract. Oma was getting older, and Josie needed to be close enough to help out.

She and Carson had only moved in a few days ago, and she already loved the place.

After weaving her way through the unpacked boxes, she set her sack on a kitchen counter.

Following, Carson left his groceries on the table, grabbed a bag of chips, and attempted a get-away to his room.

She cleared her throat. "There are several more sacks in the trunk. Please bring them in while I put stuff away."

This time, she got his patented eye-roll.

She smothered her smile and said worriedly, "Oh, honey...if you do that hard enough, your eyes might pop out and fall onto the floor."

Shocked, he paused for a whole second before catching on. Although he didn't quite suppress a snort of laughter, he still managed to look put-upon as he stalked out the door.

She shook her head. Sometime in the last few months, her affectionate, funny, sweet son had been replaced by a moody adolescent. Wasn't puberty supposed to occur later? More like thirteen or so? She wanted to bang her head on the wall and wail, *I'm not ready*.

Then again, according to her friends, no parent was prepared for the angel-to-demon transformation.

Ah, well, she'd cope. She'd had a fair amount of practice in surviving whatever the universe threw at her. By herself.

A wave of loneliness swept over her along with the longing for someone beside her. Uh-uh. Not going there. *Remember how well being involved with a guy worked in the past?*

Besides, she had no time for anyone. Not if she wanted to write for a living someday. Even though the four books she'd written were selling well, they didn't bring in enough for her to quit her bartending job.

And she needed to keep things uncomplicated for her son, especially this year. Poor Carson. His transition from elementary to middle school in September had been...difficult. Now, he had the added trauma of moving away from the apartment complex and his buddies there. Losing friends and having to go through unexpected changes hurt; she'd suffered through those changes herself.

Seeing her baby unhappy was even more painful. Everything inside her wanted to help, to make it better.

Had he been more resilient when younger? Like when he first learned to walk? He'd been so adorable. Shaggy hair falling into his bright eyes. Adorable red overalls. Knees bow-legged from the diaper. An infectious giggle when he took three steps. A heartrending wail when he toppled over.

Falls and scraped knees could be quickly cured with hugs and kisses. It wasn't so easy to ease the anguish of not being invited to a birthday party or sitting alone in the school cafeteria—and mommies were supposed to be able to mend everything.

Dammit. Her heart ached for him. Sadly, the best she could offer was stability and safety. A listening ear. And all the love in the world.

After stowing the groceries, she looked around. Where were the other sacks?

With a sigh, she walked outside. Car trunk open, groceries still there. Missing: one boy.

Aaaaand, he'd wandered next door and was talking to the tenant of the other half of Oma's duplex.

Standing with his back to Josie, the man was pointing to parts of his huge black and red motorcycle. The bike was a Harley, according to Carson, who seemed to think a motorcycle was the gateway to heaven.

Uh-huh.

Every mother in the world knew a motorcycle was the gateway to the emergency room.

Even worse, men who rode motorcycles could be...questionable. Would Carson be safe around this neighbor?

Crossing her arms over her chest, she gave him a good looking-over...and got a bit short of breath.

Oh...*wow*.

The man was tall and lean. His faded, ripped jeans covered long powerful legs. A faded black T-shirt stretched over a broad muscular back. Circling his biceps, black and red tattoos were only partially covered by the sleeves. Muscles bunched in his shoulders as he stood the bike up to show Carson something. His dark blond hair was long enough to touch his collar.

Pure man-candy and definitely on the scruffy side. A black leather motorcycle vest had been tossed over a handlebar.

Her eyes narrowed. Carson was off for Thanksgiving vacation or he would have been in class. Shouldn't this man be at work on a Friday? What did he do for a living? Then again, many people took time off at Thanksgiving.

Oma said the guy had assumed the lease from the previous tenant, Uzuri. Surely the property managers had done a background check and confirmed he was gainfully employed and all that. If nothing else, he'd managed to afford an SUV and a motorcycle.

Looking past the driveway, Josie noticed that the flowers Uzuri had planted in the front door pots were dead. How could he have let the defenseless plants die?

4

No, she probably didn't want her boy over there. "Carson," she called, picking up a grocery sack. "Let's finish this up."

Her son turned...and so did the man.

Her stomach tightened. A partially healed, red slash ran from his left temple, through his scruffy beard, to his jaw. A yellow bruise decorated his right cheekbone. More nasty cuts covered his forearms.

She stiffened. Maybe she was jumping to conclusions, but as a bartender, she'd seen far too many brawls. The man had been in a knife fight.

And he was talking to her son. Fear sharpened her voice. "Carson, *now*."

With a sullen pout, Carson trudged toward her, so obviously unwilling she wanted to shake him.

To her dismay, the man accompanied him. He was a good six feet tall.

Taking a step back, she looked up and into eyes the blue-gray of Tampa Bay just before dawn.

"Your son says you've moved in next door. Welcome to the neighborhood." He had a mesmerizingly smooth, deep voice.

His greeting was polite. Friendly. But, but, but... *Biker. Fighting. Knives.* She took another step back, and her response came out thin and unfriendly. "Thank you."

His expression went blank. "I'm called Holt." He waited a beat for her to introduce herself, then glanced at the car where Carson was pulling out sacks. Rather than offering to help— which, honestly, she'd have refused—he nodded at her boy. "Nice meeting you, Carson."

As the guy headed for his house, Carson stared at her. "Wow, Mom, way to be rude."

She *had* been, no doubt about it. When she looked over her shoulder, the black motorcycle in the driveway seemed to grow in size with her fears. "Maybe, but I want you to stay away from him."

"Mo-om, why?"

She grabbed the last sack and slammed the trunk shut. "Because I said so."

Even as the words left her mouth, she winced. Throughout her childhood, her father had shouted that rejoinder whenever she'd asked why. When Carson was born, she'd sworn she would be a better parent than her father.

Her son stomped into the house, muttering, "I'll talk with him if I want to."

She stared after him, and her shoulders slumped.

Good job of parenting, Josie. FAIL.

Jesus, the woman had looked at him as if his face was rotting off. Thoroughly annoyed, Alexander Sullivan Holt stalked into his half of the one-story duplex.

As he closed the door, a deluge of memories froze him in place. *"Bastard! She's* mine.*" A knife drove into Holt's upper back. Holt spun and cold burning pain slashed his face. He punched. Connected. Even as the man bellowed in anger, warm liquid poured down Holt's face—and more flowed down his back. Blood. A fiery pain blossomed over his shoulder blade.*

After a second, he managed to pull in a breath and shake off the flashback. *Hell.* The slices on his gut and back were burning as if brand new—no, the pain was simply because every muscle in his body had tensed.

He moved on into his place. It was a shame his new neighbor hated the sight of him...because he'd enjoyed looking at her. Although he liked long hair on a woman, her short jagged cut was damned cute, reminding him of a sprite or pixie or something. And the color—like burnished copper with lighter gold streaks—was amazing. Green eyes. Freckles sprinkled over her face and arms. Very Irish, he'd guess. She had an average sized, sturdy body, and rather than artificially glamorous, she seemed refreshingly real.

And direct. She sure hadn't hidden the fact that she wanted

her kid to stay well away from him. He'd never thought a soft Texas accent could contain so much ice. Of course, he had to appreciate a woman who looked out for her cub—he'd seen too many who didn't.

Still... It sucked to be looked at as if he was Freddy Krueger.

After punching up a Disturbed album, hearing the first strains of "The Sound of Silence", he wandered into his small kitchen and pulled out a beer. It was only early afternoon, but he didn't give a damn. He downed half of it in a long series of gulps.

Pausing for a breath, he studied the bottle for a moment before emptying it into the sink. Maybe he was screwed up—and so ugly he made pretty redheads turn pale—but alcohol wasn't the answer.

He should eat something instead. Not that he was hungry.

His cell phone rang from somewhere in the living room.

After a short search, he located the damn thing beside his recliner. With luck, the caller wouldn't be a reporter. It'd been a couple weeks or so since he'd been sliced up like mincemeat, and the news services surely must consider him old news.

The display read *Uzuri*. He swiped *ANSWER*. "Hey."

"Oh, good. I called earlier, and you didn't answer. Where are you?" Uzuri continued without pausing for air. "Are you still at Jake and Rainie's house? Or—"

Holt grinned. She really was his favorite female friend. "I'm in your place, although I should probably call it *my* duplex now. Thank you, and thank your Doms for moving my stuff from my apartment. I know you couldn't have had much spare time before your vacation." Alastair and Max had taken her to their family's ranch up in Colorado.

"Pffft, there wasn't much to do. Your moving company handled almost everything."

"And you unpacked it all. I noticed." Before all this shit happened, he'd been living in Uzuri's duplex while his apartment complex was being remodeled. After the attack, Uzuri had moved in permanently with her men, and Holt assumed her lease.

She'd called him crazy, since this was where her stalker had almost knifed him to death. He rubbed the scar on his cheek carefully. Maybe he was insane, but damned if he'd let his choices be limited by memories of that asshole.

He added, "I also appreciate that you took care of the cleanup." There'd been broken glass and his blood all over the place.

Her voice went thin. "Max's fellow cops knew of companies that handle...stuff."

"*Stuff?* You're such a girl. The company did a good job."

"I'm glad. When did you get back? I can't believe Rainie let you leave already."

His best friend's woman had thrown a fit, actually, predicting he'd die before he got through two stoplights. "This morning. Rainie fed me before I left." Then he'd taken a fucking long nap once he got here.

"Do you have food? We get back tomorrow, so I can bring some over Sunday, but if you're out, I can call some of the—"

"Zuri, I'm fine. Relax and enjoy your last day of Thanksgiving vacation. How's Colorado?" Holt sat down carefully, gritting his teeth over the sharp burn. Next time he got knifed, he'd request either the back or the gut. Not both. No matter how he moved, something felt as if it was ripping.

"Oh, Holt, the Drago ranch is huge. They have horses and are teaching me to ride. Both their dads are amazing, and everybody's so nice and not even freaked out about them both being with me. Their cousins told me Max and Alastair shared everything all their lives, so why would they ever stop?"

"I'm glad." And he was. Little Zuri deserved everything good, and the Drago cousins would make sure she had it. Good Doms; good men. Gave a man hope for his gender.

Before he'd been sliced and diced, he thought he'd found himself a sweetie like Uzuri.

Life was full of disappointments.

He shook that thought off and smiled as he listened to her descriptions of ranch life. So cute and so in love. "Do me a favor and don't pull any of your jokes while you're there, okay? You're supposed to be good."

"I am. Besides, Max said if I was bad, I'd be liable to find a rattler in my bed." She huffed. "They wouldn't, Holt, I'm sure they wouldn't...would they?"

He bit the inside of his cheek. "Oh, well, I'm sure they wouldn't." He made his tone singularly non-convincing. And didn't bother to mention that snakes were never aboveground in cold weather.

Her pitiful whine made him bust out laughing.

After more chatting, promising to behave himself, and refusing her offer of sending a bunch of submissives to care for him, he ended the call and leaned back.

He needed another nap.

His endurance was definitely shot. But, fuck, he was tired of sitting around, feeling puny and sorry for himself. There'd be no immediate cure, either. The chief at the fire station told him not to even try to show up for another couple of weeks. Human Resources for his second job as a pediatric ICU nurse said the same thing.

With the surgeon's eight pound lifting restrictions, he hadn't even been able to help his neighbor carry in her groceries. Hell, she'd probably have screamed and run if he'd offered.

He ran his finger down the long scar from beside his eye to his jaw. Here was irony. When younger, his pretty boy face had seriously affected his life. He'd barely escaped being raped more than once. Had almost gotten sold as a prostitute. Later, he'd earned a living as a model.

Few people saw past his surface to the man beneath, and he'd hated his good looks. Now he looked like someone fresh out of a war zone and hated that, too. *That's me, shallower than a California creek during the drought.*

In the hospital, his now ex-girlfriend, Nadia had stared at his ripped-up face, turned green, and hadn't even approached his bed. Her unexpected revulsion had been a kick in the teeth. He'd thought she was the *one*. That they had something special.

He leaned his head back against the chair. *No, dumbass, it hadn't been special, or she would have stuck with you.* She would've had tears in her eyes and rushed over to the bed. Instead, she'd told him she was late meeting her friend for happy hour.

Well, he'd learned a lesson about surface appearances, hadn't he? With his schedule at the fire station and the hospital, their time together had been limited—and lightweight. He'd always seen her at her best, never in a challenging situation.

He was a Dom; she was vanilla, so he'd only indulged in mildly kinky sex with her. He'd never tested her boundaries or pushed for more; otherwise, he might have discovered she was showing him only her good side.

With a grunt of exasperation, he pushed himself to his feet. Yeah, he'd been stupid. When it came down to it, he wanted a D/s relationship. While D/s in sex was a must, he also enjoyed the dynamic as a quiet, underlying thread in daily life. He didn't need a slave, but he'd prefer more than bedroom kink.

Guess Nadia had done him a favor, when it came down to it. Yeah, his heart had gotten scorched, but he'd recover. Eventually.

Now, he should move his ass and find something to eat. The surgeon's nurse had lectured him on the need for a balanced diet. Appetite or not, he didn't want a delay in returning to work. Sitting around was boring as hell, and his house was empty and silent. Times like this were a wretched reminder that he had no family left in the world.

Then again, he had great friends.

In the kitchen, he opened the fridge and saw nearly empty

shelves. Zuri and her Doms must have tossed the perishables. Good thing or he'd have been fleeing from green mold and toxic waste.

He had nothing to eat. Rainie had wanted to send food with him, but he'd accepted enough generosity.

As he started to close the door, he noticed a GET WELL card propped against the mustard. Funny place to leave a card.

He opened the card and half-smiled at the scrawling sentiments covering the inside. "Welcome home, Holt!" "We miss you!" "Get well soon!" "The Shadowlands isn't the same without you!" "Call if you need anything!" All from his friends—the Shadowlands Masters and their submissives, the Shadowkittens.

The bottom of the card read: "Food is in the freezer. Eat!"

What food? He opened the freezer door.

Ziploc bags and plastic containers filled the small freezer section. He pulled one out. "*Mexican casserole. Love you, Andrea.*" Another. "*Stuffed pork chops. Love you, Sally.*" Every single one of the 'kittens had left at least one dinner.

Warmed by their kindness, he smiled. Nah, he didn't need or want a new woman in his life. His friends had him covered.

CHAPTER TWO

Sipping his beer slowly, Holt stretched his legs out and listened to the latest firehouse gossip. Not a bad way to spend a lazy, post-Thanksgiving Sunday after the NFL game.

Sprawled in the other chairs, his three oversized firefighter friends made his backyard patio look even smaller than it actually was. Not that he was complaining. After years of apartments, he now had an actual backyard of his own—his half of the duplex's yard.

Warren, built like a linebacker and commonly called Tank, gave Holt an assessing look. "You lost some weight, but you're looking better. When are you coming back?"

"Couple weeks. The doc wants me on light duty at first, though."

Liam, the station's token Aussie, nicknamed Oz, made a disgusted sound. "Paperwork? You'll go stark raving mad, mate."

"Yeah, I know. But it beats watching the grass grow."

As one, they turned and looked at the backyard.

To the left, a four-foot brown picket fence separated his yard from the unfriendly redhead's house. To the right, a shorter fence divided the two halves of the duplex's backyard, probably to keep dogs out of Stella Avery's half of the yard.

He couldn't blame her. Her side was a lush wonderland filled with exotic tropical flowers. Holt's side had three camellia bushes against the back fence and grass that needed mowing.

"At least grass is quiet. Beats the constant racket at your singles complex." Clancy waved his hand in the air. "I like this area."

Just north of Tampa, the residential neighborhood of older one-story homes and duplexes was comfortably middle class. It was a hard-working, friendly mix of families with children, a few singles like Holt, and seniors.

"I do, too," Holt said, "especially since the apartment next to mine had a college girl who liked boy bands."

"Jesus, you got out just in time," Tank said.

Oz motioned to a corner of the patio. "You've got room there for a nice grill. Throw a few steaks on the barbie, and you'll get company." The Aussie was one pure carnivore. "That'll keep the sound of grass growing drowned out."

"Good plan." It was a good plan, actually. Might need a few more chairs, but yeah.

Long and lanky, Clancy smoothed his thick ginger mustache and pointed at Holt's untrimmed beard. "You plan to test the department regs on shaving?" Because of the need to have a seal on the respirator facemask, firefighters couldn't have beards.

"Nah. I'm just waiting for the cuts to heal." Holt ran a finger over the slice on his jaw, then the gash on his chin. Razors and sutures—not a good combination. Even now that the stitches were out, the shaver drag on the wounds was painful. "I tell you, the next asshole I take on better use a pistol, not a knife."

Tank barked a laugh. "I'll tell the Cap to mark that in your files."

"Got some scars to impress the girls with, though." Clancy

picked up the basketball lying beside his chair and twirled it on his finger.

"Don't think that's working for me." His ex had run, and his pretty neighbor sure hadn't looked impressed. Ah, well. "Any interesting fires recently?"

All three scowled.

"What?" Holt asked.

"Someone's setting fires at the middle school down the street." Oz motioned to Clancy for the ball. "Started with dumpster fires. Last week, he lit up an equipment shed."

"Amateur efforts so far." Tank finished off his beer. "With the school staff keeping an eye out, maybe we can nip this in the bud."

"Hope so. Next time might be serious." Clancy tossed the basketball to Oz.

A chill ran up Holt's spine. The car crash that killed his father had turned into a fiery blaze, and a little girl had died. Two decades later, he still had nightmares. Screaming. Fire and children—no. Just no. "Did the arsonist use an accelerant?"

"Good old gasoline." Oz dribbled the ball a few times before setting it aside. "You gotta love firebugs who stick to the classics."

"Sure, you do." If he found some bastard lighting fires near a school, he'd be tempted to administer a classic beating.

Tank glanced to the west where the sun was setting over the palms. "Guess it's time to be moving."

"Yeah. Georgina ordered me to get my ass home in time for supper." Clancy grinned. "Although she phrased it more politely."

"You're lucky you married a sweet Southern girl instead of one of our say-it-like-it-is Aussie women." Oz rose to his feet.

As Holt walked his buddies out, he spotted Oz's Harley. It now sported a fine-looking, custom paint job of a red background with black streaks. However, harassing fellow firefighters was a mandatory pastime. "Who rode in on that ladybug on wheels?"

"Get stuffed, mate." Oz grinned. "At least mine doesn't give people nightmares."

"Nah. My pretty queen wouldn't give anyone nightmares." Holt smiled at his own bike, also painted in dark red and black. It sure didn't resemble a ladybug—the gas tank displayed the terrifying queen from the movie *Alien*. "I'm considering painting teeth on the front fender."

Clancy barked a laugh. "Some snowbird from the Midwest will see you in the rearview mirror and end up in the ditch."

"And that'd mean a call-out for us. Never mind." Holt sighed. "I miss riding." In spite of afternoon downpours and the fucking bugs, Florida was almost as fine a place to ride as California. Up Highway 98 to Crystal River? The smell and feel of ocean air couldn't be beat. And he liked country rides at night like when visiting the Shadowlands BDSM club on the weekends.

Unfortunately, the surgeon had made his bike off limits for another week.

"You'll survive," Tank noted heartlessly...because he drove a pickup.

With a sympathetic grin, Oz started his bike, and the distinctive low rumble of a Harley filled the air. Waggling his eyebrows at Holt, he revved it up loudly.

Asshole, Holt mouthed. His fingers curled with the need to take his own bike out.

Grinning, Oz peeled out, followed by the other two firefighters' vehicles.

Before Holt could move, a car pulled into his driveway.

Jesus, did I put the welcome mat out or something?

The car door opened, and Max Drago stepped out. He was one of Uzuri's Doms—and another member of the Shadowlands. After Holt's knifing, his fellow Shadowlands Masters had kept as close an eye on him as had his fire crew. Maybe closer.

Lifting a hand, Holt walked down to greet the cop.

A couple minutes ago, the sudden roar of a motorcycle had yanked Josie right out of the writing zone. In her office—a bedroom that faced the street—she'd looked up from her story to see bunch of big, over-muscled brutes in her neighbor's driveway.

As one drove his motorcycle away, he slowed to wave at someone.

Josie leaned forward and saw Carson standing in the front yard, watching the biker and his friends. She hurried to the front door and leaned out. "Carson, come *here*."

Expression sulky, he returned to the house.

She closed the door. "Didn't I ask you to stay away from that man?"

"Geez, Mom. What's the deal? He's not some effing—"

"Carson," she warned.

With a sullen look, he stomped inside and to his room. The door slammed.

Oh...damn. Returning to her office, she couldn't even remember what she'd been writing, because the full weight of mommy-guilt had landed on her shoulders. How could she explain to Carson why she didn't want him over there? Especially since she tried to teach him not to judge someone on appearance. *I'm sorry, honey, but I don't like the way Holt looks...even though he's sexy enough to make a nun drool. But you have to stay away.*

Oh, that reasoning would go over well.

What kind of a name was Holt, anyway?

There must be some way to keep Carson away from the man and his friends. Bikers and leather jackets and Harleys. Talk about irresistible appeal. If Carson started going over there, he'd soon be involved with drugs and fighting and women.

She blew her long bangs out of her eyes. *Josie, you're over-reacting.*

She was. But still... Carson was her baby. A fatherless boy

might want a man in his life but a biker was *not* a good choice. Somehow, she needed to shield Carson from such a bad influence.

Shaking her head, she sat down at the desk. Back to work. She needed to answer her reader emails and finish writing the latest scene.

She pulled up an email. The girl loved the series. Couldn't wait for the next book. And added a final paragraph: "***I think Laurent and Tigre should fall in love. Pleeeze?***" Josie huffed a laugh. Young girls were so cute.

However, they lacked insight because what would really happen would go like this: Tigre would get all kissy with Laurent. Then the rich baron's daughter would latch onto him, and he'd drop Laurent like a dead mouse.

Or after luring Laurent into falling for him, he'd notice the overly endowed tavern girl, and Laurent would trip over the two rolling around in the stable. Since Laurent was a fire-starter, she'd set the hay on fire, Josie would be out a hero, and her teenaged fans would have fits.

No. Romance. Her answering email started with "I'm sorry, but..."

With the reader emails answered, Josie dove back into her world of young heroes and fantastic powers. This was her joy—touching others through the stories she shared, connecting with them in this amazing way. The only thing that came close was listening to the stories other people told, sharing and lightening their pain.

An hour passed quietly, and a glance at the clock showed it was time for her to eat something. A long night of bartending required adequate fuel, although Sunday night after Thanksgiving should be quiet.

Someday, maybe her writing would bring in enough money to live on, and she could quit the bartending job. With each new book she put out, she earned more, but wasn't it funny how the bills rose at the same time and sucked away every drop of spare money? Carson kept growing, needing new shoes, new jeans, new everything, and he ate like a sumo wrestler.

Speaking of eating...

In the living room, bag of chips half gone, her boy was watching TV. Shaggy hair, big brown eyes, growing so fast. Such a precious gift.

He was watching an old *Star Trek* episode, and wasn't that awesome? Maybe his generation would take humans to the stars. "You know, I always wanted to be Deanna Troi." Was that because she got to have a superpower—was an empath?

"I dunno, Mom. You'd have to let your hair grow long to be Troi."

"Well, never mind then. I'd go nuts." Josie ruffled at her ear-length strands.

When Carson snickered, she grinned. It seemed she'd been forgiven for being an unreasonable mom. Then again, her boy rarely held a grudge.

After watching Kirk, McCoy, and Spock argue onscreen, she asked, "Which one of those would you want to be?"

Crunching on a chip, he considered. "Kirk gets all the fun stuff, but Mr. Spock is a lot smarter. More like me, so I'd be him, I guess."

Poor Dr. McCoy wasn't even in the running. "Good choice. I prefer the smart ones, too."

"But all the women want to be with the captain."

"Seems that way, doesn't it?" Not her. Captain Kirk was a dawg, a player. Besides, Josie didn't want any man, no matter how smart. She had a child—and how would Carson react if she started dating? Talk about complicating life. Even ignoring the truth that lust didn't magically transform into a loving, happy ever after, there was the fact that a man wouldn't want to take on a child who wasn't his.

Or even a child who was.

After wolfing down a sandwich, Josie dressed for work. Black pants, white button-up shirt, black vest, ugly bow tie. Her bartending uniform.

She shook her head ruefully. Serving drinks wasn't the job she'd dreamed about while growing up. She'd planned on college with an English or history major.

Life could sure mess with a girl's plans.

But tending bar paid fairly well, and she enjoyed the work. Even better, the night hours left her time to do what she loved best—write books.

"Carson, grab your homework. Time to go to Oma's. And do remember to help her with the dishes after you eat." She ignored his usual grumbles at having to leave his show. *Thank God for Oma.* Ever since Josie's great-aunt had returned from overseas years ago, she'd babysat Carson. When Josie bartended, Carson would spend the night at his great-great-aunt's place. The two adored each other, but as a moody pre-teen, he was obligated to complain.

Smiling, Josie handed her son his sweatshirt. The night air was cool. Here in Florida, that only meant adding a hoodie at night. In Texas, she'd have needed a heavier coat.

Before getting in her car, Josie kept an eye on her boy as he trudged past the biker's half of the duplex to the half where Oma lived. As Carson went inside, Oma leaned out the door and waved.

Josie blew her a kiss, got into her car, and made a mental note to warn Oma about keeping Carson away from the biker.

———

That night, after pulling her car into the driveway, Josie sat in the dark and seethed. Not *fair*. Maybe she should do one of those FML Facebook posts. *Fuck-My-Life* sure sounded appropriate. Sheesh, had she accidentally annoyed one of the gods in Asgard or something? Was Loki, the god of mischief, following her around and messing up her life?

How many things could go wrong this month? Carson's worsening attitude. Oma's sprained ankle. Uzuri turning over her lease to a biker of all things.

And now her boss at The Highland Whisky Lounge had fired her.

Josie saw the clock on the car dashboard and scowled. Not even nine o'clock. Her boss had sent her home before she'd even worked a couple of hours. He'd tried to justify the firing by stating her work was unsatisfactory, which was such a lie. In her three years there, she'd earned glowing evaluations. Raises. The clientele and serving staff liked her.

However, as Josie'd been leaving, the head barmaid had pulled her aside for a talk. The real reason Josie'd been dismissed had nothing to do with her work—and wasn't one she could fight. Nepotism. Looked like she'd be job-hunting tomorrow.

"Loki, if you're the one messing with my life, I'm going to kick your ass," she muttered. She got out and noticed three cars parked in front of her new neighbor's duplex. Apparently, Holt had more biker friends to entertain.

Maybe she'd kick his ass, too.

As Josie reached her front door, someone else—Uzuri—parked in front of Holt's place. It was a shame she'd moved out of the duplex. Last summer and fall, Josie'd enjoyed their occasional conversations.

Before Josie could call a greeting, Holt strolled out the front door. "Zuri."

"Hey, Holt!" Uzuri hurried across the lawn, went up on her tiptoes, and kissed his cheek. With black hair, brown skin, dancing brown eyes, and in a beautifully tailored ivory suit, she was a decided contrast to Holt with his light hair and eyes, golden tanned skin, and ripped, faded clothing. To be honest, both of them were gorgeous.

Actually... As she regarded Holt's golden good looks, Josie laughed silently. No wonder she had Loki and Asgard on her brain. Her neighbor looked just like Thor, right down to the studly body, long blond hair, and I-can-deal-out-a-world-of-hurt saunter.

Whew. She needed to reserve her imagination for her writing and not let it loose in real life. Turning, she unlocked her front door.

"Hey, hey, Josie!"

Josie turned to see Uzuri run across the lawn. How could anyone run so gracefully in high heels? That was just wrong. "Uzuri, how are you?"

Uzuri gave her a happy hug. "I was so sorry to hear about Mrs. Avery's fall, only I didn't hear about it until we were out of town and in Colorado of all places when there wasn't anything I could do to help. How is she? Do you need any help? Holt said you and Carson are living here now. Are you finished moving in? How is Carson doing?"

"Was I supposed to understand all that?" Josie laughed. "Let's see... Thank you, and I hope you had a good time. Oma's doing well. No need for help. All our stuff is here now—still mostly in boxes. Carson likes the neighborhood."

"You followed what I said? Girl, *I* don't even remember what I asked. Damn, you're impressive."

"I am. How are you?" Josie held Uzuri at arm's length to check her over. "Hey, you look really good...and happy. I'm sorry you left here though." It would have been great to be closer to Uzuri; instead, she got the thunder-god-biker as a neighbor. "Did you move to somewhere awesome?"

"Ah, in a way." Uzuri's lips curved. "I fell in love with a couple of guys and live with them now."

Josie blinked. "Uh. Two men?"

"Mmmhmm. They're inside." Uzuri took her hand. "You should come in and meet them. Where's Carson?"

"He's spending the night at Oma's." As he always did when she worked. A glance at the duplex lights showed he and Oma had gone to bed.

"Perfect. Come on." Uzuri pulled her toward Holt's front door. "You're in your bartender outfit. Aren't you home awfully early?"

"I'm not working. I mean, I lost my job."

"What?" Uzuri gasped.

"Yes. I'm afraid I wouldn't be good company right now." And she sure wasn't going to Holt's place. Josie planted her feet.

"What happened? You're the best bartender I've ever seen."

Josie's eyes stung with tears at the sweet reassurance. She must've been more shaken than she thought. "It seems being good at something doesn't always help. My boss tried to say I wasn't doing the work, but the head barmaid told me the real reason I was let go. His niece finished a weeklong bartending class and wanted my job."

"What a *scumbag*." Uzuri shook her head. "He's stupid, too. An inexperienced bartender won't do well in The Highlands."

"Probably not." The clientele was older, sophisticated, and very particular about how their drinks were made. "Then again, if she's cute and fun, maybe she'll do very well."

"Doubtful. I've been in your bar, remember?"

"How could I forget?" Uzuri and a gang of her girlfriends had visited about three months before. They'd ordered samplers of the bar food, worked their way through a ton of drinks, and had a noisily wonderful time. "I thought I was going to have to demand all y'all's car keys. But then I saw your *chauffeurs* waiting."

Several of the women's men had taken over a nearby table, perfectly content to sip drinks and watch their ladies get plastered. Every time the females burst into laughter, the men would exchange pleased smiles. It had been heartwarmingly sweet.

Uzuri laughed. "It's really nice to have our own private taxi service. We're pretty spoiled."

"You really are." Josie eyed her. "And you have two *drivers* of your own?"

"I do." Uzuri didn't release her grip on Josie's hand. "You don't want to sit at home and stew about your jerk of a boss. Come and meet my guys, and let me serve *you* a drink for a change."

Josie rolled her eyes. "Uzuri, you don't live here anymore. You're not supposed to invite people to—"

"My house is her house." Holt's voice drifted through the night, as dark and smooth as black velvet.

Josie stiffened and saw him still standing at his front door.

A corner of his mouth rose...and his eyes stayed cool. "If you haven't learned yet, Zuri rarely loses an argument."

When he gestured toward the front door, Josie capitulated and followed Uzuri inside. In the entry, she stopped to look around.

Blue tile flooring opened into a living room filled with a slate gray sectional, massive flat-screen television, and black marble-topped end tables. A beautiful abstract painting in metallic blues and grays hung over a filled bookcase. Clean and contemporary. Not the biker pigsty she'd expected at all. Where was the clutter of beer cans, takeout meals, and stinky socks?

Bad Josie. How had she fallen into the mistake of stereotyping someone by his appearance?

"Everyone's on the back patio." Holt led the way to the rear of the house.

Taking Josie's hand again, Uzuri tugged her through the kitchen and out the back door. Contemporary black-finish solar lights circled the patio. The soft light revealed three men who rose when Josie and Uzuri walked out.

"Josie," Uzuri said. "Let me introduce my guys. This is Max Drago. He's a police detective."

Josie nodded at him. "It's good to meet you."

Over six feet tall, the hard-faced man had penetrating blue eyes that took her in quickly. "And you."

Uzuri put her arm around an even taller man. "This is Max's cousin, Alastair Drago. He's a pediatrician."

24

He wore his hair short, and a perfectly trimmed beard outlined his strong jaw. His brown face was a shade darker than Uzuri's, setting off his disconcertingly light hazel eyes. "It's good to make your acquaintance, Josie." He offered his hand, and she blinked at the distinct British accent.

"I'm pleased to meet you both." Josie shook his hand. "I love seeing Uzuri looking so happy."

Smiles appeared on both men's faces.

"That's our job," Max told her, and he looked quite serious.

Standing between her two men, Uzuri gestured to the third man. "Josie Collier, this is um...Zachary Grayson. He's a psychologist."

Josie frowned. Uzuri had sounded rather uncertain over the introduction; admittedly, the man was intimidating. He was older, lean and fit, his black hair silvered at the sides. Like Alastair, he wore tailored pants and a black shirt with the sleeves rolled up.

"I'm pleased to meet you." He offered his hand, and as they shook, he held her gaze. "In fact, I believe I've seen you before. Perhaps at The Highlands?"

She blinked and realized he'd been one of the men waiting for Uzuri's girl-party to end. "Yes. Your lady was the pretty blonde?"

"Yes. The very intoxicated pretty blonde. She giggled all the way home." His smile showed he wasn't put out in the least.

"They did have fun." So much that she'd been a bit envious.

He still had her hand in his, and before she could react, he'd seated her in the chair he'd been using.

"But this is—"

"Your seat now," he said firmly.

"Holt, put that chair down," Alastair said in a clipped voice.

Holt was carrying out a chair from the kitchen.

Making tsking sounds, Max took the chair and placed it beside Josie.

"Nothing like being surrounded by mother hens." Holt's wry smile indicated he wasn't truly upset. "Josie, wine, beer, or water?"

"A beer would be wonderful."

"A lady after my own heart." After bringing her a beer, he sat down beside Alastair and asked about their vacation.

Zachary took the chair beside Josie. After taking a sip of his drink, he spoke quietly, "You looked quite comfortable behind the bar at the Highlands. What is it like being a female bartender? Are you treated differently from a male?"

Trust a psychologist to ask an interesting question. "Hmm. Not really. In the past, perhaps there was more of a difference. The change is probably more noticeable for male bartenders. Their female customers are now as"—she probably shouldn't say *obnoxious*—"aggressive as my male customers."

"One of my bartender buddies often complains about how often he's getting groped these days." The low smoky sound of Holt's chuckle sent a shiver over her.

"There's progress. We now have equal opportunity groping." Max shook his head. "Male or female, touching without permission is sexual assault."

That's right; the man was in law enforcement. No wonder he looked so tough.

"True enough." She smiled at him. "Smart bartenders quickly master the ancient art of the side-step."

Zachary considered her. "Aside from serving excellent drinks and dodging straying hands, are there any particular bartending objectives you set for yourself?"

Another unusual question. She rolled the bottle of beer between her hands, trying to find the right words. "Speed, since no one should have to wait long for a drink. Courtesy, of course. But also, beyond the alcohol, to be there to...I guess...just listen, especially to the ones who don't have someone with them."

She realized the other conversations had stopped.

"You treat single customers differently than people with dates?" Holt asked.

"Dates or friends." She bit her lip. "Some people who drink

alone come in merely to be around others. Some need a person to listen to them or to laugh at their jokes or just…see them." She often had customers during the quiet hours who'd come in to sit at the bar and share their day.

"You see that as part of your job?" Zachary asked quietly.

"Not every bartender does. I do." Or did. Who knew where her next job would be? She looked down, saw her bow tie, pulled it off, and stuffed it in her pocket.

"At least you won't have to wear that ugly bow tie any longer." Uzuri said to Zachary, "Z, would you believe her stupid boss fired her? The guy's niece is fresh out of bartending school with no experience whatsoever, and he gave her Josie's hours."

"Indeed."

"At The Highlands?" Holt frowned. "The girl is in for a rough time."

Her neighbor was correct. Despite years of experience—and a superior memory—Josie had struggled for her first few weeks. "My boss thinks he's doing her a favor."

"Will you wait until she fails or go in search of a new position?" Alastair asked.

"I'll be searching. I'm sure I'll find something soon." Actually, job-hunting might not be easy. She only worked part-time and had certain…standards…as to where she'd work. She smiled. "I'd rather hear about how you two met Uzuri."

"Ah, well." Uzuri shifted her feet.

Josie brightened. Sounded like there was a story here…

Max said, "I met her at a party where a couple was celebrating the adoption of two young boys. Zuri didn't like me at all."

"You were pushy." Uzuri sniffed. "You both were. Are."

Alastair's grin was wide. "Quite correct."

Josie watched them banter. How wonderful that Uzuri had found a man—men—who were so amazing. But a party introduction shouldn't make Uzuri embarrassed. "How did you meet Alastair?"

Uzuri's skin darkened with a flush.

Josie grinned. There it was.

Zachary said easily, "I believe a friend of mine saw Uzuri's interest in Alastair and introduced them." The amusement in his gaze showed he knew why Josie asked.

When Uzuri let out a relieved sigh, Josie pointed at her. "Just you wait. I'll get you alone without all this protection and worm the real story out of you."

"You can try, snoopy-pants," Uzuri said, and a giggle escaped.

Oh, I will. "I better get on home." Josie rose and set her beer on the table. Somehow, she'd downed it all—and now had a nice buzzing in her veins. She leaned down to hug Uzuri. "I'm glad I got to see you."

"Me too."

Josie smiled at Uzuri's two men. "It was wonderful to meet you both." She looked at Holt. He was nicer than she'd thought and had good friends. But she still didn't want her boy around a biker. Her voice cooled slightly. "Holt, thank you for the beer."

His expression closed off. "Any time."

Zachary rose to his feet. "I also need to return home. Holt, I'm pleased to see you recuperating so well. You are missed."

"Good to hear, Z. And no worries about scheduling. I'll be back next weekend."

Z, huh? That was a unique kind of nickname.

"Excellent." The man looked at the Drago cousins.

Max lifted his glass. "We're on Saturday, Z. See you then."

Z's gaze turned to Josie. "I'll walk you to your door."

"There's no need."

"Of course there is." He lifted an eyebrow and motioned for her to precede him.

Well, okay then. It seems she had an escort. Here was a man accustomed to providing old-fashioned chivalry—and a man not accustomed to being refused.

To the chorus of goodbyes, she headed out, and Z strolled

beside her the short distance to her house next door. In the quiet neighborhood, the ocean breeze rustled the palms that lined the curb.

Under her bright porch light, Z leaned against the wall as she opened the door. She stepped inside and smiled at him. "Thank you for the escort."

"My pleasure. In fact, your timing was convenient. I want to ask you a question and didn't want to put you on the spot."

She stiffened. Seriously? He was going to proposition her?

"No, I'm not making an advance," he stated, although she hadn't spoken a word. "How familiar are you with BDSM, Ms. Collier?"

"What?" And he wasn't making an advance? *Right.* "What kind of a question is that?"

Even as she tried to formulate a refusal, heat swept over her face. When Carson's father, Everett, had done kinky stuff, she'd been too timid to say no. And, despite being ashamed of herself, she'd enjoyed some of what he'd done.

But...still, how dare this stranger ask her about something so intimate.

"Ah, I framed that poorly. Forgive me." Z tilted his head. "However, you didn't cringe, which is a start."

She frowned. There was absolutely no appropriate response to that observation.

His lips quirked. "As it happens, I own a BDSM club that is open only on Fridays and Saturdays. Since the club is private, alcohol is provided as part of the membership fees. Previously, one volunteer handled most of the bartending, but he recently married. Right now, we're coping with a number of members who don't enjoy the work."

Wait, what? "Are you offering me a job? In a BDSM club?" Her voice came out sounding like someone had smacked her in the throat.

"That's exactly what I'm proposing." He had a lethal grin

when he chose to use it. "Most BDSM clubs don't allow alcohol on the premises. On the other hand, I wanted the Shadowlands to be a community as well as a place to scene, and people enjoy socializing over drinks. However, since alcohol can adversely affect BDSM play, the club has a two-drink limit, and my preference is that those two drinks happen *after* a scene. Most people are quite careful about indulging, however..."

"The world abounds with idiots," she finished for him. "I understand. The bartender would have to monitor that. Why me?"

"I watched you work at The Highlands. You have an excellent memory for customers' likes and dislikes. You're polite, friendly, and careful. I saw how you assured yourself that our women weren't driving themselves home." He regarded her, his tone serious. "A BDSM club can be somewhat overwhelming. Our members, however, are more polite and less...aggressive...than a bar's clientele."

A BDSM club. *Oh. My. God.*

Yet it was a job. After years of working in bars, she had a good instinct for people—at least when they didn't look like a Hell's Angels' version of Thor. This Z had been polite and straightforward. Uzuri and her men were friends with him. He wasn't giving her any iffy vibes.

She pulled in a slow breath. "Friday and Saturday?"

"Exactly. The club opens at 8 pm and, since it's not a bar, we remain open as long as people are playing. Although scenes are generally finished by three or so, there have been occasions when we closed at dawn."

"Wow." On the other hand, she'd get in a lot of hours.

"You wouldn't collect tips. Drinks are part of the membership fees, and no one carries money in the club."

Oh no. Tips were where she made her money. "That wouldn't—"

He held up his hand to cut in. "The club will pay you thirty-five an hour."

She blinked and multiplied hours in her head. There had been a few busy nights at the Highlands where she'd made that amount...but not many. "You're on."

His smile grew. "I'm pleased. However, hear me out. There is more."

Hasty. Don't be hasty.

"Since the members indulge in unusual practices, so to speak, you will be required to read and sign the membership agreement —your fees are waived, of course. There is also a background check and physical."

A physical and background? "But...you're serious?"

"Quite. The members rely on the club to ensure their privacy and safety."

"Oh." Then again, what did she care? She was healthy and law-abiding. Sheesh, she didn't even get parking tickets. "Sure, that's not a problem."

"Good. Now, since the club is outside of your comfort zone, you may consider next Friday and Saturday a test. We'll talk afterward."

She let out a relieved breath. "That's more than fair. Thank you."

"In that case, you'll have the terms, the application and membership agreement, and an appointment for the doctor's visit in the morning."

Good grief, he moved fast.

This was good, she told herself. She couldn't afford to be out of work long. "All right."

"I look forward to seeing you this Friday. The previous bartender's name is Cullen, and he'll handle your orientation." He smiled and tapped her door. "Lock that before I leave."

He was one bossy boss, wasn't he? She shut the door, flipped the lock, and heard him stride away.

She blew out a breath. She hadn't even been unemployed for two hours.

But...a BDSM club? Lord help her.

Next door, Holt settled back in his chair and smiled at his remaining three guests. Wasn't it amazing how happy Zuri appeared? When he saw her last, she'd been terrified of meeting Max and Alastair's family. "Did you enjoy your Thanksgiving in Colorado?"

Her face lit up. "Oh, Holt, you should see the Drago ranch. The Dragos were incredibly nice. I even learned to ride."

"Mmm, I see." Holt lifted an eyebrow.

Snickering, she threw an ice cube at him. "Ride horses, you pervert. Get your mind out of the gutter."

When Max simply snorted and Alastair's lips curved up, Holt was relieved. He and Zuri had originally played together in the Shadowlands, but their relationship had changed into that of siblings. She was the little sister he'd never had.

Working in the peds ICU, he ran into Alastair now and then, and knew the doc was extremely even-tempered. The cop, Max, on the other hand, carried a weapon. So, it was nice that Zuri's two new lovers weren't threatened by the past. The little subbie'd chosen well.

"Your new neighbor seems quite nice," Alastair commented.

Holt nodded. Although Josie didn't seem to like him much, she'd charmed everyone. He glanced at Zuri. "Did you get to know her at the Highlands?"

"No. When I lived here, she'd visit her great-aunt in the other half of the duplex. I guess when Mrs. Avery sprained her ankle last month, Josie wanted to live closer."

"She found a house for rent right next door? That's luck," Max said.

Zuri snorted. "It'd been for sale for ages. The place is a dump, and they had no takers."

Alastair turned to eye the house. "That's a big building for one person."

"There are two of them. She has a kid," Holt said. "Maybe ten or eleven or so."

"Carson's eleven," Zuri said. "He's a sweetheart."

"An eleven-year-old?" Max frowned. "Unless I'm off base on her age, she'd have been a youngster herself when she had him."

A youngster? Holt considered. Josie was late twenties, maybe. Twenty-eight minus eleven...*ouch*.

"A teenage pregnancy. I bet that was rough." Zuri curled deeper into her chair and leaned her head against Max's arm. "She didn't seem very comfortable with you, boo."

Trust Zuri to have noticed. Holt's jaw tensed. "Guess some people aren't comfortable looking at scars."

"What?" Zuri said.

Oh hell, he shouldn't have said anything. The guy who'd knifed him had been after Zuri, and she still felt guilty. Even worse, she and the Doms knew Nadia had dumped him because of the scars. "It's no big deal. I—"

Zuri straightened. "Josie's better than that. She wouldn't—"

"Easy, princess." Max gave a tug on one of Zuri's corkscrew curls.

"But—"

"She might have other reasons for being uncomfortable." Alastair set his hand over hers. "Perhaps she's uneasy around men?"

"Pffft. She works in a bar, and men are always coming onto her. That shouldn't bother her." Zuri shook her head.

A bartender. That was a unique profession. He had to say, in her tailored black vest and white shirt, she'd looked both sexy and professional.

However, she didn't want to be around him. "How she feels is how she feels, Zuri. If I make her uncomfortable, I'll keep my distance."

Zuri's eyes narrowed. "I have trouble believing Josie'd be like that, but we'll see. However, if I ever run into Nadia, I'll give her a smackdown she won't forget."

"A girl fight?" Max turned to Alastair. "My money's on our subbie."

Zuri choked on her drink—then scooped ice out and shoved a handful down Max's shirt. "Cool off, dude."

His outraged shout split the night air.

Holt smiled. His fun-loving Zuri hadn't been curbed by her Dom lovers. And the contentment they'd found together made him envious. That kind of love was what *he* wanted, what he had hoped to find with Nadia.

But life went as it went. A firefighter should be accustomed to getting burned, even if he hadn't expected it from a lover. He wasn't giving up on finding himself a sweetheart like Zuri, but no hurry. In a while, when he didn't feel quite so singed, he'd try again.

Maybe next year.

CHAPTER THREE

Oh wow. Eyes wide, Josie stared through the encroaching darkness at a looming, three-story, stone mansion. *Shades of Victoria Holt and Gothic romances.* Only a formal English landscape was lacking. Instead, the long curving driveway was lined with stately palm trees.

She eyed the huge dark oak doors. *Intimidating much?* Bet the appearance of this place discouraged anyone handing out religious tracts. Her too. Tiny chills tiptoed up her spine.

She'd already been on edge because, face it, no matter how many bars she'd worked in, starting a new job was always scary. Could she do the work? Would the people she served be nice? Would they expect—and prefer—the showy, garrulous kind of bartender rather than a quiet, efficient one?

The door was as massive and heavy as it had looked—as if to warn, *Your doom awaits. Damn imagination.* Huffing a laugh, she stepped inside.

Huh. No depravity. Instead, the quiet entry was an austere room with two men in blue button-up shirts and jeans behind a desk. The clean-shaven, gray-haired man was tall and lean with a military straight posture. The other man was massively built and at least six feet five. Leather-bound light brown hair revealed a brutal-looking face.

Both frowned at her.

"Club's not open yet, miss," the biggest man said.

"I'm... Z told me to come now. I'm the bartender. Josie."

"Are you now? Welcome then. I'm Ben." He rose and held his hand out. "I used to do security here. Ghost here replaced me, at least until things quiet down at home."

"Hate to tell you, Longshot, *things at home* will get even busier after your baby arrives." Ghost stood. "Good to meet you, Josie. Sign in here, and we'll go get you a staff locker."

"Thank you."

With the slightest of limps, he walked out from behind the desk. "You can leave your belongings in the locker and"—he turned to Ben—"do bartenders get to leave their shoes on?"

"My shoes?"

"Her shoes?" Ben frowned. "But she's probably not even submissive, so—"

"She is. That wasn't my question."

"I'm what?" Josie took a step away from Ghost.

Ben scowled. "And you know that how?"

"Because Ghost is far more experienced than he's shared." The rich smooth voice came from behind Josie.

She spun and saw Z in the inner doorway.

"Josie, welcome. Let Ghost show you the lockers, and I'll meet you at the bar. Shoes are fine"—a corner of Z's mouth curved up—"when you're working."

She blinked. What else would she be doing here but working?

As the door closed behind her new boss, Ghost motioned toward a door. "This way."

Still behind the desk, Ben was sputtering. "Ghost, what exactly did he mean...experienced? Ghost?"

After stowing her purse and jacket, Josie pulled in a breath. *Okay, here goes nothing.* A BDSM club. Truly, she was out of her mind. That paperwork she'd been given had been unsettling. The first forms were normal for a new job. Income tax. Direct deposit. But then there were club rules and something titled "Limit List."

Honestly, by the time she'd finished that form—and looked some of the activities up on the internet—she felt as if she'd watched a scorching hot movie. In between giggling like a maniac. Since a bartender wouldn't be playing, she'd had an urge to check YES to the terrifying, unusual options—like asphyxiation and infantilism and branding. Then she reconsidered. What if the owner actually noticed her answers?

So, she'd answered honestly and found herself embarrassed in a whole different way. Who knew she had so many...odd...interests? Thank God the damn thing would get buried in her employment file and never be seen again.

Ghost was waiting for her, leaning against a wall by the sinks. "Ready?"

No. Not in the least. "Sure." She followed him out a different door.

"This is the main clubroom." Ghost patiently waited as she turned in a circle to take everything in. Clusters of leather couches and chairs ranged outward from a dark oval bar in the center. Around the perimeter of the room, roped-off areas held all sorts of strange devices.

So this was what a real BDSM club looked like. She'd spent the last few days researching BDSM, so she knew the X-shaped, black leather padded devices were called St. Andrew's crosses. That the sawhorse looking thing was a version of a spanking bench. That there were Masters—or Mistresses—and slaves, Tops and bottoms, Dominants and submissives. Admittedly, she didn't have them all quite straight in her head yet.

Wrought-iron sconces kept the roped-off scene areas fairly bright yet left the conversational areas in shadows. In one front corner, a caterer was setting food out on long tables. To her right was a small dance floor.

The unpopulated room smelled of leather and a citrusy cleaning agent.

Ghost nodded toward the bar where a man as big as Ben was talking to Z. "There's your destination."

"Right. Thank you." She didn't move. The entire room felt like a strange land, full of unfamiliar furnishings, behaviors, and danger. What if..."

Ghost frowned down at her, glanced at the bar, and snorted. "Come, lass. Let's get you settled." A hard hand curled around her upper arm.

"I..." She felt like a big baby and was more relieved than she could say. "Thank you."

"No thanks needed. My job is to keep the scary world at bay." He gave her a level look. "Those are two of the finest Doms you'll ever find, and oddly enough, this is one of the safest places on the planet; however, you don't know that. Yet. Until you do, I'll provide escort services."

The quivery feeling in her stomach settled.

When they arrived at the bar, he gave her a mock salute and headed back out without stopping.

She smiled at Z and the other man behind the bar.

"Welcome to the Shadowlands, Josephine," Z said.

Josephine? Oh, great, she'd had to use her legal name on the application. "Josie, please."

He smiled. "I dislike the propensity of the world to shorten names, as if an extra syllable or two is too much trouble to speak. Josephine."

"This, coming from a person everyone calls Z?"

The booming laugh came from the big guy behind the bar. "She's got you there, boss."

"She does indeed." Z chuckled. "I've been waiting years for someone to call me on that. Josie, it is."

Whew. Her boss had a sense of humor—and she wasn't fired.

His grin was a flash of white in his tanned face. "However, just so you know, Z is less of a nickname than a scene name."

Oh, that made sense. She'd read about using an alias in a BDSM setting. "I understand."

"Good." Z motioned toward the big guy behind the bar. "Josie, this is Cullen. He'll show you where everything is and explain the protocols we have in place."

As Z strolled away, Cullen lifted up the hinged pass-through, and she walked into the space enclosed by the bar. She ran her hand over the gleaming mahogany of the bar top. "This is beautiful workmanship."

"Aye and it is." A faint Irish accent lilted his words as he leaned against the bar top. "Let's start with the rules."

She nodded and leaned her elbow on the bar.

"First, the only people allowed behind the bar are you, Z, and the official Shadowlands Masters and Mistresses."

"Um. Aren't a lot of people in a BDSM club called Masters and Mistresses?"

He had a big easygoing grin. "Yes, but the club awards its "official" title to the most experienced members, ones who are willing to give back to the community. Z insists the Masters and Mistresses wear gold armbands so people can find us." He slapped the one on his massive biceps to show her what he meant. "You can consider the Masters to be Shadowlands staff. If you get swamped, someone will pop in to help. They can bring their submissives behind here to assist. Otherwise, this space is off limits."

That sounded good, both restricting the area and knowing there was help around. "Got it."

"Let's get you acquainted with where things are. Z stocks the speed rail with the standard liquors, and if a regular favors something unusual, he might add it to the stock. There's also private stock. We'll go over that later."

She nodded. "All right. So...let's start at the top so I can suck up properly. What do you and Z drink and where is it kept?"

Yeah, the guy really did have a great laugh.

———————

The weekend had arrived, and Holt was feeling pretty good as he walked with Anne and Ben up the sidewalk to the Shadowlands. The beautiful early December evening made him regret having to drive the SUV rather than his Harley. Then again, the surgeon had a point. Bumpy roads, motorcycles, and surgical wounds might not be a comfortable combination.

As the slope increased, he saw Ben take Anne's arm, as if the pregnant Domme couldn't safely walk without his assistance. Holt grinned. The woman had served in the Marines and was an ex-bounty hunter.

Her low growl said what she thought of Ben's over-protectiveness.

"Push her too far, Ben, and she'll wrap your jewels in one of her favorite nutcrackers," Holt warned.

The big guard snorted. "She can't bend down far enough to reach my package these days."

"I can if you're on the bed, tiger," Anne said in her throaty voice.

"Ah...right." Being a smart man, Ben kissed her cheek...and released her arm.

Laughing, Holt opened the heavy front door and gestured them in.

Beside the security desk, Z was talking with Ghost.

"Hey, Ghost, Z," Holt said as he followed Anne and Ben.

"Holt." Ghost studied him with a frown. "You're not moving like you're fully recovered. Tell me you're not planning to play."

Holt blinked. "Jesus, you sound like Z." Like Z at his most

protective, actually. "Why'd I get the impression you weren't in the lifestyle?"

"Indeed, that is my question as well," Z said.

Ghost's face turned unreadable. "I'm a security guard."

"Oh, you're more than that." Anne gave him a thin smile. Upon getting pregnant, she'd abandoned bounty hunting for a job with another Shadowlands Master. She was a wizard at getting information about people.

Holt glanced at her. "What do you mean?"

"Ghost was considered one of the finest Doms on the West Coast before he disappeared."

Now that was interesting. Holt eyed the guard.

Ghost's face was wiped of any expression.

"Ghost." Anne took a step forward. "If there's anything we can—"

"You three are signed in." Ghost made three checkmarks on the papers in front of him. "Have yourselves a nice night now."

"You too, buddy." Ben tugged Anne toward the door.

Holt smothered a smile. It took a brave man to cut the Domme off like that. As they entered the clubroom, he asked Anne, "How'd you find out about Ghost's rep?"

"Z had a suspicion and asked me to see what I could find."

"So, Ghost was a..." Holt caught sight of the bar, and his question evaporated. "Josie?"

In her black vest and white button-up shirt, his neighbor was serving drinks. Lights concealed in the low beams over the bar made glints in her short copper hair.

"Who's behind the bar?" Anne asked.

"Z hired us a *real* bartender," Ben said.

"What a lovely idea." Anne smiled. "I think Cullen's the only Master who truly enjoys mixing drinks."

Ben frowned. "I don't ever remember seeing you back there."

"She exchanged bartending for dungeon monitoring every chance she could," Holt said.

She gave her submissive an evil smile. "A choice between catering to idiots or terrorizing idiots—which do you *think* I chose?"

Ben snorted a laugh and told Holt, "Last week, she watched over a new Dom and made him so nervous, he dropped his flogger."

Holt grinned. He'd been in the lifestyle well over a decade, and he could still remember the first few times he'd scened in public.

"Oh, sweet Jesus, look. Master *Holt* is back." The high squeal was followed by happy sounds from the sitting area where unattached submissives congregated. The space was close to the bar where Doms could look them over and decide with whom to play.

"You've been missed, Master Holt," Anne said in a dry voice.

"You have," Ben seconded. "But remember, the colonel told you not to play."

"A colonel?" Holt asked.

"Yeah." Ben grinned. "We've traded a few war stories over beer."

"What branch of service was—" *Oh hell.* As the flock of submissives started toward him, Holt froze, unsure if he was equal to this outing.

Anne's strong hand closed halfway around his upper arm as the very pregnant Mistress lent her silent support.

"Thanks." What the fuck had happened there? After a second, he figured it out and shook his head ruefully. "I hadn't realized a minor knifing could turn a guy agoraphobic."

With an understanding snort, Ben said, "Oh hell, yeah. Any trauma can. Why do you think Z forced me to take a job here?"

Holt blinked. He'd always wondered why the famous photographer worked a security desk. Come to think of it, Ben had served overseas. "Guess I should be glad I got my ass back here before Z assigned me homework or something."

"No shit." Ben grinned.

The submissives arrived and swarmed around Holt in a flurry of breathy voices.

"Master Holt, welcome back."

"We missed you."

"How are you feeling?"

"Is there anything I can do for you?"

"Would you like me to bring you something to drink?"

Every inhalation brought him a different perfume. The variety of clothing—from long skirts and corsets to entirely naked—was almost overwhelming. Which said it was past time for him to get out more and to take up his life again. "Thank you all. I appreciate the welcome," he said gently and patted shoulders, squeezed hands, touched cheeks. Made contact.

After a minute, he took a step back. "Unfortunately, I'm not cleared by my doctor to play tonight."

Ignoring their disappointment, he added, "I'm just here to touch bases with the other Masters...and make sure Mistress Anne doesn't have her baby without supervision."

As the subbies giggled, Anne frowned at him, then patted her stomach. "This baby's getting born in a nice clean hospital with a nice *female* obstetrician, thank you very much."

Spotting three new arrivals at her bar, Josie smiled at the young Dom she'd been talking with, patted his hand, and told him, "Next time, it'll be better."

His shoulders straightened with resolution, and he gave her a nod. "Yeah. It will."

As she moved away, she shook her head. Her internet research hadn't told her how much work being a Dom could be. Or how stuff like floggings could get messed up. That poor guy felt terrible that he'd left welts on the woman in his scene.

Sometimes a bar seemed much like a confessional...and she'd sure learned a lot in the last few hours.

Josie wandered in a circle around the bar, assessing who needed refills. Two men, one in black leathers, the other in a chain harness and leather collar had nearly full drinks.

Next were three women—Dommes. Their minions—slaves, submissives, or whatevers—knelt off to one side, also talking. Nothing needed there.

Ah, she had customers waiting—three women near the end of the bar.

As she headed that way, a redhead in a golden bustier scooted onto an empty barstool. A man in a well-tailored suit joined her.

"I'll be right with you," Josie said as she passed them.

Reaching the end of the bar, she smiled at the three women. A brunette, a redhead, and a blonde...sounded like the beginning of a joke. "What can I get you?"

The platinum blonde turned to her friends as if Josie hadn't spoken. "Didn't I tell you we had a new bartender?"

Josie smothered a sigh and patiently waited.

"I'd like a shot of Scotch. Make it the Balvenie 21. It's over there." The blonde waved toward the other side of the bar before grinning at her giggling friends.

The laughter sounded nervous, and in any other bar, Josie would have carded them. But Z's background check and security guard ensured anyone in the place was over twenty-one.

"Coming right up." Josie spotted the bottle of scotch and picked it up. *Nice choice*. Aged in port wine casks, the twenty-one-year-old single malt ran well over two hundred dollars a bottle. Pouring, Josie made a mental note so she'd keep track of how much the blonde had imbibed. She set the drink in front of the woman. "Here you go."

The blonde scooped it up and moved away, followed by her friends.

"What the fuck?" a man said from behind Josie. Despite the soft voice, his irritation came through clearly.

Uh-oh. Josie turned and smiled. "Good evening. What can I get you?"

Stepping up to the bar, the man was tall and wiry, probably in his forties with short light brown hair. The coiled whip fastened to his belt sent a shiver down Josie's spine. Did he seriously use that? On a person?

His gaze was cold. "That's my bottle."

Huh? She glanced down at the bottle still in her hand. "Oh. All right. Would you like a drink from it?"

His color darkened. "I don't know who the fuck you are, but that bottle cost me a hefty penny, and I won't have you pouring it out for your subbie friends. You—"

Her subbie friends? Josie saw the women were no longer at the bar. A sinking feeling made her take a step back. She'd messed up...somehow...but what had she done? "I don't understand."

Down the bar, the man in the suit started to stand up. "Edward, might I—"

"Hey, Edward," said a very familiar voice.

Holt? Josie's jaw dropped as her neighbor strolled up to the bar. His thick, dark blond hair was loose, brushing his shoulders, and his short beard had been trimmed.

Seriously? Her biker neighbor was a member of this place?

Seeing Holt, the Dom wearing a suit silently resumed his place.

"You look riled up, Edward. What's up?" Holt's calm, resonant voice was like a flag of peace in a battle. As Josie pulled in a breath, his sea-gray eyes gaze turned to her with an appraising gaze.

"Um. Hi, Holt," she said.

Edward scowled at her. "That's *Master* Holt to you. Show some fucking respect."

Master? Josie noted the gold band circling Holt's hard biceps.

Master Holt. From Edward's irritation, apparently even the bartender should use that Master title when addressing them. Cullen had missed a few details during her orientation.

Holt gave Edward an amused look. "She's not a member. Z hired us a professional bartender." He glanced at her. "Is this your first night?"

She nodded.

"Thought so." He grinned at Edward. "We should give the poor drink-slinger time to familiarize herself with the quirks here."

"A professional bartender?" Annoyance sliding away, Edward studied her. "I've seen you before, haven't I? At The Highlands?"

"You have a good memory." She took a breath. "I'm very sorry if I messed up. Could you explain what I did wrong? When Cullen was showing me the ropes, he had a call from work and left without completing my orientation to the bar."

"Nice. Left you to the wolves and"—Holt nodded at Edward—"sadists."

She'd aggravated a whip-wielding sadist. Josie swallowed. "Um."

Edward grinned and, thankfully, didn't unsnap his whip. His mouth thinned again. "What you did wrong was to pour a drink for your girlfriend, Amber, from my private stock."

That sounded bad. Josie bit her lip. "Cullen mentioned private stock but left before he had a chance to explain it."

"Let me show you." Holt lifted up the pass-through and stepped behind the bar. Taking the bottle from her hand, he pointed to the small label on one side that said "EDWARD." "Although the bar is stocked with regularly priced alcohol"—he gestured toward the array of bottles in the speed well and on the shelves—"some members want seriously expensive shit."

Edward snorted. "That bottle ain't shit, you heathen."

Ignoring him, Holt continued, "If a member brings in a bottle, it gets labeled and kept only for them in this section."

Josie stared at the bottles in dismay. She'd given someone a drink from another member's bottle. A very expensive bottle. *But...wait a minute.* Her jaw clenched. "Does this mean if a member specifically requests a drink from a bottle kept in the private section, I should only pour if their name is the name on the bottle?"

"You didn't pick my bottle at random?" Edward's brows drew together.

"No. The lady asked for the Balvenie 21, specifically." Josie motioned toward the blonde who had taken a seat in the area for unattached submissives. "She directed me to the private stock shelves."

Both Doms turned. In the nearby sitting area, the blonde and her two friends stiffened when they realized they were being watched.

"I'm getting the impression you're not friends with Amber?" Edward asked.

"Aside from the owner, Master Holt is the only person I know here."

"Fuck. I jumped before checking the lay of the land." Edward scowled. "Sorry."

Holt stepped out from behind the bar, eyed the women, and crooked his finger. *Come here.*

Considering the stern set of Holt's jaw, Josie wasn't surprised when the three hurried over.

Holt leveled a hard stare at the blonde. "I hear you asked the bartender for Edward's Balvenie and pointed her toward his bottle."

Amber gave a shocked gasp and glared at Josie. "I did not. You're lying. You just grabbed—"

"Oh honestly, Amber." Down the bar, the redhead in the golden bustier turned. "Sure looks like the hamster is running, but the wheel isn't spinning."

Amber scowled. "What do you mean?"

"I mean if you're going to steal something, first check for witnesses. I heard you ask for the Balvenie 21. So did Master Marcus."

The blonde turned red, and then she cast a timid look at the guy in the suit—Master Marcus—who wore a gold armband.

Another Master. How many of them were there?

Master Marcus's slow Southern accent didn't lessen the firmness of his voice as he said, "Gabrielle is correct, Amber. I do believe you've gotten yourself into a heap of trouble."

He turned his attention to Holt. "You got yourself back here just in time to deal with this mess. I am most appreciative."

Josie caught the subtext—the other Master was dumping everything in Holt's lap.

Holt gave him a sour look. "Thanks, Marcus."

"Welcome back." Smiling, Master Marcus returned to talking with his redhead.

With an almost unheard sigh, Holt—*Master* Holt—turned back to the women. Ignoring Amber, he looked from the redhead to the brunette, his intense regard making them fidget uncomfortably.

After a long moment, he spoke. "You two didn't stop your friend. You didn't speak up when she lied to get the bartender in trouble. I'm displeased with such behavior from Shadowland submissives."

Both women wilted.

The redhead whispered, "I'm sorry."

"As am I. Many Doms enjoy a bit of brattiness; however, none condone dishonesty...or *theft*." His smooth voice had acquired an edge that could cut.

The two women flinched.

His tone softened. "Do you remember your first night in the Shadowlands?"

They nodded.

"Pretty scary, wasn't it?"

More nods.

"Put yourself in the bartender's shoes for a moment. Imagine it's your first night here on the job in this strange place." As Holt talked, the women looked at Josie, comprehension growing in their expressions. "You're nervous, trying to do your best." He paused...then added in a slow, disapproving voice, "Then a customer scams you and lands you in so much trouble, you could get fired. And the customer's friends think it's *funny*."

The redhead dissolved into tears.

"Oh, God, we did." The brunette closed her eyes for a second. Then, looking Josie straight in the face, she said softly. "I'm very sorry, ma'am. I was wrong. Is there a way I can make this right?"

The redhead nodded desperately.

"Ah..." Josie glanced at Holt.

"That sounds more like submissives who belong here." Holt gestured toward the bar. "Since it's tough to keep up with the drink demands, you two can help her out. For the next half hour, you pour beer, water, sodas, and clean up. Do anything she asks you to do."

More nods.

Holt added quietly, "If a Dominant asks why you're behind the bar, explain...completely."

The women winced at the thought of confessing, then ducked under the pass-through and waited for orders.

Oh...boy. Josie considered for a second before handing them bar rags. "Can you pick up the empties and wipe down the bar?" There wasn't much to do, since she tidied as she worked, but this...awkward interlude...had put her behind.

"Yes, ma'am," the redhead whispered.

"Right away, ma'am." The brunette was younger, maybe twenty-three, and her hands trembled with her relief.

As Josie started to move away, Holt gave her a slight shake of his head. *Stay*.

When he turned to Amber, his eyes were the color of sleet

and held as much warmth. "Conning the bartender, stealing, lying, and casting the blame on another person. Did I miss anything?"

Amber flushed beet red.

When the blonde's expression turned remorseful, Josie wanted to roll her eyes. She'd seen better acting from Carson's friends.

"I'm sorry, Master Holt." Amber took a step closer...and stopped when Holt's jaw tightened.

His control over his anger was impressive—and intimidating enough that Josie wanted to retreat to a safe distance. California sounded about far enough away.

"Am I the one who should get an apology?" Holt asked in a lethally soft voice.

After a second, Amber glanced at Edward and gritted out, "I'm sorry, Sir."

The sadist's expression didn't change.

Amber shrugged and offered Holt a simperingly pretty smile. "May I go now, Master Holt?"

He crossed his arms over his chest and waited.

Sheesh, Josie wasn't the one in trouble, but that silence stuff was deadly.

Amber's jaw moved sideways in an ugly fashion before she glanced at Josie. "Sorry."

That was the least authentic sounding apology Josie'd ever heard. And she was done with this. She picked up a stack of tickets a barmaid had left and started drawing a beer. Heavens knew any reply she made to that fake apology would be either rude...or dishonest. This club stuff wasn't her problem.

Nonetheless, she listened with one ear as Master Holt told Amber that her apology was as dishonest as her behavior. "Edward, could I impose on you to give Amber a paddling? Stop after each one and let her apologize. If she ever sounds honestly sorry, you can stop. Otherwise, give her the full twenty...as is listed under *punishment* in the membership agreement."

"What?" Amber gasped.

"I don't usually enjoy hurting non-masochists but, in your case, it'll be a pleasure." Smiling cynically, Edward curled a hand around the woman's arm and led her away.

Josie realized she was staring. *Not your problem. Not your business. Focus. Serve drinks.* She walked over to the two who'd spoken up for her—Master Marcus and the redhead, Gabrielle. "Thank you so much for speaking up. Now, what can I get you to drink?"

"You're welcome, and I'd love a Diet Coke." Gabrielle had a lovely smile.

Clean-shaven with short hair, Master Marcus looked like the CEO of a *Fortune* 500 business. His coloring was much like Holt's —lightly tanned, honey-blond hair, and blue eyes. But the added gray in Holt's eyes could turn them from a soft foggy color to that of a bleak winter sky.

Master Marcus's accent was pure Southern as he said, "It is truly a delight to have a real bartender working here. I'm Marcus."

Josie tipped her head in a respectful nod. "Master Marcus. Gabrielle."

"Gabi," the redhead corrected. She turned as Holt joined them and gave him a gentle hug. "Holt, it's good to have you back. How are you feeling?"

"Fine."

Marcus made a disbelieving sound.

Josie stood for a second, dying to know what they were talking about, then gave herself a stern shake and poured Gabi a Diet Coke. As she set it in front of the woman, she lifted her eyebrows at Marcus.

"Gerolsteiner on the rocks, please."

Josie scooped ice into a glass, selected the right bottle, and poured the bubbly water.

"If you're still here later, we'll join you for a real drink." Marcus smiled at Holt, then ran his fingers down his submissive's cheek. "First, I fear someone has a beatin' coming to her."

Hearing that, Josie's fingers closed forcefully around the bottle. There would be no beating of women on her watch. "Listen, you—"

Leaning across the bar, Holt gripped her wrist and gently took the bottle from her. "BDSM club, remember, pet? Everything is consensual."

Oh. Damn. She knew that, for heaven's sake. Had been watching people being whipped and flogged and caned all night. "Right." She glanced at Holt and said under her breath, "Thanks."

Master Marcus chuckled.

"You were going to come to my rescue, weren't you?" Gabi grinned. "I like you. Welcome to the Shadowlands."

"Um. Thank you." Josie exhaled silently. At the rate she was blundering from mistake to mistake, she doubted she'd be at the club for a second night. Even if the owner didn't fire her, she wasn't sure she was cut out for this place.

Holt was still holding her wrist, his gaze on her. "You okay?"

His hand was warm, the strength in it oddly comforting. And she shouldn't even be thinking that way. Leaning on a man was a good way to end up sprawled on the sidewalk.

"Fine, yes. Thank you for the help." She carefully pulled her arm away.

His gaze went flat. "No problem. If you can handle things, I need to see if Zuri and her crew are here. Excuse me."

As Holt walked toward the back, Marcus watched him for a second, then looked at Josie, eyes narrowed.

CHAPTER FOUR

The night went on.

Josie hadn't made more errors—she hoped—and she'd had wonderful conversations with the members. Well, except for a few. From the glares, Amber had friends who blamed the newly hired bartender for her punishment. She had the urge to yell, *it wasn't my fault. I didn't do anything wrong.*

Well, her father had taught her at a young age that protesting never made a difference.

As the hour grew late and the club quieter, she had the time to watch the roped-off scenes. The sessions reminded her of performance art, except...the tops and bottoms rarely seemed aware of observers. They were engrossed in what was happening and in each other.

Each scene was different. She watched canings, spankings, floggings. Dripping wax on bare skin. Tying a person up in elaborate ways. Sparking electrical wands applied to body parts—even intimate places.

One Domme had actually stuck needles into her female submissive. Josie'd kept her back turned until that scene was over.

Sheesh. However, most of the other stuff was mesmerizing. And sexy.

Apparently, there weren't any restrictions on nakedness or on sexual activity. Private parts were fondled—or slapped—or stuck with needles—or... Cullen had mentioned there were private rooms upstairs where members could play—or have sex—without being observed. But some members went ahead and had their sex right out in public.

She had no words. And she grew far too aware of the throbbing of her breasts, the dampness of her thong. Every inch of her skin felt over-sensitive.

But she wasn't here to play. She was here to serve drinks, and bartending was bartending, no matter where. She enjoyed talking with the club members here as much as she had with her Highlands customers. Once away from their roped-off areas, BDSM people were pretty normal. They, too, had the age-old problem of finding the right person or getting attached to the wrong one. Of breaking up or being cheated on.

As her customers chatted with her, she'd learned about new kinds of problems. Like "wrapping" a flogger, which meant the tips of the leather strands would curve around the target area to whip against the other side—in this case, the submissive's *breasts*. Holy hell. As she listened, Josie realized she'd crossed her arms over her chest.

A gay submissive confessed he had burst into giggles during an intense moment and annoyed his Dom.

A Top told her he'd done a suspension scene, twirled the woman in the ropes—and made her so sick to her stomach, she'd thrown up.

Then there was this woman... Josie frowned and studied the only person at the bar who didn't seem to want to talk.

In her late twenties, the tiny Latina woman sat with her shoulders slumped, drinking from her own bottle of water. Earlier, one of the woman's friends—another submissive—had come over, then given up when the Latina hunched away.

She wasn't speaking with her friends. Even though there were comfortable chairs throughout the clubroom, the woman had chosen to sit at the bar. To Josie, that was an invitation to talk or a plea for attention.

Josie walked over and leaned her forearms on the bar top. "Good evening. Can I get you something to drink?"

"No. Thank you. This water is enough." The lady didn't look up.

Since the bar was mostly empty, Josie took a glass from the rack Peggy had brought from the utility room. The sweet older woman, who did general cleanup and kept the bar furnished with clean glasses, was the only employee other than Josie during the club's open hours. Everyone else was a volunteer—including the submissives serving two-hour barmaid shifts.

With a fresh towel, Josie started buffing the wine glass to a gleaming shine—not that it needed it, but it gave her a reason to stand there. Not talking, just staying close.

The woman's shoulders straightened slightly, and she took another sip of her water. Her brows drew together. "Aren't those already washed?"

"Mmmhmm. But I like to make them even shinier."

Brown eyes lifted. "Really?"

"If I have the time, why not?"

There, the lady was breathing easier.

Josie found her own chest relaxing. "It kind of hurts to see someone looking unhappy. Do you need a buffing up, too?"

The woman gave a tiny snort of laughter. Her smile faded quickly. "It's nothing. I just get s-subdrop sometimes." The melodic Hispanic-accented voice had a hitch in it, and tears welled in her brown eyes.

"Um. I'm new to the club, and I don't know what subdrop is."

The woman's attempt at a smile broke Josie's heart. "It's like after a scene, especially an intense scene, you go from being really high on endorphins and stuff, and then everything drops out and leaves you miserable."

"That sounds horrible. What can I do to help?"

Another tear slid down her cheek. "I'll be fine."

Josie tried not to scowl. "Isn't the person you played with supposed to, like, stay with you afterward or something?"

"She...she isn't into aftercare."

Huh. Someone really needed a hug. What were the boundaries on personal touch in this place? "I'm Josie. Am I allowed to ask your name?"

Another tiny smile. "Sure. Natalia. Don't worry, Josie. I just need to sit for a few minutes before I drive home."

"You stay here as long as you need." Josie patted her hand and noticed a new customer had walked up to the bar. What crummy timing.

Stewing over her inability to help, Josie crossed the bar space. The arrival was older with silver hair and a leathery tan. Rather than flashy or black BDSM clothes, he wore jeans and a button-up shirt the pale blue color of his eyes.

Josie tried to smile. "Hi. What would you like?"

He studied her for a second. "I'd like to know why you look like someone ran over your puppy."

"I..." Josie's gaze dropped. Spotting a looped black whip attached to his belt, she stiffened. The last guy she'd seen wearing a whip had been called a sadist. Did all the sadists wear their...tools...like this?

He sure wasn't someone she'd ask for help for sad little Natalia.

"I'm waiting, girl," he growled. "Look at me."

A shiver ran up her spine at the command, but as she lifted her gaze, she saw the golden armband half-hidden by his loose shirt. "Ah." She stared at the whip and blurted out, "If someone needed your help, you wouldn't hurt her, right?"

Hard lips curved. "Not unless that was what she needed and wanted. You need help, missy?"

"Not me." Josie glanced over her shoulder at Natalia, and the Master followed her gaze. "She said she had something called subdrop?"

"That's the word. That one'd best have a female, though." He looked around and then pointed toward the middle of the room. "That Mistress there with the gold armband. You go tell Olivia that Sam wants her to help your li'l subbie there. Got it?"

"But..." Josie glanced around the bar.

"If someone needs a drink, I'll get it for them."

Right. On first sight, the guy looked like a rancher. A second look made him out to be someone extremely scary. She pulled up her own courage. "Okay, but don't scare my customers."

He barked a laugh and lifted the pass-through for her. "Half of them are here because they like being scared."

She ducked through, muttering, "Nonetheless..."

Mistress Olivia was on the stocky side. A sleeveless snug leather jacket showed off her muscular shoulders. Black latex leggings were partially covered by thigh-high lace-up boots. Her caramel-colored hair was as short as Josie's and worn in aggressive spikes. She wasn't...quite...as scary as Master Sam.

As Josie approached, Olivia stopped to talk to Uzuri and a redhead with silvering hair at the temples.

Uzuri saw Josie and grinned. "Girl, I was coming over to give you some support."

"I never turn that down." Josie turned to Olivia and hesitated. "I hate to interrupt. Sam—Master Sam—asked for your help with a...a subbie."

"Did he, now?" Olivia had a British accent and an unreadable face. "Why would that be?"

"There's a woman at the bar, Natalia, and she's got...she called it subdrop, and she's crying and that just..." Josie felt her anger rising again. "It's just not right that whoever she played with left her all alone when she's feeling so sad."

"Quite right." Olivia patted Josie's shoulder. "I got this, love."

As she stalked toward the bar like a force of nature, Josie stared after her, then looked at Uzuri. "I'm not sure whether I should be relieved or run ahead and warn Natalia to flee."

"Mistress Olivia can be scary—although nothing like Mistress Anne—but she's really nice under it all. She'll take good care of Natalia." Uzuri motioned toward the redhead. "Josie, have you met Linda? Linda, this is Josie, our new bartender."

Linda smiled. "Lovely to meet you, Josie."

"It's good to meet you." Josie glanced behind her at the bar. *I left a sadist tending bar. Bad Josie.* "I better get back."

"We'll come with you." Uzuri turned to a sitting area where some Doms were talking. Alastair's gaze was on Uzuri, and when she gestured toward the bar, he nodded.

"Did you just get *permission*?" Josie asked in disbelief.

As Linda chuckled, Uzuri headed them toward the bar. "Oh, yes. Running around here without permission isn't healthy."

Josie shook her head, then frowned. She'd already noticed submissives wore less clothing than the Dominants. Uzuri and Linda were also barefoot as well. Looking around, she spotted only one submissive with shoes, and her fancy stilettos were so high it was a wonder she could walk. "I see the lower classes lack footwear. Is that so you can't escape outside?"

Linda linked her arm with Josie's and told Uzuri, "She's so irreverent I can see why you're friends." She smiled at Josie. "The grand poohbah, Master Z, has ruled that submissives go barefoot unless they're wearing extremely sexy footwear. The security guard gets to decide."

"I used to wonder if anyone offered Ben sexual favors to get his permission to wear their shoes," Uzuri commented. "But he's incorruptible."

"Ben is the big one, right?"

Linda nodded. "That's him. Uzuri, after his baby is born, you could try bribing him with an offer to babysit." She opened her left hand. "Honor." She opened her right hand. "Crying infant." Her hands went up and down, imitating a set of scales. "Honor loses every time."

When Uzuri looked blank, Josie snickered. "I still remember my first year of motherhood. I would have done anything to have a few free hours."

"Exactly." Linda smiled. "Mine are in college, but I can still remember the horror—and delight—of a newborn."

When Josie ducked back behind the bar, Master Sam pointed her toward a patiently waiting barmaid. "Handle her tickets. I'll finish up the orders I've taken."

"Right. Thank you." As she checked the drink tickets, Linda and Uzuri settled onto barstools across the bar and kept talking about Ben and footwear.

Uzuri was enthusiastic. "I'm a great babysitter, and I have fantastic shoes he hasn't let me wear here."

Josie grinned. "I'll have to remember that about Ben. It's good to know who will take bribes."

"Isn't it though?" Linda pointed to Master Sam. "For example, that mean-looking bartender there? I hear he bribes real easily."

Josie stared. Was the woman crazy? The guy carried a *whip*. "Uh, Linda?"

Master Sam growled under his breath, leaned across the bar, and buried a fist in Linda's shoulder-length hair. She let out a yip of surprise as he yanked her toward him and took her mouth. There was no gentleness in that kiss. It was all domination.

Linda didn't struggle. She wrapped her arms around his neck.

Josie's jaw dropped.

Uzuri met her gaze, grinned, and fanned herself.

No lie, that was one hot kiss. *Whew.* The temperature in the entire bar area was rising. Josie retreated down the bar, checking for empty glasses or new customers. She picked up a couple of empties and put them on the cart for the cleaning lady.

Returning, she averted her gaze from Master Sam and Linda and asked Uzuri, "Would you like a drink?"

"A strawberry margarita, please." Uzuri's eyes were dancing. "They're together, you know—Linda and Master Sam. He doesn't just grab women. Well, not kissing-grabbing them, only it's smart to be polite around him because he's really good with that whip, and he has hard hands if he's not pleased with something you've done. I couldn't sit down for a day after he..."

Her voice trailed off when she saw Josie shake her head slightly. The submissive glanced over her shoulder and saw the eavesdropping sadist. "Oh. Oops."

Linda had a hand over her mouth, and her shoulders shook with laughter.

Cautiously, Josie assessed Master Sam. His mouth was straight, yet the crinkles beside his eyes showed his amusement. *Well, okay then.*

He nodded to Josie. "If you're back, I'll get my bag and give the redhead a lesson in manners." He glanced at Linda. "Right, missy?"

"Oh, absolutely." Rather than looking terrified, Linda slid right off the barstool. "Where to, Sir?"

Master Sam picked up a hefty leather bag from the far section of the bar. "The dungeon. Z roped off the room for single-tails."

Cullen had mentioned the "dungeon" was a separate room down a hall. Josie'd heard snapping sounds coming from that direction all night. And screams...*don't forget the screams.* Her mouth was dry as she set Uzuri's drink in front of her.

As Master Sam left the bar, he paused. "You're doin' a fine job, girl." Without waiting for her answer, he put an arm behind Linda's back and herded her toward the rear of the building.

"That is a very scary person," Josie said under her breath.

Nevertheless, she felt a warm glow. She had a feeling compliments from that guy were hard won.

"You should see him with that whip," Uzuri said. "I'm no masochist, and I never want someone to hurt me like that, but watching him turns me on like you wouldn't believe."

"He'll whip her. Hurt her." Josie shook her head. After a second, she remembered the question she'd been planning to ask. "As long as you're here, what's wrong with Holt? I noticed—" She stopped abruptly, noticing the southern, suit-wearing Dom— Master Marcus—had returned.

"Josie, I'm relieving you for a half hour. You take yourself a break now and get off your feet." He nodded to the front corner. "There's some fine food over there."

She realized she totally needed to pee. "Awesome, thank you!"

As she slipped through the bar flap, she grinned at Uzuri. "I'm going to visit the ladies' room and then will you visit with me for a bit?"

Uzuri pointed to the corner. "I'll find us food and a table."

A few minutes later, Josie found Uzuri in the munchie corner with Max. Josie dropped into a seat, considered, and put her legs up on an adjacent chair. Her feet seemed to give a happy sigh.

Max smiled. "Sore feet?"

"Always." She glanced at the people still around the bar. One was naked. One on a leash. "This sure isn't like any bartending job I've had before."

Uzuri laughed and handed over a bottle of sparkling water.

Grinning, the big cop pushed a plate across the table. "Zuri got you food."

"Thanks, Uzuri." Josie picked up a stuffed mushroom. "I'm starving."

As she chewed, she studied Uzuri's Dom. Max was dressed much like Holt. All in black—jeans, boots, heavy leather belt, and a tight T-shirt. He'd pulled his shoulder-length brown hair back in a tie. His masculine good looks with the square jaw and high cheekbones reminded her of Holt, too. Max was...powerful, with solidly packed muscles. If he was a hero in her books, she'd make him a sword-fighter. Considering Holt's steely, rippling muscles and how he moved with such breathtakingly, deadly grace, she'd give him knives—lots of finely balanced, lethal knives.

Scary Doms, really. Both of them. And Josie decided questions about her biker neighbor would wait until she had Uzuri alone.

Unfortunately, Uzuri hadn't forgotten. "You were asking me about Holt?" She waggled her eyebrows.

"Uh, right. I just wondered if he'd gotten hurt in some big biker brawl or something. He's pretty beat up."

Max's mouth pressed into a line, and Uzuri's smile died completely to be replaced by pain.

Josie froze. "Uzuri, what-whatever I said wrong, I'm *sorry*."

After a second, Uzuri shook her head. "I forgot your great-aunt went into the hospital around then. You wouldn't have heard what happened."

"Honey, whatever it is that makes you look like that, we don't need to talk about it." Josie's head was filling with all sorts of ugly conjectures.

"No, you should know. Holt lives next door to you." Uzuri curled her fingers around Max's hand as if for strength. "See, I had a stalker who was crazy. When I went to live with my dragon Doms, Holt stayed in my duplex while his apartment complex got renovated, and the stalker thought I was with him, and he ambushed Holt at home and cut him up with a knife."

The words flowed by so fast Josie needed a bit to process the meaning. A stalker? Her hands closed into fists. Was that why Uzuri had always seemed nervous? The bastard had attacked Holt? There'd been no biker brawl. *Oh my God*. A knife. Those scars.

"Last night, Max told Holt not to lift the chair." Josie's words emerged as a whisper. "How badly was he hurt?"

"Stab wounds in the stomach and back," Max said in his

rough, deep voice. "Nicked an intestine. He had surgery and was in the hospital on antibiotics for a while."

Uzuri's face was haunted. "He—"

"He'll be back at work soon." Max squeezed Uzuri's hand.

No wonder Holt had been home when other people were at work. No wonder he didn't offer to help with her groceries. That was why he walked slowly. She'd been appallingly wrong about him. Remorse ran over her, through her, making her sag in the chair.

"My fault." Uzuri stared at her hands. "It was—"

Josie blinked then scowled. She'd heard this *taking-on-the-guilt* crap before from all too many women, especially after they'd had a drink or two. "Excuse me, but did you *ask* that guy to stalk you?"

Uzuri blinked. "N-no."

"Right. I bet you told him to go away, and the asshole didn't, right?"

A nod.

"If you can't control what other people do, you're hardly to blame for their actions." Josie threw up her hands. "Next, you'll be taking on the guilt for all the squirrels that get run over, right?"

When Uzuri looked pole-axed, Max laughed.

Josie shoved to her feet. "I need to speak with Holt before I return to work. Is he still here?"

Max pointed toward the rear of the room. "He was watching a waxing scene in the left corner."

Crossing the room, Josie collected friendly nods. One Dom said to his male submissive, "Sexy outfit. We should do a bartender-biker roleplay sometime."

People here were sure different. Spotting Holt, Josie stopped.

Drink in one hand, he sprawled on a long leather couch, idly watching the cleanup of the nearby scene.

Guilt constricted her lungs.

His gaze landed on her, and his expression went flat.

Her chest felt as if someone had thumped her with a mallet.

Holt had been friendly when they met, when he'd helped her at the bar. No longer.

Biting her lip for courage, she walked over and motioned to the couch beside him. "May I?"

He moved his legs. "Of course."

What did the pretty bartender want?

Holt was fucking exhausted. He'd aided a new Dom who'd hit a submissive's trigger and needed help with getting her settled. After that, everyone he knew had wanted to talk and see how he was doing. His intended brief visit to the Shadowlands had turned into a marathon.

Now he had to deal with a woman who disliked him for some damn reason. He kept his voice level with an effort. "Is there a problem I can help you with, Josie?"

She sat down beside him on the couch. In the short time he'd known her, she'd always been remarkably self-possessed—even when dealing with a pissed-off Edward—but right now, she looked shaken.

He softened his tone. "What's the matter, sweetheart?"

"I was dreadfully wrong. I'm sorry, Holt; I've been so rude to you."

Had he missed something? He breathed out slowly and gathered energy...because dammit, he was too tired to deal with this. She wasn't his submissive. In fact, might not be submissive at all. Only, yeah, she was. And she needed help, which put her squarely into part of his Dom's duties.

All right then. "You *have* been rude," he said evenly. "Perhaps you'll share why?"

Her gaze dropped. "I thought the damage to your arms and face was because you got in a knife fight."

"I did."

Looking up, she put her hand over his. "No, you were *ambushed*. By a crazy stalker. I thought you... You have a Harley and a black leather jacket and a friend with a bike. And you're always home. I thought you were unemployed and in a gang and were fighting and brawling and..."

He eyed her, realization dawning. "You figured I was some worthless biker in a gang." Relief trickled through his veins. Her antipathy to him wasn't from his scars but the conclusions she'd drawn about them. Come to think of it, he did look damned disreputable. He hadn't even shaved for weeks.

Amusement rose. "Were you thinking Carson'd be hanging out with me, learning how to pick up biker chicks, and doing drugs?"

Her coloring made for gorgeous blushes. Gaze tipped down toward her lap, she nodded. "He's at the age where he's looking for a male role model, and you're right next door. I was scared."

He put his fingers under her stubborn chin and lifted, forcing her to look at him. Distress filled her gaze, her expression. She was more upset over hurting his feelings than she had been when Edward gave her hell. What kind of a woman got this upset because she might've hurt a guy's feelings? "No worries, pet."

Unlike Amber and her fake apology, Josie showed true repentance. The sheer honesty of her emotions pulled at the Dom in him. What she felt clearly showed in her big eyes and soft mouth.

Holt brushed her bangs out of her face and continued, "Although I ride a bike, I don't belong to any motorcycle gang or club."

"Oh."

The skin under her chin was like silk. And her mouth was damned appealing, the top lip sweetly curved. Unable to resist, he stroked his thumb over her lower lip. So fucking soft. Quivering slightly.

Her breathing changed...as if she'd become aware of him as more than someone she'd insulted.

Be good, Master Holt. He dropped his hand.

She cleared her throat. "Um, right."

Her color had risen. Yeah, she definitely was looking at him differently.

"Max said you'd be back at work soon."

"Yes. It'll be a relief since sitting at home is driving me nuts. Unfortunately, the chief benches both firefighters and paramedics until they're in fighting trim."

"I was rude to a *firefighter*—a hero?" She closed her eyes. "Just shoot me now."

She was damned cute.

"Josie." He waited until she opened her eyes. "You weren't that rude, and it's not a problem. Carson's lucky to have a mother who worries about him."

"He might do better with one who doesn't jump to idiotic conclusions."

When she bit her lip, his gaze dropped to her mouth. Color flooded her face again.

"I—uh," She jumped to her feet. "I need to get back to my bar. Thank you for being so understanding."

"Sure." Sipping his warm drink, he watched her walk away.

After hearing she'd fucked up, she'd come right to him to apologize and confess. *Repentant.* She really was a sweetheart, wasn't she? But no matter how cute and honest, she wasn't a Shadowlands member. And she was his neighbor.

Nope, not going to go there.

CHAPTER FIVE

On Saturday evening, Josie scowled at the words on the computer screen. Her heroes might have magical powers, but they were still teenagers, and she could swear that her son's new *I'm-being-put-upon* attitude was showing up in two of the team members. *You guys are supposed to be better than this,* she told them sternly.

Even worse, Tigre was still flirting with Laurent. *No, no, no.* Maybe she should turn his attention to a buxom milkmaid and give Laurent a life lesson about the duration of a man's "love".

With a sigh, she pushed the keyboard away and rose from her desk. Enough frustration. Time to dress for her second night in the Shadowlands.

As she wiggled out of her ragged jeans and into sleek black pants, anticipation uncurled inside her. The club was unlike anywhere she'd ever been. Everything had tugged at her senses.

The groans and screams and the sounds of flesh being struck in innumerable ways blended with the ominous bass-heavy music.

The scents—sex, leather, citrusy cleansers, all mingling with the aroma of beer and wine at the bar.

The sights—the darkly attired Doms and the brighter, scantily clad or naked submissives.

The majority of nightclubs catered to young, slender, hetero-sexuals. However, the Shadowlands' people came in all sizes and shapes, all gender identities and preferences. She loved the variety.

Even so, she'd had a few *moments*.

When she'd seen a Dom sticking needles into a woman's breasts—in a spiraling pattern no less—her breasts totally shriv-eled up inside her bra.

One person, attired head-to-toe as a pony, had been led around on reins. She couldn't see herself in that kind of costume, but the pony's shoe-hooved feet had been dancing with delight. *Go, pony!*

The evening had been a constant immersion in sensual sounds, scents, and sights. Honestly, she'd had sex and been less aroused. Truly, spending hours with—she rolled her eyes—with a damp pussy was most disconcerting. Was the Shadowlands truly a place she wanted to work?

And yet... And yet...

She could do the work. *Check*.

She liked the people. *Check*.

The pay was excellent. *Check*. Face it, she needed the money.

If only she didn't have this unwelcome desire to *participate*.

Her inner kinkster was struggling to emerge, wasn't it? Part of her attraction to Carson's father—*may his testicles shrivel and drop off*—was how he'd taken charge. The day before she and her father had returned to Texas, Everett had tied her up and spanked her. She'd been horrified. Cried. And orgasmed.

In fact, she'd dreamed about that spanking for years after-ward, albeit *her* hero sure hadn't been Everett. Aragorn had starred for a while. Ironman should be called Ironhand. The various King Arthurs—yep. Always someone from books or movies. Until last night.

She shook her head and felt her face flush. In her dreams last night, Holt had been the one spanking her. Kissing her.

Dominating her.

But, honestly, fantasies were one thing; real life was a whole different kettle of fish.

The security guard named Ghost had called her submissive. She scowled and yanked a brush through her short hair, then fluffed the ends. She might be a bit kinky in her dreams, but submissive for real? Doubtful. After all, she ruled this house and the youngster in it. Single mothers didn't have the liberty to be submissive.

Any woman—not just a submissive one—would enjoy watching the Shadowlands Masters. Wasn't it funny how different they all were? Sam, the rancher sadist, had dressed in jeans and a regular shirt, whereas Master Marcus's suit must have cost a pretty penny. Cullen had worn brown leathers. Holt went with all black, but nothing fancy. There was no relationship between attire and Master status.

Then—since she wrote about superheroes—she'd rather hoped their esoteric *Master* powers would hum or something. *Nada.* None of them had cool glowy auras either. Talk about a letdown.

Despite the lack of glowy auras, the power was there. Whenever one of them gave a command, she'd obeyed without thinking. That had been...strange.

It was even more unsettling to learn her new neighbor was a member of that club. Of course, she'd gotten the job because Master Z had been at his house. But still... Holt was not only a member, but also one of those super-powerful Masters.

When he'd touched her, lifted her chin, run his thumb over her lip, she'd forgotten how to breathe. Why did he have to be so devastatingly gorgeous? And kind. When she'd confessed to her rudeness, he'd been sympathetic. Even a bit amused.

He sure hadn't been amused about Amber's behavior. His

anger had been scarily impressive. He'd never raised his voice, but boy, he'd sure dealt with the problem.

Well, no matter how gorgeous, he was her neighbor and a member of the place where she worked. She wasn't foolish enough to trespass over those lines.

Eyeing herself in the mirror, she ordered, "You will stick to your bartending, Josephine, and ignore the scenes and your neighbor." *Right. No problem.*

She glanced at the clock and winced. Time to get Carson ready to spend the night at Oma's.

As she crossed the room, she tripped over a box and pain seared her toes. Hopping on one foot, she tried to catch her balance. "Dammit!"

She glared at the box and the others stacked along the wall. Every room still held unpacked boxes. On the last day of moving, they'd abandoned organizing and labeling. Everything left in the apartment had been tossed willy-nilly into whatever box was closest.

With a grin, Josie recalled Carson's appalled expression when he'd realized an unlabeled box must have the TV remote. Her boy was turning into such a guy. He'd immediately started unpacking boxes.

"Hey, Carson." She entered the living room. "Did you find the TV stuff?"

The room was empty. He wasn't in the backyard. Frowning, she checked his bedroom, bathroom, then heard noise from the fourth bedroom, currently being used for storage.

There he was, sitting on the carpet beside a box, its contents spilled over the floor.

Seeing her own face on a beach photo, she realized Carson had knocked over her memory box. It'd been filled with old photos, her diaries from teendom, her high school writing awards.

Carson was perusing a paper.

As Josie moved closer, a chill ran up her spine. That was

Everett's office paper with the dark blue logo and font...and his harsh handwriting. The blood drained from her head and left her without two thoughts to rub together, let alone explanations.

Because, even after a decade, she recognized what Carson held.

Giving in to Josie's begging, Everett's receptionist had hand-carried Josie's note into his office. Her note had said she was over four months pregnant. Carson was reading Everett's response. *Oh, God.*

Josie.

You must surely know I've been avoiding you. Since you can't take a hint, I'll be blunt. As you know, I'm married. Happily married. With a child whom I love. I never did anything to lead you to believe I held feelings for you—or to have you accuse me of being the father of your child. If you are truly pregnant—which I doubt—I'm certainly not the father. Look to one of the other numerous boys you've been with.

If you persist in harassing me, I will be forced to take legal action.

Everett

Josie closed her eyes. Reading the letter had been like being on the receiving end of a beating. So many blows straight to her heart, driving her back, hurting her. *Bam, bam, bam.*

He'd been *"avoiding her"*. She'd told herself he was busy. After all, he'd told her repeatedly how much he loved her. He'd said he couldn't wait for her to return to St. Petersburg.

He was *"happily married"*? Then why had he said he was separated and getting a divorce from his hateful wife? He'd sure never mentioned a child.

"I'm certainly not the father." Her teeth gritted together. He certainly *was* Carson's father. During her high school Christmas break, her father had taken her to St. Petersburg so he could go deep-sea fishing with his friends. He figured she'd enjoy the beach. Seeing her sitting alone, Everett had flirted with her, charmed her, and then banged her every spare moment of every

day. He'd taken her more than once without a condom. *"I'll pull out, sweetheart. Don't worry."*

She should have worried.

The ugliest part was the statement she'd been with *"numerous boys"*. Everett knew he'd been her first. He'd gloated about it.

Legal action. She'd been so stupid, so naïve. A terrified teenager. Otherwise, she'd have known the legal action taken should have been hers. She'd have known to demand a paternity test and gotten child support. Instead, when he'd threatened her with legal action, she'd panicked.

She swallowed. The pain of that letter still lingered, like an open wound in her chest.

The paper shook in Carson's hand as he stared at her with his big brown eyes—his father's eyes. "Is he my father? Everett Lanning?"

She'd dodged this day for years, even while telling Carson the truth—that his "father" hadn't wanted to be a parent. That they did fine on their own. "Yes, he is." Her voice sounded dry as the dust covering the box lid. "He was—"

"You were—you *fucked*—a married man?"

The coarse accusation made her flinch. Because she had...oh, she had. How could she tell her little boy that infatuation didn't look for the lies beneath the words? That hope swept uneasy doubts away. Everett had treated her like someone special and said he loved her. Back then, she'd yearned for kindness and love with all her heart.

"I'm afraid so." She pulled in a breath. "He told me he was getting a divorce."

"Oh, please." Carson's voice cracked and dropped to a baritone that sounded like Josie's father—scorn and all.

When she'd told Pa that she was pregnant, he'd gone into a rant over her ingratitude and lack of morals...and over the damage to his reputation. He'd given her an hour to pack and leave—and told her never to come back.

She'd driven straight to St. Petersburg, certain Everett would take care of her. He loved her, after all.

Looking back at that time, over a decade ago, she could forgive herself. She'd been awfully young.

Well. Young or not, she'd learned how the world worked. And, as she often told Carson, life lessons tended to be the ones that hurt. She'd discovered how quickly a man—father or lover—would jettison an inconvenient woman. She'd also found out she could make her own way, even as she raised a child on her own.

Knees shaking, she sat on a box. Where were all the calm, reasonable explanations she'd practiced for this moment?

"Yes, I was stupid, Carson. However, your birth father"—damned if she'd call him a *real* father—"lied to me, got me pregnant, and then wanted nothing to do with me."

Carson's gaze dropped to the note. "But he didn't believe you. Didn't believe you were pregnant."

In hindsight, she could see how carefully Everett, an investment banker, had tried to cover his ass. How could she explain that to her son? "He knew I wouldn't lie—and knew I hadn't been with anyone else."

"He was, maybe, really mad. After I was born, did you go back and tell him he had a kid? Try to talk with him?"

"No, Carson." She nodded at the paper. "His opinion seems rather clear, don't you think?"

Carson looked away.

She bit her lip. Her tone had been too harsh...because she hurt. After this many years, her wounds had healed, but her son's disbelief was ripping the scars open. She held her hand out. "Honey, I know this is hard."

He pushed her hand away. "You didn't even *try*. Didn't try to get my father to want me."

The stubborn set of her boy's chin—something she saw in her own mirror—let her know any explanations at this point wouldn't be heard. Her arm dropped.

He shoved to his feet, kicked the box over, and ran for his room. The door slammed with a finality she could hear echoing in her heart.

Closing her eyes, she pulled in a despairing breath through her nose and tried not to cry.

Tomorrow. Surely, he'd be ready to listen to her tomorrow.

"Oh, Master Holt, your poor face."

The submissive's gooey sympathy set Holt's teeth on edge, as did the way she stared at his scars. She wasn't the first. A shit-ton of the Shadowlands members—especially the younger women—acted this way.

"It's healing." He forced a smile and patted her arm.

As he turned away, he noticed Nolan and Beth nearby. They'd undoubtedly overheard.

Nolan pointed to a chair. "Sit with us and take a load off."

"I look that bad?" Holt sat and hated that it felt so damn good. Then again, he'd insisted on taking a dungeon monitor shift and had been on his feet for far too fucking long.

"Not bad, just tired," Beth said in her soft voice. She shook her head. "I know it's draining when people get all focused on the damage instead of seeing...you."

The pretty redhead would know. Her psycho ex-husband had left scars all over her body. Holt's anger rose on her behalf. Sure, he didn't like people staring at him, but he could take it. No one should treat sweet Beth that way.

After a calming breath, he gave her a rueful smile. "Not to be conceited, but when I was younger, I made a ton of money because I had a pretty face. It's disconcerting when a subbie bursts into tears on seeing me now."

Nolan took Beth's hand before running a finger down the scar on his own cheekbone. "Yeah, the reactions can be a pain. On the upside, a nice long scar is handy when you want to scare li'l submissives."

Beth snorted, and then grinned at Holt. "When we met, he had me so terrified I almost puked."

Yet she'd married the Dom. The tension knotting Holt's shoulders eased away.

"The scars fade so they're not as noticeable," Nolan said. "People who aren't shallower than a puddle will notice the scars and see past them."

"So I'm finding." It also seemed there were a lot of shallow women in the world—like his girlfriend who'd walked out of his hospital room. Holt leaned back. "Our new bartender's reaction was unique. She's my neighbor, saw my Harley and these scars, and decided I was some murderous biker and should stay far away from her son."

Ignoring Nolan's burst of laughter, Beth turned an angry red and pushed to her feet. Her hands were fisted. "I'm going to have a chat with her."

She got one step before her Master yanked her down onto his lap. "Uh-uh, sugar. Holt's problem."

Beth's fury on his behalf was heartwarming, but no longer needed. "It's all good, sweetheart. When Josie found out the truth, she came straight to me to apologize. Was damn upfront about it, too."

"Oh." Beth's frown faded. "Well, all right."

"Seems like Z warned you about fighting in the Shadowlands, didn't he?" Nolan asked her.

"He knew I was protecting my Master from a nasty she-predator," Beth muttered. "It's not like I punched her or anything."

Damn. Holt wished he'd seen that altercation. He grinned. "You're a lucky guy, King."

Nolan's instant "damn straight" made Beth smile.

"I should head on home." Holt gave them a smile, started

toward the locker room, and found himself detouring toward the bar.

Josie wanted to be home and talking with Carson about Everett's letter. She tried to focus on dispensing drinks, but worries kept bubbling to the surface. Surely time would heal the breach between them.

It helped to remember that her boy wasn't one for holding on to his anger.

Okay, then. She took a long, slow breath to get her mind back into the proper workspace. At least this shift was going better than last night's. Or maybe she was adjusting to the strangeness of her surroundings. The costumes—fetwear—weren't as startling, although she was still wincing at the sight of clamps and leashes attached to balls and cocks, nipples and labia. *Sheesh.*

She definitely liked the music. The songs had a pronounced beat that kept her feet dancing, her hips swaying, and she had to remind herself she was at work and shouldn't be adding in a shimmy now and then.

Of course, her added comfort level meant she watched more of the scenes and now totally wanted to participate. The thought of being on the receiving end of a sexy—*not* a punishing—flogging made her insides all quivery.

Don't be foolish, Josephine.

One: She worked here.

Two: She didn't have anyone to wield the flogger.

Seriously, this wasn't anything she wanted to get into. Heck, she didn't even date. What kind of disaster would she make out of a BDSM scene?

As she looked out over the room, she glimpsed Holt...and a zing shot straight to her girl parts.

Again. Surely those electric zaps should have stopped, as often as she'd seen him tonight. Okay, she had to admit she'd watched for him as he went about his monitoring rounds. Honestly, what woman wouldn't watch him? Every time he moved, muscles rippled under his sleeveless, black T-shirt. Would his biceps be as hard as they looked? It was insane to have such a craving to touch.

To be touched.

Such thinking was simply crazy. Even if she dated and even if she was into the serious Dominant/submissive stuff—and she wasn't—Holt was out of her league. She was pretty...in a healthy sort of way. Master Holt looked like he should be on a magazine cover.

True, he did have scars, the dark red one running from his temple to his jaw and a more jagged-looking one under his chin. It hurt to see them—to think of the pain he must have endured, to see the perfection of his face marred. Yet the scars added a deadly edge to his appeal. He'd been in a knife-fight and survived.

With a huff of exasperation, Josie yanked her gaze away. *Bad Josie. No leering at Master Neighbor.* Unfortunately, returning her attention to the bar meant she saw who was at the barmaid station. Amber.

Josie gave a quiet unhappy sigh. Most of the volunteer barmaids were friendly and fun. However, Amber was making it clear she blamed Josie for her punishment last night and had grown increasingly rude.

Josie smiled politely and held her hand out for the tickets.

Amber tossed the tickets, scattering them over the bar, then slapped down her tray. "Hurry it up, would you?"

Somebody should have had more time-outs as a child.

"I'll have these for you in about five minutes." Josie kept her tone even and started working her way through the list.

Amber's sighs of impatience grew louder. Her fingernails drummed on the bar. "I don't have all day."

Josie tilted her head in acknowledgment. Early in her bartending career, she'd learned that reacting to rudeness only escalated the unpleasantness. Bartenders who lasted soon developed armor impervious to insults, aggression, and leering.

As Josie set the last drink onto Amber's tray, the blonde

snapped, "Finally. I've never seen anyone so slow. Who hired you anyway?"

"That would be me." The darkly resonant voice held an edge of steel.

The barmaid spun. At the sight of Z behind her, she went pale. "Master Z!"

"I've been quite pleased with how efficiently our new bartender fills the drink orders." His icy expression contrasted with his measured words. "The only complaints I've heard are from the submissive who stole a drink from the private stock."

Amber sank to her knees.

Master Z looked down at her. "After being punished, a submissive is forgiven and her slate wiped clean. It seems you haven't extended the same courtesy to the person you attempted to wrong. Rather than trying to make amends, you're taking out your resentment on her."

The woman's head bowed until her forehead touched the floor.

"I'm disappointed in your behavior, Amber. If your discourtesy loses us the bartender, the Masters will have to resume tending bar, and *none* of them will be pleased with you. Neither will I."

The submissive's squeak was like a tortured sparrow. "Oh God, oh God, I'm sorry, Master Z. It won't happen. I'm sorry, I'll behave."

There was a long silence before he spoke. "You're normally a good girl, one a Dom could enjoy. Before you leave tonight, I want you to write an essay explaining why a submissive should release all the anger in her heart after her punishment. Just as she hopes her Dom will do."

"Yes, Sir."

"Very good. Continue."

Master Z nodded at Josie and strolled away as if he hadn't just reduced a person to a quivering mess with a few words. He hadn't even raised his voice.

Amber scrambled to her feet, saw Josie, and grabbed her hand. "I'm sorry. I'm really, really sorry. It wasn't your fault, and I shouldn't be mean to you, and I'm sorry. Please don't quit. Oh God, don't quit."

Good grief. The woman sounded so much like Carson that the annoyance drained out of Josie's heart. With her free hand, she patted Amber's arm. "It's all right. Shhh. I'm not quitting—it'll be fine."

Tears filled the blonde's eyes, and she whispered, "Thank you. You really are nice, aren't you? Thank you!" Grabbing her tray of drinks, she hurried away.

Josie stared after her and then scrubbed her hands over her face. "Sheesh."

A low chuckle resonated up her spine, and she turned.

On a barstool, Holt sat close enough to have heard the whole show. "You look shook up, sweetheart." When he smiled at her, a sexy dimple appeared in his left cheek.

The easy affection added to his melted-chocolate voice made her knees weak. "This place sure has some strange...customs." With a towel, she restored the bar top in front of him to the proper gleam. "What can I get you, Sir?"

Amusement glinted in his steel-blue eyes. "Did you just call me sir?"

She had, hadn't she? Why in the world had she done that? "Um...I guess all this military lingo is catching."

"You do it very nicely." As his eyes held hers, the floor sank a few inches under her feet.

When he finally released her gaze, goosebumps covered her arms.

"Holt, I do believe you're looking better today." Master Marcus sat down beside him.

Turning away, Josie busied herself with tidying up the drink well...and tried to get her wayward responses under control. What in the world was wrong with her?

When Master Holt returned his attention to her, the intent look in his eyes set up a flutter in her stomach. "I'll take a Mountain Dew if you have one on hand."

"Coming right up." This time, she managed to bite back the *sir* that wanted to follow. He was her neighbor. They weren't even friends, although she found his presence oddly reassuring, like she wasn't alone amidst strangers. Only, really, he was a stranger, too.

As she went through the sodas to find a Dew, she took a few glances at him. Tonight, she could finally see the tattoos covering his very ripped biceps. A dark dragon on one arm, a red and black phoenix on the other. Beautiful work. Destruction and rebirth.

When he leaned his forearms on the bar top, she saw more slashing knife scars marked his golden tan, starting at his wrists. The sight made her eyes burn with tears. *No, you can't go give him a hug, Josephine.*

Instead, she turned her attention to finding the right can of soda. After opening it, she held up a glass. *Glass or straight from the can?*

He nodded, accepting the glass. As a bartender, she had a well-tuned antenna for facial expressions and body language. While he wasn't snooty or rude, it was clear he was accustomed—and comfortable—with being served.

Why did that seem sexy, too? Yes, she was being silly.

As she poured, a man in a black vinyl tank and black jeans approached the bar. Medium height, stocky build, sandy hair and ruddy complexion. He looked like a sales rep who sold liquor to The Highlands.

Wait... She took a second look. "Peter?"

"There she is." The rep took a barstool next to Holt. "Good evening, Holt."

Holt nodded. "Peter."

Peter grinned at her. "I was hoping to find our lost bartender from The Highlands. Quite the change for you, isn't it, Josie?"

Wow, more people were into BDSM than she'd ever realized. "Sure is. Have you been a member here very long?"

"A year or so. The newsletter said Z'd hired a bartender named Josie, so I decided to find out if he meant you."

"Well, as you see…"

"It's great to have you here." His smile widened. "The Highlands regulars have been grumbling quite loudly about losing their favorite bartender."

"Really?" Smiling, she served him a drink and got caught up on the news. She had to laugh at his wry description of a lost sale. He was a sociable guy, always polite, and had asked her out a couple of times in the past. When she told him she had a child and didn't date, he'd taken the refusal good-naturedly.

He took a sip of his drink. "What do you think of the Shadowlands?"

As she considered her answer, she noticed Master Holt had stopped his conversation with Marcus and was openly listening. Her cheeks heated. "It's different, but I'm enjoying the change. I hadn't realized how nice it is when no one gets drunk."

"What about the kinky stuff going on all around you?"

She avoided looking at Holt. After a night of dreaming about him, she felt off-balance seeing him in person. Especially in the Shadowlands. "I can see why *50 Shades* was so popular. I've never… Well, it's…interesting."

"Good." Peter leaned forward and put his hand over hers. "You know, we should play a bit on your break. I could give you an idea of what it's like. Nothing intense."

She stared at him. And hated—*hated*—that she wished Holt had made the offer. What in the world was wrong with her? "I… um, surely that's not allowed. I'm here to work."

"Josie." Master Holt broke in. "Did you sign membership papers and get the physical and background check?"

She nodded.

"Then you're allowed." He smiled slightly. "Z handles the

employee applications much like membership ones in case a person decides to participate."

"That's very foresighted of him." Downright cautious to boot. She glanced at Holt, felt the impact of his eyes, and looked away.

"Perfect. So, Josie?" Peter prompted.

But, but, but... With relief, she spotted someone waiting for a drink at the other end. "Let me take care of that person. I'll be right back."

She took orders from a cute male submissive with big brown eyes and netted time to think as she mixed the two gin and tonics.

Admit it, Josie, you want to see what a scene would be like.

However, she'd be in front of everyone. Not so good. Of course, a bartender was always on stage.

The bondage stuff would be rather unsettling. Still, she wouldn't mind trying it.

But...she hardly knew Peter.

"Here you go." She handed the drinks to the young man and watched him prance back to a tough-looking Dom. Upon receiving an approving smile, the submissive glowed with delight.

Huh. She couldn't imagine being overwhelmed at a compliment from Peter, although he was a likable man. She sure hadn't realized he was a Dom. She had noticed, however, when he and his friends were drinking in The Highlands, he was always the one in charge.

A man who was confident—a boss type—was quite attractive.

The young submissive with the drinks knelt in front of his Dom. Happily. He sure acted as if he found his Dom to be more than just attractive. He really showed that whole dominance-submission stuff. Like... She could see he had an overpowering need to do as told. The way he took so much pleasure in his obedience was eye opening.

She sure couldn't be much of a submissive since she didn't automatically obey any order given—well, not always. In fact, these Masters here had managed to circumvent her customary *think first, act if agree* habit.

Moving down the bar, she gave a Domme a Diet Coke and bottled water. Politely, she answered a younger Dom's request for another beer by saying he'd reached his two-drink limit. Giving him a sympathetic smile, she offered a Red Bull and was pleased when his scowl turned rueful and he thanked her. Members here responded far more politely to getting cut off than her nightclub customers had.

She saw Peter was patiently waiting for her return. *Decide, Josie.*

Why not try a scene? It wasn't as if this would be a date or anything. She'd watched lots of what they called "pickup scenes." Face it, she was dying to see what it was like. Maybe she'd even find out if she really was submissive.

When she reached Peter, she put her forearms on the bar. "I'd love to have an actual introduction to this stuff. Yes."

When Holt's pretty neighbor agreed to a scene, he frowned. Sure, he'd stepped in to clarify the paperwork, but he hadn't thought she'd agree to play with Peter. He'd figured her for being more conservative. As he sipped his Mountain Dew, he studied her.

A flush nearly hid the scattering of freckles over her nose and cheeks. Her gorgeous green eyes held a hint of wariness. So fucking appealing. He wanted to explore those emotions with her, heightening the excitement, easing the wariness...at least for the first scene.

No, he knew better than to mess with a neighbor. *Don't be an asshole.*

He did notice she showed no sexual interest in Peter, which wasn't uncommon. A good scene didn't require sex. However, the Dom had a definite interest in Josie.

Holt tightened his jaw, trying to conquer the need to warn the guy to watch his step or better yet, tell Josie to say no. *Getting a bit overprotective here, dumbass?*

She was fine. Even if the two didn't negotiate, she'd been quite clear she wanted only an introduction. Smart girl.

Sitting beside Holt, Marcus said under his breath, "This should be interesting." He raised his voice. "Darlin', I'll cover your break."

She glanced around the bar. "It's pretty busy. I don't—"

"I can draft Holt to help out. He needs to move some."

Hands on on delightfully curvy hips, she scowled. "No, he doesn't. He should be taking it easy, not working."

Now, just listen to her. As the sweetness of her concern warmed him, Holt smiled and gave his Aussie buddy's favorite retort, "No worries, love. I'll let the lawyer do most of the work."

"I guess that'll be all right." She frowned at Marcus. "You'll watch him?"

"Certainly." After Josie had exited the bar space, Marcus glanced at Holt. "I do like this one."

"Z did well." And Holt liked her a bit too much for his own comfort.

He followed Marcus through the pass-through and started filling drinks on one side. He was doing fairly well until one submissive ordered a mojito. *For fuck's sake.* He didn't have the time to squish up mint, mess with the sticky shit, or do the shaking crap. He gave her a frown. "For that, you'll have to wait for the real bartender."

"Sure," she said. "She made me a couple last night, and they were the best."

Holt eyed her. Two drinks at once? "Did you play afterward?"

"No. Josie said if I even looked like playing, she'd rat on me to Master Z." The subbie grinned, so Josie had apparently delivered the warning without upsetting the young woman.

"Good girl." Holt smiled at the subbie, saw Marcus had over-heard, and they exchanged satisfied glances.

Holt understood Z's affection for the socializing effect of drinking; however, alcohol was a risk in a BDSM club. When Cullen—who had a cutting-edge memory—decreased his hours, they'd had a few problems.

But apparently, pretty Josie could and would police the bar.

Finished with open drink orders, Holt looked around. Where had Peter set up with Josie? He wanted to be sure the Dom wasn't pushing her too much.

Hey, she was a neighbor—under his protection, in a way. All right, that might be over the top, but dammit, she was.

And he wanted to see how she reacted to a scene.

No, be honest. He wanted to be the one tying her to a cross...*dammit*.

Near the dance floor, a handful of people watched a Domme doing knife play with an older male submissive. Next was a standard spanking scene on a sawhorse-type bench. Then wax play, a caning, a...

"North wall," Marcus murmured as he walked past to deliver a drink.

Holt moved to the other side of the bar. Near the munchie area, Vance and Galen were playing with their submissive, Sally. Holt watched for a minute. Although he'd never been interested in sharing a woman, the two Doms made co-topping look like a dance. Very nice work.

The next scene was a Master with two slaves. The two females waited on their knees as he chose the toys he'd use.

In the adjacent roped-off area...there she was.

She'd removed only her vest and shirt.

Well, that probably made sense. She and Peter weren't on intimate terms.

She had gorgeous shoulders and upper arms. Creamy skin. Did she have freckles sprinkled over the tops of her shoulders?

As Marcus joined him, Holt muttered, "Did you see? She still has her shoes on."

She was talking to Peter as he tied her wrists to the upper bars of the X-shaped St. Andrew's cross. Her head was up, posture erect, eyes bright with interest.

No signs of submission.

"Interesting dynamic," Marcus commented.

"She's not anywhere close to the right headspace." Holt glanced around the bar, saw no one waiting for a drink, and continued watching.

Peter did a hasty warmup of her skin before starting in with a fairly heavy flogger.

Holt exchanged frowns with Marcus, before shrugging. "He *is* on a time limit."

"True enough. A half-hour timeframe won't give her more than a taste." Marcus frowned. "Is he more to her than a casual friend?"

"Doubtful. Her great-aunt told me today our little bartender hasn't dated anyone in years. Not since her son was a toddler." And hadn't that been a surprise? What the hell was wrong with his fellow males that they'd let her isolate herself?

Marcus glanced at him. "How is it that you're acquainted with the great-aunt of our new bartender?"

"Stella lives in the other half of my duplex, and I drop over now and then to check her blood pressure." Damned if he'd let the sweet old woman stroke out on his watch. "She worries about the lack of men in Josie's life." Holt grinned. "From what I've seen, Stella isn't lacking for male admirers. She could probably teach Josie how to get on."

Marcus chuckled. "And why doesn't our Josie date?"

"She has a son."

After a second, Marcus glanced at Holt. "That's it?"

"It's the reason Stella gave me. I figure there's more to the story."

"There must be."

As they watched the scene, Holt's frown returned.

Marcus shook his head. "She's getting a taste of impact play, but I see no submission going on."

Holt leaned his forearms on the bar. No, she wasn't in a submissive frame of mind. She was simply satisfying her curiosity. Tugging on the restraints. Feeling the flogger. Testing the cross. The excitement she'd shown before had disappeared. She was having fun—a degree of fun—but it sure wasn't what he'd call a successful scene.

Damn. She wasn't his, and Peter wasn't doing anything that required intervention but... "It's sad to see a submissive not receive what she hoped for," he murmured.

She'd hoped for more, Josie thought, as the flogger fell across her back, although the physical sensations were interesting. The flogger thudded over her bare shoulders like tapping fingertips.

The sensation changed when the strands hit her pants instead of bare skin. She hadn't stripped down like most of the "bottoms". At Peter's urging, she'd removed her shirt and vest. Her bra and everything else stayed on.

He'd restrained her arms upward to the X-shaped equipment in a high V. Earlier, she'd seen a naked submissive whose ankles were cuffed to the lower part of the X, and the Dom had taken advantage of his submissive's widespread legs to play with her pussy. Watching the Dom work the woman had been hot.

A non-self-induced orgasm might've been amazing, but Josie wasn't interested in going there with Peter. She did appreciate how nice he was being.

He was talking with her, telling her about the flogger, and asking her every few strokes how she felt. His attentiveness was reassuring...also awfully distracting. She had to keep assessing herself, then turning her head to answer. The constant interruptions took her out of...well, whatever she should be feeling.

The stuff she'd read about BDSM made it sound as if she should be floating around in her head or something.

Not.

How long had they been doing this, anyway? Surely, it was time to be done. Funny how she'd started all revved up, and now a dull sense of disenchantment weighed her down—like she'd expected a smooth Glenmorangie 18 scotch and gotten moonshine instead.

"We still have a few minutes left. Did you know there are private rooms upstairs?" Leaning against her from behind, Peter pressed his chest against her back and his erection against her ass.

Oh, ew, that wasn't good. She hadn't wanted to get him interested in sex; she should have known better. Guys were awfully predictable that way. But sheesh, even if she was interested, she needed to be back to work within five minutes. *Seriously, Peter?*

Gently, Josie. Sure, she was disappointed in the scene, but she mustn't be rude. "I'm really sorry, but I need to get back to work. I don't want to make my boss unhappy." She smiled at him. "Thank you for letting me see what it's all about."

"Ha, I *knew* you'd like it. Subbie."

Subbie? What she felt wasn't submission; it was impatience and a craving to be safely ensconced behind her bar again. Seeing the arousal in his reddened face, she closed her eyes.

Finally, her arms were free. Stepping away, she pulled on her shirt and vest.

When Peter sprayed down the cross, she grabbed a paper towel and helped clean.

"I could hold you for a couple minutes, do some aftercare," he offered.

She'd noticed that post-scene, many submissives were sweaty and shaking. Some were even crying. Almost all of the Doms provided blankets, water, and cuddles. Carefully tended the bruises or cuts. A few lucky submissives even got chocolate.

Josie hadn't even broken a sweat. "That's sweet of you, but I'm fine. I should get back. Thank you again." She kissed his cheek lightly and headed for the bar.

Well...at least she'd tried something new. She gave herself two points for being adventurous. Could she give herself a few points for—what would it be called—self-discovery? She'd discovered watching BDSM stuff didn't necessarily mean she'd like it herself. She now knew she didn't have a submissive bone in her body.

As she neared the bar, the two Masters were watching her.

When Holt's slow perusal sent heat shooting through her, she stiffened. "*What?* Did I forget to button my shirt?"

He raised an eyebrow at her defensive tone, then answered mildly, "Unfortunately not."

An embarrassed flush warmed her cheeks.

Chuckling, Marcus told Holt, "She's got a sassy mouth on her. Reminds me of my Gabi."

The corners of Holt's mouth tilted up. "God help us. If she starts sounding like Gabi, I'll find a gag. Bartenders don't need to talk, right?"

Laughing, she joined them behind the bar. "You should stop now while you can still get a drink that lacks arsenic, Master Holt."

His expression darkened. His step forward put him right in front of her. "Did you just threaten me, pet?"

His proximity made her realize how tall and muscular he was. Her pulse quickened.

Her quick retreat halted with her spine against the bar. He simply followed.

She stared up into penetrating slate-blue eyes, seeing the dark gray ring around the iris. His body radiated warmth—and sparked an answering surge from her own.

Expression stern, he curled his big hand around her nape, holding her in place. His tone lowered. Darkened. "As it happens, I like gagging little subbies." He ran a finger over her lower lip. "Listening to the helpless sounds, the whimpers, the begging they can't voice."

As her mouth went dry, she stared up at him, feeling a quiver deep in her core.

"Would you like to apologize?" he asked ever so softly.

She wasn't sure her voice would even work. She swallowed. "Sorry, Sir." The breathy sounding words were barely audible.

"Very nice." Humor lightened his eyes to the mesmerizing color of sunlit fog. Leaning down, he kissed her lightly. "Get to work, subbie."

As he followed Marcus out of the bar, she stared after him.

Because when he'd called her *subbie*, every bone in her body had turned to jelly.

CHAPTER SIX

On Sunday evening at Oma's dinner table, Josie watched her son fidgeting with his silverware. Her heart ached for him. For her.

He finally pushed his plate away. "I gotta go do homework." When his great-great-aunt lifted her eyebrows, he recalled his manners. "May I be excused, please?"

"Of course, Carson," Oma said.

With a sigh, Josie watched her sulky boy slink out the door.

As usual when she bartended, Carson had spent the night and next morning with Oma while Josie slept late. Unfortunately, at breakfast, Carson had begged Oma for permission to go to his friend, Isaac's, after church. The rascal had known she wanted to talk with him. He didn't return until suppertime, and from his behavior, he was still angry with Josie.

What should she do? Force him to listen to her explanations? Her excuses? Trash talking about Everett could make his son feel as if he came from bad seed. Josie took a sip of water, hoping to dissolve the lump in her throat. Maybe tomorrow night he'd be ready to talk this out.

"What in the world is wrong with that boy?" Oma asked.

Josie looked across the table at her great-aunt with a loving smile. Oma was white-haired and a bit stooped, complaining she'd shrunk at least four inches as she approached eighty. Her skin was creamy white despite all the gardening hours, because she slathered on the suntan lotion. She was the sweetest, most even-tempered, and sociable person Josie knew. And those sharp blue eyes didn't miss a thing.

Josie only hoped she'd be as amazing when she got to her senior years. "Carson found a note from his birth father. It was the one Everett wrote when I told him I was pregnant. It says he wasn't the father, that it was obviously one of the other men I'd been with, and he was happily married."

"Covered his bases, did he?" Oma pursed her lips. "It's a shame we humans don't geld our males as ruthlessly as we do horses and cows."

A castrating knife, Everett's balls... "Don't tempt me, Oma."

"Carson wants a father, so he can't get angry at Everett, which means he's blaming you instead." Oma gave her usual succinct summary.

"He's definitely blaming me. He feels I should have tried harder to get Everett to accept fatherhood."

"Ah." Oma gave Josie a sympathetic look. "Children who want something rarely have empathy for anyone else involved."

"I know." It still hurt that her son had lashed out—and hit his mark. She'd been raised to believe sex outside of marriage was wrong—and Carson's accusations brought the guilt back full force. "Maybe he's right. I could have tried harder. Or tackled Everett again after Carson was born."

"Josie, you'd barely turned seventeen, and he threatened you with the law. A more experienced youngster might have managed better but not an innocent from Podunkville, Texas." Oma considered. "When I found you after I returned from Europe, and we talked, you told me why you didn't go after him for child support. Do you remember the reasons you gave me?"

"Yes." Josie pushed her uneaten food away. "He's not the type of man to let a cent out of his grasp. He'd have fought me."

"But you would have won." The lack of doubt in her great aunt's voice was heartwarming.

"Yes, a blood test would've proven my claim." And there would have been child support. Her anger rose as she remembered how hard she'd worked to support herself and Carson, especially at first. Even a small amount of money would have helped. Carson wasn't the only one who'd been betrayed. "But a public legal battle would have devastated his wife and child. And Pa, too."

"I do understand you not wanting to destroy a marriage." Oma slapped her napkin down beside her plate. "But your father... Although one shouldn't speak ill of the dead, your father was an insufferable prig, not worthy of kissing my niece's shoes. Or yours."

"He was pretty rigid," Josie admitted. Every year until his death, she'd sent him holiday cards. He'd never responded. Never forgiven her. Never met his only grandchild. She looked away, blinking hard. Harsh and often cruel, still, he'd been her father— and she'd loved him. "It's hard for Carson to have no family except the two of us."

"He has two people who love him, and that's two more than some children get in this life." Oma started stacking the dirty dishes. "Our boy has a good heart. He'll get past this."

Carson did have a good heart. A tender one. Unlike his grandfather, he knew how to forgive.

Mood lifting, Josie carried the plates into the kitchen to load the dishwasher. "What day should we do some heavy-duty cleaning? Are you hosting the book club meeting this week or next week?"

"You don't have to be my housekeeper, child."

When Josie gave her a stubborn look, Oma simply chuckled and moved to the calendar.

A few hours later, Josie realized she'd fallen asleep on her living room couch. It wasn't surprising, considering how late she'd worked at the Shadowlands the past two nights. Well, she'd better get used to it. Master Z had caught her last night before she'd left, said he was pleased with her, and hoped she'd continue.

Coming from someone so intimidating, the compliment had felt amazing. And she'd agreed to be the Shadowlands bartender. She sure wouldn't get bored with her job anytime in the near future.

Yawning, she sat up. The house was quiet, the only noise the hum of the fridge in the kitchen.

After Carson had come out of his room...once...to bid her goodnight, she'd put on a chick-flick DVD to try to lighten her unhappy mood. The movie was long over.

She glanced at the clock. Midnight. It was definitely time for bed. As she headed for her room, she paused outside Carson's door. *Dammit, my sweet son.* How could she explain that his father had played her? That all he'd wanted was sex with a young inno-cent girl. Somehow...she'd have to talk to her boy, embarrassing as it might be.

She stroked her hand over the wood on his door. Where had the years gone? When he'd been a baby, sleeping next to her bed, every time she'd rolled over, she'd check on him, smile down at him, touch his tiny fingers. However did such an immensity of love fit into a human-sized heart?

Now he was older...and she only peeked in when she knew he was unhappy—like during the miserable days when he'd started middle school last September.

She tiptoed into the dark room. The nightlight and glow from his digital clock and electronics let her avoid the scattering of shoes, soccer balls and shin guards, and dirty clothes. There was enough light to see that his bed was empty.

She stared. Turned in a circle. Turned on the light. No boy.

He wasn't in his bathroom.

In the kitchen, she flipped on the light. Empty.

The living room? Empty.

As she lit up each silent space, her anxiety increased.

The front and back doors were still locked with security chains in place.

She returned to his room, hoping against hope that he was hiding. But Carson had never hidden from her, not even when just a little guy and in a rage. He had never run away. Her boy tackled every problem head-on, even when he felt his mother was the problem.

A paper lay in the middle of his bed. She picked it up— Everett's note. As fear ate the strength in her muscles, she leaned against the wall...and a breeze ruffled her hair.

The window was wide open—and the screen was off.

Eyes closed, Holt sat on the back patio, feet up on another chair. The night air was pleasantly cool and smelled of the briny Gulf and the tropical flowers in Stella Avery's half of the backyard.

How long had he lived in this duplex now? He considered. Since late October when Uzuri'd tried living with the Drago cousins? Yeah, about a month and a half, although he'd only officially owned the lease for a couple of weeks. Damned if he didn't like living in a residential neighborhood where the loudest night noises were a barking dog or someone coming home late.

A job as a firefighter and a paramedic could leave ugly shit in a man's head. How a human body looked after a head-on collision or a house fire was...bad. Losing the fight to save someone's life hurt. And those memories could turn into a knotted tangle of pain. Here, in this quiet backyard, he'd learned that simply sitting and watching the grass grow could drain away the tension.

A noise broke the silence, and Holt glanced at the other half of the duplex. No lights. Stella tended to retire early.

At the sound of footsteps, he checked the left and saw Josie walk into her backyard. His momentary annoyance at the disturbance disappeared when he realized every light in her house was on.

He set his beer down and walked over to the chest-high picket fence. "Josie."

She spun, hope in her gaze. "Is Carson with you?"

"No. I saw him going into your house earlier, around sunset, when I was over talking to Duke."

Worry tensed her face.

He glanced at her house. "I take it he's not home?"

"He climbed out his bedroom window sometime in the last couple hours." Her Texas accent had grown thicker with her upset. She stared around the empty backyard. "Oma would have called if he'd gone over there. He's not in the house, not out here. Where could he be?"

"Maybe at a friend's?"

"Oh, God, he might have gone to Isaac's." She pulled out her phone and quick-dialed a number. Holt heard the ringing, then a woman's sleepy voice.

"Courtney, I'm sorry to bother you this late, but Carson isn't in his room. I was hoping he'd snuck away to see Isaac." A pause. "That would be great. Thank you."

Josie could feel the hard edges of the phone digging into her clenched fingers as she waited.

"He's not here, Josie. Let me wake Isaac and see what he knows. I'll call you back," Courtney said in Josie's ear.

"Okay. Thank you so much." Carson wasn't at his best friend's. Stuffing her phone in her jeans pocket, Josie looked around again —and realized Holt had disappeared. He'd probably gone inside. Gone to bed. The unexpected pang of disappointment annoyed her. What had she expected? She didn't know him and this wasn't his problem.

Hearing footsteps she spun. "Carson?"

"No, sorry." Holt walked out of the darkness beside her house, coming into the backyard. He wore only a pair of jeans, his broad chest bare. "What did your friend say?"

"She's checking with her son." Josie shook her head. "I'm sorry. I didn't mean to disturb you."

He put a hand on her shoulder, a firm hand, steadying her. "Breathe, sweetheart. We'll get this worked out." His voice was low and soothing. "Come. No need to stand out here."

With an arm around her, he guided her inside and pointed to her couch. "Sit."

As she did, he disappeared into the kitchen and returned with a Diet Coke. Opening it, he put it into her hand. "Drink that, and let's think a minute."

Think? Under his level gaze, she dutifully took a sip. It burned going down, but the act of swallowing forced her to set her fear aside for a whole second.

When she put the can down, he took her hand, engulfing her cold fingers in warmth. "Now, it's tough to think like a youngster that age, but let's give it a try. He's eleven, right?"

"Yes. Just started middle school this fall."

"Mmm. Probably no girlfriend, then."

"No."

"Did you two have a fight about anything in the last couple of days?"

"We did..." But was his anger toward her about his father enough reason to run away?

"That looks promising. What are you thinking?"

Josie looked up into Holt's blue-gray eyes and drew strength from the steady gaze. "We fought over his father."

"Ah. You think he's gone there?"

She shook her head. "Carson's never met him." She closed her mouth over the rest. Holt was her neighbor, not a friend. She shouldn't—

"Because..." he prompted.

The feelings flooded back, and her eyes started to burn. She realized she still held Everett's note, the one that had made her son hate her. Her hand started to shake as she stared at it.

"Why don't you show me what you're holding, pet?" Holt held out his hand.

When she hesitated, his voice lowered. "Josie."

She set the paper in his hand. "It's not..."

Ignoring her, he read the contents in a glance, and his mouth tightened. "Pretty fucking cruel. Carson saw this?"

She nodded. "He found it while he was unpacking boxes, and now he blames me that his father didn't want him. Like I should have forced Everett to see him and..." Tears spilled over. "My baby h-hates me."

His arms closed around her, pulling her up against a solid, warm body. "Sweetheart, being of the male gender, I can tell you adolescent boys are dumber than rocks and constantly say shit they don't mean. He'll figure it out."

She leaned against him, her cheek pressed to his chest, and his voice was a soft deep rumble. As he ran his hand up and down her back in slow soothing strokes, for a long self-indulgent minute, she took comfort in being held.

When she finally pushed upright, he let her go immediately... and she felt awfully alone without his arms around her. *Josie, you idiot, you don't even know him.* Turning her head, she wiped her eyes.

His voice was gentle as he asked, "Do you think Carson ran away or did he go to his father?"

"Carson's never run away, ever. He sulks for a while, then comes out and battles for what he wants."

Holt half-smiled. "You're a good mom."

"What?"

"To be willing to do battle, a kid needs to feel he has a chance of winning. I'd say that shows he's not afraid of you and thinks you're reasonable."

Oh.

"If he didn't run, do you think he's at his father's?" Holt asked.

"No, he doesn't know where Everett is."

Frowning, Holt held the letter to the light again. "This is on office paper. Has a bank address. Is it Everett's business?"

"Oh, God."

"Aaaaand, that sounds like a yes." Holt ran a finger down her cheek, making her want to press her face into his hand.

"Holt, I don't know if Everett even works there now. That was over a decade ago. And this is Sunday night."

"Good point. I daresay Carson's smart enough to know a bank would be closed."

At a loss, Josie stared at him. What should she do now?

"Easy, pet. If Carson's trying to—"

Her phone rang right then. *Oh please, let it be Carson.* But the display showed COURTNEY. Josie swiped the ANSWER with a trembling finger. "Hey, Courtney. What did Isaac say?"

"Oh, wait till you hear what our two young monsters did." Courtney sounded thoroughly exasperated. "Isaac says Carson wanted to meet his father. So our computer nerds dug up the guy's home address and phone number. It's really true—nothing is secret on the internet."

"Everett's home address?" She blinked. "I don't even know that."

"You do now." Courtney recited the address and phone number, and Josie repeated it back. It seemed Everett was now living north of Tampa.

"Would you text me when you find him?" Courtney asked. "I won't sleep until I know he's all right. Or if there's anything I can help with, call me."

"I will. You're wonderful. Thank you." Josie's hand trembled as she put her phone away. Was Carson really trying to see his father?

"Here, I wrote the info down." Seated on the couch, Holt pushed a paper toward her. He tapped the address. "Looks like he lives near the Avila Golf Course, north of Lake Magdalene. Maybe nine or ten miles from here. It's pretty far to walk."

Carson's bike. Josie ran through the kitchen and outside to the carport. She turned to see Holt behind her. "His bike is gone."

"Then we have a destination and a method of travel. I don't like that you didn't hear from either Carson or his dad. Have you tried calling Carson?"

"He doesn't have a phone."

"Ah." Holt handed her the piece of paper. "Then call his father and see if contact was made."

"No," she whispered.

She looked up into firm gray eyes. "I'm sorry, pet. But it needs to be done." His low voice was even but unyielding.

Call Everett. Everything inside her cringed. Yet Holt was right. All that mattered was Carson's safety. She entered the number and waited as her phone rang and rang. When it stopped, she hit redial. Again. And again.

"Who the fuck is this?" a man snarled, and she recognized Everett's voice.

"This is Josie Collier. My—*our* son—Carson found your address, and we think he might have—"

"Jesus fuck. Wait."

Josie heard a woman murmur, and Everett saying, "Got to take this. It's a client."

A few seconds later, he came back on. "I cannot fucking believe you sent your bastard to harass me at my door. What do you want? Money?"

Rage filled her. "I didn't know he was going to your house, and I certainly didn't send him there. But for some foolish reason, *he* thought you'd like meeting your son."

"He's not my son."

"I agree. You only provided the sperm. You're certainly not any kind of a father. What did you say to *my* son?"

"What do you think? I told him to get lost. Jesus, it was a

good thing I answered the door and not—"

Her anger tipped over. She punched END CALL and threw the phone as hard as she could.

With a quick snatch, Holt caught it. "Uh-uh. Your boy might want to call you, baby."

Her throat clenched at the disaster he'd averted.

Absently, he handed her the phone, even as he spoke into his own cell phone. "Yeah, sorry about the late hour, Dan. I need a favor. My neighbor's son attempted to see his absentee father over in Lake Magdalene and got the door shut in his face. Kid's only eleven. Could you ask a local unit to swing by the area and see if they can spot him? We'll be on our way there too."

Josie heard Dan's growling reply in the affirmative and something about Zane.

Holt grinned briefly. "Okay, I'll owe you a night of babysitting. As soon as I'm allowed to lift more than eight pounds, yeah? Here's the address." He read it off.

A murmur came back.

"That's it. Thanks, Dan." Holt tucked his phone away and told Josie, "Dan's a cop. He should be able to get a patrol car to that neighborhood. The officers might spot him—and if nothing else, their presence in the area will make it safer for Carson."

"Thank you, and thank your friend for me." She rose. "I'll be on my way and—"

"No, you won't." His smooth voice sharpened to edged steel.

"But—"

"We'll take your car, because Carson will recognize it, but I'm driving. Grab your purse and leave a note here for your boy in case he gets home before us. Have him call us if he does."

"You—"

"You can't drive and look for a boy in the shadows at the same time." His eyes darkened, and he gripped her shoulder. "Car crashes aren't pretty, sweetie. Your son needs his mother in one piece."

Under that unwavering determination, all she could do was nod and hurry to get her purse.

Holt turned off Bearss Avenue into the smaller residential streets and glanced at the woman in the passenger seat.

Her short dark red hair was tousled, and the ends flipped out in all directions, making her look like an upset sprite. The ear-length cut emphasized her big green eyes and the sweet curve of her wide mouth. Her face was rounded with a pointed, stubborn chin, and he'd say his pretty neighbor resembled the stereotypical wholesome girl-next-door.

"Almost there, sweetheart," he said.

She stopped searching the street and turned to look at him. "I wish I'd bought him a phone like he wanted. Why didn't I buy him a phone?" The tremor in her voice broke Holt's heart.

"Because cell phones aren't especially good for children, especially young ones?"

She nodded, but he doubted she'd even heard him. "He hasn't gotten home yet, or he'd see my note and call. Do you think he's on his way home?"

Holt tried to think himself into the kid's shoes. "Probably. He's had his hopes stomped on. He might even think you haven't realized he left."

"Right. Right." She slowly sat back, her fingers resting on her phone. Hoping. There was so much love in that patient waiting.

His mother had loved him like that. But he'd lost her well before he'd turned eleven. Did Carson realize how lucky he was?

Now, they just had to find him.

At a long stoplight, he punched the address into his phone's navigational app. As the directions started—in Yoda's voice—Josie gave a snorty laugh of disbelief.

Following the Jedi Master's instructions, Holt reached an

upscale neighborhood with stately palms along the wide side-walks. Two and three story houses were set well back from the street. A few had wrought iron-and stone privacy fences. "I got the impression Everett didn't mention Carson to his wife."

"Apparently not. But why should he? He got rid of me easily enough when it happened."

Holt eyed her. She was perhaps a bit younger than he was. "How old were you when Carson was born?"

She shrugged. "It doesn't matter."

Didn't like to share, did she? Some people would dump their life stories on perfect strangers. Most people answered questions when asked. Then there were the ones who raised a wall around their world. He had a feeling he knew when a young Josie's wall had gone up.

As a kid, he'd loved jumping over fences. These days, the walls he tackled tended to be emotional rather than physical. He reached over and took her hand. "Don't make me play guessing games, pet. How old?"

"Seventeen."

A teenager. His jaw tensed. That note was on office paper, so Everett had been employed, not in high school. "And how old was his father at that time?"

She looked out the window. "I'd guess mid-thirties."

Nine months pregnancy meant she'd probably been sixteen when the asshole got her with child. Holt kept his voice level with an effort. "I'm surprised your parents didn't go after him with statutory rape charges and a paternity suit."

When she didn't answer, he glanced over.

She was still looking out the window. The hand in her lap was fisted.

On the phone, the navigational app kicked in, and Yoda stated, "Reached your destination, you have." Holt slowed the car. The bastard's house was a pretentious colonial mansion style. Yeah, why was he not surprised? Inside, the lights were off.

He saw no child lurking in the yard or under the dimly lit portico.

Josie had the window down and leaned out, searching the street for her boy.

They cruised past the asshole's home, reached the end of the street, and spotted a police patrol car moving slowly down the block.

Holt pulled to the curb, got out, and flagged the car down.

The patrol officer lowered his window. "Can we help you?"

"If you're looking for the eleven-year-old, I have the boy's mother in the car. Have you spotted him?" Holt noticed Josie had gotten out and stood close enough to hear.

The young officer shook his head, as did his female partner in the other seat. "All quiet."

Dammit. "We'll keep cruising around, so if you get calls about a white Honda Civic scoping out the neighborhood, you'll know it's us."

"Good point. I'm glad you stopped us." The officer handed over a card. "This is our station. If you find him, have them relay us the message that he's safe."

"Will do." Holt pulled out his own card. "My cell phone is on here. Same deal."

With nods, they separated.

As Josie jumped back into the car, she said, "Now what?"

"Now we circle this neighborhood and start back...slowly. We know he got here. Let's make sure he didn't run into trouble on his way home."

———

Carson pushed his bike down the sidewalk, scowling at the flat front tire...and trying not to cry. When he and Isaac had figured out how to get to Lake Magdalene on his bike, it'd looked easy. The ride there hadn't been bad.

Walking back? It was going to take him *forever*.

He had a feeling it was awful late. Trying to get up the courage to ring the doorbell at his dad's—at *Everett's*—house, he'd walked around the block a bunch of times first.

Then he'd rung the doorbell.

Tears spilled down his cheeks, and Carson roughly swiped his arm over his face. The door had opened, and a smiling man had answered and asked if he was a Boy Scout or selling stuff for school.

Carson hadn't been able to talk.

His dad hadn't recognized him. Shouldn't a father recognize his son...somehow? So Carson had blurted out, "My mom is Josie Collier. I guess you're my dad, and I wanted to meet you." When the man just stood there, Carson figured he had the wrong person, only then a lady somewhere in the house had called, "Everett, who is it?"

Yeah, Everett was the right person. Besides, the man kinda looked like Carson. Same straight brown hair. Same hook on what Mom called a Roman nose. Same brown eyes.

But his father'd stared at him like he was...a cockroach or something. And he'd whispered, real mean, "I don't fucking believe this. You're not my kid. Get away from here, you little bastard," and slammed the door. As Carson'd stood there, staring at the closed door, he'd heard the guy tell the lady, "Just some homeless bum, darling."

His dad was a dick.

Swallowing hard, Carson kicked a soda can and listened to it clang down the sidewalk. He'd hoped his dad would be happy to find he had a son. Would...*like* him.

Mom was really awesome—some kids had horrible mothers—but most of his friends had dads, too. And their fathers would hang with them and watch football or shoot some hoops. Sure, his mom and dad wouldn't, like, get together or anything, but it would've been nice to *have* a dad. Sometimes. To visit or something.

More tears made his eyes burn, and he blinked them back. *I want to be home.* Home and curled under the covers...where he could cry.

The noise of traffic increased. The nice houses were behind him, and he was close to another big street. *Dale* something or whatever. It was all parking lots and most of the stores were closed and dark.

Creepy.

Skin prickling, he walked faster, feeling...small.

Even as he thought that, a big guy came out of a dark parking lot and onto the sidewalk. He had a shaved head, a straggly beard, and missing teeth. "Yo. You lost, brat?"

Carson stopped, retreated a step, and turned to run the other way. He rammed right into another man, and the guy grabbed Carson's arm in a painful, biting grip.

"Got him." The guy had red and blue tats from wrists to shoulders—and he stank.

"Let me go!" Heart pounding, Carson kicked at the man. "Let me—"

The man slapped him.

Fiery pain burst in Carson's cheek. He cringed.

The man spun Carson around and put his forearm across Carson's throat. "Shut your trap, or I'll shut it for you."

Carson's yell strangled along with his air. He couldn't *breathe*.

The bald guy with the beard shoved his hands into Carson's pockets, searching him. "No fucking wallet?"

"How about a phone?" the tatted man asked.

"Nope. Got shit." Baldy stepped back.

"Wha'd'ya wanna do with him?"

"Pretty boy like this? I can think of—"

Carson kicked Baldy hard in the knee, frantically scratching at the arm across his throat.

A white car screeched to a stop at the curb.

The tatted creep holding Carson jerked around. He didn't let go, despite Carson's kicking and scratching.

The driver of the car sprang out and charged straight for Carson. Holy shit, it was their neighbor, Holt.

Carson tried to call out and couldn't.

"Get the fuck out of here, asshole." Baldy stepped in between them.

Holt ducked a swing, grabbed Baldy, and heaved him at a parked car so hard the man went headfirst over the hood.

The tatted guy holding Carson gave an ugly grunt, and his arm across Carson's neck loosened.

Carson ripped himself loose and scrambled toward Holt who pulled him up against his side.

"Easy, buddy." Holt pulled him closer. "Fight's over."

But...the other guy. "What about..." Carson spun around.

Hand to his head, the tatted guy was on his knees, swaying like he'd fall over. Blood poured through his fingers.

Mom...Carson's *mom*...stood behind the man, a broken, bloody chunk of concrete in her hand. She tossed it away and held out her hand to Carson. "Oh, honey."

"Mo-om!" Carson lunged across the space, buried himself in her arms...and cried.

Safe, her baby was safe.

Josie was shaking so hard that it took a minute to realize her son was trembling even more. He held her as if he'd never let her go—and dear heavens, he hadn't cried like this in years.

Pulling in a breath, she realized they stood in a dreadful part of town at night, easy targets for someone to... She frantically looked for Carson's attackers, but they'd disappeared. Then she spotted Holt.

Big and muscular, black leather jacket, black boots, bearded. Steely gaze alert, he radiated menace, even as he leaned against her car and spoke on his cell phone.

God, she was glad he'd come with her.

Call finished, he shoved the phone in his pocket. He never stopped scanning the area as he opened the back door and told her, "I called off the search party and reported the attack. Let's get you two home."

"C'mon, honey. Let's go." Arm around her son, Josie tucked him into the back seat and hesitated.

"Stay beside him, Josie." Holt helped her in beside her boy.

After putting the bike in the trunk, Holt slid into the driver's seat and glanced in the rear view mirror. "Buckle up, you two."

In the middle seat, Carson didn't move. Josie buckled his seat belt and fastened her own before wrapping her arms around him.

Safe, safe, safe.

"That guy called me a pretty boy," Carson finally whispered. "I kicked him."

"I saw that," Holt said. "It was a good kick, ace."

A good *kick*? Her baby had left the house at night and been assaulted by two men. He could have *died*. Furious words piled up in her throat. *Don't yell, don't yell.* Her jaw cramped from holding everything back.

Her boy had been terrified. Alone. Lost. He'd suffered more than enough consequences for a foolish action. "Why weren't you on your bike?"

"Got a flat tire." He tried to sit up straighter.

Despite the pang of letting him go, she opened her arms. "You went to see your birth father."

"Yeah. I told him I was his kid." He stared at his sneakers. He had big feet, like a gangling dog still growing into his paws.

"It didn't go well," she prompted.

The streetlights outside the moving car provided enough light to see tears fill his eyes.

She would have killed Everett if he'd been in reach.

"He said I wasn't his." Carson's lower lip trembled. "Only I know I am. I look like him."

She forced her tone to stay quiet and even. "Yes. You do."

"An' you don't lie. You never lie."

When she heard the certainty in his voice, tears blurred her vision. Her son had watched her deal out truth even when she hadn't wanted to, when it was awkward or ugly or had unhappy results. He believed her.

Don't cry. Blinking hard, she drew in a breath through her nose. "There is no doubt he is your father, Carson. I'd never been with anyone before him and wasn't for years after."

Only her voice and the low hum of the car engine broke the silence in the car. She took her son's hand. "I was young and foolish. He said he wasn't with his wife and was getting divorced, and I believed him. When I was pregnant with you, he was afraid his wife and friends would find out."

She swallowed and continued. "He's never been willing to risk losing what he has, even to gain an amazing son."

Carson returned to staring at his feet, and his mouth twisted into an unhappy line.

"I'm sorry this didn't turn out the way you wanted it to."

His short nod acknowledged her words.

The rest of the drive was in silence.

Holt pulled her car under the carport and opened the back door.

The anger and worry had drained her, and as she tried to stand, her knees buckled.

"Whoa, pet." With a muscular arm around her waist, he steadied her until her legs stopped wobbling.

"Thank you," she murmured.

"Mmmhmm." Keeping his arm around her, he waited for Carson to jump out, locked the car, and escorted them into her house.

Once inside, Holt released her. Looking down, he gave Carson a half smile. "Considering the level of hygiene your muggers displayed, you might want to take a thorough shower and toss your clothes in the washer."

"Oh. Gross." Carson's nose wrinkled.

Josie couldn't suppress a laugh. She waved toward his bedroom. "Agree. Shower and laundry."

Carson took two steps, turned, and looked at Holt. "Thank you."

Rather than laughing it off, Holt tilted his head gravely. "You're very welcome."

As Carson trudged toward his bedroom, Josie faced Holt. "You have my thanks as well. So many thanks. I wouldn't have..." She was going to have nightmares about those two men. "You saved him."

"Hey, we're neighbors. Neighbors help out." He glanced toward the bedroom. "You've raised a good kid, Josie. You should be proud."

Startled by the unexpected compliment, she looked up...and into his eyes. Eyes the color of a windy sky, only so very warm. Heat pooled inside as she saw him for what he was—more than just a gorgeous male. He was an incredibly confident, masculine man whom she'd leaned on all evening. He'd soothed her panic without making her feel inadequate. His sensible orders, given in a firm, controlled voice, had calmed her even more.

He'd kept her boy safe.

"Will you be all right?" He curled his hand around her nape in a warm grip.

His touch was so comforting she rubbed her cheek against his forearm. "Yes, Sir. I will now."

"Then get some sleep, sweetheart." The sun lines at the corners of his eyes deepened. "You'll have a sulky boy on your hands tomorrow." After kissing her forehead, he tucked her keys into her hand and walked out, closing the door softly behind him.

CHAPTER SEVEN

Josie tossed and turned all night. But what mother wouldn't? Her son had run away and been attacked. She'd finally pushed those nightmares aside only to dream of Holt. Of repaying him...in a very carnal fashion. She'd rewarded him and been rewarded in turn. Those steely blue eyes had watched her as he'd ordered her to...to do all sorts of erotic activities that weren't appropriate at all. *Bad Josie.*

She needed to keep her distance from him. Carson was in a vulnerable state, especially since Everett had crushed his hopes. And here was Holt who'd saved the day in a tough-guy fashion that had to impress a young boy. He'd sure impressed her.

But if they got involved at all, Carson couldn't help but view Holt as a father figure. And when the man realized how much work a child and a baggage-ridden woman were and moved on, her son's heart would be broken. She couldn't risk her baby's heart.

In the shower, she scolded herself for even dreaming about Holt.

While she dressed, she lectured herself about the responsibilities of motherhood.

As she fixed a hot breakfast—a treat for Carson on a school day—she reminded herself of what was important in life. Her son was first on the list.

When Carson emerged from his bedroom, his apprehensive expression reminded her of when he was four and had broken every egg in the carton to see what was inside.

She knew he was eleven, could see how big he'd grown, and yet her heart saw him as her baby. Did that feeling ever go away?

Last night, he'd told her what Everett had said. Her boy had tried to pretend he didn't care. But he did. His father who should have been so proud of him had acted as if his son was something he loathed.

She knew...oh, she knew exactly how Carson had felt at that moment. Even though her son knew how much *she* loved him, he would hurt for a long time to come.

"Good morning, honey." She patted him on the shoulder. "I made pancakes. Do you want a couple of eggs with them?"

"Uh. No, thank you. Not today." Far too quiet, Carson set the table and got out butter and syrup.

Anger at Everett simmered inside her, yet what could she do? Sure, she could lawyer up and create hell for the jerk. What about his innocent family? What about making Carson an object of gossip at his school? The collateral damage for getting revenge seemed excessive.

She set the plate of pancakes on the table and joined Carson, seeing he'd poured milk in the glasses. He was on his best behavior...and she wished she had her sullen pre-teen back again.

Once finished, she started cleaning up while Carson got ready for school. At the sound of a door shutting, she glanced out the kitchen window.

On the other side of the fence, Holt sauntered into his backyard. His thick blond hair was tangled, his eyes, heavy-lidded. He was obviously just out of bed...and the knowledge sent a wave of warmth through her.

Dammit, no. You will not go there, Josephine.

Monday afternoon, Holt sat on his patio, feet propped on a chair, and contemplated what boring task to take on next. The sky was a clear blue, the temperature a perfect seventy degrees with a light breeze from the Gulf. December in Florida was one of his favorite months, and the perfect time for chores outside.

Rebuilding the patio or fence came to mind, but he didn't own the place and wouldn't live here long. Hell, he'd only taken over Uzuri's lease to get out of his singles complex where he would constantly run into his ex, Nadia. However, the duplex lease would be up at the end of March.

No, he was done with apartments—and duplexes, too. It was time to buy a house, one on a quiet residential street like this.

Unlike some of his friends, he didn't need lots of land for privacy. He liked having neighbors. In fact, when the time came to move, he'd miss playing basketball with teens across the street, visiting Stella Avery for coffee, cookies, and blood pressure checks—and rescuing distressed mothers with runaway kids.

His smile faded. Carson had fucked up by running away—and not having backup. That mugging could've been ugly. But, damn, the kid had kept his head and never stopped fighting. And his mother—Holt shook his head—Mama Bear had charged right in to save her cub. She'd snatched up that block of cement and smacked the bastard hard enough to scramble his brains.

There was a woman after his own heart.

No. Don't go there. Dammit, he'd broken up with Nadia only a month ago. But the pain had faded fast, maybe because he'd discovered he didn't even recognize the real Nadia. Didn't *like* the real Nadia.

Despite the short time, he knew Josie far better than he had Nadia—at least in the ways that mattered. Josie'd apologized for her rudeness when believing he was a biker. When her kid was in danger, she'd risked herself to save him. In the Shadowlands, she listened and tended to the members with as much care as she mixed their drinks. She'd uprooted her life to move close to her aging great-aunt. Even the neighborhood teens said she was cool. She listened to them—and gave them cookies.

Aaaaand now, he had a craving for cookies.

Holt grinned. As a guy, he'd noticed how well her round ass filled her jeans, her eyes turned greener in sunlight, and her mouth curved into a smile. Damned if he didn't want to nibble on that soft lower lip of hers. To see what color her nipples were and savor the weight of her breasts. To strip her down, physically and emotionally.

To take her under command.

Because, Josie *was* submissive, and the sweet yielding look in her eyes ignited a fire in his belly.

Hell, now he was an idiot. Starting anything with Josie was a foolish idea ripe for ugly complications. She was his neighbor. Worked in the Shadowlands. Had a child.

And according to Stella, Josie didn't date. At all.

Why?

A noise made him look to the left, and he turned.

Carson stood on the other side of the fence, the sun glinting off sandy brown hair a few inches longer than his Mom's. Ill at ease, the boy shifted from foot to foot. "Um. Hi."

"Hey, kid. Jump on over."

The boy's brown eyes lit. His hop over the fence was effective, if not graceful. He jogged to the patio.

"Want a Coke or Dew?" Holt held up his Mountain Dew.

"Uh, sure. Coke. Please."

"Be right back." When the boy followed, Holt halted. "Nah, it's best if you stay outside."

Carson looked confused, then hurt.

Shit. Jesus, this kind of warning should come from the parents, shouldn't it? But teaching was what a nurse—and Dom—did, even if the subject matter was difficult.

Holt leaned a shoulder against a patio pillar. "You're not a girl, Carson, but there are perverts who'd hurt boys your age. Outside, where people can see you"—Holt waved at Stella who was puttering in her garden—"you're pretty safe. However, if a man asks you into his house, say no."

Carson turned red.

"Your mama ever talk to you about this?"

More red. The kid looked at his feet. "Yeah. She did."

Not a surprise. Josie seemed like a mother who'd tackle hard subjects. "See, this, right now—that's what she meant. I'm a good guy, but you don't know that for sure. Assholes are easy to label when they act like the two last night. But some bad guys are sneaky. They'll seem nice—might even be friends or relatives."

With luck, the kid would never learn how a friendly personality could conceal ugliness beneath. "Learn to be cautious until you're sure. Which means you take a seat out here and keep safe, yeah?"

After a second, Carson nodded with a half-smile. "Yeah."

When Holt returned, the kid was slouched in a chair. He took the Coke with a muttered, "Thanks."

"You bet." Holt settled into his own seat and put his feet back up on the empty chair. His belly and back were sore today—not surprising after the way he'd tossed the mugger into the car last night. Didn't feel like he'd ripped any internal stitches open though. He should be good to return to work at the hospital on Wednesday. "How's your mom? Is she doing all right?"

Carson's surprised blink showed he'd expected questions about himself, not his mother. Ah, boyhood. "Um, sure. She's fine."

"I'm glad to hear it. She was pretty distressed last night when she couldn't find you."

"I know." Guilt chased over Carson's face. "I shouldn't have

---

taken off like that. If I got hurt… She doesn't have anybody but me an' Oma."

Good, the boy *did* have a heart and conscience. "So…did she ground you for life?"

Carson's lips curved up. "Not that bad. She said she considered it but figured I'd already suffered the consequences…been punished." The boy's smile faded. "Because my father turned out to be a dick, and I got kinda beat up."

"Yeah, those are definitely consequences." And Josie was a great mom to leave it at that.

"But she said I owe you two hours of free labor."

Holt lowered his drink. "What?"

"Because you lost time because of my incon…condiserateness" —Carson frowned—"I forgot the word, but I'm supposed to pay you back. Mom says you're not supposed to do heavy work, and I'm strong. I can mow your lawn. Clean up around the bushes. Wash windows. Whatever."

Well, damn. Holt started to refuse and stopped. Josie wouldn't give her boy the assignment unless she'd thought it out. "Well, Stella would probably appreciate it if you mowed and cleaned up my half of the backyard. Every time she looks over at my side, she gets this…look on her face." Imitating the elderly gardener's expression, Holt pursed his lips, frowned, and shook his head.

"She does." Carson laughed, then sobered. "Thanks, though. For getting rid of those guys."

The kid's eyes showed he hadn't forgotten the terror of being helpless. Holt wished he'd had the freedom last night to beat the assholes senseless. It was a sick world where children weren't safe. "I enjoyed having something to do. It's boring sitting around on my ass."

Last night, he'd felt useful for the first time in over a month. Huh. Maybe he had some bizarre hero complex buried in his subconscious. Actually, considering his choice of jobs…*yep*.

As if following his thoughts, Carson said, "Mom says you're a firefighter."

"Sometimes." Holt gave him a wry smile. "I started out chasing fire. These days, there are more medical emergencies than fires, and I ride the ambulance some days, fire engine on others."

"So you're like an EM...something?"

"EMT—a paramedic." Holt took a sip of his soda. "I also have an RN license, so I work the fire station on Mondays and an intensive care unit in the hospital later in the week."

Carson wrinkled his nose. "A hospital isn't very exciting, is it?"

"That was the point." How to explain to a starry-eyed boy? "I've been a firefighter since I was eighteen. A human body can get pretty mangled up, and seeing that can make it tough to sleep. I found it's good to get a break."

The kid thought it over before voicing a comprehending, "Huh."

Yeah, Josie had a smart lad. And a brave one. He'd done well during the fight. And now, much like his mother, he took responsibility for his mistake without trying to blame anyone else. Too many so-called adults weren't as mature.

When the boy set his soda on the table, Holt noticed the dark bruises on his face, arms, and neck. "You catch grief at school about the bruises?"

"Yeah," Carson muttered. "The teachers asked. And some of the guys."

"Guys? Not friends?"

The kid's brows drew together. "My best friend's only in one class with me now. I didn't even see him today. An' a lot of my other friends—I don't see them."

"You lost me. Why?"

Carson shrugged. "When we got into middle school, half my friends went to other schools. The rest who're at my school take different classes and eat lunch at other times."

Holt tried to remember middle school, but that was about

when he'd been running drugs at his aunt's and then he and Aunt Rita had been homeless...with no school at all. "Sounds like you're going to have to find new friends."

"Yeah." After a heavy sigh, Carson brightened. "Brandon an' Yukio are okay. Not total losers, you know. Gamers an' stuff."

"That's a start." Smiling, Holt rose. "C'mon. Let's see if we can get Zuri's old lawn mower started."

———

That evening, as Holt and Carson discussed Xbox games, Josie leaned back in her chair with a pleased sigh. Her impromptu supper had gone nicely, hadn't it?

Maybe life would settle down now.

After Carson had left for school this morning, she'd written an excellent fight scene by channeling her fear from last night into her heroine. The chapter had been bloody and scary...and the evil reptilian attackers had lost.

And hey, she'd been able to describe the sights, sounds, and feeling of hitting someone with a rock quite authentically.

When Carson had returned from school, they'd talked, gotten everything out, and she'd sent him off to work for Holt.

In the quiet house, she'd tried to dispel her lingering anger and fear with a cooking marathon. The enormous amount of food had reminded her of her own debt to pay, and she'd sent Carson over to offer Holt a neighborly invitation.

That, perhaps, hadn't been the...wisest idea. Sure, she had a debt to pay, but after last night's off the scale, erotic dreams, she was having trouble remembering Holt was a neighbor and that she didn't date or...anything. It sure didn't help that he was a more muscular, much smarter version of Thor, and that his darkly masculine laugh could make her heart skip beats.

You're being a weak female, Josephine. With a silent sigh, she turned to watch him.

On her right, he'd leaned a thick forearm on the table as he and her boy argued about a gaming technique. His blue-gray, button-up shirt matched his eyes so perfectly she'd bet Uzuri— a Brendall's fashion buyer—had bought it for him. He sat close enough his muscular shoulder occasionally brushed against hers.

She got a hot tingle every time.

He caught her staring and captured her gaze with a long look. When he finally smiled, she had to remind herself to breathe. *Honestly, Josie.*

Forcing her gaze away, she tried to study her dining room. She'd dressed the table with a white tablecloth, and her dark red stoneware looked festive—and reminded her she and Carson needed to buy a Christmas tree and figure out which boxes held holiday decorations. Tomorrow, for sure.

The room needed a lot of work though. Boxes needing to be unpacked were stacked in the corners. The sickly pale green walls and trim needed new paint. But the beautiful antique chandelier softened the ugly hue...and brought out the sun streaks in Holt's caramel-colored hair.

Good God, she was back to staring at him. *Stop.*

"Mom, I'm finished. May I be excused?"

Ah, wasn't it awesome when her son actually used the manners she'd tried to teach him? Josie smiled. "Sure. Do you have homework?"

"Of course," he grumbled. "I know—do it first."

"Good plan. Don't forget your dishes."

With a heavy sigh, Carson picked up his plate and silverware and trudged to the kitchen as if the chore required all his strength.

Holt chuckled. "Makes me want to talk about how I suffered when I was his age and how easy kids today have it."

"I know, right? Only I didn't, really. Now Gramps, he boasted about having to walk across town to school because the school bus was only for the ranch children, not anyone inside the town limits."

"Ah, one of those. He had to struggle through snow drifts up to his waist, right?"

"In Texas?" She gave him an outraged look. "The cattle would have heart failure."

"There is that." He grinned. "I knew that was a Texas accent I was hearing."

"Accent?" She scowled. Dammit, she'd been sure she'd lost it years ago.

"Yes, pet, you have a pretty Texas drawl."

She could feel herself flush at the compliment.

With a slow smile, he ran a finger down her hot cheek.

"Done, Mom. See you, Holt." Cookie in hand, Carson headed for his bedroom and homework.

In the now silent dining room, Josie settled back in her chair and eyed the man beside her. The one she barely knew. "I just realized I don't know your name. Is Holt a nickname?"

"Last name. My first name is Alexander."

"But...that's a wonderful first name." He even looked like an Alexander. "Why not use it?"

"Ah, well, when I was young, I spent some time in a place"—his eyes darkened—"where there was another Alex. After a while, people simply used my last name, and I got used to it."

Where had he been that gave him such a haunted look in his eyes? "I see."

"One syllable. Nice and short." The shadows disappeared as his lips curved. "I did some modeling way back when, and my agent used simply 'Holt'. Said it was memorable."

Modeling. And with only a one word name. She smiled slightly. Yes, he had the self-assurance of someone who would say: This is who I am. Take it or leave it. "You went from modeling to being a firefighter and RN?"

"Yep. Actually, the money I banked from doing commercials

paid my college tuition." Holt finished the last bite of roast beef on his plate and leaned back in his chair. "That was an amazing dinner, Josie. Thank you."

"It seemed the least I could do for your help last night. Would you like some dessert?"

"No room right now. How about we try out that dessert wine I brought?"

"Sounds perfect." She picked up her plate, pleased when he followed and loaded the dishwasher with his own dishes.

After pulling the corkscrew from the drawer, Josie saw Holt studying the fridge. Between snapshots of Carson and Oma and Josie were the grocery list and a list of emergency numbers. Taking the pen dangling from a string, Holt added his name and cell phone number to the emergency list. Seeing her watching, he said casually, "Feel free to call me when things go thump in the night or you find ogres under your bed."

The offer left her speechless. She hadn't had anyone to scare away monsters since...since she was Carson's age. "Thank you," she whispered.

Feeling flustered, she opened the bottle of Tokaji and poured two glasses. When she felt his eyes on her, she hesitated. Was she supposed to have let him do this task? Had she upset his sense of masculinity?

He only grinned. "It's a pleasure to watch a master at work."

Of course he didn't mind. She'd never met anyone so down-right confident.

"I was wondering," he said. "The Shadowlands is only open two nights a week. Do you need help getting a job at another bar, as well? I know a fair number of people."

His concern warmed her heart. "Thank you, but there's no need. I don't want to work more than part-time."

His head tilted slightly in an unspoken direction to continue explaining.

"I'm an author of teen fantasy novels." She took a sip of the wine, enjoying the gentle bouquet of sweet flavors. "Although the four books I have out now sell well, I still need a day job."

"An author—that's fantastic." The respect in his voice was heartening. "You bartend part-time and spend your days writing?"

"Writing, promoting, researching. Yes." She grinned. "This afternoon, I researched medieval punishments. I always thought putting a person in the "stocks" meant she stood bent over with her head and wrists restrained—but that's a *pillory*. A stock is the board with semicircles cut out and hinged to another stock to make circles. Traditional stocks restrained a person by the ankles."

"Good to know. The Shadowlands has a few wooden stocks—both head and wrists post restraints or seated ankle restraints, but we lump them all under *stocks*."

"Exactly. The things you learn..."

He leaned against the counter and studied her. "And are you interested in that kind of restraint?" His smooth voice flowed over her like poured honey.

Then she realized what he was asking. "Me?" She actually squeaked. *But, oh, my, God.* There were pillories in the Shadowlands...and he wanted to know if *she* liked them? The zing went right through and straight to her pussy. "I...um...hadn't thought... I just wanted to avoid having my hero sent to a jail where a rescue would be too tricky."

"Of course." He pushed a lock of hair out of her eyes with the merest brush of his fingers. "Now tell me, which would be more exciting—being restrained by your ankles?" He paused. "Or bent over with your neck and wrists imprisoned?"

The minute he said *bent over*, heat engulfed her.

"Ah." A corner of his mouth lifted. "I'll let Z know the pillory is your choice of discipline."

She gave him a reproving look. *Bad Dom.*

With an easy grin, he picked up the glasses of wine. "Let's take this to the living room, shall we?"

How did he make a suggestion sound like an order? "Sure."

He led the way and set both glasses on the coffee table. It wouldn't be polite to pick up her glass and choose the chair across the room.

In response to her narrowed eyes, he merely smiled and opened his hand toward one end of the couch.

Were Doms sneaky as well as bossy? Giving in and taking a seat, she picked up her wine and kicked off her shoes with a sigh of relief.

He sat down near the other end of the couch. Not close enough to make her uneasy, but still...close enough.

She studied her wine for a second before looking up. Although he was disconcertingly easy to talk with, she never seemed to find her balance around him. Maybe because the mere sound of his resonant voice sent champagne bubbles through her veins.

Sipping her wine, she shifted uneasily and finally settled on a cross-legged position. The quiet, softly lit living room was far more intimate than the brightly lit dining room with Carson talking about school. "This is a great wine," she said. "Very, um, pleasant."

"I'm glad you like it."

The top two buttons of Holt's shirt weren't fastened, and as he leaned back, the edges gaped, revealing hard pectoral muscles. He'd held her against his solid chest last night. Wrapped iron-hard arms around her. And oh, she wanted to be in those arms again.

Her gaze dropped. His forearms were thick with muscle and lightly dusted with golden hair. Strong hands, corded wrists. A shiver shook her, and she saw her wine start to splash in the glass.

No. Stop it. She didn't want a man. *Stop, stop, stop.*

"Josie."

She looked up and met amused winter-blue eyes.

"Relax, pet." He studied her for a long moment. "What's going through that head of yours?"

"Ah..." She gave him a rueful smile. "I'm feeling awkward, I guess. I can't recall the last time I entertained a man."

"I see. I'm assuming that's lack of desire and not opportunity? I did get the impression Peter would've been happy to break the dry spell."

Oh, God, Holt had watched her scene with Peter, hadn't he? As her face turned hot—*again*—she wondered how many times a person could flush in one evening before dropping dead of cardiac shock? "Aside from the fact that I'm not interested in Peter, I simply don't date."

"I see." Holt twisted to face her, leaned forward, and grasped her ankles. Pulling firmly, he set her feet onto his lap.

"What are you—" When he closed his hands around one foot, and his strong thumbs pressed against the aching spot under the arch, her eyes almost rolled back in her head. She waved a hand at him. "Never mind. Carry on."

He grinned. "Are you worried about introducing a date to your son? How Carson would react?"

His hands massaged her foot in slow, rhythmic strokes, pressing deep enough to release tension she hadn't even realized was there. Leaning her head against the back of the couch, she closed her eyes to savor the sensation. What had he asked? As he pulled, then rolled each toe, she quivered with the pleasure.

Oh, Carson and men. "Exactly. Avoiding dating saves me all sorts of worries."

The hands on her feet stilled for a second, then resumed. "That's one way to look at it."

"Uh-huh. What about you?"

"Hmm?"

"Girlfriend? Fiancée? Wife?"

"None of the above."

Shame on her for feeling pleased. "I'm sorry."

"So what did you think of your scene with Peter in the Shadowlands?"

Dragged into reality, she opened her eyes and glared. "You're ruining my massage, Master Holt."

His grin was a quick flash of white. "Sorry, baby. Guess you'll have to learn to multitask. Tell me about the scene."

She studied him. All his laid-back friendliness wasn't a...lie. He really *was* easygoing and sociable; however, at his core, he was as much a Dominant as Master Z. No wonder he'd taken charge of finding Carson last night.

Now he wanted an answer and wouldn't be deflected with a pout. "I suppose you won't do my other foot until I answer?"

He pinned her with a level gaze. "Josie, I asked because I want to know. I hope you'll answer for that reason alone."

She put her hand over her stomach, which felt quivery or something. She didn't want to discuss the scene with Peter—and yet the thought of disappointing Holt was equally uncomfortable. "The scene was...all right."

His gaze kept hers trapped. "Sweetheart, in my opinion, an evasive answer is worse than none."

She flinched. That's how she felt when Carson played games with her.

"Let's try this—did you expect more from the session? Want to...feel more?"

How did he know? "I...yes. It was kind of a let-down." She shook her head. "I didn't want him to hurt me, but it just... Something wasn't there."

As if rewarding her for speaking, Holt massaged her other leg. His strong, warm hands surrounded her foot. "You're submissive, Josie, at least in some respects. With Peter, you experienced no loss of control, and I'd say that was what you missed."

Holt thought she'd wanted to give up control? The idea was wrong—and so appealing her mouth went dry. What would it be like to let someone else take charge? Peter had tried during the scene. "Maybe."

Holt's eyes crinkled as if he knew she was bullshitting him.

"It doesn't matter anyway," she said hastily. "It's not like I'll participate in a scene again. It didn't work for me—probably because I'm not submissive."

"Oh, you are, pet," Holt said softly. "However, playing in BDSM is a lot like dating. A failure could be the guy or woman's fault. It could be there's no chemistry between them. Or it could be the venue or choice of equipment—like taking a cowboy to a chick-flick."

She laughed. "I'm not going to—"

"You never did tell me what you thought of working in a terrifying BDSM club." Holt tilted his head. "I know all of us Masters are pleased to have you there."

"That's what your Master Z said. He talked with me before I left on Saturday." She laughed. "Working at the Shadowlands is a bit frightening but exciting, too. And everyone"—almost everyone—"has been very welcoming."

"Good to hear." He pressed her toes upward, stretching the muscles on the bottom of her foot. "You found watching the scenes exciting?"

"Uh." She felt warmth rising upward again. "I meant exciting like interesting, not exciting like...like sex-exciting."

"Mmmhmm." His hum was one of disbelief.

She scowled down at her wine because he had read her well, and her correction had been a token protest. In all reality, she'd found the atmosphere totally erotic. "Fine. Yes. It's exciting in all shades of the words."

"I like when you're honest, Josie." He leaned forward and cupped her cheek. "Good girl."

At the warmth of his hand and the approval in his low voice, she stilled, her insides melting like butter in a hot sun.

"I'll see if Z will let you off early at 1 a.m. on Saturday so you can do a scene with me." His steel-gray gaze held hers, holding her protest in check. "If nothing else, when we're done, you'll know more about BDSM and what you want and need."

When he moved his hand, her cheek felt cold.

Swallowing hard, she stared at him. A scene with *him*? The thought was terrifying. And the interest she saw in his eyes was purely electrifying. "I-I'm not sure that's a good—"

"You don't know me well enough to trust me completely, and that's all right. But can you trust me with this one scene in a public place?"

He'd touch her. Maybe tie her up. Use a flogger on her. And it would be *Holt* holding the flogger. Quivers of desire ran across her nerves, and she dampened between her legs. Oh, God, this would be such a bad idea. "I don't know." Her voice came out disconcertingly husky.

"Josie, if you don't like how it's going, one word will stop everything."

"Just say no, huh?"

His laugh rolled out, wickedly sexy. "Actually, the word is *red*, not *no*."

Right, a safeword. She'd read about them. "I never quite understood why y'all don't use *no*."

She was beginning to wonder if she could refuse Holt... anything...and she shivered.

His eyes narrowed. "I think you need to be closer when we talk about this. Come here, sweetheart."

Moving to the middle of the couch, he settled her in his lap.

She smacked his shoulder. "No, dammit, you had surgery. You're not supposed to be lifting or putting people on your lap or—"

"Guess you better sit still then," he murmured. He positioned her so her legs were on the couch, and she sat sideways, leaning against his chest. "I enjoy holding you, Josie, in case you haven't noticed."

She caught her breath at his words, and his arms came around her, holding her firmly against him. As she felt the thick erection pressing against her hip, she felt herself melting. Because she'd wanted to be here—right here—all night.

"To continue our discussion," he said. "Some Doms do allow the use of no. I don't—for two reasons."

Feeling daring and absurdly happy, she put her arm around his shoulders. A deep breath brought her the fragrance of his soap and freshly laundered shirt. So clean and masculine and perfect. "Why wouldn't someone prefer a clear *no* instead of a safeword?"

"One is due to our society. Even now, too many females are raised believing respectable women shouldn't want sex. If she doesn't make at least a token protest, she doesn't feel as if she's a good girl. That kind of idiotic pressure on women means it's difficult for a guy to know if a *no* is a symbolic protest or a definite, absolutely not. A distinct safeword lets her use *no* as a token protest and ensures there's no confusion as to when she really does want to stop."

He stroked his hand up and down her back. It should be comforting...except her nipples bunched into hard throbbing peaks.

Her palm against his chest, Josie could feel the slow lub-dub of his heart. "I'd like to say your reasoning is wrong...except that's how I was raised too. I tell myself women deserve sexual freedom, and I should be able to jump into bed with no worries—but part of me feels it's wrong."

"Yeah." Holt sighed. "Society doesn't do right by the female gender."

"What's the second reason?"

"Ah, now, that one's more fun." Holt nuzzled her hair, sending a tremor from her head to her toes at that sign of his interest. His voice was husky. "Some women enjoy rough—forced—sex. They don't need to be relieved of the guilt; they simply get off on being physically dominated. Yelling *no, no, no* is part of that roleplay, and —again—the aggressor needs to know when she truly wants to stop."

A frisson of interest went through Josie, and when she heard Holt's low chuckle, she realized she'd squirmed.

Oh God. When she tried to slide off his lap, his arms tightened and trapped her against his chest.

"You're not ready to go that far yet, pet. We're going to keep things simple on Saturday." His firm statement swept her objections away.

She was committed to a scene with him. As anticipation roared through her, her heart set up a hard, fast thumping like every bottle in the whisky bar was falling off the shelves. *Thud-thud-thud-thud.*

CHAPTER EIGHT

On Saturday night, near midnight, Holt crossed the Shadowlands toward the bar and damn, he was looking forward to seeing Josie. It'd been far too long.

On Wednesday and Thursday, he'd returned to work at the hospital, which had been a relief. He'd missed the bustle and camaraderie of the pediatric ICU unit. Unfortunately, working again had kicked his ass, and he hadn't made it into the Shadowlands last night.

Tonight, he'd planned to arrive early and treat himself to watching Josie at work. Raoul had screwed up that plan. Having volunteered to teach sailing to some of Marcus's high-risk boys, the Dom asked for help. Holt enjoyed working with the kids and loved to sail. The damn cruise had gone longer than anticipated or he'd have been in a fuck-of-a-lot earlier.

As he headed for the bar and Josie, he had to shake his head at the scenery. Z had chosen a Cops and Robbers theme for tonight, and yellow-and-black crime scene tape now marked off the scene areas.

The costumes were a bit confusing. Either side of the power exchange could be a good or bad guy. "Cops" could be any form of law enforcement. "Robbers" were anyone who veered toward the wrong side of the law.

Holt had already planned out the scene for tonight. Depending on the negotiation he and Josie would conduct, he'd incorporate a bit of tonight's theme. Josie might enjoy—

"Good evening, Holt." Olivia wore a sleeveless, blue latex "uniform" top with a silver badge. Shiny black boots covered her black leggings to above her knees. A black duty belt held a long baton on one side and a golf-ball-sized gold bag on the other. A conical custodian helmet with a London Metropolitan Police badge covered her spiked hair.

"Mistress Olivia, you look sexy as hell," Holt said, surprising a smile out of her.

"Thank you, love." She gave him a slow perusal. "You're finally looking back to normal. All trimmed up and everything."

"The long hair got annoying." He ran his hand over his bare jaw. "But the shave is due to firefighting regulations. I gotta say, after a month of being bearded, I feel naked without it." At least the wounds on his face were closed up enough he could wield a razor around them.

Would Josie be bothered at the sight? The scars were still fucking red and visible.

An outraged shout drew his attention to the center of the room. An agile submissive in skimpy shorts and a ragged top dodged around chairs waving a gold bag and laughing maniacally. A Dom in a sheriff's khaki shirt and badge pursued. Catching her, he took her to the floor—carefully—and applied handcuffs. Her struggles earned her a noisy slap to the back of one thigh.

"Police brutality! Someone call the papers. Police brutality. I'll sue!" A second later, the sheriff shoved a ball gag in her mouth, and then all that escaped was "Mmmph, mmmph, mmmph!"

The observers roared with laughter.

When the sheriff picked up the bag of gold and attached it to his belt, Holt noticed other gold bags. "What's with the pouches?"

"Z filled a table in the munchie corner with extra props, including these coin bags." When Olivia shook the gold pouch, it clinked. "He handed me one and ordered me to wear it."

"You specifically?"

She snorted. "He thinks I intimidate the submissives. That they don't know how to catch my attention. The man's barmy."

"Sorry, sweetie. The shrink is right." Holt studied her. Olivia wasn't fashion plate beautiful, yet was too striking to be merely pretty. With a well-padded, sturdy body, short spiked hair, diamond stud in one ear, and an assessing look in her brown eyes, she was a total submissive magnet. And yet... "To a timid subbie, you look as attainable as Mount Everest."

"I never noticed."

"Because you simply pick who you want out of the masses." Holt smiled. "The way Z set this up, the ones you've overlooked get a chance to catch your attention."

"He's quite the sneaky bastard, isn't he? Fine. I'll wander about and see if someone bites."

As she sauntered away, Holt spotted a tiny Hispanic submissive wearing a ripped-off prison-stripe T-shirt that exposed her belly. Long dark hair, huge brown eyes. Quite pretty. When Olivia walked the other way, she wilted as if the sun had set on her hopes.

Too cute. Holt caught her eye and nodded encouragingly toward the Mistress, mouthing, *go for it.*

The submissive hauled in a visible breath, tensed, and dashed after Olivia. She grabbed the golden pouch, yanked, and lifting it over her head, ran away.

"Bloody hell!" Olivia gave chase.

As the submissive's terrified giggles trailed behind her, Holt grinned and murmured, "Good luck, little one." He continued across the room.

Yes, Josie was there behind the bar. Through the crowd, he caught a tiny glimpse of her...and heard his name called again. *Dammit.*

"Holt, good to see you." In a torn T-shirt, ripped jeans, and full sleeves of gang-related temporary tats, Vance Buchanan was sitting on a couch, feet up on an ottoman. "I heard you've returned to your hospital job."

Of course he'd heard. The Shadowkittens knew—and spread —all the gossip in all the world, and Buchanan's Sally was one of the worst offenders. "Yeah. It was good to be back."

"Being laid up can drive a man stir-crazy." The FBI agent had taken a bullet in the leg a year and a half ago.

"It did. So how is married life?" Holt's train of thought left the station as the people around the bar parted enough he could see Josie. *Well now...* "I see the new bartender decided to join in the roleplay fun."

A police hat covered Josie's short hair. She had on a short-sleeved blue uniform shirt with a badge, and her gun belt held a tiny plastic pistol and baton. Holt's smile grew. No police officer had ever enjoyed herself so thoroughly. Hands a blur as she mixed drinks, Josie was laughing and chatting with the members around the bar...and bouncing with the beat of the music. She was adorable.

"Ayuh. She's having a good time." Also dressed like a gang member, Galen walked over. He had an arm wrapped around his and Vance's submissive, Sally, pinning her to his front. Leaning down, he handed Vance one of the two beers he carried in one hand.

"Evening, Galen." Holt's lips quirked. "Gotta say, your patrol officer there looks somewhat the worse for wear."

The short brunette wore an over-sized, long-sleeved uniform shirt. One of the Doms had pulled her sleeve cuffs past her hands and knotted a rope around the wristbands, effectively restraining her. Tears had streaked dark mascara down her cheeks, and she had the unmistakable glassy-eyed appearance of someone who'd enjoyed a long, painful—and pleasurable—session.

"Ah, well, she's new to law enforcement and didn't check she had backup before chasing a suspect." Galen shot Vance a look. "Rather like someone I know."

The two men had been partners in the FBI before Galen quit and started a business. Vance smiled. "She'll be more careful, I'm sure."

"Next time, I'll shoot first," the irrepressible brat muttered under her breath.

Holt winked at her before asking his fellow Masters, "When I checked the schedule yesterday, I saw I'd been taken off DM duty tonight." It was why he'd gone on the boat when Raoul had asked for help. "Was there a reason?"

"Z knew you returned to work at the hospital this week and would be dragging." Vance took a good swallow of his beer and sighed appreciatively.

"Mother Z." Holt shook his head ruefully. He was fine. In fact, anticipation rolled through his veins at the thought of the scene with Josie. "Is Z around?" He should take care of the protocols first.

"Yeah. Anne volunteered to babysit Sophia, so he's brought Jessica for a scene." Galen grinned. "Poor subbie. She turned bright red when he said they'd be playing in the dungeon."

Holt laughed. The curvy blonde both hated and loved doing scenes in public.

Vance glanced at his watch. "They're probably finished by now."

"Good enough. I'll wander on back."

"You should wear a gold coin pouch and make the submissives happy," Sally piped up. "They've missed you."

"It's good to be missed. But I have something else in mind for tonight." Near the rear, he spotted Z and Jessica leaving the back hallway.

Short and curvy, the blonde wore a black and white striped "prison" outfit. The skimpy halter-top and short skirt were less a uniform than an excuse to riot. Her hair damp with sweat, Jessica looked as if she'd had a good hard session.

Z had his arm around her, half holding her up. The Shadowlands owner had on a black uniform shirt complete with silver badges and insignia. He gave Holt a swift perusal. "You survived returning to work, I see."

"The first night, they stuck me on the desk, doing paperwork, and relieving people for breaks. I had to beg to get to do something on Thursday night."

"It's good to see you back," Jessica said.

"Thanks, sweetie." He smiled. "Now that I'm out and about, can I stop by and play with Sophia sometime?" Z and Jessica's baby was around six months old and cute as a button.

"Of course." Jessica gave him a stern look. "But you have to stop spoiling her with a toy whenever you show up."

"She's smart; she's brave; she's inventive. She deserves some spoiling." He turned to Z. "On another subject..."

Z chuckled. "What can I do for you?"

"Let your bartender quit at 1 a.m. so I can see how she does with a real scene."

Jessica's mouth dropped open. "You want to play with Josie?"

"Excellent idea." Z didn't appear surprised. "You have my permission...if she agrees."

"Of course." The little bartender might have had second thoughts, but he didn't think so. She'd wanted to play. And damn, he wanted to show her the joys of true domination and submission.

"You be careful with her," Jessica demanded. "She—Mmmph, mmmph." Master Z's hand over her mouth reduced her admonishments to unintelligible sounds.

"Kitten," Z said gravely, "a submissive giving orders to a Dom in the Shadowlands rarely ends well."

"Mmmph...mmmph, mmmph, mmmph." The last one ended in a high note and a glare.

Holt smothered a laugh.

Z grinned. "I have a theory that crime might decrease if police officers were allowed to spank impertinent prisoners. Let's test that, shall we?" The Master took a couple of steps back, sat on a couch, and pulled his pretty subbie belly-down over his knees.

Grinning, Holt headed for the bar.

Behind him, the first loud smack was accompanied by an outraged shriek.

Midnight had come and gone, and the crowd in the Shadowlands was thinning.

Holt hadn't showed. Disappointment was a hard coil in Josie's chest.

With a sigh, she pushed her police hat back and leaned against the bar. She'd been...foolish. Too excited about being with Holt. She should have known better.

Aside from Holt's nonappearance, she'd had a great night...and was adapting nicely to the Shadowlands. On her first weekend, in addition to learning the members, the bar setup, and the protocols, she'd had to work past the shocking costumes—or lack thereof—and the distraction of the scenes. And the conversations. "*She screamed so loud...*" "*His testicles turned blue and I knew...*"

Last night, she'd found her footing, and tonight, she'd thoroughly enjoyed being the bartender. Smiling, she set a vodka Collins in front of a brunette submissive in a half-ripped-off prison uniform.

She'd even found herself some sexy cop apparel. The approving glances and smiles she'd gotten from the various members felt good.

This place sure knew how to throw a costume party.

The munchie table had cookies in the shape of police badges and an incredible variety of donuts.

Bad submissives were imprisoned in the iron-bar cages placed in a row down the center of the room. The short cages forced the prisoner to kneel. Two were tall, upright, and coffin-sized, keeping the submissive standing. One cage displayed a sign: PLEASE TOUCH and passing Doms would reach through the bars and fondle the naked captive.

The variety of costumes was amazing. She watched a Dom in cop uniform leading his *horse*—a male submissive in full "pony" regalia.

Josie had assumed a police uniform would indicate she was in the untouchable Dom category. Then she'd seen two Doms dressed like slum escapees hauling around a restrained, very subdued submissive in a cop's uniform.

Apparently, no matter the costume, the Dominant always won.

And boy, people really got into this roleplaying stuff. Submissives kept snatching the coin pouches and getting chased. One Domme officer dragged a submissive to a couch and spanked him for *"excessive speed when walking"*.

She glanced around. The few people lingering around the bar still had full drinks.

"Looks quiet." Smoother than an aged Glenmorangie whisky, the dark smoky voice stole her breath. *Holt.*

He was *here*. Her heart started doing disconcerting somersaults in her chest. She turned...and her mouth dropped open.

He'd cut his hair to ear-length. And shaved. Oh...*wow*. He'd been gorgeous before, but now nothing concealed the sharp, stern angle of his jaw or the firm line of his mouth. The now completely visible scar made her want to kiss it and make it all better.

And kiss his lips right afterward.

He leaned on the bar, his gaze on her. The masculine appreciation in his gaze was heady. After a second, she noticed his clothing. Interestingly enough, the firefighter hadn't donned a uniform. He wore a black leather vest over a skull-decorated black tank top. Black dragon tats—real ones—wound around his muscular biceps, and he'd roped a dark blue and black bandanna around his head.

"You really do look like a biker tonight." Her voice came out disconcertingly husky.

"Guess it's a good thing I have a bike." His voice dropped. "You wanna ride?"

"Oh my God, that sounds incredibly perverted."

His grin flashed white in his tanned face. "Little girl, you're in a BDSM club. We *are* perverted."

A delicious thrill seared over her nerves at the reminder. "Of-of course. What can I get you to drink, Master Holt?"

"Nothing." He smiled slowly. "Z gave permission for you to abandon the bar and have some playtime."

Holt still wanted to do the scene. Her mouth went dry. She took a step toward him. "B-but what if someone needs something?"

After a quick scan of the area, he called to an approaching man, "Cullen, I'm going to go beat on the bartender. If someone is desperate for a drink, can you handle it?"

"Aye." The giant Dom who'd trained her had his arm around Andrea, his tall, lush brunette wife. He grinned at Josie. "Go have a good time."

"Thank you." She turned to Holt and hesitated. Those clothes made him look awfully mean. And she hadn't ever seen him play. What if he was a sadist or something? "You...wouldn't really..."

He gave her a level look. "You can trust me, Josie."

She did, really. Mostly. "I... Okay."

"Good girl." The purr in his resonant voice sent warmth curling inside her.

He lifted the pass-through to let her out and then stopped her with an upraised hand. "Let's keep you out of trouble with Master Z. Leave your boots and socks here."

"What?"

His lips twitched, but his face held no laughter. "The correct response is: *Yes, Sir.*" And he waited, not for her argument but for her to comply.

"Right. Yes, Sir." Come to think of it, Zuri and Linda had discussed barefoot submissives. She toed off her boots, removed her socks, and set everything on an under-bar shelf. She was instantly another inch shorter...and this Dom already loomed over her.

"Good." He studied her for a second. "My subbie, you're still over-dressed. Let me fix that for you."

"What?"

His arched eyebrow reminded her there were rules to the game. This *was* a game, right? "Uh, yessir."

"Better." He pulled her tucked-in shirt out of her jeans and unbuttoned it, pushing her hands out of his way. Rolling up the shirttail, he tied the ends beneath her breasts, snugly enough her breasts were forced half out of her bra. When he ran a finger over the plumped-up curves, her nipples bunched with excitement.

"Holt," she protested.

"You have beautiful breasts, Josie." His gaze held hers. "If I want to share the sight with others, that's my prerogative for the next couple of hours. You think about that before we start. Because I intend for you to be wearing a lot less than this."

The entire room had heated to that of a sauna, and with every brush of his fingertip over her skin, the temperature went up another degree. She swallowed hard. "Yes, Sir."

He nodded approval and curled his hand around her nape, his grip not painful, but...firm. The heat of his hand seemed to sear her skin as he guided her toward the back of the room. "Let's talk for a minute."

Foliage plants in tall planters divided the sitting areas, lending privacy and muting the sound of the music and various scenes. When he sat on a couch, she moved to sit beside him.

"No, sweetheart." He pointed to the floor directly in front of him. "Let's start with the basics. Kneel, please."

She closed her eyes. Years of not buckling under to a man warred with the bewildering need to obey. "That's so wrong."

"I understand," he said evenly. "Josie, submissiveness has nothing to do with being male or female. You've been here long enough to see men kneeling as well."

She had. And there were female Dominants. In all reality, female equality was perhaps honored even more in the Shadowlands than outside its doors.

And when it came to her and Holt, there was sure no question of who was the Dominant.

She knelt.

"Very nice." He leaned forward, muscular forearms resting on his knees. "Straighten your spine and lace your hands together behind your back."

The posture arched her spine, pushed her breasts outward, and made her shirt gape.

"Good." He brushed his knuckles over her collarbone and between her breasts. "Some Doms prefer their submissives to look down. I'd rather have your eyes on me. Always on me. Clear?"

Her lips were dry. "Yes, Sir."

"For this scene, I'm not planning on having anyone else involved. It'll be just you and me for an hour or two. Nothing terrifying. I'd like to give you a taste of bondage and see how you like various impact toys. On a pain scale of 1 to 10 where 10 is bad, I don't plan to go over a 3 to 5, and any red marks will disappear within a few hours."

In rehab, Oma's nurses had used a pain scale like this. Hadn't Carson mentioned Holt worked in a hospital as well as the fire station? The knowledge was reassuring. "Okay."

"And, as I warned you, the amount of clothing you'll wear is up to me."

She pulled in a breath. Submissives here were often stripped down to briefs...or nothing. Oh, God. But skin didn't...really... bother her. Mostly.

"I need a verbal yes or no, pet."

"Okay. Yes, Sir."

"Brave girl."

He brushed his knuckles over her cheek and the knot of worry relaxed...slightly.

"I looked at your application file. You have no medical problems, no triggers, no phobias that you know of, right?"

Oh, God, he'd actually looked at that embarrassing Limits List. Her stomach felt as if she'd swigged an entire bottle of fizzy water. *Answer him, Josie.* "No problems, right, Sir." The words were coming easier the longer she was on her knees.

"We'll use the club safewords. Yellow means you're uncomfortable, emotionally or physically, and you want me to pause and fix the problem. Red means everything stops, and the scene is over." He smiled. "But tonight, because you're new, I'll also quit if you say no. However, *ouch* isn't a safeword in any way, shape, or form."

She snickered—and made a mental note. *Use red and yellow.*

"Good. Next, let's come to agreement on sexual contact." He smiled into her eyes and ran his fingers over the top of her breasts. "This, by the way, is considered sexual contact. If you're comfortable with my touch, I'd like to be able to play with your breasts and your pussy—outside and inside, with toys and fingers only."

A flush scorched its way from her breasts to her face. Her heart had sped up...and his palm was pressed against her sternum. Maybe she could tell him she didn't want him to touch her.

He would know she lied.

"Okay." She licked her lips. "But what about you? I mean—do I touch you?"

"No, baby. Not this time." He brushed her hair out of her eyes. "That's not what this scene is about."

This scene sounded like there might be others in the future. Sexy ones. What a terrifyingly exciting thought.

"Do you have any questions or concerns?"

There was a riptide in her brain, drawing her thoughts away from logic and out into an ocean of desire. She shook her head.

"All right." He studied her for another minute, then leaned forward and kissed her. Lightly. Gently.

She sighed and started to put her arms around his neck and heard him chuckle. "No, sweetheart, you weren't given permission to move. Arms behind your back."

She stared at him. Not allowed to touch him? He wanted her to stay in position while *he* touched *her*? Doing what he wanted? The floor seemed to drop slightly under her knees as she slowly put her hands behind her back again.

He watched her obey, his face unreadable, then a dimple appeared in his cheek. Again, he leaned forward and kissed her, his hand curling behind her nape, holding her as his kiss deepened, as his tongue took possession, as he nibbled on her lips, and then he took her mouth again.

And she wasn't permitted to move or touch. A shaking started up deep inside her.

When he sat back, her gaze dropped, only to have him remind her, "Eyes on me, Josie."

As her gaze met his, he simply regarded her, and it felt as if he saw...more. Too much, too deep. Could he see her trembling?

After studying her for an eternal moment, he grasped her arms and lifted her to her feet. "Let's go visit the dungeon—or, I should say, the jail."

He held her hand and led her to the very back of the clubroom. A small hallway had rooms on each side, each with a large display window. One was set up like a medical exam room. Across from it was an executive's office. The back left had a room almost filled with a mattress. On the right was... She glanced at Holt.

"This is the dungeon." He swung open an actual door with wrought-iron bars. An ancient prison cell door.

The room felt very medieval with stone walls and roughly fashioned black iron sconces that gave off a red-tinged light. A Domme sat in an ornate throne near the back wall. Her legs were propped on a naked man's back as she talked with another Domme.

A leather sling—a sex sling—hung in one corner, and Josie stiffened. *Please, not that.* But, no, he said it would only be touching, not fucking.

Holt led Josie to the other corner. A steel bar dangled from chains attached to the exposed beams of the ceiling. Nearby sat a black leather bag—a Dom's toy bag. Holt slid the bag to one side with his foot.

She bit her lip, feeling her anticipation...and worry...rising. Was she sure about this?

Smiling slightly, he kissed her again, even as he pulled off her police hat. He tossed it next to his bag and slipped off her shirt. When she stared up at him, his eyes danced with laughter—and she realized he'd managed to get her bra off, as well.

"What—" Shocked, she crossed her arms over her breasts.

"You wouldn't believe how hard I practiced that move when I was a teenager."

She choked. "I can't believe you told me that." Couldn't she just see him—a lanky blond teen, elated with how expertly he'd removed a girl's bra?

Her anxiety eased when he grinned at her. Weren't BDSM scenes supposed to be all serious and ominous and stuff? But... he'd seen her fear, hadn't he? Relaxing slightly, she smiled back at him.

"That's better." He ran warm hands up and down her upper arms. "Breathe, pet. Nice deep breath."

She sucked in some air.

"Better." His hands closed on her forearms, even as he held

her gaze with his. "A submissive doesn't hide her body from her Dom. Arms at your side, please."

She swallowed, and her arms dropped.

"There's a good girl," he murmured. He stepped back and looked at her, openly, not embarrassed in the least, even as the heat of a blush filled her face. "You have a beautiful body, sweetheart."

As the air wafted over her bared skin, he took leather cuffs from his toy bag. He wrapped a cuff around her left wrist, and despite the soft fleece lining, she couldn't escape the feeling of... imprisonment...when he buckled it. After cuffing her right wrist, he fastened each cuff to the steel bar over her head. When he finished, her arms were raised over her head in a wide V.

A tremor surged over her. When Peter had restrained her arms to the St. Andrew's cross, it hadn't felt like this. It'd been entertaining. Kind of fun. She'd felt a bit silly. Not...vulnerable.

She gave a tug on her arms. Restrained.

And naked from the waist up. She tensed, waiting for him to fondle her. To touch. To...

Arms crossed over his chest, he stood still. Waiting.

Slowly...slowly, she realized he was in control, not only of her but of himself as well. Her muscles unknotted.

"There we go," he murmured. He moved close enough she could feel the warmth of his body. With a hand at her waist, he ran his fingers through her hair, massaging her scalp gently, sending happy fizzles up her spine. His fingers were firm. Just right.

He finished by cupping her cheek and ran his thumb over her lips, leaving tingles behind. Taking a knee in front of her, he removed her duty belt and unzipped her pants.

As her slacks and thong dropped down around her ankles, her hands fisted. She'd told Peter not to mess with her clothes. Why hadn't she refused Holt? A sound escaped her.

His steely-blue gaze lifted, and he ran his hand up and down her bare thigh. "It's tough to be naked, isn't it? Almost all of the submissives and bottoms have a...moment...the first time they're stripped down."

The sympathy helped. Kind of.

He patted her left knee. "Lift, pet."

A second later, her pants and thong were tossed on top of his toy bag. Oh, sweet heavens, she really was naked and not in her own bedroom. Suddenly, she realized how many people were in the room. The Dommes and their submissives. Someone using the leather-covered table. Another over—

"Josie. Where is your gaze supposed to be?" Holt was still in front of her, on one knee. His voice was soft but held a stomach-quivering warning.

She'd screwed up. "On you, Sir." She looked down at him and realized he wasn't angry. Just correcting her.

"Better." Buckling cuffs around her right ankle, he ran a finger inside to ensure the fit wasn't too tight, and drew her leg outward. He lifted a stone in the floor to reveal a chain attached to an embedded ring, then hooked her ankle cuff to the chain and repeated the process on her left leg. After an assessing look, he adjusted the attachment to force her legs open into a wide V.

The position wasn't uncomfortable...exactly...but she now realized how useful her thighs had been at concealing and guarding her vulnerable bits.

As he rose, he validated her concern by cupping her mound and pussy.

Shocked, she sucked in a breath. He was touching her...*there*. Intimately. As if he had the right. The possessive, authoritative gesture shook her.

He didn't move. Slowly the warmth of his powerful hand seeped into her skin, heating her insides—and making her clit swell in response.

Biting her lip, she stared into his perceptive eyes.

He was like a chameleon, so sociable with his caressingly

smoky voice and easy smile, but at his core, there was an almost terrifying Dominant. One who didn't care what anyone thought. Once they entered this room, he'd never looked around; all his attention was on her. "Josie, tell me what your safeword is again."

Her what? *Oh. Safeword.* "Red to stop. Yellow to slow?"

"Very good." His lips curved again. "You may also use green to say everything's great and keep going."

"Oh. Okay, cool." Why did it feel as if her skin had tingles of electricity running over it? "What now? Sir."

He chuckled and ran his finger down her cheek. "Now I enjoy myself and play with this curvy body you've so sweetly offered."

"I did what?" Offered? She hadn't offered...only, she really had, hadn't she? Just by agreeing to this scene.

"I'm going to learn what you like, what you don't like...and then mix everything up until that busy little mind of yours shuts down." The words sounded almost like a threat—and yet melted every bone in her body.

He saw that too.

Damn, Josie was sweet. He'd removed her clothing, her mobility, and opened her to his touch. As he'd slowly eliminated her choices, one by one, she'd slid further into a submissive state.

Holt grasped her nape, ran his fingers through her short hair, and gave the strands a firm tug.

Her soft exhalation told him all he needed to know. Some places on a woman's body were erotic; some increased her sense of vulnerability. In Josie's case, pulling her hair did both.

Interesting. He liked long hair—winding it around a fist was fun. But her short cut was perfect for both her personality and her face. And was much safer around floggers.

He kissed her, taking his time, nibbling on her plump lower lip, licking the curve of the upper, before aggressively taking his fill of her mouth. The way she responded stirred all his senses— and melted his heart.

When he stepped back, her eyes had a slightly unfocused look.

"Let's get you warmed up."

Her brows drew together in confusion since she undoubtedly already felt toasty after that kiss. He sure did. But he didn't mean sexually heated—he meant the blood flow to her skin.

He took his time, rubbing his hands over her shoulders, back, ass, and thighs, waking and tautening the skin. Reaching around her, he did the same on her front—and pleased himself by fondling her cute breasts, her soft stomach, her upper thighs. Rubbing changed to patting, light slaps, light pinches.

Her brows drew together sometimes when he did something unexpected, then she'd relax again. Her eyelids had lowered; her lips parted. She was slowly getting drawn into simply...feeling. He kept his hands on her, never moving away, keeping the tie between them—physical and emotional—strong.

The lightweight flogger had falls thick enough to give her a thuddy sensation. He teased the strands over her back, her ass, her stomach and breasts. Such a pretty sight—her tight pale pink nipples through the brown leather strands. When he stroked over her neck and shoulders, she'd inhale the scent of the leather with each breath.

Watching her closely, he lightly flipped the falls against her shoulders. Her lips curved up slightly. He worked his way from side to side, avoiding spine and kidneys, moving down toward her ass and upper thighs. Down, then up, repeating the cycle until her skin was an attractively rosy color. Her muscles were loose, and she was still smiling. Yeah, she was enjoying herself as much as he was.

To keep her from getting too relaxed, he moved to her front. This time he started with her thighs, lashing gently. He grinned when her eyes flew open.

Upward. He avoided her pussy—for now—and sent the falls flicking lightly over her belly.

She was holding her breath as he danced the flogger over her lower breasts, over her nipples and upper breasts. The delicate, untanned skin over her breasts turned a clear pink color.

Stepping back, he studied her. Hands open. Arms, shoulders still relaxed. He liked how her nipples pointed outward in opposite directions and had formed hard peaks. Her eyes were half-lidded. *Mmmhmm.* Looked to him like light flogging went into the plus column for her. As did bondage. And the humiliation of nudity in the club environs.

Fuck, he liked her.

Time to push a bit. He abandoned the flogger and chose a light cane.

As he straightened, he noticed Raoul entering the room. In the gold-trimmed vest of a dungeon monitor, the Master checked Josie in one comprehensive glance, smiled slightly at her dazed expression, nodded at Holt, and moved to check the other scenes.

As the music changed to Razed in Black's "Sacrificed", Holt caned his little submissive, using the rhythm of the music as he dealt out a series of quick light taps on her sweet round ass and her upper thighs. She lacked adequate padding on her shoulders, so he moved around to her front. Upper thighs got light whaps. He skipped the belly. *Hmm.* How would she react to a bit of pain on her breasts?

He'd have to go quite light. He flicked the thin cane over her left breast—tap, tap, tap.

Her eyes widened, and she pulled in an audible breath. But her nipples bunched into invitingly hard peaks. *Very nice.* He wasn't planning to hurt her. At least not this time. But she apparently enjoyed a dash of pain—and fuck, he did enjoy hearing the sound of a subbie sucking in air. He teased each breast, pattering the cane around the outside and beneath, and tapping over her nipples.

Her pupils dilated until her eyes looked almost black. Her lips turned a dark pink and now matched her nipples.

Giving her a break, he cupped her breasts, circling the stiff, swollen nipples with his thumbs, and pulling until they formed long, distended points.

She whimpered.

When he rolled the peaks between his fingers, he got a husky moan. Fuck, she was adorable.

Stepping back, he studied her nicely exposed pussy. Her lower curls were trimmed to a tidy copper-colored fuzz, long enough to be soft, short enough her engorged clit was in sight. *Beautiful.* Being in the medical field, he'd never been an advocate of completely bare pussies. As far as he was concerned, this was the perfect compromise.

And she was slick with arousal.

Her eyelids rose, and she blinked slowly. After a second, she realized where he was looking. The pretty freckles on her cheeks disappeared with her blush.

"While you're in my bonds, you're mine to look at," he murmured, holding her gaze with his.

"Mine to kiss." He bent down and kissed her, deliberately rough and deep and invasive. Feeling her shock—and capitulation.

"Mine to touch." He ran his hand down her stomach and lower. With one finger, he stroked around her clit and down between her folds before pressing up inside her. Hot velvet wrapped around his finger.

She made a shocked sound against his mouth.

With a hand behind her ass holding her still, he explored her in the most intimate way possible. When he was finished, he'd verified she hadn't had a man in a long while, and her clit was delightfully sensitive. If he put a clamp on the swollen nub, they'd probably hear her in downtown Tampa.

He stepped back and licked his fingers clean. Delicately musky—and damned if he didn't want to tease her with his mouth and tongue. Her surprised expression as she watched saddened him. Had she only been with men who wanted her smelling of chemicals and soaps? He liked the flavor of an aroused woman.

Now to take that arousal up a notch. He picked up a heavier flogger.

Unsure as to how long had passed, Josie felt as if her entire body hummed with desire. The alternating flogging and caning had left her skin tight and burning as if she'd been out in the sun too long. Although a few places stung, she couldn't even tell exactly where. Her breasts were swollen, her nipples throbbing. Her pussy was awfully wet, and her burning clit was making urgent demands.

"Josie." Holt's voice slid over her like warm molasses, perfectly steady and even. He was totally in control of himself—and her. "Look at me, sweetheart."

With an effort, she opened her eyes. God, she felt almost drunk. Her field of vision encompassed his wide shoulders, his corded neck, his strong jaw. Words spilled from her. "Are we done now? Are you tired? I'm green, not red. Just so you know. All green. You know, like the Hulk."

"Good to know." Still laughing softly, he kissed her. Oh, he had amazing lips. Firm, yet so soft. She really wanted those lips...everywhere.

As he caressed her breasts, the caned skin burned, and her nipples were extremely tender and sensitive. His hands hurt her, only didn't really, and when he pulled at the peaks, everything inside her throbbed with need.

Her moan was urgent. Greedy.

"That sounded nice," he murmured. Even as he nibbled down her neck, he cupped her mound.

The light pressure on her clit made her jerk, and the need grew, pulling at her, blurring her thoughts until her attention was all concentrated...there. "Oh, oh..."

"I know, sweetheart," he whispered. He pressed a finger

inside, past slick swollen tissues, making her core bloom with heat. His thumb settled beside her clit—and it was vibrating.

Oh, my God. The fine vibration continued, steadily and far too effective. Her clit hardened and swelled even as her pussy clamped down around his invading finger.

He bent and took one nipple in his mouth, teasing it with his tongue.

Each lick and suck made her insides clench around him.

He slid his finger out, back in, repeating, each movement deliberate and slow. The tiny vibe attached to his thumb settled directly on top of her clit.

Her hips jerked, pressing forward. Anticipation stilled her breathing until nothing existed except his lips on her breast, the exquisite thrumming sensation on her clit, and the slow, merciless thrusting of his finger.

Sweat broke out on her skin. Her muscles grew taut. Her legs trembled. *Please, just a bit more...* She whimpered.

Reaching around her, he closed his free hand over her flogged bottom.

The shocking pain erupted into a surging, boiling pleasure—and ignited everything inside her. Driven up and up by the vibrations, by his touch, the waves of incredible release rippled upward and outward through her entire body, filling her so full of sensation that she could only hang from the chains and shake.

"There's a good girl." The smoky voice crooned in her ear as Holt held her against his hard body.

As her breathing eased, and her heart slowed, he drew back slightly. "Hey, Raoul, could I have an extra hand here?"

"Easy, sweetheart," Holt murmured, his words so calm, she could let herself relax into a happy lethargy.

Her arms were released and lowered...and her legs gave out. Someone's arm caught her around her waist and held her up. A blanket was wrapped around her.

"I've got her. Thanks, Raoul."

"It was my pleasure, my friend." The voice had a Hispanic accent.

"Down you go, pet." Holt helped her to a sitting position on the floor, half-leaning against the rock wall. The floor was made of rocks, too. Pretty rocks. Not as bumpy as they'd looked...

Holt snorted. "Time to come back to reality." An unyielding hand under her chin lifted her head. "Drink some of this for me, sweetie." He put a straw between her lips.

She sucked some of the cool liquid, and the flavor of lemony-lime filled her mouth. She'd never tasted anything so wonderful. "Mmm."

"Good girl. Hold still a second." After wiping off her sweat-damp face, he gave her the straw again.

After a few more swallows, she felt the world steady. Kind of. She looked up at him.

He smiled. "Think you can hold the bottle?"

"Uh-huh. Thank you."

"No, baby. Thank *you*." Cupping her cheek, he kissed her gently and put the bottle in her hand. "Sit there and drink. I need to pack and clean up the area."

"I can—"

"If you move, I'll restrain you and put you back on the ground."

She blinked at him, heard the implacable note, and muttered, "I think I'll sit here and drink this stuff."

"Good choice."

She wasn't sure how much time had passed. Somehow, she'd ended up in the main clubroom, lying on the couch with her back against Holt's chest. His right arm and shoulder were under her head, and he'd turned so he could look down at her. She felt his chest rise and fall with his slow breathing. His left hand rested on her stomach.

He hadn't let her get dressed.

Her clothes were stacked on top of his toy bag at the other end of the couch. She was wrapped in a blanket—and what had felt amazingly soft and comfy when it first went around her began to feel scratchy. Only, the fabric wasn't the cause. Her skin had been...tenderized. She frowned. "How long were we in there?"

"Mmm, maybe close to two hours."

She stiffened. "Seriously?"

"Yes."

Whoa. She looked around the dark club. Only an occasional person strolled past. Almost everyone was gone.

"Since you're tracking on all levels again, talk to me. How do you feel about what happened?" When she didn't answer, he gave her a gentle squeeze, as she would a teddy bear. "How did being restrained make you feel?"

"I don't...I don't like to—"

He put her bottle of Gatorade in her hand and let her sip. "I know you're not used to sharing your feelings, but this is part of BDSM, pet. Communication. Before, during if needed, and definitely after. Talk to me."

"Boy, you're stubborn," she muttered and got another teddy-bear squeeze as if he could press the answers out of her.

She'd rather not think about how much she liked what he'd done to her. But he'd spent two hours just on her. She owed him the truth.

What had it felt like when he'd chained her arms over her head and her legs to the floor? "The restraints were scary and somehow sexy and—I know it's weird—but having them on felt almost safe. Or not safe, exactly, but...it was kind of freeing, in a way. Maybe because I didn't have to worry about doing anything... because I couldn't."

The kiss on top of her head made the space around her heart feel all warm.

"Very good. Now, so I don't stress you too much, the next question is about all the impact toys. We'll cover each one individually some other time." He chuckled. "Did you enjoy getting flogged and caned and all that?"

"Yes." Wait, that couldn't be the right answer. She tried to sit up—and his hard palm on her stomach kept her pinned to his lap. "No." A breath. "Yes."

When he laughed, she'd have thumped him if she'd been in any position to do so. Being flat on her back made reprisal...difficult.

"Does that mean you figure you shouldn't like it but you did?"

Her grumble was all the answer he apparently needed.

"Then the—"

"All fine," she hastily interrupted, because she just knew he was going to talk about the sex stuff. And she so wasn't. "No one could complain about getting off, right?"

"Actually, yes." He tipped his head and rubbed his cheek against her hair. "Some people find any sexual intimacy within a power exchange to be uncomfortable."

"I don't understand."

"You climaxed because I wanted you to. I, essentially, *made* you get off. Not everyone likes losing that control."

"Oh." He really *had* taken any option of how she responded away from her, hadn't he? The way he touched her, played her body... She'd have come whether she wanted to or not. A shiver chased down her spine.

But she was okay with it...because the Dom was Holt. Her mouth turned down. If someone else—like Peter—had done what Holt had, she'd have found out if that safeword stuff worked. "I liked it with *you*."

She watched how the left corner of his mouth quirked up slightly, making his dimple appear. Dimples often made a man look like a boy. Holt's made him even more masculine. "Why do you have to be so gorgeous?"

The dimple disappeared. "Sweetheart, I'm scarred up enough to make you think I'm a biker."

"Oh, please." The shake of her head make her brain spin. "Like a line on your face can diminish the appeal of the Thunder God."

His laugh was as sexy as his face. "Sweetheart, you're rambling. We'll talk about the scene more when you've had time to process. I'm tied up for a couple of days, but after that... Let me think."

He wanted to make plans? For the future? Oh, no. He was too good-looking, and she'd let him play her like a piano—and that would've been okay, but now all she wanted was to stay tucked in his arms and on his lap. This BDSM stuff was more dangerous than she'd realized. Not because she'd had fun, but because of the way it made her feel about the person doing it. For heaven's sake, she hardly knew him.

"I can't think about next week. Really, I need to get going." She pushed at the hand on her stomach, sat up, and slid her legs off the couch.

He hauled her back. "Josie. What's going through your head?"

"Nothing. Nothing important." She shoved his arm away. "I'm all recovered, and right now, I need to get back and close down the bar."

He let her rise. As he sat, arms extended along the back of the couch, his frown showed his...not annoyance...but concern. His intent gaze said the Dom would figure out why she was running.

And the idea of him getting deeper was simply terrifying.

CHAPTER NINE

On Monday evening, Carson looked through the stacks of books at the book fair and gave a sniff. As he'd feared, he'd read most of them at least two years ago. But there was a bunch of books for advanced readers and... Huh, some of them looked pretty good. *Ghostopolis*? Maybe. *Trapped*. Yeah, that had potential. He'd never seen a blizzard, after all.

"Cars, dude. You're looking at *books*?" Brandon nudged his shoulder and snatched the book out of Carson's hand.

Annoyed, Carson grabbed it back. "What're you doing in here?" It wasn't as if Brandon was into books. He was into games —and good at them.

"The mom's here, selling books. Figured I could hit her up for some cash." Brandon smirked. "She won't want to look cheap in front of the other parents, so she'll give me some."

"Pretty smart." Carson considered, then shook his head. Messing with Mom that way seemed kinda mean. She wouldn't cave anyway. She was always talking about not doing stuff just to impress other people...and she didn't.

"I know, right? C'mon." Brandon headed for the front.

Carson hesitated. There were other books to pick out. But

Brandon was cool, even if he didn't play soccer, and apparently, he had a bunch of *Mature* Xbox games. It might be fun to see them. Brandon wasn't a total geek either. Sure, he had a gut, but he was bigger than Carson and knew karate. Not that he practiced since he said his dad wasn't on his case anymore.

Turning, Carson followed with his two books. The cafeteria section had been roped off and the tables piled high with books. Near the "entrance", three women stood behind the checkout table. One of them was Carson's mom.

"Hey, my mother, how about giving your one and only son some lunch money?" Brandon started on his spiel.

Carson caught his mother's eye. She was biting her lip, trying not to laugh. Yeah, she'd seen right through Brandon. Mom was pretty okay.

Carson held up the books he'd chosen, and, as he'd expected, she nodded. She was a soft touch when it came to books. But just handing out money without a reason? Not a chance. She wouldn't fall for something like Brandon was pulling.

She sure hadn't when he was five. Imitating another kid, he'd thrown a screaming fit in a grocery store to score some candy. He hadn't gotten any candy. Mom'd leaned against the counter and told everyone who walked by what he was doing and why. Every adult thought she was a great mom. Jeez, one group of old ladies had even applauded her—and told him he was a bad boy. He'd been the one who was embarrassed. And he hadn't gotten to go shopping with her for a whole month afterward.

He handed her the books. "Thanks, Mom."

"That's your mom?" Brandon looked at the women. "Since you two know each other, is it okay if Carson comes over after school?"

Visit Brandon? Carson would've bounced on his toes, only that wouldn't be cool. "Mom?"

"Ah…"

Brandon's mother smiled. "I don't have a job, so I'm home when Brandon is out of school. Carson would be very welcome."

"All right." Mom nodded. "Have fun then."

"Awesome." Brandon held out his fist.

Grinning, Carson fist-bumped him. *Yes!*

Josie watched the two boys swagger out, all arms and legs, like ungainly puppies. "When did he get to be that tall?" she muttered.

Cecily laughed. "I know. I have to buy Brandon a whole new wardrobe every few months."

"And shoes." Josie sighed. "Shoes are the worst." One of the presents under the Christmas tree held the new soccer shoes Carson wanted. Just in time, it turned out, since the middle school soccer season started in January.

"Here, let me give you our address." Cecily scrawled on a piece of notepaper, then pulled out her phone. "What's your phone number?"

Josie recited it and received a text. "Got it." Wasn't it funny how quickly smartphones had been incorporated into the *making friends* ritual?

She eyed Cecily. Nicely dressed, well educated, polite. "Can I assume no drugs, no alcohol, guns are locked up, and the boys aren't left with anyone I haven't met?"

Cecily's eyes widened before she laughed. "You did all that in one breath. Amazing. But it's all good. No drugs. I have a bottle of wine in the fridge, but children don't get any. I don't own any guns."

Josie waited.

The woman's gaze dropped. "I'm the only one at our house. My husband and I divorced not long ago. You know the cliché— the CEO finds himself a younger, prettier wife? He did."

"Oh. Oh, no." What could she say? An *"I'm sorry"* wasn't suitable, since, obviously, the woman was better off without the jerk. "Divorces are rough."

Fiddling with the receipts on the table, Cecily shrugged. "At least I received a hefty settlement—mostly so he could get everything finalized quickly. His chickie gave birth a week later."

"How awful."

Cecily's glare was hot enough to scorch the receipts. "He seems very happy with his wife and new son over in St. Petersburg. He could have weekends with Brandon, but he doesn't bother, even though St. Pete's only an hour or so away."

"Poor Brandon. That must be a blow."

"His father's such an asshole." Cecily pushed the papers away. "When I called him about him neglecting his firstborn, the dumbass said I'd ruined Brandon. That I'd turned him into a sissy, a coward, and a wimp who only fights on the computer."

Josie stared. "That's unbelievably harsh."

"Isn't it? But my bastard ex was a football star in college and served as a Marine. He expected Brandon to be a chip off the old block. Made him take karate and everything." Cecily shook her head. "But...when we were talking, Brandon was on the other line. He heard his father call him those names."

"Oh no." Josie knew too well the mother's pain. She closed her eyes for a moment, remembering the hurt in Carson's voice when he'd shared what *his* father had said. Yet nothing could be done. No matter how much a parent wanted to spare their children, the world held a wealth of disillusionment and heartache. "I'm so sorry."

"Brandon took it hard—not that he talks about his feelings with his mother." She gave Josie a rueful smile. "Going from elementary to middle school's made his life even worse, what with the changes and losing friends."

"Carson's having the same problems."

"Well, let's hope they both adjust." Cecily smiled at an approaching teenager. "Did you find everything you wanted?"

Still thinking about Cecily's husband, Josie let out a breath. When his son wasn't what he wanted, he'd dumped poor Brandon like so much garbage. Like her father had done. Like Everett had done with Carson.

Men were sure difficult.

She sighed. Despite her resolve to keep her life simple, she'd complicated everything by doing that scene with Holt. But, okay, she was human and female—and he was appallingly sexy and appealing—and dominant. She'd loved everything he'd done to her last weekend. Sheesh, the mere memory could arouse her.

And it was more than just the...sexy stuff, dammit. She...liked him. A lot. He was amazing with Carson. He paid visits to Oma to check her blood pressure and see how she was doing. The teens in the neighborhood adored him. He'd helped her when Carson ran away—insisted on it, no less—and had been so damned strong and capable.

The three C's—he had them in abundance: competent, confident, and caring. She'd never been so...attracted...to anyone before.

The trouble was that now, she couldn't stop thinking about him. When in the office writing, she'd keep glancing out her window, hoping for glimpses of him. Her heart rate would increase at the sound of his motorcycle.

She wanted to feed him, worry about him...care for him.

With the hours he worked, she might not see him until the Shadowlands next weekend. And she had to wonder... Although he'd mentioned talking, maybe the scene was all he'd wanted from her. It wasn't as if a BDSM session was a...a date or anything.

And really, that one scene should be all she wanted, too. *Really.* To get involved with a neighbor and one who belonged to the club where she worked was foolish. Add in the BDSM stuff? Purely foolhardy, and she just wasn't that kind of a person. She was a *no complications* person.

Dammit, I don't want to care about him.

CHAPTER TEN

Carson wiggled his knife in the mashed potatoes. Two eyes. Big nose. Eyebrows pinched together to match the turned-down mouth. Ugly face for the crappiest teacher in the school. Mr. Jorgeson. The big jerk had picked on Juan all during their science class. With his fork, Carson squished the face.

"What school do you go to, Carson? The one down the street with the fires?"

Startled, Carson looked across the table at Holt who'd come to supper. "The dumpster fires? Yeah, that's my school." Blazing dumpsters—kinda awesome. No one knew who was doing it, but the teachers were sure all freaked.

"Fires? More than one?" Oma asked.

"Um, yeah." Carson shrugged. "Two."

Holt's mouth went tight. "An equipment shed was also burned."

"Was anyone hurt?" Mom looked upset. She always got worried if she heard about anything interesting. She sure found a lot of stuff dangerous. Isaac's mother was the same way. It must be a mom thing.

"No one hurt, and not too much damage, thankfully," Holt said.

As Mom sat back, Oma started telling about the guy down the street who'd lit his house on fire by falling asleep with a cigarette.

Talk about embarrassing. Chewing on a bite, Carson shook his head.

As the grownups talked, Carson dished himself more mashed potatoes and gravy. No one made better food than his mom did.

Sure looked like Holt liked it, too. Like Carson, he'd taken seconds.

He was pretty cool. Picked great music when he and Carson worked on his backyard. And Wedge and Duke—the fifteen-year-olds—said he had a huge TV, and if there was a game on, he'd let them come over.

Today, Holt'd seen him and Mom putting up Christmas lights around the door and windows, and he'd walked over to help. They'd gotten done really fast that way.

And Mom'd invited him to supper. Mom did friendly stuff like that.

Only not with men. Last week when Holt came to supper, well, that was Mom's way of saying thanks for saving Carson. Was today just a thank you sort of supper again?

Or...did Mom like Holt, as in *like* the way a girl would?

Carson eyed the guy. He'd shaved his beard off. Looked good, kinda normal. The girls would say he was hot, Carson figured. Would Mom? Judging grown-ups ages wasn't easy. Holt might be around Mom's age or a few years older. And he'd gone to college, so he was smart.

He kept touching Mom. Not like laying a big, wet one on her, but gripping her shoulder or putting his hand on her back. It was really creepy to think about a guy making moves on his mom.

If she and Holt were just friends, he wouldn't touch her like that, would he? But they must be. Mom didn't have boyfriends or anything.

Thinking of friends... "Hey, Mom, Brandon asked me to go over to his place on Saturday. Yukio and Juan are going. Can I?"

"Who is Brandon?" Oma asked.

"He's in a couple of my classes," Carson said.

Mom added, "I met his mother at the fundraiser book sale. She seemed nice, although unhappy."

"Why would that be?" Oma asked.

"She got divorced this year, and it sounds like she and Brandon are taking it hard."

Yeah, Brandon was messed up about the divorce. And even more pissed off his father was so into the new baby and didn't want Brandon any more. Kind of like ol' Everett, the douche. *"You're not my kid. Get away from here, you little bastard."*

Carson frowned. "I don't know why people get married anyway. They just end up hating each other and getting those divorces and stuff."

His mother straightened. "Not everyone gets a divorce," she said, mildly.

Yeah, because some—like Mom—don't even get married. He bit back the words. It wasn't her fault Everett was an asshole. Carson'd told Juan about his father last week; Juan's mother hadn't married either. Juan had made him see what kind of jerk Everett was. And, although Mom was smart about people now, she might not have been back when he was born.

"A wedding is like a celebration and announcement all in one," Holt said. "It's something like a school graduation ceremony where you're telling everyone you made it through high school and you're an adult. People get married to tell everyone they found their partner and are starting life together."

"Huh." Carson half grinned. "I thought a wedding was just a reason for a girl to wear a fancy dress."

Oma's lips twitched. "That, too."

Carson noticed the way his mother was looking at Holt. That was a *girly* look. He stared at Holt. "So do you have a wife?"

The guy smiled. "I did. And yep, we ended up divorced."

"How come?"

Both his mother and Oma gave him the "*Carson*" at the same time.

Holt shook his head. "It's all right. I don't mind talking about it." He turned to Carson. "Bear in mind, some breakups are ugly, so asking the reason can be awkward."

Carson nodded. It was probably like when Mindy stopped talking to Addison, and everybody knew not to ask why or Addison would start bawling. "Uh. Yeah. Got it."

Holt smiled at the boy. Josie's son was a good kid. And observant. It wasn't surprising the boy had edged toward being rude. The kid had eyes, and Holt hadn't concealed his interest in Josie. The boy was old enough to want to defend his territory against another male.

"We were pretty young when we married." Holt nodded to Carson. "If you can, wait until you're older to jump into the marriage stuff. Even in your twenties, you're still figuring out what you want, and often, a couple ends up going in different directions."

Carson took that in without a challenge.

"I take it you and your wife went in opposite directions?" Stella asked.

"We did. She liked being married to a firefighter. And although I like being a firefighter, the job is hard on the mind and body. With an eye to the future, I started college to get my bachelor's in nursing."

The kid snorted. "Girls think firefighters are hot, not nurses."

"Sad, huh? I think she agreed," Holt said. "We broke up when I was in college. She wanted to party when I needed to do homework."

Josie nodded. "You grew up first, and she wasn't ready yet. Then again, when a baby arrives, it's more often the mother who grows up faster."

"That adulting stuff can come as a shock." Eating the last bite of his chicken, Holt leaned back with a sigh. "You're an amazing cook, Josie. Thank you."

"I'm glad you liked it." She checked that everyone was finished before rising and starting to clear.

Holt stood to help. "Did you get saddled with a ton of homework tonight, Carson?"

The boy was picking up Stella's dishes with his own. "Nope. I'm helping Mom with her job." The tone was clear. *We're busy here; don't let the door hit you on the way out.*

Holt looked up. "Bartending or writing job?"

Stella chuckled. "Writing. Nevertheless, drinks *would* be nice. Carson, could you bring us all some lemonade?"

"Yes'm."

As Holt set his stack of dishes on the counter, Josie looked up from the dishwasher. "You know, while I hope to make a good living at writing, I'm not sure I'd want to give up bartending. I'd miss talking with people."

Last weekend, the club members had hung around the bar in a way they hadn't since Cullen cut back. Because Z had hired them a warm and caring bartender. Smiling, he pushed a lock of her hair behind her ear. "Your customers would miss you too."

She stilled at his touch, and again, he felt the link between them. The sizzle that accompanied sheer liking. She cleared her throat. "Anyway, about tonight. When I run into a tricky action scene in a book, Oma and Carson help me act it out."

Action scene? Holt looked over his shoulder at the woman at the table. He'd guess Stella was over seventy.

Josie followed his gaze and snickered. "No, I'm not doing martial arts with my great-aunt. You can stay and help if you want."

"Little author, you couldn't get me out of here with a crowbar."

Carson gave a dish sponge to Stella to wipe down the dining room table, then returned with a box of small dolls.

Josie dried her hands on a towel. "Let me get my notes and we can get started."

At the table, Carson was arranging the dolls.

Sitting across from him, Holt picked one up. He was used to seeing Barbie dolls in shorts or fancy evening gowns or swimsuits —and as carefully made up as women hitting the nightclubs. These looked about the age of high schoolers. No make-up. And... "What is this—Barbie in the Middle Ages?"

"That's right." Laughing, Josie joined them, setting down a notepad and pen. "When Zuri visited Oma, she saw my notes and crummy drawings of the clothing my characters would wear. A couple of weeks later, she showed up with these dolls. She's so talented."

"She is that." Had Josie seen the kinky BDSM ones Uzuri made for the Shadowkittens? Holt studied the dolls. Tunics, trousers, cloaks. And swords. "One girl gets a sword and the other doesn't?"

"She has magic. It doesn't react well to all that metal."

"Got it." The one with the sword was obviously female, but her hair was cropped short. Holt glanced at Josie. "The hairstyle seems...off...for that time period."

"She ran away from an arranged marriage. Everyone thinks she's a boy."

"Ah. Good for her."

His comment won him smiles from both Josie and Stella.

He saw Stella had put two male dolls with the two females. "Is there a love story going on as well as fighting?"

Carson snorted. "They're too smart for that."

With a light laugh, Josie told Holt, "No romance. I don't believe in it."

Holt's smile faded. She didn't believe in romance, so her son was growing up thinking love was for idiots.

Shaking her head, Stella said, "Not all romances end badly, my dear."

"Maybe not for men," she said under her breath, then winced and looked at him. "Sorry."

Holt leaned back in his chair, watching her thoughtfully. She had trust issues. Considering she'd had a teenage pregnancy and her lover'd turned out to be a bastard, he could understand why. Trouble was, the longer he knew her, the more he liked her.

The more he wanted her for his own.

How could he not? She was submissive—so the Dom in him was happy. She was fun with a sense of humor that was never cruel, just quirky. He'd probably laughed more this evening than he had in a long, long time. He'd enjoyed simply putting up Christmas lights and arguing over whether *Star Trek* or *Star Wars* had the better technology. Jesus, she liked fantasy and sci-fi—how could he help but like her?

Most of all, she had a caring heart.

The question wasn't whether he wanted her, because he did. Now he just had to help her see that romance wasn't inevitably bad.

And that her anxieties were affecting her son's outlook on life.

"Holt can be the bad guys." Carson pushed over a box of horses, wolves, elephants and oversized...somethings.

Holt held up one ugly-ass doll. "What is this?"

"Ogres. That box also has trolls." Josie picked out more dolls. "Tonight, the team is taking on the reptilian race of Grestors. And they have a troll with them."

She described the talents of her young team. The heroine, Laurent, could ignite her hands and throw the flames short distances. The thought made the firefighter in him wince. The hero, Tigre, was a knife-fighting ninja type who could become invisible.

Interesting. When he got home, he'd boot up his eReader and

pick up her first book. Why should kids get to read all the good stories?

Josie waved at the table. "The neighboring country is softening our land up for war, and the team has been sent out with a teacher to defend a border village."

"Aren't they rather young?" Holt frowned. Children shouldn't be going to war.

"Even in our history, a squire was usually around fourteen years old and often went into battle to guard his knight's back." Josie gave him an understanding smile. "At eleven, Carson would've been serving as a page, working his way up to squire."

Carson grinned at the thought.

Holt didn't. "Hard times."

"Exactly. When there's a need, children grow up fast. Our team will do their best, no matter how frightened they are."

Holt gave her an understanding nod. "Heroes in heart as well as skills."

"The world needs heroes, and our children today need role models," Stella murmured. "Courage and self-sacrifice. Honesty and integrity."

Josie shot her a smile. "All of that—and learning to work together." She checked her notes. "Carson, if you'll take the two boys. Oma, the girls. Holt, you get the bloodthirsty Grestors and the troll."

Bowls provided boulders for protection—and a way to jump down on the bad guys. Holt lost two reptile-men to the damn knife-boy. Josie stopped the action occasionally, reworking the choreography to be trickier. She redid one mini-fight to force the air mage and the knife boy to work together. Carson got infuriated when Holt's troll hurt a wolf the animal mage had called in.

In the end, Holt managed to save a few of his Grestors. As they ran for the edge of the table, he turned his leader around and shouted, using an Arnold accent, "I'll be back. You wait. I'll cut off your nose next time."

Carson burst out laughing, and Stella sent a lightning bolt—a gummi worm—after Holt's guys. For all her church attending, the woman had a vicious streak.

After giving Stella a disapproving frown that made her grin, Holt ate the gummi worm and eyed the other woman at the table. *Josie.* There was so much more to her than met the eye. An author, one who was trying to improve the world with her stories. One who let her family help and cheered them on in the battle.

She really was amazing.

Grinning at him, she asked, "What do you think?"

"You may call on me anytime you need assistance in destroying the world, sweetie." He winked at Carson. "It's my duty to help." And his duty to help get the sweet author past her aversion to romance as well.

Because he fully intended to sweep her off her feet and into his arms.

And keep her there.

CHAPTER ELEVEN

On Friday, Holt finally had the energy and time to clean up his place. Fuck knew, he didn't like living in a mess.

After a couple of hours, he had the kitchen and bathroom scrubbed down, his laundry done, and he'd moved on to the living room. Swiping at a cobweb, he caught an eight-legged inhabitant with it. "Sorry, guy, you need to live outside."

As he walked out the front to shake the cobweb—and spider —off the duster, he heard Imagine Dragons playing from Josie's house. *Interesting.* Her appearance would suggest a Celtic music fan. Her Texas accent said country-western. Instead, she liked alternative rock and the odd mixes Z played in the Shadowlands. Everyone in the club enjoyed watching her dance in place as she mixed drinks.

He smiled. Last Saturday with her had been amazing. She'd been nervous, but she'd trusted him to take care of her. Was authentic in her physical responses. Had loved being bound and taken to the edge of pain, over and over. The way she'd felt in his arms had been...right.

Too right. He'd been a Dom a long time and couldn't remember when he'd felt so close to anyone. From the way she'd watched him, softened against him, listened to him, she'd felt the same way. He'd been the entire focus of all her attention—just as she'd been his.

There was something between them—and it was a hell of a lot more than just lust. Hell, his spirits lifted at the mere thought of seeing her.

He'd never met anyone quite like her. He loved the way she saw the world with a child's eyes. Hell, she probably wouldn't be surprised if fairies danced in the garden at night or if Carson started to levitate. Yet she was uncommonly down-to-earth, able to deal with everything from unhappy teenagers to upset Dominants. And she listened to people with all her attention and with an open, caring heart. Whatever she'd suffered in the past had left her wary of men—and had given her an ocean-deep empathy for others.

Yeah, he'd fallen right into caring a fuck of a lot for her.

He took a step toward her house and stopped.

No, dumbass, this was her writing time. Even more than that, he didn't want her to feel pressured by a man living next door. He had a wary submissive here, and he'd have to take care.

Frowning, he turned and went back inside. She reminded him of some of the trauma patients he'd cared for, the ones unable to move, stuck in replays of what had happened. Josie wasn't playing games with him. After being burned in the past, she simply didn't want to be vulnerable again. In fact, she might not even realize how thoroughly she'd fenced herself in.

Yet her response to him showed she wanted more.

He'd give her more.

Tonight, he'd assess and then slowly and steadily take this relationship a step further.

As he stowed the vacuum away, he heard a car pull into his driveway. The guys from the firehouse tended to swing by if they were in the area.

He opened the front door...and scowled.

Dressed in one of her fancy stockbroker suits, Nadia was strolling up the sidewalk.

Well, fuck. "What brings you here?" His tone wasn't welcoming.

"Holt. You look much better. Your poor face." Her pale green gaze tracked the scar from his temple to his mouth and lingered on the rougher scars on his chin.

"I'm doing well, thanks. Are you here for a reason?" he asked again.

Her strawberry-blonde hair was loose. Fluffy. The way he'd told her he liked...and she'd rarely worn.

Josie was a green-eyed redhead, too. But different. Her short hair was dark copper, and her eyes held the mesmerizing darkness of evergreens. And, like an evergreen, she had an unshakable character. Nadia was more like a hothouse orchid.

Yeah, there we go, good analogy, he decided, amused at himself. Nadia would wilt at the first frost. Josie would stand strong through a blizzard.

"What are you smiling at?" Head tilted, Nadia looked up through darkened eyelashes. Flirting, for fuck's sake. "Are you pleased to see me?"

"No. I'd like you to—"

Before he could finish, she went up on tiptoe and planted a kiss on his lips. "I missed you, my darling."

Leaning into him, she flattened her palms on his chest. "I'm sorry I wasn't there for you, but I just...I couldn't stand seeing you so hurt. It destroyed me."

Destroyed her? He hesitated. Had he been too harsh? No. In the hospital, she stared at his scars—and looked repulsed, not destroyed. There'd been no tears. In fact, even before she'd seen him, she'd arranged to hit happy hour with her friend. She sure hadn't planned to stand vigil at his bedside. This wasn't love.

He waited for the pain to hit. *Nope, no pain.*

He'd been in love with an imaginary person. It had hurt like fuck when she walked out of his hospital room without even coming close enough to touch him. Didn't hurt now. Sure, she was smart, and they'd had good times together, in bed and out. He missed having someone in his bed and in the evenings. Not especially *her*.

Her lips curved up in a satisfied smile. While he'd been thinking and not moving, she figured she'd gotten to him. "You know, the winter charity ball is coming up. I'd like to go with you. It will show everyone we're back together."

Not happening.

He shook his head. "We're not back together, Nadia. In fact, it's time for you to leave."

Her smile disappeared. "You can't mean that."

"I do."

"Did you forget something, Josie?" Oma called from her kitchen as Josie hurriedly stepped back inside and closed the front door.

"Ah, no." Despite the stabbing pain in Josie's heart, she forced her voice to stay light. "Your next-door neighbor is having an intimate moment on his front stoop. I'll give him time to take it inside."

"The fancy redhead?"

Fancy? Mmm, that would be a good word for the woman. Her tailored mint green suit showcased a tall slender figure. Matching green fingernails had sparkled when the redhead spread her fingers over Holt's chest.

"Yes, she's a redhead. I take it he has a girlfriend?"

"Well, I never saw any women there except that one—and Uzuri, of course. Uzuri said Holt went through women like Moses parting the Red Sea until this one. She thought he might be settling down."

Josie swallowed. "Oh. Well, that's good." The words...hurt. *Went through women. Settling down.*

He and the redhead looked good together. Both were stunning.

Feeling as if she'd been punched in the stomach, Josie sank down on the couch in Oma's living room.

How stupid could she be? She'd gone and done what she'd told herself not to do—fallen into...caring...for the damn man.

Reality check, Josephine. Holt wasn't her lover, wasn't a boyfriend, wasn't even anyone she'd dated.

Just because he was a Master at the Shadowlands and had indulged her in a scene, well, it didn't mean anything, now did it? They'd had a...a *pickup* scene which was the equivalent to dancing with someone at a nightclub. No strings, no promises. Fun was had by all. Just because he'd...looked...at her and taken charge and touched her in a way that fulfilled all her dreams didn't mean anything.

At least to him. It shouldn't have meant anything to her, either.

But, dammit, couldn't he have told her he had a girlfriend? She'd even *asked* him. She didn't poach on other women's men. Why did men think it was right to touch other women when they were already in relationships? Did the redhead know Holt had spent a couple of hours kissing and touching Josie intimately?

Her teeth clenched as the wounds from Everett's letter reopened. "*I'm married. Happily married. With a child whom I love. I never did anything to lead you to believe I held feelings for you...*"

Why did men lie? But they did. All right? *Just...get over it.*

She tried to rub away the ache that had centered under her sternum. Maybe BDSM people didn't consider participating in a scene to be cheating. After all, some club members were involved with a multitude of people, like the woman who had a "vanilla" husband, served as a slave to her Master, and topped other women. Josie's eyes had almost crossed.

Maybe Holt didn't think he'd done anything wrong.

But Josie wasn't in the BDSM lifestyle, and he should have told her he had a girlfriend. *Master* Holt had talked about being honest; yet it seemed the truthfulness went only one way.

Her jaw was so tense it ached.

No. More. Men. Ever. She *knew* better.

She heard a car start up and leave. A glance out the window showed the redhead's car was gone. "Looks like the road is clear. See you tomorrow, Oma. Enjoy the cake."

As Oma called her farewell, Josie crossed the front lawn and hurried past Holt's half of the duplex. To her relief, his front door was closed.

Please, God, don't let him be at the Shadowlands tonight.

CHAPTER TWELVE

That night at the Shadowlands, Holt greeted a new security guard, crossed through the empty clubroom and went out the side door to the Capture Gardens where the festivities were being held. He stopped in surprise.

Well. The physical landscape hadn't changed—the wide green lawn still sprawled between the mansion and the densely landscaped acreage. But the atmosphere? Totally changed. Rather than the ominous, dark area used for catch-and-fuck games, the ambiance was that of a party.

The Shadowlands was celebrating Saturnalia—the hedonistic holiday of ancient Rome.

Z hadn't made costumes mandatory, which Holt appreciated. He hadn't wanted to figure out an outfit. Some subbies were in variations of Roman attire, including a couple of bedsheet togas.

The buildings and tables were illuminated by strings of tiny clear lights. More colored lights in shades of blue wound around the dwarf trees. Gilded low shrubs and plants sparkled. Sun symbols and the two-headed face of Janus dangled from everywhere...and damned if that wasn't the soundtrack from *Gladiator* playing. Z was a crazy bastard sometimes.

BDSM equipment alternated with king-sized mats around the edges of the lawn—and everything was in use. The center and left of the lawn was filled with Doms reclining in the low lounge chairs, submissives at their feet.

The food and bar area was to the right. A portable bar was set up, but empty. No Josie. The feeling of disappointment was...not surprising. But he'd find her.

Food was being served on both wooden tables and human tables.

In a variation of the Japanese *nyotaimori*—sushi served on a human body—several naked submissives were on hands and knees with platters of food on their backs.

Two more reclined face-up on coffee tables. Toothpick-speared appetizers on napkins covered their bodies. After eating, the members would use the toothpicks to torment the subbies.

Holding a cane, Ghost sat on an ottoman within the circle of human tables.

Holt wandered over. "I wondered why you weren't at the door. I see Z put you to a different task."

The gray-haired guard pressed his lips together. "He's pushing the boundaries of guard duty."

A brunette submissive tried to look up at Holt—and almost tipped her food over.

"Tables do *not* move." Ghost's deep rasping voice held enough authority to make everyone in the area freeze. His cane hit the submissive's ass with an audible *thwack*.

At the subbie's pained inhalation, pleasure glinted in Ghost's eyes.

Holt raised an eyebrow. It appeared the ex-military Dom was also a sadist...and a very well controlled one. Only a small red mark showed on the subbie's white skin. Rumor had it that Ghost had been out of the lifestyle for a while...and now, Z'd handed him a cane with orders to control some submissives. Hell, that was like offering a three-course meal to a starving man.

Z was a sneaky bastard.

"How long are the tables lasting?" Holt asked. He checked the face-up serving tables. Both—one male, one female—were masochists. In fact, they all were. Yep, Z had loaded the dice.

"They're rotating every half an hour. It's good discipline for them, having to stay immobile, no matter *what* happens." Ghost deliberately smacked his cane over a bare thigh.

The male submissive's eyes dilated with pleasure as he held perfectly still and absorbed the stinging pain.

"They're improving," Ghost said with a faint smile.

The circle of submissive "tables" brightened at the hard-ass Dom's words. If they could have wiggled in pleasure without earning punishment, they would have.

After eating a couple of quiches from one face-up table, Holt started to move away, but Ghost shook his head. "Reward the table for being a good girl."

With a huffed laugh, Holt drew the two sharp toothpicks in a slow line down her bare stomach, increasing the pressure as he went...until the happy masochist moaned in pleasure.

"Good," Ghost told Holt, and then slapped the cane across the subbie's breast in reprimand. "Tables do *not* make noise."

She quivered her delight at the added pain...silently.

Nodding to Ghost, Holt moved on.

Josie was still missing from the bar. As Holt crossed the lawn, he noticed a Dom was using a tall wooden frame for a suspension scene. Beautifully meticulous rope work patterned the submissive who was already well on her way into subspace. *Nice.*

Near the scene, Anne lay on her side on a long lounge, one hand on her gravid belly as she watched. Kneeling on the grass, Ben was feeding her grapes.

Holt slowed. "*Io, Saturnalia*, you two. How goes the count-down to delivery?"

"You just had to ask, didn't you?" Anne pushed a lock of brown hair back and scowled. "I wanted the baby to come early.

But *noooo*. This kind of fucking behavior does not bode well for our future mother-child relationship."

As Ben tried to cover his grin, his Mistress backhanded him in the belly hard enough to get an *oomph*. "It's not funny."

Giving up the struggle, Ben roared with laughter. "Yeah, it is." When he took her hand and kissed her fingers, her glare softened.

"Mistress Anne, I have your drinks."

Hearing the light Texas accent in a husky voice, Holt felt his spirits lift. He turned.

Josie's attire looked vaguely Roman. Her white halter-tie sundress had a gold metallic rope tied below her breasts. The sprinkling of freckles on her bare shoulders cried out to be kissed.

As she set drinks on the low table beside the food, Holt smiled at her. "I didn't know you waited tables."

"I make exceptions for women who carry our next generation." Her glance at him was cool, her tone even colder.

What the fuck? Holt gave her a long look. The last time they'd spoken was Tuesday when she'd walked him to the door after supper and acting out the book's action scene. Out of sight of Carson and Stella, he'd taken himself a long, warm kiss—which she had enthusiastically returned.

Tonight, she acted as if she'd be happy to walk over his corpse. In stilettos.

Turning away, she patted Anne's shoulder. "I remember my last month of pregnancy. My feet hurt, I needed to pee constantly, and I walked like a penguin. I just wanted the nine months to be done."

Anne grinned. "You nailed it."

"Josie," Ben said, "I'm capable of fetching drinks for my Mistress."

"I know, but I'd rather you stay beside her." Josie glanced around. "Out here, if she needed help, it's possible no one would hear her yell."

She made sense. Scenes were going on around the perimeter

of the lawn as well as farther back in the secluded nooks of the Capture Gardens. Considering the screams, groans, and shouts of pain, one more yell might go unnoticed. So Josie had carried Anne and Ben's drinks over herself. She had a caring heart.

And she still wasn't looking at him. *Hmm.* He stepped in front of her as she started to leave. "How is bartending going tonight?"

"It's busy enough that I need to get back. Enjoy your evening." Her nod to him could be considered polite...if a man didn't mind having his balls frozen off. With a quick sidestep, she moved around him and away.

Anne looked up. "All right, Holt, what did you do to our new bartender?"

"The way she talked to you, she could have iced the drinks without adding the cubes," Ben said.

"Very funny." Holt watched Josie take her place behind the makeshift bar. As she chatted with members ordering drinks, her smile lacked the joy and enthusiasm normally present. "Unfortunately, I don't know what I did."

"I hate when that happens," Ben said seriously. "*Women.*"

Anne raised an eyebrow. "Don't make me hurt you, guard dog."

"Mistress, I'm fucking looking forward to when you can," Ben said, his voice a low rumble.

"Oh, me, too. It's been forever." She heaved a frustrated sigh before turning her attention back to Holt. "We're having a barbecue tomorrow afternoon if you're free."

Wasn't she due...like now? Without thinking, he looked at her belly.

Ben barked a laugh. "Yeah, the gathering is a last minute deal, mostly to keep someone from stewing."

Holt didn't even have to think. "Sure. Want me to bring something?"

"Yes." Anne smiled slowly. "Bring the bartender if you manage to get back into her good graces."

"I'll do that." Holt patted Anne's shoulder gently and headed for the bar.

When a honey-smooth deep voice said her name, Josie turned with a smile...and wanted to smack herself. *Holt.*

In a black vest, black T-shirt, and black jeans, he leaned on the bar. As he smiled at her, she saw he hadn't shaved. His beard stubble, shades darker than his hair, shadowed the stern line of his jaw.

And why was she noticing that?

She lifted her chin. "Good evening. What can I get you?"

It was annoying that her mouth wanted to add "Sir" to the end of the sentence.

"Answers would be good, thank you," he said politely, despite the unyielding expression in his gaze. "When's your break?"

"I-I'm not a-available for anything." She firmed her voice back to cold. "My break time isn't your concern."

"I see." He glanced behind him at the closest sitting area where several people were gathered. "Raoul, can you babysit the bar for fifteen? The bartender and I need to chat."

"Of course, my friend." The Dom's Hispanic accent was familiar, but she didn't remember meeting him. His black leather vest couldn't conceal the thick muscles of a bodybuilder...or the gold band around his arm.

Wait, was he the Dom who'd helped release her from the restraints last weekend? When she was naked? She felt herself flush.

Raoul—Master Raoul—reached down to the slender brunette kneeling beside him. "Come, *gatita*. We have work to do."

"Yes, Master." The woman with vibrant blue eyes took his hand and rose.

And Josie was losing control of the situation. *No.* No, she wasn't going to get pressured into a...chat. She set her hands on her hips. "Listen, Master Holt, I'm an employee here and not at your beck and call for a chat or a scene or anything."

His expression didn't change, as if her words had hit a shield and bounced off. "No scene. Merely a chat—an honest one."

"Honest? You?" Her laugh came out bitter. As she turned her back on him, her gaze ran right into Master Z's. Oh...*damn.*

A bartender's personal life was never supposed to affect her work. Talk about unprofessional. She pulled in a breath. "Can I get you a drink, Sir?"

Master Z studied her for a long, uncomfortable moment. "As an employee, you are not required to participate in any activity here. However, you did—and there appears to be a problem."

"No, there—"

He kept talking. "A submissive may always say no to a scene— or any advances, for that matter. However, if a Master wishes to discuss a problem, especially one related to a session in the Shadowlands, you *are* required to listen and be respectful."

She stared at him in dismay. *Seriously?*

Running straight for the exit would be immature. Still... *Note to self: No more scenes in this place. Ever.* Then again, since she'd sworn off men, that shouldn't be a problem, right?

Aaaaand, her boss was still waiting for her response. How someone could be both reasonable and terrifying, she didn't know. He sure hadn't left her any choice. It seemed she'd be talking with Holt. *Fine.* "Of course, Master Z. I'll listen and be respectful," she said ever so politely.

His lips quirked.

Oh, he thought this was *funny?* Jaw tight, she turned. "Master Holt. If you wish to speak with me, I'm ready."

"Very good." His steel-blue eyes held no amusement.

When she moved from behind the bar, he led the way to two chairs at the far edge of the lawn. "Sit, please."

Stiffly, she settled onto one chair. "Well?" She lifted her eyebrows.

He took the other chair and leaned forward with his forearms on his thighs. His gaze slowly ran over her face, down her body, and back to her face in a measuring look rather than a sexual one. "You're angry with me. Tell me why."

"Seriously?" Was he insinuating she was unreasonable? She wanted to throw something at him. Was it a law of nature that testosterone and truthfulness couldn't exist in the same body? "I don't see the need."

"I do. I obviously hurt you enough to cause this anger; however, I don't know what I did. I'd like to know."

All right, since this *Shadowlands* was all about open communication, maybe it was time someone laid some honesty on him. If he could even recognize it. "You told me you had no girlfriend, fiancée, or wife. You said '*None of the above*,' in fact."

He looked puzzled. "That's right."

She stared. He was still holding to that story? Her anger rose until it felt as if it would shear off the top of her head. "You are such a *liar*. I saw you, you—" She bit back the ugly word. Adults didn't name-call; that's what she told Carson. "I saw you and your redhead earlier, and Oma said you've been with that woman for a while now. So, *Mr. I'm-Single*, what about *that*?"

He looked as if she'd slapped him, then leaned back. "Got it."

"Can I go now?" She rose.

"Sit. Down." His voice had gone dangerously low.

To her annoyance, her knees obeyed and dropped her back onto the chair. "You can't—"

"It's your turn to listen without interrupting. That's how this works, pet."

Pet? How dare—

"Nadia—the redhead—showed up today because she wanted to get back together. I said no."

She had a second of hope and then shook her head. Another lie. She gave him a cynical look and let her disbelief show in her words. "You're saying you broke up with her."

His smile held no warmth as he ran a finger down the long scar from his temple to his jaw. "She visited me in the hospital, saw this, and couldn't bring herself to get near me. I told her we were done. Today was the first time I've seen her since."

Come to think of it, she'd have remembered seeing that flashy red BMW if it'd been in his driveway before. "Oh." *Weak, Josie.* Her gaze dropped as guilt slid a knife between her ribs. She hadn't waited to ask. Had simply assumed he'd lied. "I jumped to conclusions."

"Yes, you did." Taking her hands, he pulled her up, over, and onto his lap. His grip on her hips kept her firmly in place.

"Holt, this—"

"You screwed up, sweetheart, because you didn't come and talk with me. Even yelling at me would have been better than the cut-and-run." He brushed a strand of hair out of her eyes. "In a relationship, you first try to work shit out. And then, if you can't, you walk away."

She tried to rise, but he didn't release her. With an annoyed sound, she sat still. Each breath brought her his clean scent—that of a beach after a thunderstorm.

Dammit, she hated that he was correct about her behavior and hated that she had to say the words. "You're right. But we don't have a relationship."

"No, not formally, but we're neighbors and I thought, friends." He waited.

Neighbors, *true.*

Friends...he'd saved her son. Had been over for meals. *True.*

She nodded.

"And more," he said softly. "Josie, to me, the scene we did was more than a simple pickup scene. Didn't you feel it?"

His words were like boulders being piled on her chest until she had trouble drawing in air. Their scene... She'd watched other quickly arranged scenes and the aftercare. How Holt had treated her and how she'd responded hadn't been...casual. There *had* been more, during and afterward. *True.*

The words wouldn't come. She nodded.

"Ah, progress. So, you decided I'd lied rather than checking." Keeping one arm around her waist, he picked up her hand, tracing the veins and ligaments. "All because of Everett?"

She stiffened.

And he waited. Silently. Expecting her to answer.

She didn't want to wade through the bitter memories again, yet his silent patience was a trap.

"Not all, but mostly, yes." The sigh she gave was a capitulation. "I believed all his lies. I was so...*stupid*."

Holt's mouth thinned into an angry line. "And, at sixteen, you'd have had a wide experience to call upon?"

He was angry for *her*?

"No experience at all, actually." Small Texas town. A church-going, honors student. A virgin. "You read his letter. At the time, it was...devastating." She'd adored him with all her sixteen-year-old heart. How could she explain the pain of realizing he'd lied just to get in her pants? Of learning she'd never been more than a fun diversion?

"And...? You said *not all*. What's the rest of it?"

She sighed. "As a bartender, it feels as if I'm surrounded by deceit. People lying about relationships, jobs, finances, interests. Women, sometimes. Men...a lot."

"Ah. I hadn't considered that ugly aspect of your profession." Holt's gaze ran over her face. "Josie, I don't lie." His lips curved slightly. "Of course, any liar would say that. You should check around. I've been a member of this club for quite a few years now. Ask the members about me."

"But..."

"It's always wise to research the reputation of the person you want to play with."

Actually, from what she'd heard, the Shadowlands Masters were extremely well vetted by Z and the membership. How had she forgotten that? He had a point, though, about checking with the members if she ever played with someone besides Holt.

The thought was unpalatable.

Taking her courage in hand, she looked him in the eyes. "I'm sorry for jumping to the conclusion that you lied to me. I should have talked with you."

"Forgiven." Gently, he pushed a strand of hair behind her ear. "You know, a past betrayal is a kind of a trigger. And a trigger can mess with a person's thinking."

Oh. She hadn't thought of that.

With firm hands, Holt pulled her against his chest. "There. I've missed holding you."

And she'd missed being held. Bending slightly, she buried her face in the hard curve between his neck and shoulder. "Thank you for dragging me away for a talk."

"Mmmhmm. However," he murmured against her hair, "the next time you go cold and silent instead of talking, I'll call you on it, get it hammered out, and then spank you so hard you won't do it again."

She froze. "You...what?"

"You heard me." He lifted her head, forcing her to meet his steady gaze. "If you are not honest with me, I will bare your ass and spank you."

"You...you..." Her sputtering made him laugh, and he bent his head and took her mouth. His free hand gripped her hair, holding her head imprisoned as he kissed every protest right out of her.

Releasing her, he smiled into her eyes. "To reiterate, I'm totally free and single, not in any relationships. I like you, Josie. *More* than like you. I'd like to play with you here...and outside of the Shadowlands as well."

Even as a thrill went through her, she wasn't sure if she was ready for such honesty. Or the next step. She swallowed. "I like you, too."

He chuckled. "I know. Or you wouldn't have been so pissed off."

Rising, he set her on her feet. "Go on back to work. I'll be by in a while to talk with you about a barbecue tomorrow."

———————

Hours later, after finishing a stint as dungeon monitor, Holt stopped at a hail.

Talking with Cullen, Dan stood near the bar. Dressed in his usual black leathers with a Master's gold armband, the cop looked almost as lethal as he probably was. "You owe me a babysitting gig."

"Trust you not to forget either. How's Zane?" Holt did a quick calculation and was surprised at the result. "Jesus, he's over two now?"

Cullen snorted. "And he's mastered the art of saying no."

"At the top of his lungs," Dan admitted ruefully.

Holt laughed. The police detective terrified felons as easily as he did submissives—but a two-year-old had him cowed? "The 'no' stage is healthy, even if it is a pain in the ass." In fact, Holt cheered when his little patients started giving him the big *no*. It meant they were on the road to recovery.

"So Kari says." Dan looked to where several Shadowkittens clustered around his wife, and his gaze softened. The hard-ass cop was still gone over the pretty schoolteacher.

Since Holt's fellow firefighters went through women faster than they did beer, it was reassuring to see the Shadowland Masters and their strong, enduring relationships—especially since many of them lived a form of D/s lifestyle.

As Dan told how his munchkin had spattered their enthusiastic German shepherd with oatmeal, Holt kept an eye on Josie. She looked up, saw him...and her smile smacked him right in the fucking chest.

"You know, buddy," Cullen said, his gaze also on the bar, "I've been missing my old job."

Catching his drift, Holt snorted. "Sure, you have. Nah, it's okay, bro. I live next door to her. It's not like I can't spend time with her when she's not working."

"Sure you can. But this is a party, and our bartender should have a chance to enjoy it. As it happens, I like tending bar. Gives me a chance to talk with members I haven't met." Cullen crooked his finger at his submissive who was talking with Kari.

Kari looked over and smiled at Holt. Dan's pretty school-teacher submissive was a sweetheart.

"It's nice to see you both here," Holt told Dan.

"It's good to be here—and easier now that Zane's bigger." With a wry grin, Dan shook his head. "I can't believe we're thinking of having another."

"A-huh." It wasn't a surprise to Holt. The last time he'd visited Dan and Kari, the cop had been on the floor, helping Zane pile up blocks and knock them down. Dan's grin had been as wide as his son's. "Count me in as a babysitter."

"Good evening, lads." Olivia smiled as she strolled past.

"*Io, Saturnalia*, Olivia," Cullen said. "Nice pet you picked up."

"Yes, Natalia's being quite the good girl," Olivia agreed.

The pretty Hispanic submissive was exactly one step behind the Mistress. Holt smothered a smile. Natalia wore one of Olivia's temporary collars...and a thrilled, terrified expression.

As the two moved on, Andrea appeared in front of Cullen. "You wanted me, *mi Señor*?"

"I'm going to kick the bartender out and take over for a while." Cullen glanced around with a frown. "And I want you with me, love. Can't have you getting dragged down on one of the mats."

In Roman days, the Saturnalia orgies were infamous—and the Shadowlands members were doing their best to uphold tradition. Although some used the Capture Gardens' secluded nooks for private interludes, the less inhibited members were enthusiastically fucking on the thick mats around the lawn's perimeter. The giant ocean of mats in the center had turned into a free-for-all orgy.

Considering the Shadowlands' stance on consent, Cullen knew Andrea wouldn't get dragged onto the mats unless she wanted to be. He just wanted his subbie at his side.

She knew it, too. Her eyes danced as she tucked herself against his side. "You're very good to protect me from all the evil Doms."

He grinned. "I know."

For a moment, Holt watched Josie and all the people around the bar. She'd think better without an audience. He turned to Cullen. "Thanks for freeing Josie up. Do me another favor and send her over to Raoul with a couple of Sierra Nevadas?" Each small sitting area had a number taped on a table, and Holt squinted to get the number. "At sitting area nine."

Relieved of her bartending job, Josie planned to head home after she dropped off a couple of drinks. Cullen had asked her to deliver them to Raoul.

Carrying the two bottles, she wended her way through the chairs and groups of people. *Seven. Eight. Nine.* Yes, there was the muscular Master in a patio chair. His black-haired submissive was on her knees in front of him.

Josie smiled at the two, glanced around the area, and froze as a winter-blue gaze met hers. *Holt.*

Her heart set up a disconcerting thudding in her chest, and she swallowed. "I, um, Master Raoul. I have the drinks Master Cullen sent over."

Master Raoul gave her a quizzical look before holding up his nearly full drink.

"One is mine," Holt rose and took a beer, then seated her beside him on the loveseat. "And one is yours."

"But…"

"You're off duty now. It's time for a drink…unless you don't want it."

She did. She just wasn't sure if sitting beside this...Dom...was her wisest choice. Especially since, as usual, an evening in the Shadowlands had sent her hormones whirling.

Looking away, she realized the conversational area was close to the center of the lawn. And the biggest mat area. Her eyes widened. A woman was taking on three men—one in each orifice —and seemed to be loving it.

Putting an arm around Josie, Holt followed her gaze. "Ah. The center mat is gang-bang central."

She took a hefty swallow of the icy beer. "Are you... into...that?"

He didn't appear especially interested in the moans and slapping sounds of flesh. "I must lack a good imagination, since I had to check out everything for myself. Which means, back in my decadent days, I tried various multiples." With a smile, he brushed her cheek with his knuckles.

She frowned. "Did you like the gang-bang stuff?"

"Yes and no. Sex is rarely bad—especially for a guy. With more than one man, it's easier to drive a woman mindless. That said, I'm also possessive and don't want anyone touching what's mine."

"But..." Josie well remembered how he'd made her strip.

"Oh, they can look. I do enjoy sharing your beauty." His warm gaze made the heat rise in her cheeks. "They just can't touch."

How did he make her feel so stupidly flustered? Looking away, she realized Master Raoul was listening—and amused.

"Josie," Holt turned her chin so she saw only him.

The firm hand, the way he didn't ask, melted her bones. "Yes?"

"Do you want to take the next step and explore dominance and submission for an entire evening?"

Her breath clogged in her throat. "With you?"

"Yes, pet," he murmured. "Totally and only with me."

With his fingers still under her chin, he stroked his thumb over her lips. "I'll push you...a bit...but you'll be safe, baby."

She knew that, actually. Well, she'd be safe physically.

Emotionally...might be a different matter. But the funny sinking feeling she got every time she looked into his eyes made her want to say yes. Her tongue wetted her dry lips, brushed his thumb, and his eyes heated.

A shiver danced across her nerves, because...he wanted her. And she wanted him. In this place and this night, they'd have sex. "Yes," she whispered, flinging common sense to the winds. *Yes to everything.*

"All right then." He leaned forward and kissed her, slowly and gently.

When he released her, she blinked.

The other two were watching. And, hmm, Master Raoul's submissive was on her knees while Josie was sitting on the lounge. Holt had made Josie kneel last week. "Should I be on my knees?"

Holt eyed her thoughtfully. "Do you want to be on your knees?"

"What? What kind of a question is that? No one wants to be on their knees."

"You're making an interesting assumption." He pulled her closer. "I'm not sure you've actually met everyone. Master Raoul, this is Josie, our bartender."

Interesting. Holt's innate manners implied he knew a man should be presented to a woman. But she'd been presented to Raoul. In the Shadowlands, a Master ranked higher than...gender? Unsure what to say, Josie hesitated.

"I'm pleased to meet you, Josie," Master Raoul said in a Spanish accented voice. He put his hand on the kneeling woman's shoulder. "This is my Kim."

Whoa, that was awfully possessive. And demeaning. Yet the pleasure and pride in Raoul's voice was heartwarming. Leaning against his legs, Kim rubbed her cheek against his forearm before smiling at Josie.

"With that out of the way," Holt said, "permission to speak with your slave, Raoul?"

"Granted."

Josie stiffened. Slave? That beautiful woman? The term was one Josie had trouble getting her mind around.

Holt leaned forward. "Kim, how do you feel about kneeling for your Master? Especially when everyone else is sitting?"

Kim straightened, pushing back a wealth of long black hair. Smiling, she spoke to Josie in a soft Southern accent. "Actually, it bothered me at first, especially if I was the only *slave* in the group. But then I realized not everyone has a Master personality. It's a lot of work, after all. Not everyone is suited to be a slave and give up so much control. Being a Master or a slave isn't a good thing or a bad thing, any more than it's good or bad to be an introvert or extrovert, or to be an athlete or musical."

"You're saying you weren't pushed into being a slave," Holt said.

"More the opposite. Master R let me—made me—try not being a slave. This is what I chose, because it's what makes me happy."

Josie studied the...slave. She sure didn't look beaten down or miserable. She practically glowed with happiness. "I think it'll take me a while to truly understand."

"It did me, too." Kim grinned. "You asked about kneeling. To me, this is comforting. There is no safer place in the universe than at my Master's feet, and safety is something I cherish very much."

Well, that was straightforward enough. Josie glanced up at Holt. "I'm not sure what to think."

"I see that. But thinking isn't what is required." He ran his fingers through her hair, then nodded at the grass. "Kneel for me, pet."

It wasn't a request.

She slid off the loveseat to the grass and took the posture from last week.

"Very pretty. You have a good memory, sweetheart." Holt's low approving voice in her ear made her quake. "That is exactly what

I want when I say *kneel*. If I say 'be comfortable', you can relax and let your hands rest on your lap and can rest some of your weight on a hip. So, get comfortable now, since you'll be in place for a while."

Rules. Yet knowing exactly what to do was oddly reassuring. After she clasped her hands on her lap and relaxed, he pulled her between his knees and leaned forward to rest his hands on her shoulders. "Raoul, are you going to Anne's tomorrow?"

As the two Masters talked, Josie relaxed. The grass was cool on her bare legs. A tiny breeze ruffled her hair and carried the sounds of conversations, of sex, of the more distant scenes. The warm, solid strength in Holt's hands on her shoulders was a comfort.

"Josie." Holt's voice broke into her floating quiet place. "Bring us a tray of the vegetables and dip, please."

"Of course." Seeing Kim grin and shape a word with her lips, Josie added hastily, "Sir. Of course, Sir."

Holt leaned over and rubbed his beard-rough cheek against hers. His smoky chuckle resonated through every nerve. "Good save, pet." With an easy strength, he put his hands on her waist and set her on her feet. "Off you go."

As she headed for the food area, Kim was sent to fetch soft drinks.

After securing a vegetable tray, Josie turned and bumped into a man who was standing way too close. "Excuse me," she said politely.

"It's the pretty bartender." The man was dressed in black vinyl pants and a tight shirt, meaning he was probably a Dom. "They're almost finished on the gangbang mat. How about you join us for a turn?"

She almost said *ewww* and changed it to "No, thank you."

As she tried to sidestep around him, he blocked the move and ran his hand down her arm. "C'mon, you know you want to. Every woman does."

Anxiety rose in her. Throwing the tray at him might cause a fight. However, being polite hadn't worked. What could she—

"Josie, please return to our area, put the tray on the table, and resume your position."

Relief was a sweet rush as she looked up into Holt's hard face. He wasn't upset, but had quietly told her exactly what he wanted her to do. "Yes, Sir."

"Very good." He squeezed her shoulder and stepped out of her way. As she moved toward the sitting area and Master Raoul, she heard Holt say calmly, "She gave you a clear, polite no, and you didn't listen. You didn't pay attention to her body language either. As a Dom, it's your job to both hear and see what a submissive—or any woman—is saying."

After setting her tray on the table, Josie knelt.

Master Raoul picked up a piece of broccoli and then studied her with dark eyes. "You look worried, *chiquita*."

After a quick glance at Holt, Josie relaxed. As Holt talked, the jerk bowed his head, his shoulders slumping. "I was afraid they might fight. It seems Holt has it covered."

Eye on the two men, Raoul smiled slightly. "Our Holt is a master of diplomacy. He has the ability to control almost any situation, to calm people down, to quiet fears, to bring reason to a problem."

While setting drinks on the table, Kim laughed.

"Yes, *sumisita*?"

"He does try diplomacy, but he has his limits. Remember that gay Top who ignored the bottom's safeword?"

"What happened?" Josie asked.

"Holt was dungeon monitor. He stopped the scene and was releasing the bottom while telling the Top how he'd missed seeing all the signs." Kim grinned. "Master Holt is very into teaching."

"But the Top didn't listen?"

"Oh, it was a mess. The Top was yelling and pissed. The bottom collapsed in tears and the Top actually smacked him again with his cane. Holt...you could see his jaw set...and he simply swung the jerk into the wall. Face first. Busted the guy's nose. Blood everywhere. Before he could stand again, his bottom was gone."

Josie grinned, remembering how a certain mugger had hit a car and gone skidding over the hood.

"It was a pretty sight, yes," Raoul said.

Kim snickered. "Master Holt never raised his voice. Not once."

Master Raoul opened a soda for Kim and handed it to her. He smiled as Holt dropped down on the loveseat behind Josie. "Can I assume the Dom will accept a no next time?"

"I think so." Holt motioned toward the orgy-like activity in the center of the lawn. "Seems like watching too much of that shuts down higher brain functions."

Josie frowned. "And that makes it all right?"

"No, it doesn't." Holt's brows lowered. "No more than it's allowed to break into McDonalds because you're hungry and smell a Big Mac. And so I told him when he tried to give me excuses."

"Oh." Josie laughed. The Dom had been mid-twenties. "That's a good analogy. He looks like someone who loves fast food."

"What I thought, too." Holt smiled and pulled her back between his knees. "Then I told him if he touched my submissive again, I'd knock him into next week."

Over the next hour, Holt enjoyed giving the little bartender lessons in what he expected. He wasn't much into strict high protocol, so the rules weren't too difficult. During parties, he didn't mind if his submissive looked around. He wanted her comfortable in a sitting-kneeling posture. Talking, though? Not without permission, which Josie actually picked up from watching Kim. Eating—again, not without permission.

For his own pleasure, he hand-fed her, making mental notes of which foods she took eagerly and which were greeted with a slight pulling away. When he sent her for a dessert tray, he memorized the contents, figuring she was smart enough to choose only items she liked.

It was a delight to have a smart submissive on his hands.

After their drinks were finished, he took her for a stroll, stopping to tell Z which path in the Capture Gardens he'd check on. There were always dungeon monitors on duty; even so, every Master tried to keep an eye on the secluded nooks.

As they walked down the grassy paths, Holt paused at each scene to check the safety of the participants—and to let Josie get a good look. Her reaction to a suspension scene showed him she wasn't ready for that level of bondage. Eventually, maybe. Restraints—he knew she liked those. He hadn't anticipated her interest in gags. Interesting.

The way she clung to him after seeing Edward using a bullwhip in a wide clearing had been delightful.

Bare-ass spanking—that was a definite go when they had the chance.

During their scene last week, she'd enjoyed being flogged, not so much the caning. From the way her pulse increased at the sight of one couple, he might try light breast and pussy spanking in the future.

Severe pain, blood-play, fisting, face-slapping—he now knew to avoid those. Not a problem, since he didn't enjoy them particularly.

When they returned, he gave her a bathroom break and picked up a couple bottles of water.

"Holt, join us."

He turned to see Nolan hailing him from a nearby sitting area. Black straight hair pulled back, black eyes, forbidding face, the general contractor occupied a patio chair with his delightful redheaded wife at his feet. Across from them, Max and Alastair had taken over a blanket and leaned on a pile of pillows with Uzuri kneeling between them.

"Hey, people." Holt eyed a blanket with more pillows. No, this would be more fun. He chose a long lounge chair and raised the back to a semi-reclined angle.

Returning from the bathroom, Josie started to kneel close to Holt's chair...and hesitated. Half of her wanted to be as close as possible. The other half felt out of control and wanted to be out of easy reach.

That tour of the Capture Gardens had been overwhelming and far too arousing. By the time they finished, her skin was so sensitive that the slightest brush of Holt's body against hers gave off sizzles. She wanted his hands on her more with every breath she drew. And that feeling scared her spitless.

So, she knelt now...just out of his reach.

His eyebrow lifted, and he swept her with an assessing stare. Then smiled slowly. "Too far away. Sit between my legs, pet."

"But..." She looked around the group. No other submissive in the group was seated.

"I don't care what other people are doing." A smile softened his features. "When we're in scene—like now—the only opinion you have to worry about is mine. You don't have to think or plan, simply follow my directions. Clear?"

Don't do anything except follow orders. The lack of control was a comfort in a way. It helped, knowing he was a paramedic and nurse. He wouldn't ask her to do anything unhealthy or illegal.

"Yes, Sir." She rose.

"Before you sit, remove the underwear."

"*What?*"

"Language, pet, and this is your last warning." His quiet, steady gaze made her stomach feel as if she were on an elevator going down. "You heard me. Underwear off."

Okay, his order wasn't unhealthy or illegal. Only...*dammit*. She already knew he wouldn't let her go to the restroom to take off her briefs. A glance showed her the others were watching. Not only the Doms, but Zuri and Beth, too.

She bit her lip. Surely, this wasn't more embarrassing than stripping completely naked like last week.

Only it *was*. "Yes, Sir."

With cold fingers, she reached under her mid-calf-length skirt and lifted it far enough to catch the bottom of her briefs and work them off.

Without a word, Holt confiscated them and tucked them into the inside pocket of his black leather vest.

"Thank you. Now sit." He patted the extended lounge between his bent knees.

As she planted her butt between his legs, he pulled her back against his chest. With a sigh, she relaxed and smoothed her skirt down over her knees. This wasn't so bad.

Holt picked up a blanket from beside the chair and shook it out over both of their laps.

She gave him a quizzical glance over her shoulder.

"I thought you'd prefer not to flash people when I did this." Reaching down, he put his hands under her thighs and lifted her knees. Ignoring her attempt at resisting, he parted her knees until they leaned against his bent legs. Thank heavens he'd put a blanket over her.

"Now, let's explore a bit of bondage." Her right forearm lay on the armrest, and he drew a padded short strap over the top of her wrist, securing the fabric on the underside of the chair arm. Where it stayed.

Her mouth dropped open. The...the jerk had restrained her wrist to the chair arm. She tugged at her wrist, realizing if she really, really wanted loose, she could get free.

And even as she thought that, he secured her left wrist to the other armrest.

"How did you do that so fast?" Buckles should take longer.

"Velcro is an amazing invention."

Something slid over her breasts, and...she gasped, realizing he'd undone her halter-top. She'd put a knot in the ties, dammit.

She tried to pull up the top—and her arms didn't move. Turning her head, she growled, "What are you *doing?*"

"I'm letting my fellow Doms enjoy the sight of my submissive's breasts. They're very pretty breasts."

"You...you—"

The laughter in his eyes cooled. "Your language is becoming increasingly disrespectful, subbie." He looked past her. "Nolan, you got any extra leather strips? Two, if possible?"

"Got you covered." Nolan's bag was at his feet. He rummaged and tossed something over.

Holt caught the leather strips. He moved sideways slightly, so she could see his face without craning her neck. "Now, pet, you've been in the Shadowlands long enough to know that a submissive's body belongs to her Dom—even if it's only for the course of an evening."

She nodded despite the sinking feeling in her stomach. "But...but..."

"You were completely naked last weekend, were you not?"

A flush rose in her cheeks. That had been *different.* Here, she was sitting in a group of friends, expecting to have a conversation. This just wasn't...right.

His eyes held hers. "This, Josie, is the heart of submission—obeying even when you don't want to. Open your mouth."

She knew her glower was singularly ineffective when laughter lightened his eyes. Her defiance found nothing to fight, as he simply waited, knowing she'd give in.

Her mouth opened.

He pushed the thick strand of leather between her teeth and knotted it behind her head, "Since you can't talk, if you need to safeword, I want you to hoot—or scream—three times in a row." He held her gaze with his until she nodded.

Oh, God. She could see Beth's sympathetic look, the amusement in Nolan's black gaze, Uzuri's—

The other strip of leather appeared in front of her, and she involuntarily shut her eyes. The leather pressed against her eyes... and he knotted it behind her head like the gag. He'd *blindfolded* her.

She tried to say, "Take it off," but it came out "Aaa-iii-ooo!" When she tried to get up, Holt pulled her to him, her back against his chest. He anchored her in place with his hand over her right breast. Her very bare breast.

"Mmmph!"

"I know." His whisper was low and smooth, his breath warming her ear. "Giving over control isn't easy, but sweetheart, you have no choice."

His hand gently caressed her breast and heat surged over her skin, in spite of her dismay. She couldn't even see who was watching.

She was gripping the armrests so hard her hands ached.

"Relax." He rubbed his cheek against hers. "You'll give me what I ask of you, because that's what a submissive does for her Dom."

She could safeword. She knew she could safeword.

How could she totally hate this and want this? Why did letting him take control from her make her want to give him more? Make her anxious and...happy?

"That's a good girl," he whispered. His fingers tugged her nipples lightly, the pressure forceful enough to send an ache of need through her. He lifted his voice. "Is anyone going to Anne's tomorrow for her barbecue?"

"Can't," Max said. "I'm on duty, Alastair's on call, and Zuri won't go without us." Max chuckled. "She doesn't trust Anne's temper these days."

Josie couldn't believe Holt was touching her even while he participated in the conversation. Under his ruthless touch, her breasts swelled and her arousal surged.

"Ben does a good barbecue," Nolan was saying.

Holt's right hand stroked down her stomach beneath the blanket. Slowly, he drew her skirt up, and his fingers slid through the wet folds of her pussy. His cheek rubbed against hers. "You're wet, Josie." And he proved it by spreading the moisture over her throbbing clitoris.

She almost, almost lost control and moaned. Were they all looking at her?

A pinch on her breast derailed her thoughts, and the sharp pain zipped like a bolt of electricity to her pussy. He moved slightly, reached farther, and slid one finger past her folds and up inside her pussy.

She inhaled sharply.

Slowly, he slid it out, circled up and around her clit, and thrusting back in. Harder.

Her hips wiggled slightly.

His voice was low as he warned, "Don't move, Josie, or everyone will know where my hand is."

She froze. It was bad enough they could see him fondling her bare breasts.

"If you make any noise or move, I'll know you want to share, and we'll finish without the blanket."

Her breathing stopped in her throat. *No, no, no.*

His fingers on her pussy never ceased the slow, ruthless stimulation. Sliding in and out of her, making circles around her aching, swelling clit even as his other hand played with her breasts.

And he continued to chat with the other Doms. The...the *bastard*.

The soft background of their conversation disappeared beneath the hammering of her pulse. Sweat bloomed on her skin as her excitement rose. She was at the edge of coming, so close...

"I think you can wait a while longer," he whispered in her ear and resumed talking with the other Doms. His finger slowed, lightened. Each touch on her clit pulled her close and then he'd pause. Slide in. Out. Touch.

"Hey, Z, I heard Ghost was a Dom in Seattle," Max called.

"He was," Z said in his rich deep voice.

Her jerk of surprise pushed her hips against Holt's fingers, and she was too, too close, and... An immense tidal wave of pleasure crashed over her as wave after wave of exquisite sensation poured into her veins. *Don't move, don't move.* Yet holding still made every spasm of pleasure more intense, and it went on and on until even her fingers and toes were tingling.

As the breakers receded slightly, and her breathing started to slow, she heard the men discussing the security guard who'd turned out to be a Dom. And a sadist.

And then she heard Z's quiet voice. "Thank you for sharing, Holt. She is lovely when she comes."

"Isn't she though?" Holt agreed easily. "Will you need her back at the bar tonight?"

Master Z chuckled. "You may keep her."

Despite the sweet languor of her body, Josie felt the heat of embarrassment cover her like an added blanket. Had Z truly told Holt to keep her?

She struggled to move...and heard Master Holt's voice in her ear. "Uh, uh, little bartender. Be still."

The stern order sapped the strength from her muscles, and she lay quiet. Between her bent knees, his palm covered her mound, as if to hold in the lingering, throbbing pleasure. His other arm held her still, his warm palm cupping her breast.

"You don't have anything to do right now, pet, and I like holding you." He rubbed his chin over her hair and returned to talking with the others.

Relaxing, she realized she was breathing in time with him. And she loved the feeling of being held—not allowed to move— not having to make any decisions.

After a few more minutes, he kissed her cheek and removed the blindfold and gag. "This is our last chance to have something to drink. I'd like you to get us a Mountain Dew and a root beer, please."

Blinking, she looked around. Everyone was still there. Had seen...everything. Heat rose in her cheeks again.

"Josie?" Holt said.

"Sure."

When his one eyebrow rose, she hastily amended, "Yes, Sir. I'd like to fetch us drinks."

"That sounded very nice. Thank you, pet."

Why did the approving sound in his voice soothe every worried rumple in her body?

He reached under the blanket and pulled her skirt down, undid her wrists, and helped her sit up. "Off you go, then."

She started to tie up her halter-top, caught the stern shake of his head, and dropped her hands. *Dammit.*

Beth and Zuri waited off to one side for her to join them.

Oh, God, they'd have watched the whole thing. She wished the ground would swallow her up. What must they think?

A hand took hers and squeezed. Zuri grinned at her. "Relax, girl. You're not the first or the last to be on display."

Beth took her other hand. "You're so lucky—you got a blanket. Master Nolan put me on the bar—naked—where everybody could watch."

"When I first started, I thought Master Cullen's *bar ornaments* referred to the big chains over the bar. I have since learned up close and in person all about being a bar ornament." Zuri rolled her eyes.

Beth burst into laughter.

Josie frowned. "What are bar ornaments?"

"Us, girlfriend. Naked submissives are the bar ornaments." Zuri shook her head. "Haven't you noticed the chains dangling from the ceiling beams?"

She'd noticed. "I figured the chains were there before the bar was built. Seriously? Those are for...restraints? On my *bar*?" Outrage made her voice louder.

"Oh yes." Zuri shook her head. "That's why Beth is laughing. I

pranked my Dragon Doms, and I not only got secured to the bar
—naked—but they made me come so many times I was begging
them to stop."

Josie stopped dead. "You're joking."

"'Fraid not."

Beth gave Josie a sympathetic look. "It's a shock when a
Master makes himself free with what he considers his property. I
have to say Master Holt was pretty careful with you."

Nolan had put his pretty redhead on the bar. Naked. As a bar
ornament. The Drago cousins had done that to Zuri.

Josie huffed out a breath. "I guess he was."

CHAPTER THIRTEEN

Mountain Dew in hand, Holt frowned as he watched Z walk across the lawn to the center. What was he up to now?

On her knees in the grass, Josie was leaning against Holt's lounge chair, obviously enjoying having him play with the soft, short strands of her hair and with her bare breasts. Gradually, she'd relaxed, more comfortable with his hands being on her.

And hadn't she been gorgeous earlier, the way she responded to his touch despite her embarrassment? The way she'd climaxed so beautifully.

When the time was right, he planned to take her into the Gardens and take her more thoroughly.

"People." Z lifted his voice...just enough. Like a wave, silence rolled outward from where he stood. When the grounds were quiet, he continued. "During Saturnalia, the Romans would conduct a power exchange and switch roles between a Master or Mistress and their slaves. Tonight, until I announce differently, the Dominants and Tops will serve the submissives and bottoms. Aside from food service, consent is still mandatory."

As voices rose in elation—and complaint, Z simply strolled away.

Holt glanced around.

Nolan and Alastair wore frowns.

Max was laughing. "Z's sure upset the apple cart."

"This should be an interesting hour." Holt rose to his feet.

Startled, Josie stared. "But—"

"I guess it's our turn to work." Max stood and lifted Uzuri to her feet. "Here, this is your spot, my lady." He carefully seated her in the nest of pillows he'd been using.

Catching on, Uzuri smoothed down her slinky white dress and straightened regally. "Where's my scepter? Don't I get a scepter?"

Chuckling, Alastair reached into his bag. With a low bow, he handed her an oversized pink dildo. "Your scepter, my lady."

"Pitiful," she muttered, then waved it at Josie who still looked unsettled. "Get with the program, girl."

"But..."

When Nolan rose, Beth stared. "*Sir*? You're going along with this?"

"When the Lord of Misrule speaks, the guests obey." Nolan's amusement showed for a second. "Have a seat here, my queen, while I bring you some sustenance."

Lady for one. Queen for another. Well, his Josie should outrank them. Holt held his hand down to her. "Let me assist you into your place, my empress."

Catching the rise in hierarchy, she huffed a laugh and settled into the lounge chair.

Indulging himself shamefully, Holt stroked her smooth legs as he straightened her skirt. Then he retied her halter-top to cover her breasts. "Might your humble servant bring you and your friends a drink?" Since she was new to command, he added, "Please make your instructions clear for your somewhat foolish minion."

Looking uncomfortable, she glanced at the other women. "What would y'all like? Holt's fixin' to fetch us drinks."

Ah, her drawl turned thicker when she was uncomfortable. Good to know.

Beth considered and ordered herself a Bushmills with a Corona for Master Nolan.

Uzuri added her preferences and glanced at Alastair. "Would you like a—"

"My queen's presence is the only refreshment I need," the doc said smoothly.

His cousin Max made gagging sounds.

Uzuri glared. "Such unseemly noises." She waved her hand at Max. "You get no refreshment. Be off with you and assist Holt with his task."

"Me?" Max scowled at Alastair. "She likes you better. I knew it."

When Uzuri's mouth dropped open in dismay, Holt chuckled. His sweet friend had a tender heart—and a huge phobia about being rude. He bent down to whisper in her ear, "Max is pulling your chain, sweets. Teach him a lesson and tell him he can't talk."

Zuri's shoulders straightened. "Max, you may not speak the remainder of this time. Go with Holt. Now."

After shooting Holt a laughing look that promised retribution, the Dom sketched a salute of silent obedience to his queen.

"My empress, what is your desire?" Holt asked Josie.

Her lovely green eyes showed her discomfort. She'd been well into the submissive mindset, and now Z had jerked her out of her comfort zone. The next hour should be interesting for both of them.

Josie swallowed. "Well, I'd like an iced tea. And would you—" She broke off and firmed her jaw. "You may have a beer for yourself if you are quick about it."

"You are most generous, my empress." He gave her a polite bow and headed off with Max to the bar.

Max was laughing as he said under his breath, "Z sure put a damper on the festivities."

Looking around, Holt saw that most submissives were sitting in chairs, uncomfortable and uncertain. A few were grinning widely, snapping out orders.

Overhearing Max's comment, Z turned from the bar with an unperturbed smile. "Would you believe the Romans did this for a week? Of course, the servants weren't slaves by choice, so for them, Saturnalia provided a welcome break."

After giving Andrea the drink orders, Holt asked Z. "Aside from honoring tradition, was there another reason to the power exchange?" Z's games often held an underlying lesson.

Cullen set the beers on the wooden bar top. "It forces people to see what the other side feels like."

"Exactly." Z tilted his head. "A few members might well discover they prefer the other role. Or both roles. The rest, whether Dominant or submissive, will be unsettled by the power exchange."

Ah-hah. That was the reason. "And they'll resume their places with fresh appreciation for being in the role where they belong."

"Exactly."

Years ago, while training as a Dom, Holt tried out being a bottom. It'd given him a unique perspective of what he was asking of a submissive. Now that he'd been a Dom for a decade or so, switching roles was...interesting.

He didn't mind serving others, or he wouldn't be in a health occupation. Taking orders at work rarely bothered him...as long as he agreed. In a sexual context? He liked making a woman happy... but it would be in his time and in his way. He didn't take orders at all in bed.

After handing out drinks, he studied his little submissive.

Perhaps the most difficult part of this role reversal was seeing Josie's discomfort.

But since this was a lesson, he'd do his part. He knelt. "My empress, would you like me to feed you—or rub your back? Or your feet? Or might I drink my beer?"

Josie closed her eyes in frustration as Holt tossed out a list of choices for her to select. Honestly, why was this so hard? She made decisions for herself all the time. And for Carson, too, although it'd been easy when he was younger.

But making decisions for another adult? Choosing what another person should do or might want? Especially for a...a person she was in some sort of a kinky relationship with? She hated it.

Tonight was worse. The questions Holt had asked niggled in her head. Maybe she should pick something he hadn't offered. Tell him to do something else for her. Unfortunately, her mind was blank when it came to demanding service from someone.

Woman-up, Empress. But...what would Holt prefer to do? She wasn't sure. With an effort, she made her voice firm. "Rub my back."

How did he make everything look simple when he was in charge?

He stood behind her, and his massage was awesome, but she couldn't relax...because she kept wondering if he was getting bored or tired. Maybe she should be bossier and move him to other things. Did he need a drink? Should she tell him to stop and enjoy his beer?

"This is crazy," she finally burst out.

He lifted his hands, and she twisted to face him.

As he knelt beside her, his gaze was on the ground.

Her stomach flipped over with distress. When he didn't speak, she realized he was following the strict protocol some Masters and slaves used.

"No," she whispered. "I don't like this. Please..."

"Time is up, people. Return your power exchange to normal," Master Z announced. "Then I'd like you to discuss the experience. Did you learn anything new?"

Holt rose. "Subbie, you're in my seat."

Sweet relief streamed through her veins. "I don't like your seat," she said under her breath as he lifted her to her feet.

"Mmm, I'm rather glad about that." Rather than letting her kneel, he put an iron-hard arm around her. His hand on her ass pressed her against the thick ridge of his erection. Fisting her hair, he ruthlessly pulled her head back and captured her mouth. His kiss was deliberately hard. Ravaging. Devastating.

Oh, yes. This was what she wanted. As she sagged in his arms, heat spiraled up her spine.

Lifting his head, he smiled down at her and ran a finger over her damp lower lip. "Ready to kneel again?"

Her sigh of relief made him laugh.

The others had already changed positions.

Queen Uzuri had punished Max by putting tiny braids in his shoulder-length hair. Now, kneeling between her Doms, she was giggling and undoing her handiwork.

Beth was on her knees between Nolan's legs. Her arms were around his waist, cheek pressed to his belly. She was visibly trembling.

What would it be like to reverse years of being submissive?

Head down, Josie knelt in the soft, cool grass and started to shake.

When Holt pulled her between his legs, he must have felt the shivers coursing over her skin. His hands stilled, and he gripped her waist and hauled her into his lap. Wrapping his arms around her, he pulled her against his hard chest. "Easy, pet, it's over."

Shaking, she burrowed her face in the curve of his shoulder and neck, breathing in. His masculine scent mingled with the crisp rain-freshness of his aftershave. Oh, she'd needed to be held so badly.

After a couple of minutes, she tried to sit up.

"Stay here," he murmured, one rigid arm around her waist. He stroked her back soothingly. "I'll start picking on you in a while. For now, rest against me."

His resonant voice warmed her, calmed her, and with a sigh, she went limp against him.

"It was interesting how our submissives felt." Alastair's British accent was pronounced as he spoke. "Uzuri enjoyed the treat at first but was pleased it was over. Beth didn't like switching roles at all. Josie was quite uncomfortable."

Josie closed her eyes, only half listening as the Doms discussed the range of behavior—and how they themselves had felt.

After a few minutes, Nolan left with Beth and then Uzuri and her Doms said good night.

After smiling a farewell at Uzuri, Josie leaned against Holt.

"Better?" Holt cupped her cheek, his gaze roaming her face. "You're steady again."

"Sorry, Sir."

His lips quirked. "You weren't the only one to be unhappy with Z's game."

"Telling you what to do was awful. I got torn between what I wanted, and what you might want, and whether I knew what you wanted, and not wanting you to be unhappy and..."

He chuckled. "You're a submissive who takes her pleasure from making someone else happy. There's a reason you enjoy bartending, pet, and why you're so good at it."

Takes pleasure from making someone happy. It was a bit scary how well he knew her.

He ran his fingers through her hair, teasing the short ends. "In a sexual context, your need to please would be even stronger."

Wasn't that the truth? She let out a disgusted sigh. "You don't seem to have any trouble taking the lead."

"I like making decisions and being in charge. It's how my brain works. Like you, I enjoy making people happy. The difference is"—he grinned—"I figure I know what's best for my charges."

Huh. No, she sure didn't have that certainty. She frowned. "Why didn't you become a doctor?"

"I considered it. But a doctor only gets about fifteen minutes per patient. A nurse spends an entire shift with his patients." He shrugged. "And ICU nurses have a lot of autonomy. It suits me."

Wasn't it amazing how well he knew himself—and how comfortable he was with himself?

Another question surfaced, and she tried to shut it down.

"Ask, Josie."

How did he read her so easily? And, actually, that was part of her question. "Um, can we walk and talk?"

"Of course." He rose with her in his arms, set her on her feet, and steadied her until she found her balance.

Glancing at her bar, she saw Cullen, arm around Andrea, was surrounded by people and obviously enjoying himself.

Holt followed her gaze and read her worry. "He doesn't want the job back, Josie; he doesn't have the time he used to before Andrea. But I'm sure he'll slide behind the bar now and then when he needs a people fix. Will that bother you?"

She shook her head. "Not at all. I'm used to working with another bartender during rush hours."

"Good. Now, before we go walking, your clothes need adjustment." He untied her halter-top again, exposing her breasts. With callused hands, he kneaded and fondled her breasts. "Have I mentioned how much I enjoy playing with your breasts?"

Her nipples puckered into throbbing peaks, and a sizzling stream of lust arrowed straight down to her pussy.

"I have something else for you to wear." He went down on one knee and pulled something from his vest pocket. "Lift your left foot. Now, right."

He drew the underwear—it wasn't *hers*—up her legs under her dress. This wasn't a thong—there was no crotch at all, but something came to rest against her clit. His fingers rubbed her gently, making her inhale sharply. "You're still wet. Very nice." With a hum of approval, he secured straps around her thighs and waist to hold the thing in place.

"What are you doing?"

His lips curved, his gaze steady. "Whatever I want, Josie."

Rising, he held his hand out to her. "Let's walk."

The thing over her clit rubbed slightly, but wasn't uncomfortable. Just...odd.

Holt led her down a quiet path they hadn't taken before. The Capture Gardens contained several spectacularly landscaped acres of winding paths between tall shrubs and trees. There were hidden nooks and unexpected flower gardens. Fountains of various sizes were scattered here and there, adding the sound of flowing water to the music from the mansion.

"What did you want to talk about?" Holt asked.

"I'm just curious. The Master title implies you're very experienced, but you can't be much older than me."

"Thirty-one, and yes, I've a fair amount of experience." He kissed her fingers in an absent-minded gesture. "Looking back, I realize my parents lived a D/s lifestyle, so maybe dominance runs in the genes. But I didn't know that when I discovered the lifestyle in college. At the time, BDSM was exciting and different... and then it became essential."

Essential. "I, uh, I know some of the members only play..." They walked over a tiny bridge with a gurgling stream beneath it.

"During sex. Yes, many people enjoy a bedroom-only power exchange."

From one clearing came distinctive noises—wet sounds, slapping flesh, a man's moan.

Josie felt herself dampening even more. Why in the world had she started this conversation in this place? But she couldn't stop. "And...and you? What do you want?"

"I stay in charge during sex." Releasing her hand, he curved his fingers around her nape, sending a rush of heat down her spine at the firm grip. "I'm also more than happy to take control outside the bedroom, too, if my partner consents."

Despite the way her mind blurred when he touched her, she had to wonder how the "outside the bedroom" stuff worked.

After pulling something out of his pocket, he leaned forward and kissed her slowly. His beard-stubble was a soft rasp over her skin, his lips warm and questing.

Something tingled against her clit, and she jumped. *What?* Her mouth dropped open. "That thing is a vibrator? Seriously?"

He gave her a *Look*, and she realized her misstep. "Sorry, Sir. But we're out for a walk, not—"

"No worries, sweetheart, you're going to enjoy the walk, and when we get a bit farther, I'll enjoy the walk, too."

His evil smile couldn't be mistaken. He intended to have...sex. With her.

Every hormone in her body broke into a happy dance, warming her core. She swallowed. "Oh."

His low chuckle sent more heat through her, and he leaned down. His kiss was deep and forceful—and a hand behind her back held her still as he fondled her breasts. Her nipples were already tender, and he deliberately pulled and pinched, adding an exquisitely pleasurable edge of pain.

Oh, God.

He kept her pinned against him as the vibrator sped up.

At the increased hammering on her already swollen, sensitive clit, she tensed. The vibrations weren't hard enough to make her come, but oh, she really, really wanted to.

"Feel that, do you?" Smiling slightly, he moved his hand down and pressed the vibrator more firmly against her clit. The burst of sensation made her almost moan.

His gaze stayed on her face as he ran his thumb over her lips, making them tingle. "More questions?"

How could she think when he was doing this stuff to her? "Have you had...um, D/s relationships, then?"

"My wife was submissive," he said softly, guiding her down the grassy path, "as have been the three long-term relationships I've had since." He ran his hand up and down her arm. "Pet, you don't need to look as if you're poking through someone's underwear drawers. These are questions you have a right to ask."

She shook her head. "I don't—"

"Josie."

"We're not..."

He stopped and turned her to face him. "You know better than that. What we have at the moment isn't defined, but there's something between us. We just have to see what."

Oh. My. God.

No, wait. She didn't even date. She didn't want any relationships. Only...she did. She wanted him.

"Now, I have a question for you. Do you notice how I'm being a kind Dom and giving you a choice?" Arm around her waist, he turned another corner and lifted a hand to a Dom wearing a gold-edged vest. "Jake."

The Dom glanced at her, smiled, and nodded at Holt. "See you tomorrow."

"Say hi to Rainie for me." As the Dom strolled away, Holt veered off the path into a quiet niche filled with the scent of night blooming jasmine. "I'm going to take you now. Your choice is the location—here in the Gardens or back on the lawn where more people can watch."

Her heart thumped her ribs hard enough to make her gasp. "You wouldn't."

"Mmm, yes, I would." Drawing her down onto a hard stone bench, he kissed her slowly. "Where?"

"Not the lawn," she said quickly. The Gardens would be...kind of private.

He reached behind the bench and drew out his leather toy bag and a thick soft blanket. "I had a feeling you'd choose here. I had Peggy drop my bag off."

Studying her face, he waited for her to respond.

What could she say? He was utterly self-confident and comfortable with pushing her, yet she knew if she gave him a safe-word, he'd escort her back to the mansion with equal grace.

The realization was heady. She let out the breath she'd been holding.

He smiled. "Brave girl." He pulled her to her feet.

On one side of the clearing were three knee-high gnomes holding glowing lanterns. Tiny lights twinkled from the encircling five-foot high bushes as if someone had scattered stars from the sky.

Off to one side of the clearing was a post with a very recogniz-able T-shape. The top of the "T" was two hinged boards with circles cut out and designed to restrain a person by the neck and wrists. She took a step back. "That's a pillory," she whispered.

"When you talked about your research, you seemed to have a certain...interest." He tossed the bag and blanket onto the soft grass next to the post. After lifting up the top board, he grasped her wrists. "Hands in the small openings."

When her wrists lay in the semi-circles, he gripped her nape. Under the pressure of his hand, she bent from the waist...down.

As her neck touched the coolness of the large semi-circle, he closed the top, and her arms and neck were secured in place. She felt him run a finger around the padded openings, making sure they weren't too tight.

Crouching, he pulled her right ankle outward and secured it with a strap anchored in the grass. He repeated the procedure on the left. "That looks nice," he murmured, running his hands up and down her widely parted thighs. She felt him lift her skirt up, exposing her bottom.

A shudder shook her as coolness touched her hot flesh.

On top of her clit, the vibrator was still humming along. When he slid his fingers upward and over her very wet pussy, she almost came. "Mmmm, *God*."

"And that sounded nice." He chuckled. "Be aware that your pretty noises might attract observers. I don't mind, but I thought you should know."

People watching them? "Noooo." She tried to straighten, and the pillory held her mercilessly in place.

"Then you might want to be fairly quiet." Standing behind her, he ran his hands over her back and then around to her dangling breasts. Waves of heat seared up her center as he pinched the nipples and rolled them between his fingers. One pinch grew harder until felt as if teeth had closed over her nipple. "Holt!"

He slapped her bottom, and she jumped at the sharp sting. "By now, you know how to address a Dom in the Shadowlands."

A flush of shame heated her face. She did. "Sorry, Sir."

She tried to see her breast, but the pillory board blocked her view. Only...she knew he'd put a nipple clamp on her breast. Oh, sweet heavens. He was really using that stuff on her. A shudder of excitement shook her...until he fastened a clamp to her other nipple. This time the bite was worse, and she whined a protest.

"Breathe, Josie. Blow out the pain, breathe in, accept it."

As she did, the sharpness eased to a heavy throbbing, one that seemed to increase her skin's sensitivity. The light breeze wafted cool against her hot, damp skin. The grass tickled her feet. The calluses on Holt's palms scraped teasingly over her waist.

And the vibrations against her clit grew lighter.

Holt returned the remote to his pocket and stepped back to enjoy the view. Josie's breathing was fast, and her heart-shaped ass wiggled adorably as she fought her need.

Running a hand over her shoulder to let her know his location, he moved in front and dropped to his haunches. "Look at me, pet."

Even in the dim light, he could see her face was darkened with arousal, her lips swollen. Her gaze lifted to meet his, sweetly submissive, sweetly pleading. She wanted to come. Needed to come.

He'd pushed her as far as was appropriate, and in fact, it would have been better if the Saturnalia party had happened later in time. As aroused as they both were—and had been all night—this was going to be a hard, fast coupling. Next time they were together, though, he'd show her the softer, sweeter side of sex.

"Josie. I'm going to take you now. If anything is too much, remember red is your safeword. Use it and everything stops. That applies if something emotionally bothers you, too, pet. Is that clear?"

He waited for understanding to bloom in her eyes.

"Yes, Sir."

"Good. For now, aside from being restrained"—he smiled and ran a finger over her flushed cheek—"are you all right?"

She licked her lips, making him imagine those lips around his cock. "I'm all right. Sir."

Wasn't she being a good girl in not whining that she needed to come? Because yeah, he could see she did. A butterfly vibe wasn't that effective at getting a woman off—not by itself—but for teasing? Worked great.

He rose, tugged her hair lightly, squeezed her hands to check circulation, and circled behind her. Her ass was perfectly positioned, her legs wide, her pussy open and wet and available.

One day, he'd have to fuck her outside during the day so he could enjoy the sunlight glinting off her coppery curls.

For now... To tease them both, he stroked his fingers through her slick, hot folds and heard her breathing stammer to a stop. She was beautifully ready.

Still, he'd go slowly. She hadn't had sex for a while, and he needed to see if she could take him without a problem.

Pulling out a condom, he opened his jeans and suited up. With his cock touching her entrance, he reset the vibrator to high, then reached around her waist and pressed his palm against the soft plastic device over her clit.

She gasped as the increased vibrations hit.

Yes, now. Slowly, he entered her, past the soft lips of her pussy and into the hot silk of her cunt. Deep enough he felt her stretching around his girth.

She gasped and tried to pull away, tried to straighten up—and was halted by the restraints.

Her body shook with a hard tremor as she realized she couldn't escape being penetrated—and fuck, he loved the way her pussy clenched around him in response. Yeah, she liked being trapped and taken, probably as much as he loved doing it.

He held in place a moment and ran his hands over her back and shoulders. "I love the way you feel around me, Josie," he murmured. "Breathe, pet. Because you're going to take all of me."

As her panting slowed, he started again, pulling back slightly, then pressing in, moving farther each time. Her warm, soft walls pulsed around him. Time to give her something else to think about. He moved the butterfly vibrator sideways to hit a different area on her clit.

Her whine made him grin. Her buttocks clenched even as her slick cunt gripped his shaft like an oiled fist.

Another inch and his groin pressed against her round buttocks. "All in, baby."

And she was damn close to coming. Breathing hard, whimpering slightly.

"All right, pet. You've been a very good girl." Inch by inch, he pulled back, savoring the velvet grip her cunt had on his erection. Almost out, he paused—and slammed in, hard.

"*Aaaah.*" Her back tried to arch, her ass tilted up slightly, and her pussy clamped down on his dick and began to spasm as she climaxed with sobbing gasps. "Oh, oh, *oh.*"

With one hand, he unsnapped the butterfly, letting it fall loose, as he thrust several times to keep her orgasm going.

And then he slowed to an easy in and out. His cock was so damn hard it was painful, but he wasn't ready to finish. Nothing in the world compared to the feeling of having her all around him, feeling her soft body under his hands. She was so fucking sweet.

He moved his hand up and set his palm between her dangling breasts. Her heart was still hammering against her rib cage.

Oh, oh, oh, she'd come so hard. Josie could feel her heart slamming within her chest, and she was sucking in air like a runner finishing a marathon. When her knees wobbled, Holt's left hand under her pelvis held her in place. His cock pressed in, filling her impossibly full, and then he'd slide out ever so slowly. And back in. The thick heat penetrating her made her shudder.

He'd...taken her. Hard. Not asking, not pausing.

And he wasn't finished, she realized belatedly. Oh, heavens, he hadn't come when she had.

"You feel fantastic, sweetheart," he murmured, his speed not increasing. His right hand moved over her stomach, over her mound, and back up.

She gasped as he captured a breast and fondled it firmly. He jostled the clamp on her throbbing nipple, deliberately tugged on it.

Squirming, she tried to get away. *She. Couldn't. Move.* She was totally restrained. He could play with her body...and she couldn't stop him. Couldn't even see him. The feeling sank deep in her core, even as her excitement increased.

"Mmm," he murmured, "I love your breasts."

"You're a guy. Of course you do." Her voice came out hoarse.

"Uh-uh, little bartender," he said reprovingly. His cock slammed into her hard, sending after-orgasm quivers through her. "You're in no position to be sassy."

"S-sorry, Sir." How...how in the world was she getting aroused again? She'd just come. The low moan she couldn't prevent gave her need away.

"No worries, pet, I'll fuck some of that sass out of your system." His low smoky voice wasn't angry, but...amused.

His fingers slid back over her clit, making her jolt. When he rubbed one side, she wiggled at the exquisite feeling—so very different from a vibrator, so much more exciting because...it was *his* hand. With a frighteningly knowledgeable touch, he ran a slick finger over the sides, teased the hood, flickered over the very top.

Impossible need clawed into her system. Her hips twisted uncontrollably as a keen rose in her throat.

As his thrusts quickened and deepened, the rhythmic hammering set up shockwaves in her core. The feeling of being *taken* increased, and then with a quick two-handed movement, he removed the clamps on her nipples.

Blood surged back into the abused peaks with a hot, liquid, throbbing pain, and she yanked at her hands, needing to hold her aching breasts, and couldn't move.

As if to emphasize her helplessness, he possessed one aching breast in his big hand. His other hand stroked her clit—and his merciless cock never slowed.

Too much. The far-too-knowledgeable torment of her clit. His thick shaft stretching her unbearably full. The fingers tugging her rigid, tender nipples. The sensations multiplied, engulfing her, pushing her to the edge...

She squirmed helplessly in his grip. Restrained, held, taken.

"You're going nowhere, Josie."

At his low growl, everything inside her tensed to an excruciating point—then exploded in huge, impossible waves of sensation, one after another. The unbearable pleasure grew and grew with every hard thrust of his shaft.

And then he pressed, deep, deep inside her, and she could feel his cock jerking as he joined her. "Mmmm." His hands moved over her, touching, sliding, drawing her orgasm out until she was drowning in pleasure.

When he finally stopped, her head was spinning.

"That's a good girl," he said, running his hands over her. "Stay put a moment while I clean up, then I'll get you free."

She was still gasping as he opened the pillory and helped her straighten.

Laughing, he caught her when her knees gave out. "Easy, baby." Gently, he laid her down on the blanket and joined her, pulling her into his arms.

Her head rested on his shoulder, her arm over his waist, her knee over his thighs. She squirmed slightly, trying to get even closer. Under her ear, she could hear the thudding of his heart... slightly faster than normal.

"Okay, pet?" he asked quietly, his hand stroking her damp shoulder and back.

"Yes," she breathed. And then she womaned-up and gave him the truth. "I've never...felt anything like that."

"Mmm. For a submissive, being pushed adds an extra kick."

Yes, it had. But that wasn't...all. Admittedly, she didn't have much experience, but she'd been with Everett and a couple of men when Carson was a toddler. They'd tried to push her.

Slowly, she inhaled, breathing in Holt's masculine scent, all man, all strength.

There was being ordered around, and there was really submitting, and that was more emotional than physical. She didn't submit to men. But because this was Holt, who would take care of her, she'd let him in and lowered her defenses and given him...everything.

And oh, it had been wonderful.

But when he'd been inside her, physically, mentally, spiritually, he'd stolen more than her defenses.

She closed her eyes. Appalled. *No. Do not be crazy, mushy, stupid.* She hadn't changed. No, she *hadn't.*

Only, each time he stroked her arm or spoke to her in that smoky, firm voice that exuded confidence—every single time—he took more of her into his keeping.

This couldn't be. Part of her was thrilled at the connection, and the other part inched back, step by step, toward the cave that was her refuge.

A soft gong sounded three times, and Holt sighed. "Z's closing down the Gardens. We have to get back."

She started to sit up, and he brushed her hair out of her eyes. "Rest here, sweetheart. I need to clean the equipment, and then we'll be off."

"I can help." Her legs felt weak, but she'd—

His grip on her shoulder tightened, and he lifted her chin with one hand. "What did I say?"

His jaw was stern.

She should know better by now, shouldn't she? "Um. I'll stay here. Sir."

His lips twitched. "Good answer."

CHAPTER FOURTEEN

On Saturday afternoon, the sun bright and hot on his shoulders, Carson steered his bike around a corner. Shifting his backpack to a better position, he pedaled faster to catch up to his friends.

He was kinda sorry they hadn't stayed at Brandon's. Since Mom was going to a barbecue, she'd said Carson could spend the whole afternoon with his new friends, which was awesome. Brandon had video games Carson wanted to try.

Turned out Brandon had different plans. They were going to their school.

Carson lifted his head. Brandon was at the front, followed by black-haired Yukio, ginger-haired Ryan, and dark-haired Juan. They sure didn't look at all alike. Brandon was tallest and, along with Ryan, the most muscular. Juan was short and skinny. Yukio was built like Carson, kinda tall and lean.

But they were all smart and at the top of their classes. Well, except for Ryan who aced everything but couldn't stop talking and ended up in trouble. Especially with the science teacher who was a sarcastic a-hole.

Brandon had decided the science teacher needed to pay for

how he treated Ryan—and Juan, too. He thought a sackful of poop in the classroom would piss off old Jorgeson, especially since the bag might not get found until after Christmas break. Brandon called it a *mission*.

Carson fell back slightly. A mission was what a superhero would do—which was really cool—only he couldn't see Spiderman throwing shit through a window. But Ryan and Juan thought Brandon's plan was fantastic.

Before reaching the middle school, Brandon turned a corner and down a street to the athletic fields so they could approach "the target" from the rear. Quietly. Like spies.

Carson swallowed. This really wasn't a good idea...

With the others, Carson hid his bike in the bushes near the soccer field and jogged toward the school buildings. Yukio pointed out the security cameras—his family had just put in a home security system—and led them around.

Finally, they came to the building that held Jorgeson's science classroom.

At Brandon's gesture, Juan stopped at the end of the sidewalk to keep watch. He was too short to see in the high windows anyway. The rest of them squeezed behind the man-high, sharp-edged palmetto bushes lining the back of the stucco building. Carson hissed as one sharp leaf stabbed his arm.

The classroom should be somewhere in the middle. On tiptoes, Carson peered in a window. The room was dark. "English." Were they really going to do this? His hands were cold even though sweat made his T-shirt stick to his back.

"Music room," Brandon said from farther down.

"Here. This is Jorgeson's room." Yukio stepped back to let Ryan look.

"That's it. There's that ugly-ass, dried-up frog he keeps on his desk." Ryan turned to Brandon. "You got the bag of shit?"

"Oh hell yeah." Brandon took off his backpack and pulled out a small blanket. "Yukio, hold this in front of the window. Carson, grab a rock and hit the blanket. Bust a hole in the glass."

"Noise control." Ryan nodded approval. "Smart."

Me? Why do I have to break the window? Carson's heart hammered. *Say no. Leave.*

"Hurry up, Cars," Brandon snapped.

Carson looked around and found a big rock.

God, Mom would *kill* him if she ever found out about this. Did they send kids to jail for busting a window?

But Jorgeson was a total asshole. Carson'd had strict teachers before, and even if they were a pain, they were fair. Jorgeson was purely a jerk, especially to mouthy kids like Ryan or the ones who couldn't keep up, or didn't do their homework. And he picked on girls and anyone of color, too. He'd get all sarcastic and nasty, and he'd made Ryan cry. Not sobbing or anything. Still, everybody could tell cuz Ryan's eyes and his freckled face got red, and his lips pinched together, and he kept swallowing. And he wouldn't talk with anyone for the rest of the day.

That wasn't right. It wasn't. Mom always said to stand up for his friends and not give in to bullies.

Jorgeson deserved a bag of shit in his classroom.

Exchanging unhappy looks with Yukio, Carson gripped the rock and smacked the blanket-covered window.

Nothing happened.

"Use some muscle, wussie," Brandon hissed.

This time, Carson swung hard. The cracking sound of glass made him cringe.

"Again," Yukio whispered.

Gritting his teeth, Carson hit the window hard, and it gave. Glass tinkled into the room. He ducked down behind the palmettos.

Yukio crouched beside him.

After pulling on thin gloves—like in those criminal shows—

Brandon pulled out a bottle filled with clear liquid. When he unscrewed the lid, the scent of gasoline filled the air.

Carson's mouth dropped open. "What are you *doing*?"

"My bag-of-shit idea was okay; this is better," Brandon said.

"I don't know, BB," Yukio whispered. "Fire?"

"It'll make a statement." Brandon snorted. "But not much of one. The sprinkler systems'll go on before anything much gets burned."

Start a *fire*? Horrified, Carson stared in disbelief.

Ryan frowned, and then shrugged. "It's not like anyone's here over break."

Yukio looked worried, but he didn't say anything.

Biting his lip, Carson took a step away...and stayed silent.

Brandon stuffed a long wadded up paper towel into the end of the bottle to plug the top. "Is there anybody around?"

Looking down the line of palmettos, Ryan asked in a loud whisper, "Juan. Are we clear?"

Juan gave a thumbs-up.

"Here goes." Brandon used a lighter and set the paper towel on fire. Standing up, he flung the bottle through the window. Sideways.

Carson heard the bottle break and a sound—*foomph*. Frigging-A, they'd really set something on fire!

"Let's get out of here." Brandon ran down the side of the palmettos, and the rest followed with Carson in the rear. He glanced back and could see that the science room's window was no longer as dark as the others.

When they reached their bikes, Brandon was giggling. Bouncing on his toes, he ordered, "Split up, and we'll rendezvous at my place. See you there."

Carson pedaled to the left with Yukio beside him. As they turned the corner off the grounds, the fire alarms came on.

Yukio looked back, then at Carson. "That was crazy."

"Yeah." Carson's palms were sweaty on the handlebars. "Let's get out of here."

Pleasantly stuffed with barbecue and potato salad—and the cherry cobbler Josie had made—Holt stretched his legs out and tilted his face up to the afternoon sun. Below the deck where he sat, a long expanse of white sand rolled down to the blue Gulf waters. The air was laden with the scents of brine and seaweed.

Anne and Ben had a hell of a beach house—and Ben could grill a mean steak.

Lazily, Holt watched Ben, Josie, and Rainie stroll the beach. Rainie's fluffy dog, Rhage, and Ben's beautiful golden retriever, Bronx, danced around them.

Farther down, Cullen and Andrea, hand-in-hand, were walking off the big meal—or, as Cullen said, making room for more dessert.

Jake had gone to the kitchen for more drinks.

Holt glanced toward the house behind him, then up at the balcony overlooking the shore. Earlier, seeing how tired Anne had grown, Ben had taken his pregnant Mistress upstairs for a nap.

Must be hell having an extra twenty pounds to lug around.

A high yipping drew his attention back to the beach. Charging a gull, Rhage sent the bird screeching into the sky, before prancing proudly back to the women. Josie bent to ruffle his furry head, and Holt could hear her husky laughter.

Her laugh had been mostly absent this afternoon. She'd been uncommonly withdrawn.

Because she was reassessing what was between them.

Because of last night.

He'd never enjoyed an evening as much. She was a delight as a submissive and a lover, both responsive and intelligent. Not a pushover, but sweet and giving. Truly someone who took delight in serving. When she'd given him her trust and her body, he'd been honored. Last night, they'd been as close as two people could be.

And he had a feeling it had scared her.

Today, she'd pulled away. His sweet submissive was reestablishing her boundaries and shoring her defenses. That was her head talking. Her body—and her heart—disagreed, and today, every time she relaxed, she'd lean against him, all soft and submissive female. If he touched her, her eyes would heat...and then she'd take a step back.

Her trust in him was warring with her distrust of men. Yeah.

Trouble was, he was falling for her, hard and fast.

He rubbed the back of his neck and sighed. Hell, it wasn't as if he hadn't known she had trust issues. That didn't worry him. Working through problems was part of a Dom's duties. Besides, he had a few potholes in his own past that'd keep life interesting.

"Here you go." Returning from the kitchen, Jake handed over a Mountain Dew, then dropped onto the love seat next to Holt's chair.

"Thanks." Holt popped the top. He and Jake had been friends for a couple of years since the day Holt took a burned, bleeding poodle to the veterinarian's not-yet-open clinic. A house fire had sent the dog's family to the hospital. Rather than turning Holt away, Jake'd cared for the dog and taken it home with him until its owners recovered. The vet was good people.

Holt took a long swallow of the Dew. Cold carbonated caffeine—what could be better?

"I see our women are having a good walk." Jake leaned back and stretched his legs out. "I like your subbie, by the way. Did you happen to see her with Anne?"

"No, did they talk?"

"While you were helping Ben repair the broken step." Jake opened his soda. "After a few minutes with Josie, there Anne was, telling her about the difficulties of being pregnant and how Ben was driving her nuts, although she also loved being pampered."

"Compared to your Rainie, Josie doesn't talk much, but people open up to her."

Jake took a sip of his drink. "It was impressive. The Mistress doesn't share easily."

"Josie's amazing. People trust her." Holt watched as Josie and Rainie climbed the deck steps. Bronx chose a corner to wait for Ben. Rhage, however, bounded across the deck, leaped, and landed in Jake's lap. Obviously used to the maneuver, Jake had his drink out of the way and laughed as the fluffy black-and-white mutt frantically licked his neck, acting as if they'd been parted for years.

Smoothing down her blue sundress, Rainie settled beside Jake on the love seat. The Shadowlands submissive had colorful flower tats, brown hair streaked with red and blonde, and an equally lively personality.

She sure as hell had enlivened Jake's life—and Holt thoroughly approved of her for his friend.

Now, he had his own submissive to capture and win.

Looking undecided, Josie stood in the center of the deck. He could see her desire to be with him...and her unease.

"Come here, Josie," he said softly. When she got close enough, he took her hand—and pulled her firmly into his lap.

"Hey. There are other chairs."

"I like having you here." He molded her against him, loving the way she fit. She wasn't tall and slender like Nadia. Wasn't short and round either. Josie was what his father would have called sturdy Irish stock. Resilient in both body and personality.

After brushing the wind-whipped hair out of her eyes, he took himself a kiss, enjoying the quiver of her response.

"What was that for?" She blinked at him, her eyes a gorgeous green in the sunlight.

"Dom's privilege," he told her.

She gave him a wary look. "This isn't a scene. Sir."

"Very true." He wrapped an arm around her waist, securing

her nicely. "But you should know, for a lot of us, dominance isn't something to turn on and off."

"Does that mean you try to boss your fire chief around?"

"No." He smiled. "But in the absence of someone officially in charge, I'll take the reins. And when around a submissive"—he ran his finger over her full lower lip—"the need to take charge is difficult to shut off."

She scowled at him.

Fucking cute.

"This submissive stuff...I'm a mother, and I give orders all the time. I don't think I'm all that submissive."

Oh, baby, yes, you are. Last night, she'd known and accepted her nature. Today, she was over-thinking it all. "Parents are in a whole separate category. When you work with other bartenders, do you give orders like you do with Carson or do you let someone else take the lead?"

Silence was his answer.

He took a moment to nibble on her neck and breathe in the musky smell of woman with the lingering fragrance of her soap.

She was slowly melting against him.

"As you probably noticed, I enjoy telling people what to do," Holt murmured. "More than that, I like looking after people, making sure things are done right, and everyone is protected."

"You and Jake." Rainie rolled her eyes at Josie. "I swear, dominants can't handle when a submissive is in danger or hurt. Whoa, mama, they go cray-cray."

"What do you mean?" Josie frowned at Jake's submissive.

"Like when Zuri's crazy stalker grabbed me, Jake went all overprotective on my ass."

"Damn straight," Jake muttered.

"He kept asking how I felt and..." Rainie looked at Holt. "After your surgery, when you were staying at our place, Jake said he was glad you were there, not just for your recovery, but for mine, too."

"Your recovery?" Josie leaned over and grasped Rainie's hand. "Did you get hurt by that man?"

"Not physically." Rainie wrinkled her nose. "I was just having nightmares."

"And she refused to go to a counselor." Jake scowled.

Holt had known about her refusing to get help. Women could sure be fucking stubborn.

Rainie told Josie, "Mr. Paramedic-Nurse there made me work through everything—even though I didn't want to talk about being kidnapped or scared or anything. He ignored me being rude and just...persisted."

Josie gave Rainie a worried look. "Did your nightmares go away?"

"They did, thanks to Holt." Rainie smiled at him. "In case I didn't say thank you—*thank you*."

Jake gave him a nod that said the same thing.

"Seems like I got board and room and care," Holt said lightly. "I think we're even."

On Holt's lap, Josie turned and curled an arm around his neck...and relaxed completely.

Rainie glanced over, and her lips curved in a pleased smile. She'd known how her story would affect a nervous submissive, hadn't she? Had realized Josie needed the extra assurance he was trustworthy.

Josie was frowning again, her gaze on his face.

"What, pet?"

"It bothers me...how close you must have come to getting killed." Her voice was a tiny thin sound. "Did you get help, too? Do you have nightmares?"

The depth of her concern shook him. Pleased him. "A few nightmares, at first." He stared off at the dark blue Gulf and sighed. "For a while, every time I walked back into the duplex, I had a flashback."

She stared at him, her beautiful green eyes appalled. "Then why ever did you stay there? Are you insane?"

Holt glanced at Jake. "I think I've just been called crazy by two women within five minutes. That's a record."

Josie's eyes narrowed.

He was looking forward to seeing that passion in his bed. "I like the duplex, and I wasn't going to let the bastard drive me out. It took a while, but the flashbacks are gone."

"You're even more stubborn than I realized," she said under her breath.

"Yes, I am." He smiled slowly. "Keep that in mind, pet."

In her bedroom, Anne woke to the sound of laughter. Groggily, she yawned. Good, their friends were still here at the barbecue. She could go down and join them...and her Ben.

The crazy man had thrown the party to keep her from fretting about when the baby would get around to arriving.

He'd been right. A party was a hell of a diversion. It was amazing how much energy she'd had while cleaning the house and preparing side dishes. Then, during the barbecue, Cullen and Holt had been full of fire and arson tales, Rainie and Jake with puppy stories from the clinic. Anne hadn't had a chance to stew about labor.

Later, she'd taken the opportunity to talk with Josie. Alone.

Anne grinned. On the way upstairs, Ben had accused her of planning to interrogate the poor girl to see if she was good enough for Holt.

Her tiger knew her so well. That'd been the plan.

Only, somehow, the discussion had rolled around to pregnancy. And how disconcerting it was to have her athletic body distorted and weakened. To need help for the stupidest things—like putting on shoes. To have back pains and need to pee all the damn time and... Anne shook her head. Rather than an interrogation, she'd ended up confiding in the submissive. And she found out what she needed to know. Holt's submissive not only had a solid core of practicality and kindness but also listened with her whole heart. Josie would do well for him.

Yes, it'd been a great barbecue, Ben.

Perhaps a bit uncomfortable. Despite the interesting conversations, she'd had to shift positions constantly to relieve the pressure on her back and ease the annoying Braxton Hicks contractions. And it sucked to need a *nap* like a damn toddler... and to have Ben escort her upstairs, no less.

Son-of-a-bitching, over-protective subbie.

Damn, she loved him.

Rolling over on her back, she stretched. Air ruffled the curtains at the open window, bringing in the heartening scent of ocean and sand. Nothing in the world smelled as fresh. Voices drifted up from the deck. Time to rise and shine, even if the *rising* part was like juggling a massive watermelon.

I want my body back. There wasn't any position that was comfortable, and her back always hurt.

"Not that you haven't been wonderful company," she murmured and patted her stomach. He or she was quiet today— not trying to roundhouse-kick her bladder every few minutes. Maybe she wasn't the only one who'd needed a nap.

Bet those damn Braxton Hicks had livened up the kid's naptime. She let out a grunt of annoyance as her belly tightened. "Still? Seriously?" She'd hoped the contractions would disappear during her nap. Sometimes they did. Not today, apparently.

A shame the "false labor pains" weren't the real thing. She gave a snort of laughter. Positive that Anne was having the baby, Ben'd called the obstetrician three times this week. Each time, the doc had patiently explained that if the contractions were erratic and didn't really hurt that Anne wasn't in labor.

Of course, as a sadist, Anne knew "really hurt" was a subjective term. No one in their right mind would say that those squeezing sensations felt *good*.

As she walked—waddled, dammit—to the bathroom, she passed the hospital bag beside the dresser and sighed. *Soon.*

After using the toilet, she started to stand and felt an odd popping sensation. A gush of fluid spilled into the toilet bowl. *What the fuck?* Had her bladder lost control completely?

A huge, painful contraction gripped her insides.

Dropping back on the toilet seat, she curled over her belly. *Oh. God.* That one had hurt.

And, hello, that fluid hadn't been her bladder—her water had broken. If her water had broken, then...it was time to have a baby. Heart picking up speed, she swallowed hard.

Oh, fuck, am I ready for this?

After a moment, she shook her head. Not like she had a choice. And wasn't it clever of her to have her water break right there on the toilet?

She cleaned herself, yanked her loose pants up, washed her hands—and bent in half with the next contraction.

Holy fuck, weren't the damn things supposed to work up gradually to hurting like this? Kari and Jessica had said they'd puttered around and watched movies and spent hours before even breaking a sweat.

Anne wiped her forehead and set her jaw. Damned if she'd be more of a crybaby than the submissives. She'd served as a Marine, a police officer. She was a Domme. Pain didn't slow her down.

The next contraction caught her on the way to the bed—and sent her to her knees.

Inside the house in Anne and Ben's living room, Josie crouched to pet their orange tabby. All length and legs, the teenaged kitten reminded her of Carson.

With a long, annoyed meow, the cat expressed his displeasure at being shut in the house during the party.

"Aw, poor baby." Josie picked up the young cat and cradled him in her arms, smiling as his meows turned into purring.

The barbecue was over, and Cullen and Andrea had left. Near the kitchen, Jake was laughing as Rainie tried to talk Holt into adopting a puppy.

Josie grinned. Rainie was such a wonderful mixture of humor and kindness, and her Dom obviously adored her.

Everyone here was friends with Holt, and she'd been watched and weighed as they evaluated whether she was good enough for him. She, honestly, wasn't sure of the answer herself. Sure, she was a fine person. Really. But she might not be all that perfect a girlfriend, let alone a submissive.

She...didn't see a good ending to her and Holt starting a relationship.

Carson needed a stable home. And face it, even a wonderful guy like Holt would have second thoughts about taking on a single mother with a grumpy, almost teenaged boy. Holt could break Carson's heart.

Giving Holt up would break hers.

Last night...last night, she'd felt like someone had taken all her fantasies and dreams and longings, stirred them together, and poured them out into an evening made just for her. Gaining her trust, Holt had swept her along, teasing and ordering and...taking her further than she'd ever dreamed of going. Making her come harder than she'd ever thought a person could.

Making her want...more. Want *him*. And now she felt almost incomplete when he wasn't beside her.

Oh, this was so wrong.

She rubbed her cheek against the purring cat and wished her heart didn't feel as if it were fracturing.

This morning, she'd known she should pull away before she

got more involved with him. Before Carson got used to seeing him around.

But when he'd appeared at her door and she'd tried to back out of this barbecue, he'd smiled and tucked her into the car. And now, when she tried to keep her distance, she ended up on his lap.

Her father had been all thunder and noise when he demanded his way. Holt was like...like the ocean, infinitely powerful, calmly wearing away the beach, the cliffs, vanquishing obstacles without fuss.

Holt glanced over at her, as he did so often. His gaze ran over her, and his eyes darkened slightly as if he could hear her worried thoughts.

"Josie, I see Coltrane has you under his paw." Ben grinned. "He may never let you leave."

She laughed. "Even a Dom kitty has to give in to necessity. My son is due home soon, and his homework won't get done without a nudge."

"My mother did the same thing." Ben's smile faded. "I'm not sure my sisters and I would have survived without her. Your boy is lucky to have you."

That was so nice to hear. "Thank you. And thank you for having me over to the barbecue." She glanced at the stairs. Bronx sat on the bottom step, a worried look on his furry retriever face. He adored his mistress. "May I run upstairs and tell Anne good-bye? I won't wake her if she's asleep."

"Sure. I was going to sneak up and check on her, even though she's threatened to flog me when I hover too much." He grinned. "You have a better excuse."

Josie patted his arm and handed him Coltrane. "Anne's lucky to have you, and your child will be, too."

Somehow, she couldn't see Ben disowning a daughter if she was with child. And he'd already shown how he'd react if his lover turned up pregnant.

With a smothered sigh, Josie headed up the stairs. Anne was a lucky woman. Josie'd had no barbecues thrown to keep her happy. No protective boyfriend. She'd "celebrated" her seventeenth birthday in a homeless shelter.

At the top of the stairs, she heard an odd sound. Was Anne on the phone? No, that was a groan.

Josie ran the last few steps. The door was open.

Kneeling on the floor, Anne was bent over, hands clutching her stomach. A sound emerged—a low, teeth-clenched moan of pain.

"Oh no, this isn't good. Hold on a second, Anne." Josie ran to the head of the stairs and yelled, "Ben. Holt. Get up here!"

When Josie dropped down beside her, Anne whispered, "Good subbie. I tried to ye—ooooooh."

Josie's eyes widened. Those contractions shouldn't be so close together.

Pounding on the stairs announced Ben's arrival—and Holt's.

"Jesus fuck, woman." Ben scooped Anne off the floor.

"Hold her for a moment, Ben." Holt grabbed towels from the bathroom closet and spread them over the bed several layers thick.

Anne groaned again as Ben laid her on the mattress.

"Another pain? Already?" Holt's expression changed, holding worry. "You weren't in labor when you came up for a nap."

She gasped for air. "I had contractions earlier." Breath. "Wasn't anything." Breath. "Didn't hurt." Breath. "This is insane. Owwwww, fucking *hell*."

"Close the door, Josie, to keep the pets out. Ben, take Anne's pants off and do you have gloves in here? Let's see if there's time to get to the hospital." Holt disappeared into the bathroom to wash his hands.

Door closed, Josie picked up a clean beach towel and draped it over Anne's bared legs and groin, getting a look of approval from Ben.

"There's lots of light in here, at least." Cleaned up, Holt

walked over to the bed, bent Anne's legs up, and moved the towel. His jaw hardened. "Ooookay, then. Ben, call 911 and tell them precipitous labor."

"What?" Ben said. "She needs to get to—"

"She's having the baby now, bro." Holt patted Anne's leg and met her eyes. "You're almost fully dilated, sweetheart. Labor pains this fast are hell; however, the good news is you're having the baby really, really soon. This won't last long."

"Oh. Good." Anne gasped...and curled up again with a whine of, "Fuck, fuck, fuck, *fuck*."

"Josie, please get my first aid kit out of the car. It's in the cargo space." Holt gave her a reassuring smile and tossed over the keys. "Tell Jake and Rainie to direct the first-responders."

"Yes, Sir."

As she ran out of the room, she heard Anne's grunted approval. "Well trained."

After telling Jake and Rainie what was happening, Josie grabbed the bag from the car, dashed up the stairs and into the room.

Nothing had gotten better. Anne's face was a dark red, and her hands were fisted as she screamed through gritted teeth. *God.* Josie'd thought her own hours of lonely labor were bad. This was horribly worse. Anne hardly had a chance to breathe between the long contractions.

Josie unzipped the bag and set it close to Holt. He dug inside.

Sweat poured down Anne's face, and her eyes were glazed as she got lost in the pain.

"Do we need to boil water or something?" Ben asked frantically. Holding Anne's hand, he wiped her face with a cool towel. "I don't—"

"No worries, Ben," Holt said. "The ambulance crew will have sterile equipment and can cut the cord. It's better to let the cord go uncut for bit anyway."

Gloves on, Holt checked Anne again. "You're there, Anne. Fully dilated."

"Fucking go me." Anne groaned again.

"Josie," Holt said quietly. "Can you sit behind her and give her some back support?"

"Got it." Josie toed off her flip-flops, crawled onto the bed, and braced Anne from the back. "Lean against me. I've got you."

At the foot of the bed, Holt waited for the next contraction. "Hang in there, Anne. You're almost done." He patted her leg, radiating confidence and competence.

Josie's racing heart slowed.

His steady gaze met hers, took in how she was bracing Anne, and his nod of approval warmed her through and through.

"Push. Have to," Anne gasped. She bore down with a high-pitched keening sound.

"Won't be any postponing this baby." Holt motioned to Ben. "Come here, bro. Let's get your baby birthed."

Anne gave another bit-off scream as Ben moved. When she stopped and gasped for breath, Josie reached around and took her hand. "I've got you," she whispered. "Ben is here. You're having the baby now—just hang in there."

Anne clutched her fingers, took another breath, and pushed again.

Holt murmured quiet instructions to Ben. "No cord problems, we're all good. Put your hands here."

As the sound of sirens filled the air, Ben let out a shout of joy. "Anne, we have a baby."

Anne sucked in air in deep gasps, her hand shaking in Josie's. "Healthy?"

"Let me have him, Ben." Holt took the baby, drying and rubbing with a clean towel. A sputter sounded, then a heart-warming high cry. "Perfect," Holt murmured. "Here, Dad, put your son to his mom's breast—and cover them both up."

Josie slid off the bed and turned to help Anne lay flat.

The look of love on Ben's face as he sat beside Anne brought tears to Josie's eyes. Blinking hard, she looked at Holt.

He smiled, a dimple appearing, his eyes alight. "Best feeling in the world, isn't it?"

Oh, *hell*. She was falling for him. Right into that four-letter-L-word.

Two hours later, when Holt walked Josie to her door, she felt as if she'd been wrung out to dry. The remnants of adrenaline were long gone... and the joy remained. She'd helped a baby get born.

Josie smiled up at Holt. "Anne is sure a stubborn person. I didn't think she'd ever agree to go to the hospital."

Holt chuckled. "I can see her reasoning. Why bother when the baby'd already arrived?"

Anne had finally agreed to go to the hospital, only because neither the pediatrician nor obstetrician made house calls—and Holt had said having a baby that quickly was hard on both participants and they should be checked.

Josie shook her head, remembering her own labor. It had seemed to last forever, but at least, there'd been plenty of time to realize the baby she'd carried for nine months was on his way out. The actual birth and separation had been...a kind of grief. Anne, though, had been in too much pain and labor had gone too quickly for her to process the parting. "She looked shell-shocked."

"Yeah. Precipitous births are...unsettling. I've seen a couple. Both times, the women had given birth before—and they'd still looked as if they'd taken a header off a cliff."

"I think I prefer the slower way."

"Speaking from the paramedic's point of view, so do I." Holt leaned forward, pinning her against the door. "In case I didn't tell you, you were wonderful."

She lifted her lips to his, feeling as if she was absorbing his strength, his control. He'd been so calm. Just hearing his smooth, resonant voice had been heartening. "I merely followed orders. Anne was awfully lucky you were there."

All your patients are damn lucky.

He laughed. "I doubt she'll even remember who attended her. But it was a hell of a party. I'm glad I got to share it with you."

"I..." Actually, she'd be happy to share anything with him. Everything. And that was something she mustn't say. She breathed in his scent, longing to get closer, to have his mouth on her, his shaft inside her, to be—

His gaze heated. He ran his hands up and down her arms and then lifted her chin. "Little subbie, I'd like to take you up on that invitation, but your son is probably over at Stella's and watching for you."

She closed her eyes. What was she thinking? She needed to pull away from him, not...not extend unconscious invitations. "He is. I saw his bike over there."

"Then I'll let you go. You need to eat and get ready for work." He ran a finger down her cheek. "I won't be at the Shadowlands tonight. However, tomorrow, I'd like to see you."

She eyed him. "Uh...let's not make plans. I'm really busy, and I should spend time with Carson, and really, it was fun today, but..."

Her excuses fled when his gaze darkened. His voice dropped to a warning rumble. "Josie..."

Her mouth went dry.

"Second thoughts are normal, pet, but don't let your fears get in the way of something wonderful." He kissed her lightly, strolled off the porch and across to his duplex.

This wasn't fair. It *wasn't*. The one man she most wanted to be with—and most needed to be away from—lived next door.

God truly was a male—and a sadist.

Anne couldn't quite remember the afternoon. The events had all run together in a ghastly montage of pain-filled moments.

She remembered the barbecue. That'd been fun. She'd taken a nap. Gotten up. Then pain, pain, and more pain. And although they said she'd had a baby, nothing felt real.

Now she was here, spending the night in a damn hospital, by herself rather than with Ben snuggled around her. Had he left? Gone back to the house?

She couldn't remember. Everything was all mixed together. Ambulance. Baby. No baby. Ben. Forms and questions. Her OB guy had been in to see her, hadn't he? Hell, this was worse than any blackout hangover—ever.

And she hurt, like everywhere, as if someone had used a baseball bat on her belly and ribs and arms. And even her pussy. Oh, right, the OB guy had sewed her up...down there.

Lovely, she had stitches in her hoo-hah. She rolled her eyes. There were masochists who enjoyed having needles poked through their labia. No fucking way. In fact, she'd never jammed needles into any of her boys' packages. Good to know that she was entirely right.

Well, time to see if she could move. She flipped the covers off and blinked. Whoa, look how flat her gut was now. No belly. She ran her hand over her stomach, feeling...empty. And lost. Tears prickled her eyes.

No. No crying. Josie had warned her about hormonal up-and-down swings after the birth. For fuck's sake, it'd been bad enough having them in the beginning of the pregnancy. More now? Didn't seem fair.

And hormones or not, she felt lonely and empty, and no one was here for the celebration, even if, dammit, she didn't feel there was much to celebrate.

She'd had a baby and felt...nothing.

Blinking hard, she sat up and bit back a grunt of pain. Yeah, her abdominal muscles were strained like she'd done a year's worth of sit-ups in an hour. That labor shit wasn't for wussies. The chair beside the bed looked comfortable, though, and maybe she wouldn't feel like a...sick person...if she was out of the damned bed.

Moving like a...sick person...dammit, she shuffled the few steps to the chair and settled down despite the complaints from her stitched-up crotch.

Yeah, this was better. But still lonely. She pulled in an unhappy breath, trying to get her wayward emotions to settle.

And then the light from the open door dimmed as a huge man filled the space and walked in.

Ben.

"You're up. Shouldn't you be..." His heavy brows drew together. "What's wrong, darlin'?"

The concern in his voice was heartwarming. Strengthening. The lump in her chest, in her stomach, in her heart lightened as he walked over, a blanket balled up in one arm. He went down on one knee.

She pressed her hand against his rough cheek, and a day's worth of beard growth scratched her palm. "I'm all right. I just feel..." She shook her head. "Empty?"

"Of course you do." He smiled slowly. "Maybe this will help." And he set the blanket in her lap.

She looked down, startled that she actually had a lap now, and stilled as he pulled a fold of the blanket back.

Oh. So *tiny*. Above a scrunched face, little fists like pink walnuts waved at her. Her baby was a grumpy pixie with half-closed eyes and pursed lips.

"Oh, Ben," she whispered. She stared down. Ever so slowly, her heart filled, reached over-flowing, and expanded to the point of pain trying to accommodate the love. "We have a *son*."

Ben's gaze met hers, his eyes shiny. "Yeah," he said, his voice gruff. "We do."

CHAPTER FIFTEEN

I t was Sunday afternoon, Eagles vs the Giants. And halftime.

As the teens and preteens raced out of Holt's living room in search of provisions, he exchanged grins with the other two adults. Hell, if he'd known he'd be hosting a horde, he'd have stocked up. Duke and Wedge, the teens from across the street, sometimes came to games. Today, though, they'd brought along Carson and two of *his* buddies.

Then, before the teens had even settled, Jake had shown up. Apparently, Rainie and some friends had commandeered the television to watch *It's a Wonderful Life*. "*They were starting to cry, bro. I had to get out of there*." Duke had shaken his head—"*That sucks, man*" —and handed over the bag of Doritos.

The game had barely started when Vance arrived. Turned out his wife's family from Iowa was visiting, and he and Galen had wanted Sally to have some alone time with them. Remembering Holt's 65-inch, wide-angle television, the Fed had swung by to catch the game.

Eight people had sure made a serious crowd in the tiny living room. At least he'd staked out his recliner before everyone'd arrived. Holt looked over at Jake on the couch and Vance in an armchair. "I think I need a bigger place."

Jake snorted. "I've been telling you that. There are a couple of places out by me."

"Country living isn't for me. I like having neighbors." Holt pointed to the house across the street—the one with the basket-ball hoop. "With teens around, I always have someone to shoot hoops with." He wadded up a Dorito bag and tossed it into the corner wastebasket. *Two points.* "However, if I'd known I'd be entertaining so many of them, I'd have bought more food."

Vance glanced at the empty bags of junk food and grinned. "Teens are a black hole for snacks."

"No shit."

"They seem to be good kids though," Vance said. "Did you say one of them is Josie's?"

"Yep. Carson. He's one of the younger three—slim, light brown hair."

It was a shame Josie hadn't shown up. Then again, yesterday, when he'd said goodbye, she'd looked as if she wanted to retreat again. Poor subbie. She really was torn. If she thought her doubts would make him back away, she was in for a surprise.

Did she know her kid was at his house? Probably not, but if she didn't find him, all she had to do was listen. Being prudent, Holt'd left the front door open. Any touchdown got rowdy cheers and fumbles garnered so many catcalls the entire neighborhood must know where the kids were.

Jake laughed. "Carson might be smaller, but he ate as much as the rest of them did."

And, in fact, here the kid came, leading the other two through the door. Yukio lugged two six-packs of sodas, Brandon had a container of cookies, and Carson carried a huge tray of something that smelled amazing.

"What've you got there, Carson?" Holt asked.

"Chicken wings. Whenever Mom gets stuck on some plot

thing, she cooks. Or if she's upset or worried or pissed-off or whatever." The kid's laugh was that of a boy who knew he was loved no matter how annoyed his mother got.

Holt noticed the other two Doms had the same smile he did. "I take it she's cooking?"

"Oh, boy, is she cooking." Yukio shook his head. "She was, like, all pissed-off that the hero in her book wants to kiss the girl."

Vance blinked. "That's bad?"

"She doesn't want any gaggy kissing or anything. Ugh." Carson gave a nod of agreement.

"She said if Tigre started any romance stuff, she'd geld him, even if he is the hero." Yukio scowled. "Tigre should be allowed to kiss Laurent if he wants to."

"I agree," Holt said. "Gotta say, Tigre better make his moves carefully, or he'll get his package crisped." Holt grinned at Jake and clarified. "Josie writes paranormal fiction, and the potential girlfriend has a pyrokinesis ability. She can manipulate fire."

Jake snorted. "Talk about a talent that'd give a firefighter fits."

"It really does."

Carson looked between Holt and Yukio. "You read Mom's books?"

"Sure, they're really good." Yukio grinned. "I read them even before I knew the author was your mom."

"I've got 'em all, too," Holt said. "She writes a great story." So much of her personality and beliefs—and humor—went into the stories, how could he not enjoy them?

"I wish my mom would cook instead of throwing shit when she's mad." Brandon grabbed three more cookies and settled onto the floor. "Wish we'd had these cookies yesterday."

Carson didn't say a word.

Holt eyed Carson. "I hope Brandon's mom was in a good mood yesterday. What'd you guys end up doing?"

"Not much." Carson's shoulders hunched, and he turned away from Holt.

Before Holt could say anything, Brandon spoke up, "Just video games...at my place. It was quiet."

The older teens trotted in then with more soda, more chips and dip, and whoops of joy when they saw the container of chicken wings.

"All *right*." Wedge made a beeline for the wings. "Josie makes the best food."

"How do you know? I thought she just moved here," Holt took a wing, sampled, and had to agree. Perfectly seasoned.

"She 'n' Cars have been coming to see Mrs. Avery, like, for years." Duke grabbed a couple of wings.

Carson grinned. "Cuz Oma said the guys helped out—like taking the garbage cans to the curb—Mom started making cookies and stuff for them. Like for thanks."

"Yeah, Josie's cool," Wedge said. "Even about our music, you know?"

Duke snorted. "Mostly. She has a thing about women being called hoes and bitches."

"Does she?" Obviously, Josie not only fed the boys, but listened to them as well. Holt smiled and took another wing. Somehow, he wasn't surprised in the least.

Carson dropped down beside Yukio in the pillow pile in front of the couch. "When the game's over, I'm supposed to bring everybody back over to our place, and if we have any room left, she'll have nachos, tacos, and burritos. We can kick a soccer ball around in the back, too."

Duke grinned and instructed Holt, "Never turn down her food, man. It's dope."

"All right then." Holt smiled and wondered if she knew exactly who she'd invited over.

Twilight had set in by the time everyone trooped over to Josie's house, and to Holt's surprise, Jake and Vance decided to join in.

Holt was pleased with the chance to see her. He didn't want her to get the chance to solidify her fears about having a relationship with him. *Uh-uh.* If she didn't like him, that would be different. There was a fine line between being persistent and stalking. However, Josie was delivering mixed messages, retreating then advancing. He'd have to observe with all senses in case her uncertainty turned toward a definite *no.*

After cleaning up the living room, Holt, Vance, and Jake headed for Josie's house. The older teens had halted in the front yard, texting for permission to eat at Carson's.

Holt, followed by Jake and Vance, stopped in Josie's living room to admire the holiday decorations. In the front corner, the six-foot Christmas tree was covered in blue and gold lights and science fiction/fantasy ornaments. A tiny black dragon had a Rudolph-red nose. A hobbit-hole was circled with tiny lights. Darth Vader wore a Santa hat...as did the Predator. Holt snorted. Now, that was just wrong.

As Holt entered the kitchen, Carson, Brandon, and Yukio were already there, chattering away to Josie.

"Carson," she asked. "Food will be ready soon. How many will be here?"

"Me 'n' Brandon 'n' Yukio," Carson reported.

"And Duke and Wedge," added Brandon.

Yukio nabbed a black olive and popped it into his mouth. "The vet and the Fed and the firefighter, too. They said they know you."

"The...firefighter?" Josie turned.

And there—that was delight in her eyes, in her expression, in her posture. The worried expression took a good ten seconds to appear.

"Josie." Vance moved forward as the three boys grabbed soccer balls and went out the back door. "Carson invited us over, but if this is an awkward time, we can take a rain check. I know you've been smothered in names the past couple of weeks. I'm Vance Buchanan, married to Sally."

And to Galen, Holt added silently. The two Doms shared their submissive wife.

"It's good to see you, Vance," Josie said, smiling. "You, too, Jake. And Holt. How was the game?"

As Vance answered, Jake glanced at Holt and said quietly, "She's still not sure if you're worth the risk."

"Yeah, I know," Holt said, equally quietly. "She's picked up some scars in the past."

"Mmm. Dodging old hurts is tricky."

No shit. "She's worth it."

Jake's smile widened, and he slapped Holt on the shoulder in approval. When Josie looked at him, he said, "Do you need a grocery store run? Anything picked up? Rainie has me well trained."

"Well trained?" Vance snorted. "You two need to get away from the dog kennels and out with humans once in a while."

Laughing, Josie shook her head. "I always make tons of food. Carson knows he can bring people home and feed them anytime."

The two older teenagers came in, saw the food, and exchanged fist bumps.

Josie moved forward to give one a pat on the shoulder and the other a fond smile. "Carson and his friends are in the backyard. We set up a soccer goal this morning, and he's been eager to give it a try."

"Cool," Duke said. He and Wedge jogged out the back door, obviously already familiar with the house.

Josie told the three men, "Food won't be for a few more minutes if you want to join the boys and do something active."

"Sounds good." Vance and Jake sauntered out, and Holt heard Jake call, "Vance and I will defend the net. Let's see if you can get anything past us."

Whoops of enthusiasm came from outside.

"Looks like they're all busy." Holt straightened. "Now who is going to defend *you?*"

Josie bit her lip, a flush rising in her cheeks.

Lovely. Moving forward, he trapped her against the counter with an arm on each side of her.

"This isn't a good idea, Holt," she whispered. "I-I don't date."

"That's fine, pet. We can just hang around at home and fuck," he whispered back.

She gave an indignant sputter of laughter and that was when he took her mouth. Her lips quivered against his and then...she surrendered.

Was there anything sexier than a woman who put her whole heart into a kiss? One who softened against him. One who didn't want to kiss him, yet ended up plastered against him.

The thump of approaching footsteps broke them apart. By the time Brandon appeared in the kitchen, Holt was nibbling on shredded cheese instead of a little submissive's neck. A pity that.

"Brandon." Josie gave the boy a sweet look. "I take it soccer isn't your game?"

"Nah," the kid said. "My father wanted me to play football and baseball. He didn't like soccer."

Holt gave him a closer look. The boy was tall and hefty; he was also out of shape. Doubtful that he played any extracurricular sports. "I better go save Vance and Jake from the under-twenty crowd. Thanks for the treat, Josie."

From the way her color increased, she knew he didn't mean the cheese. "Tell the boys they still have a few minutes to grind you old guys into the dirt."

"You're a vicious woman, Josephine."

As Holt walked out, he heard Brandon laugh.

Ten minutes later, he headed into the house on a bottled water run. He'd expected to see Brandon watching TV. Instead, the kid sat at the kitchen island, cutting up black olives for the tacos, and pouring his heart out.

Yeah, Josie had a talent for listening.

After a moment, Holt silently headed back outside. The boy was talking about his father and a divorce and never being good enough, and his emotions were bouncing from tears to sheer fury.

Best that everyone continue with the soccer for a few more minutes.

Duke and Wedge were taking on Jake, Vance, and Yukio. And Carson had been sidelined while he knotted together a busted shoelace. He looked up at Holt. "We get a few extra minutes?"

"Eh, I didn't ask. Your buddy is talking with your mom, and I didn't want to interrupt."

After a second, Carson nodded his understanding. "That's good, yeah. He's had a hard time—and Mom'll help. She's good at that."

"She is." Holt leaned against the picnic table. "I'm pretty good, too...if you ever need to talk about shit."

Carson looked up. "Huh?"

"My father died when I was around your age. It made it rough since sometimes a guy has questions—ones he can't ask a female." Holt ruffled the kid's hair. "Just remember you can call me if you get into trouble you can't handle."

The kid flushed and nodded, gratitude in his eyes. "'Kay, thanks."

At a yell from Yukio, Carson darted out, swept up the pass, and kicked the ball right past Jake and into the net.

Holt grinned and let out a whooping cheer.

Startled, Carson turned. The boy had his mother's grin.

CHAPTER SIXTEEN

Christmas day was almost over. That evening, Josie walked around her house, picking up stray pieces of wrapping paper and ribbon.

It'd been a very nice day.

Oma'd invited two women to their holiday dinner. One was a widow from Oma's bridge club, and the other was a divorcee whose ex had the children for the day. The poor woman.

The two guests had been delightful, even showing up early to help prepare dinner. Carson had been on his best behavior, peeling the potatoes and running errands.

Her boy was feeling better these days. He'd sure had fun last Sunday, watching football with the crew over at Holt's. When they'd all come over afterward, well, she'd never laughed so hard in her life. Men had the oddest perspectives on life. And Holt kept the conversation hopping. The man could quite simply talk about anything. No one stayed a stranger around Holt.

Despite her good intentions, she wasn't managing to stay a stranger either. It was as if when they'd had sex, he'd awakened her sleeping desires. Now she wanted him with every cell in her body. She wanted to touch him, to hear his voice, breathe in his scent.

He'd driven her crazy last night during church.

Yesterday, when Holt had checked Oma's blood pressure—something he'd been doing frequently since he moved in—Oma had ordered him to join them for Christmas Eve service. Admitting he hadn't been to church in years, he'd thanked Oma for including him.

During the service, he'd captured Josie's hand and refused to release it, despite her tugging. Taking it a step further, he'd put his arm along the back of the pew so his hand rested on her shoulders.

And kissed her forehead when she frowned at him.

He wasn't just a man, but a Dominant, as well. A determined, unshakable one.

Why did that simply melt all her resolve?

Shaking her head, Josie stuffed the wrapping paper into the recycle bin. The Christmas tree certainly looked bare without presents beneath it.

It'd sure been fun to open those presents. Her great-aunt had been delighted with her new eReader. Quite a few members of Oma's book club had embraced the technology, especially loving the ability to increase the font size.

Carson had loved his presents, which was a relief. He sure was more difficult to shop for the older he got. Who knew how much she'd miss buying cute stuffed animals and toy trucks? Now it was Xbox games and music. And soccer shoes.

However, getting a cell phone had totally made his day. She foresaw many future arguments about its usage. Still, all that mattered was that he could now call for help if he got in trouble.

After the service last night, she'd given Holt his present. Last Sunday, the men and teens had argued over their favorite cookies. She'd memorized Holt's choices, done a cookie-baking marathon, and filled an oversized Christmas tin for him.

He'd opened the tin right then and there to sample the contents—and realized it held his favorites. His stunned expression had been worth all the time in the kitchen.

The gifts hadn't been one-sided. This morning, Carson had found presents from Holt on the doorstep.

Josie grinned. He'd given her boy a Lego starship model. *Score.* Carson had already started building it.

Her present had been a gorgeous leather notebook, colored pens, and a mug that said, I *WRITE.* WHAT'S *YOUR* SUPERPOWER?

When she'd opened it, Carson told her Holt'd read her books and thought they were great. She'd come very close to crying. The Dom liked her stories—and gave her presents for a *writer.*

Poor Holt was working today. He said that since he didn't have children who'd be crushed if he wasn't home, he preferred to work so nurses with families could have the day off. *God, Holt.* She'd never seen anyone who would appreciate a family more.

While she'd been unwrapping presents, singing carols, enjoying a big Christmas feast and socializing, he'd been caring for children who were so ill they were in ICU. He'd spent Christmas stuck in a cold, sterile building.

Feeling tears prickle her eyes, she went into her office and looked out the window. His lights were on. He was home. Damned if he shouldn't have a bit of Christmas, too.

After piling a plate with baked ham, cheesy potatoes, and various side dishes, she tapped on Carson's door. "Hey, you. I'll be back in a few minutes."

"'Kay, Mom."

At Holt's, she rang the doorbell.

And waited.

She'd turned to go home when the door opened. "Josie?" He stood in the doorway, hair wet and shoved out of his face. Jeans zipped up, yet unbuttoned. No shirt.

She'd never thought she'd be the type to drool about a man's chest. Dark blond hair, golden tan. And muscles so hard and ripped that her mouth went dry. Her fingers quivered with the urge to touch.

Instead, she held up the covered plate. "I...brought you some Christmas dinner. Since you couldn't come."

"Did you now?" His lips curved in a pleased smile. "I'm starving. The unit was crazy, and I never did get a break. I was about to open the cookie tin—and I'm not going to tell you how many of those I already ate last night." He took the plate from her, closed his hand around hers, and pulled her into his living room.

"No, I didn't come—"

"You'll keep me company while I eat, won't you?" His hard arm around her waist didn't relax at all. Every breath brought her his clean, just-out-of-a-shower scent.

"Holt." She looked up at him, had a moment to see the pleasure in his gaze, and then his lips were on hers and he kissed her with all his devastating skill. When she sagged against him, he took her weight with an approving hum.

"I can't leave Carson alone."

"Does that mean you're inviting me over to your house?" He had a wicked glint in his eyes.

"You know, Master Holt, you're awfully sneaky."

"I am. And I can't think of anything nicer than spending the evening with you both."

The sincerity in his smooth voice shook something deep inside her, and it took her a moment to recover and keep her tone light as she said, "You're not fooling me, Sir. You simply want someone to serve you your food, don't you?"

He brushed the backs of his fingers over her cheek. "Yes, sweetheart. I'd like that very much."

CHAPTER SEVENTEEN

On Thursday, Josie poured herself a glass of sparkling cider left from yesterday's Christmas dinner. As she walked down the hall to her office, her footsteps echoed in the empty house.

Since Carson had winter break from school, she'd agreed he could spend the night at Isaac's house. Their move to this part of Citrus Park meant her boy didn't get to see his buddy often. Although Carson had new friends, it would be a shame to lose the old ones.

Like Josie had lost hers. Because of Pa. She shook her head. After Mama left them, her father had decided Josie spent too much time on "frivolous" activities like being with her friends, and her friendships had soon withered from lack of contact. She'd do her best to keep that from happening with Carson and Isaac.

Even if it meant the house felt hollow-hearted. She frowned. Funny, she never thought much about Mama—her abandonment had cut deep. Her mother had always been busy, a whirlwind of noise and activity, singing and humming, cooking and cleaning. After Mama ran off, their house had been cold. Unhappy. Josie'd come to hate empty houses.

Josie and Carson's apartment buildings had been filled with noise, and she never felt totally alone, even when Carson started school. Maybe that was why she'd never wanted to move into a real house before.

For a couple of hours, she worked on her book, right up until Laurent started flirting with Tigre. *Again*. The heroine sure wasn't listening when Josie scolded her and said, "No romance."

Frustrated, she abandoned the manuscript and took a shower instead. Only her long hot shower turned into a short one when she started thinking about empty houses and knives and *Psycho*.

Having an active imagination had a serious downside.

Grumpily, she pulled on her great-uncle's old work shirt and pajama shorts—her comfort clothes—and stomped into the living room. Watching a movie by herself wasn't appealing. Maybe Oma would want to have some hot chocolate or... No, Oma wasn't home. This was her church group night.

The woman had a better social life than Josie did.

Josie huffed a laugh. When she grew up, she wanted to be Oma. A brilliant career, a loving marriage before losing her husband to a heart attack, then working overseas for years, and... Josie's smile faded. In a way, Oma had taken those international assignments to escape her own empty house.

Josie looked around the living room. Last night, Holt had been on that couch, arm around Josie's shoulders, teasing Carson about the excessive collateral damage in a car chase scene. The evening had felt...different...with him there. Fuller. Richer.

What would it be like to have a man around? Someone to talk with in the evenings, to cuddle up to on the couch. To cook for and have the joy of seeing him enjoy the meal she'd made. She didn't *need* a guy, not for doing chores or fixing things—she'd learned how to do stuff herself and to hire people when needed.

It was tough to hire someone to assuage loneliness, though.

Or to help with parenting. That was a biggie. She got so tired of making all the decisions. Like earlier when she'd tried to decide whether to let Carson spend the night with Isaac. And when she was trying to figure out why her boy was being so quiet and whether she should try to discuss his moods or leave him alone. It was...scary...to be a single parent.

It was even scarier to realize she was whining and dragging her mood even lower. With a grunt of exasperation, she abandoned the hollow-sounding house and went outside.

Here was noise. Finding a smile, she walked over to the tall maple and leaned against the trunk. Frogs croaked in the ditch behind the fence. With quiet cheeps, birds were settling in for the night. A hum of traffic came from the distant highway. She could hear a sitcom's laugh track from Percy's house next door. Rock music drifted from across the street with occasional discordant notes. Wedge was practicing his bass guitar.

Small neighborhoods were never truly silent. And she'd been lucky in her neighbors. Even the dominating, Harley-owning hottie was quiet. Smiling, she glanced over the fence. She'd hoped he might come over after he got off work, but his windows were dark. Maybe he went somewhere else.

As she turned, she spotted a motionless form on his patio.

Intending to tease him about his silence, she wandered closer to the fence and frowned. Usually, he sat on his patio with his feet up, head tilted back to enjoy every moment of being outside. Tonight, he was hunched forward, leaning on his forearms with his head down.

"Holt? Is something wrong?" The question popped out before she could think. Boy, talk about intrusive. She was peering at him over the fence like a snoopy neighbor in a sitcom. What if he wanted to be alone?

His head came up. "Josie." He stood and walked over. "It's a pretty night out, isn't it?" His tone was dull.

Yes. Something's wrong. "It is. You know, I have a couple of cold beers in the fridge. Why don't you come over and sit with me."

She winced. Her invitation was as romantic as talking to Carson. Well, aside from the beer.

He shook his head. "I wouldn't be good company tonight, pet."

"I realize that." At his quizzical look, she straightened her shoulders. If she needed to be blunt, so be it. "That's why you need to come over."

His lips curved slightly, and in the moonlight, she could see the smile didn't reach his eyes. "Aren't you a bossy subbie? All right, I'll join you for a while."

"I'll let you in the front." She started toward the back door—and he simply put a hand on the top of the fence and jumped over.

Wow. The athletic grace gave her libido a lovely shimmer.

He followed her to the back patio and patted the long porch swing. "New addition?"

"It was my Christmas present to myself. We had one in Texas when I was growing up, and I loved it." She pointed to one end. "Sit."

At his long look, she felt a quiver in her belly as if she'd poked a wolf with a stick. "Um. Please, Sir, have a seat."

"Better." He brushed his knuckles over her hot cheek in a gentle caress. "Thank you."

God, how did just the merest touch of his fingers make her tingle? "I'll...uh...be right back."

In the kitchen, she pulled in a slow breath. That "Sir" word had popped out...because that's how she felt. Holt had gone all Dominant and turned her submissive with just a look. But he didn't usually pull that Dom card on her.

Tonight might be different. She shook her head. As a kid in Texas, she'd tried to help a starving dog and made the mistake of cornering it. It hadn't attacked, but its terrifying growl had sure made her retreat.

Apparently, bossing around a Master when he wasn't feeling up to par netted the same response.

When she returned with two bottles of beer, he'd taken a seat. The swing rocked gently.

After handing him the beer, she sat on the other end.

He took a long drink of the cold beer and straightened. In fact, she could almost see him trying to change his mood to a sociable one.

That wasn't the point. How blunt could a person be with a Dom? Did Doms let other people help? She shoved her bangs out of her face and ventured forth. "So...what happened today to make you so unhappy?"

He stiffened, and this time, his attempt at a smile wasn't convincing at all. "Nothing worth discussing. How's Carson doing? He looked as if he was—"

"Holt. We're friends...and we have something between us. You *said* so." Carefully, she reached over to stroke her hand up and down his arm. His scarred forearm was thick with muscle—very tense muscles. "Tell me what's wrong."

He turned his hand over and interlaced their fingers. "I know you want to help, but you don't need to hear about this. It's ugly, sweetie."

Wednesday and Thursday were his hospital days. She slid across the swing until their hips and shoulders touched. "Cops, soldiers, firefighters, medical people, the ones who share last longer. Manage better. And you know, everyone talks to bartenders."

His fingers tightened around hers. "This—"

"Holt, I don't break easy."

He let out a huffed breath. "No, you don't, do you?"

She waited.

After a pause, he shook his head. "I love working the pediatric ICU. Children are...magic. They're resilient. Hopeful. Motivated. But sometimes, nothing works. We had a baby, not even a year old, who was taken off life support today. The decision was correct, but he was a champ. He fought so fucking hard." He paused, and his voice came out raw. "It's hard to give up."

"He wasn't getting better?"

"He was born with a bad heart. It's fucking unfair to be born with the odds already against you. He hadn't done anything, didn't deserve any of it."

Oh God, to lose a baby. Tears burning her eyes, Josie took the beer out of Holt's hand, set it down, and wrapped her arms around him. "I'm sorry. So sorry."

Stiffly, he held it all in, and then his arms came around her, holding her against him so powerfully that her ribs creaked. She held him harder. If that baby had been hers, she would have been so grateful to have this amazing man taking care of her child.

But this kind of heartbreak was the price he paid for the work he did.

Pressing her face against his shoulder, she rubbed his back.

Slowly, his muscles unknotted. When an owl hooted from the neighbor's tree, his head tilted slightly as if he was letting the world back in. She could almost feel the flow of life around them refreshing his spirit—and she willed some of her own into him as well.

Eventually, he drew away. Silently, he used his thumbs to wipe away the tears spilling from her eyes. "Thank you," he said softly and kissed her.

He retrieved her beer for her, picked up his, put his arm around her shoulders, and set the swing to rocking slowly. "Where's Carson today?"

"How'd you know he wasn't here?"

"No light in his room. No music from the house." Holt ran his hand up and down her arm, leaving tingles behind. "It's a good thing I approve of his taste in music...mostly. At least he likes Green Day and Linkin Park."

"Sorry if he gets too loud. We've battled about the volume."

She still considered the music too loud, and Carson was convinced he'd gotten the worst of the deal. She took a sip of her beer. "Anyway, it's school vacation, and I let him spend the night with a friend."

"The whole night?"

The darkly masculine question made her mouth go dry.

A smile curved his lips.

She swallowed hard.

Then he tucked the hunger away and tugged a strand of her hair teasingly. "Don't worry, pet. I thoroughly enjoyed having sex with you, but if you're not ready to play privately, it's all right. I don't want you worried that having an empty house will mean your neighbor puts the moves on you."

She hadn't even gotten to that worry, and he'd eased it.

He wanted her...and backed off to keep from making her nervous.

She leaned her head back against his upper arm. Each breath carried his clean scent. Each gentle slide of his fingers through her hair sent quivery chills along her skin. She wanted to ask him questions, just to hear his whisky-smooth voice.

"Josie?" He set his beer down and lifted her chin. "What's going through your head?"

I love you. No, that wasn't something she'd say. Probably not ever. But tonight could be hers and she could be honest about that. "I want you."

He chuckled. "I do know that, pet. But are you ready to show me your bedroom? Otherwise we can sit out here and enjoy ourselves in a less...comprehensive...fashion."

Comprehensive sounded perfect. She wanted his hands on her. All over. And wanted to touch him in return.

In answer, she wrapped her fingers around his hand and rose. "You never got to see all of the house. Let me show you."

She was a brave one, wasn't she? As she led him into the bedroom, Holt could feel her nervousness, hear it in the heightened Texas drawl. It made him want to pull her into his arms and say *there, there*.

When she stopped in the center of her bedroom and looked up at him with those wide eyes, he nearly told her to get used to having him around. Whether she realized it or not, he planned to keep her. When she'd comforted him tonight, she'd sealed her fate.

"Um. This is my bedroom."

He glanced around the shadowy room, knowing she was too nervous to turn on the lights. Well, he'd give her that option...this time...but eventually, he intended to see her orgasming when the lights were on.

The heavy wooden bed and nightstands didn't match, were probably secondhand since her budget would be tight. Yet it was a treat to see she'd indulged her romantic nature with Arthur Rackham's fairy prints and blue satiny, lacy bedding.

She'd look lovely in that bedding.

After a visible breath, she straightened her shoulders and grasped his T-shirt. Started to lift the hem.

The action—and the sweet vulnerability in her gaze—drew out the Dom in him. Rather than cooperating, he took her wrists and crossed them behind her back. "I want your arms to stay right there until I tell you differently," he murmured.

The way her mouth dropped open made him grin.

"I did mention that dominance occurs outside of the club, didn't I?" He ran his hands through her hair, ruffling the silky strands until she looked like an annoyed Tinkerbelle. He kissed her temple, her cheek, then tangled his fingers in her hair and used it to pull her head back so he could pillage her mouth. Fuck, she had a kissable mouth.

Releasing her...slowly...he stepped back.

More light would be better. Flicking on the master bath light, he closed the door partially and did the same in the hallway. Enough so he could assess her responses but not enough to make

270

her feel awkward. Eventually—if he kept her naked often enough in the Shadowlands—she'd learn to be more comfortable in her own skin.

And she had lovely, pale skin with golden freckles spattered over her arms, shoulders, and cheeks.

He walked back to stand in front of her and look down into her big eyes.

"You didn't move. That's a very good girl." He ran the backs of his knuckles over her washed-to-thinness white shirt and felt her nipples rise to hard peaks. No bra. His cock thickened painfully.

With slow movements, he undid the first button on the shirt. Kissed her jaw.

Undid the next button. Kissed her neck. She'd showered within the last hour or so...and she smelled like tropical flowers—a Florida woman with a Texas accent.

Courageous and vulnerable. Practical and romantic...yet didn't believe in love.

The next button. He pushed the shirt back far enough to nuzzle the sweet curving junction of shoulder and neck.

Her breathing deepened.

The next button. The hollow between her breasts had a muskier scent.

She started to tremble. Shifted her weight.

"Don't move," he cautioned and felt her shiver at the sound of his voice.

The last button came undone. Stepping back, he indulged himself in the sight of her breasts shadowed by the open shirt.

"Holt," she whispered.

He moved close enough to cup her breasts, using them as playthings—and leashes. "In the club or in any sexual situation, call me Sir. It's an audible reminder of our roles, of the power exchange we're in. Using my name anywhere else is fine. But no matter where or when, if you're feeling submissive, go ahead and use Sir."

Being new, she might not realize how easily and often a submissive could slide into handing over control and relaxing into a service state of mind.

Her brows drew together. As aroused as she was, her mind might not be processing well. She nodded finally. "Yes, Sir."

"Now, baby, in any sexual situation—even if we're not in the Shadowlands—I keep the reins. You never have to worry about how to please me, because I will tell you."

Her eyes got wider, yet...no fear. If anything, she looked relieved.

"You will need to ask my permission to come."

And wasn't that the cutest glare in the world? She sure didn't like that idea.

"Sweetheart, scowling at me won't change my mind. Begging sometimes works."

Before she could say something he'd have to punish her for, he rolled her nipples between his fingers and watched her brain shut right off. After a quick kiss, he continued, "No matter what we're doing, I'll never forget your safewords are red and yellow. You're safe with me, Josie."

Her next breath was deeper. Easier.

Before she got too comfortable, he moved her hands and slid the shirt off her shoulders. As the garment fell to the ground, he crossed her wrists behind her again.

Such pretty breasts with the rosy nipples pointing outward. As he indulged in a nice long look, her face colored. "You're gorgeous, sweetheart."

With one finger, he stroked the bottom curve of one breast, establishing he could and would touch her when he wanted. No need to manhandle her...one finger was all that was needed. He walked behind her and brushed his fingers over her spine, then followed the edge of her shorts from the back to the front. "Cute shorts."

They were gold with tiny bunnies. Another glimpse into the

soft, whimsical side of the practical bartender. He undid the drawstring tie, putting a finger under the waistband to stretch it, and let go. The shorts slid down to her ankles.

Seeing her aborted move to catch them, he managed—barely—to smother his laugh.

"Sorry, Sir," she whispered, her hands behind her back again.

"Well, you might have been sorry." He took some time to enjoy her breasts. They fit into his palms perfectly, a satisfying, sensual weight. Warm and heavy with satiny skin. Her nipples puckered into hard buds when he ran his thumbs around them.

Her lips parted, her eyelids drooping slightly.

Damn, he liked watching her responses.

Crouching, he ran his hands down her waist, hips, and outer thighs. When he nuzzled the sweet spot between her hip and pussy, she trembled. He breathed her in—no perfumes, simply shower fresh and aroused woman—and wanted to toss her on the bed and bury himself deep.

No. Tonight would be slow. An affirmation of life. For them both.

Besides, the Dom in him would enjoy drawing out her antici-pation. He rubbed his chin over her mound, letting his light stubble rasp over her delicate skin.

Her knees wobbled. In fact, he doubted she could remain upright if he started on her pussy.

Rising, he gripped her waist, lifted her so the shorts fell from her ankles, and sat her on the bed. "Keep your arms behind your back, baby."

She had the most beautiful vulnerable eyes.

Now...what furniture and toys did he have to work with in her bedroom?

The bed was a great height and had a lower upholstered bench at the foot. No footboard. Yeah, that would work nicely—make it easy for him to play. With his foot, he moved the bench a couple of feet out from the bed.

He eyed her. Her need to serve also meant she wasn't comfortable with receiving. She'd enjoy what he planned, but undoubtedly would try to give him "his turn" far, far sooner than he intended. A bit of bondage might be in order.

The bathroom yielded a pair of scissors that he set on the nightstand.

In the closet, he found belts and scarves, including a long wool belt from a winter coat. Perfect.

He buckled a leather belt around her waist. "Drop your arms." Wrapping the coat's oversized belt all the way around her above her elbows and below her breasts, he pinned her arms to her sides.

"Holt—um, *Sir*." Josie felt her pulse pick up when she couldn't lift her arms. Her hands were useless. She should have known he wouldn't do simply missionary style sex. But still...bondage? "What if..." *What if you leave? What if you drop dead of a heart attack?*

He studied her face and then cupped her cheek. "Because we're alone here, any bondage I use will be possible to get out of, pet. If needed, you could work your arms out."

She wiggled slightly and realized it was true. It would take a while, but she could get free. Her muscles relaxed. "Thank you."

"No worries." He kissed her lightly. "I like you on edge—but not terrified. Josie, for pain or pleasure, I will not give you more than you can take."

His gaze met hers. Under his absolute confidence and the sheer force of his personality, she...let go. The control was his.

He nodded slightly and with an easy movement, scooped her up and laid her down on the bed. Her legs dangled off the end of the mattress.

Well, this was different.

He bent her right leg up, wrapped a scarf just above her knee, and knotted the end of the fabric to the right side of the waist belt. When he did the other side, her knees were secured up and close to her sides.

"Yeah, that's nice." He smiled and laid his palm against her very exposed pussy. "Easy access for whatever I want to do."

His hand was warm, intimate, and the light pressure on her clit made her squirm.

"Since you're a practical woman, you probably have a battery-operated-boyfriend." He didn't even wait for her answer before rudely opening her nightstand drawers.

"Don't you dare—"

His frown silenced her. "Best remember the terms of respect, baby. I wouldn't want to have to punish you more than you've already earned."

"What? Earned?" When his eyebrows rose, she hastily added, "Sir."

Ignoring her, he made a pleased sound and pulled out her rechargeable wand vibrator. "Nice." He flicked on the wand and smiled at the hum. After turning it off, he tossed it on the bed.

She felt the mortified heat in her face and glared at him.

"None of that, pet. Let me explain. If you're single, your toys belong to you alone." He stood at the foot of the bed and leaned over her body, bracing himself with a hand beside her shoulder. He ran his fingers through her hair—and fisted the loose strands —holding her for a deep, demanding kiss.

Lifting his head, he whispered against her lips. "However, if you're with a Dom, your toys get added to his arsenal...and your orgasms belong to him."

The words took a second to register. *What?* "No."

His look was full of sympathy. "I'm afraid so." He kissed her again, so thoroughly her arguments disappeared, and she felt only the heat of his body over hers, the velvet of his lips, the firm grip in her hair.

He nipped her bottom lip before kissing his way down her neck, to her collarbone, between her aching breasts. When he finally closed his mouth over a nipple, the hot, wet feeling was so intense she gasped.

Ruthlessly, he fondled her breasts almost painfully, except she was so excited, his every touch felt amazing. Streamers of liquid heat ran down to pool in her core. He pressed the peak against the roof of his mouth and worked it with his tongue, then sucked gently.

The tingles zinged all the way to her toes.

Gradually, he moved lower, alternating kisses with scraping his scratchy chin over her belly until she was half-squirming, half-laughing, and totally aroused.

Would he...

He pulled the bench closer and sat on it, then gripped her hips and pulled her ass right to the edge of the mattress. "Perfect. I can play with your pussy while sitting down. Now that's being indulged."

Before she could answer, he ran one finger between her slick folds, eased the hood up, then circled his finger around the edges of the exposed nub. The blast of heat and sensation sent fire through her veins.

Oh. My. God.

His fingers opened her folds more widely, and then his tongue swirled around her clit—hot and wet and far too effective.

Her last lover, so many years ago, hadn't known where a clit was. Master Holt not only knew but was terrifyingly good at what he did.

Her core turned to molten heat.

When he lifted his head, she tried to move and grasp his hair. The restraints kept her arms in place.

He licked his lips. "You taste like the sea, pet."

Oh. Was that good or bad? There was no way she'd ever ask that question aloud.

He chuckled. "I'm a California boy, Josie. I love the ocean, and I love the way you taste."

The worry died before it had a chance to take her over.

Sitting back slightly, he teased her pussy with one finger,

watching her with steel-blue eyes. Stroking one side of her clit, then the other. When he rubbed over the top with a callused finger, she winced...and he returned to the sides.

She could feel her clit swelling, hardening.

With his other hand, he slid a finger inside her.

An excruciatingly delicious burst of pleasure swept her body, and she moaned.

Smiling, he pulled back and inserted two fingers, thrusting in and out with slow tortuous movements. His other finger teased her clit.

Her whole pussy came alive and throbbed with need.

Three fingers. His fingers were too big, almost painful and—

He went back to two, sliding them in and out. His gaze never left her face. Leaning down, he licked over her clit. His tongue was so wet and hot as it flickered around her.

The combination of fingers and tongue lit her up like wildfire, and the seething tension inside her grew.

His fingers thrust in harder. Faster. His tongue worked her up and up.

She was almost...almost...

He lifted his head. "Do you have permission to come, little subbie?"

"Wh-what?" He wasn't serious. He couldn't possibly...

Her need was a churning, aching hunger. His fingers inside her had gone motionless, and she throbbed around him. *Permission to come?* She stared at him in disbelief.

His return gaze was steady. "I don't want you to orgasm yet, Josie. Fight it off. Can you do that for me?"

He didn't want her to come. *But I want to. Need to.* She bit her lip. *"Can you do that for me?"*

She'd do almost anything for him. Panting in frustration, she fought her climax down, drawing away from the edge of coming.

"There's a good girl." His approving smile sent joy singing in her veins, and then the bastard lowered his head and started licking again.

This time the urgency rose even faster, a terrifying pressure inside her, ready to explode. He lifted his head to murmur, "Not yet, Josie," and waited for her to fight it down.

How did he know?

He started again. Every thrust inside her pulled her closer, every light touch on her clit made it more swollen, more taut—and she fought back another climax. Every exhalation held a moan of need and pleading.

He paused. Paused. Paused.

"I'm proud of you, sweetheart. You can come now." His lips closed around her clit, his tongue teasing and tapping.

Under the exquisite torment, the pressure inside her built to a razor's edge.

His fingers thrust in just an infinitesimal amount harder.

"Oh, *God*." The explosion hit in a wild eruption. Spasm after spasm of billowing pleasure poured through her, right down to her toes like molten hot lava flowing to the sea.

As her orgasm eased and she sucked in air from the after-shocks, Holt laughed—*laughed*—and suddenly his fingers moved, thrusting hard and fast inside her.

With a shocked gasp, she stiffened, and her center spasmed hard again in fresh waves of pleasure.

Oh God, Oh God.

The rolling climax lasted and lasted.

Finally, as her heart began to slow, his mouth came down on her exquisitely sensitive clit. He curled his fingers upward inside her pussy and massaged a place that sent amazing sensations careening up her spine. Rather than dancing lightly over the nub, his tongue rubbed firmly. Demandingly. And the fingers stroking that internal spot were relentless.

Her body shot back into monstrous need. My God, she'd already come twice. "No," she whispered. "I can't."

"You can. You will." He blew a puff of air over her sensitive nub and made her tremble. His eyes met hers as his lips curved into a wicked smile. "Sweetheart...we're just getting started."

He licked over her clit, each flickering touch a merciless wonderful torment as he pushed her back toward the precipice. And then, his mouth closed over her, and he sucked.

Exquisite heat roared into her core, and her whole body arched upward as she came again. The stunning pleasure whipped through her body in a fireball of sensation. "Noooo." Her hips tried to buck—futilely.

Inside her, his fingers pressed deeper, thrusting in and out, before he returned to massaging her G-spot.

Her knees trembled in the restraints as pleasure after pleasure engulfed her. Her whole core was one tingling lake of sensation.

Mercilessly, he kept her going. His tongue flickered over her just enough to spark another wave. His fingers rubbed inside her. And her orgasm went on...forever.

When Holt finally straightened, sweat beaded on her skin, and her body was limp with satisfaction.

Amusement and heat shone in his eyes. "You're gorgeous when you come, Josie. I'm tempted to keep this going a while longer."

Still gasping for air, she stared at him in disbelief.

After removing the belts and releasing her arms and legs, he massaged the aches from her stiff shoulders and hips. "But I owe you a spanking, and it's not good to defer a punishment."

Her sluggish mind grappled for what he meant. Punishment? *Wait.*

As he picked her up and positioned her belly-down over his knees, she realized she should have *run.*

"No, no, I don't—you *can't.*" Her hands were flat on the carpet on one side of his legs and her feet on the other.

He caressed her bare bottom with his large, callused hand. "You have a great ass, have I mentioned that?" His palm stroking her felt so good in the aftermath of all those orgasms. "With your fair skin, my handprints are going to look very pretty."

Hand prints? Oh, Lord, no one had mentioned the man was a sadist. "Why do you want to hurt me? I'm not..."

"Not a masochist. I know, pet. It's like this—when aroused, many people will process pain as pleasure. Of course, not everyone does, so we'll explore and see where you fit on the continuum. This will be a bit of punishment and perhaps a lot of fun."

Fun? She'd never seen "spanking" listed in the dictionary under the definition of "fun".

He reached between her legs. At the sound of a familiar hum, she realized he'd positioned the wand vibrator to poke up between his thighs. With firm hands, he repositioned her hips, placing her pussy directly over the vibrating head.

As the vibrations struck her clit, and she jumped. "No. I'm too sensitive." She squirmed sideways so her nub of nerves wasn't touching the device.

"No worries. I'm going to move all the blood away from your pussy." His hand came down on her ass with a stinging whack.

"Ow!" Twisting, she put her hand over her butt to guard it.

"Uh-uh, sweetheart." He caught her wrist, pinned it to her lower back, and then smacked her harder. *Whap, whap.*

Tears filled her eyes and spilled over.

"I want you to keep both hands on the floor, Josie." His voice was...level. Firm. No anger—just instruction.

Even as she choked on a sob, the melting sensation started in the pit of her stomach again. He'd said he would tell her what he wanted. And that he wouldn't go further than she could take.

Only...her bottom was *stinging*.

But she trusted him.

Nevertheless, agreeing to be hurt wasn't easy at all.

I don't want to.

I will.

She pulled in a breath. "Yessir." When he released her wrist, she braced her hand on the floor. The sensation of relinquishing control was like opening a fist and feeling the blood flow back into cramped fingers. Achy and warm and wonderful.

"Good girl. I know that was hard." He massaged her stinging bottom. "Now breathe through the burn. And, by the way, you have permission to come."

Come—during a spanking?

With hard hands, he shifted her hips—and with his first slap on her bottom, she realized the new position put her clit directly over the device.

Stinging spanks rained over her burning skin—and from under her, the vibrator hammered her clit, sending her up and up. Gradually, the pain melted into a roiling hot pulse of sensation, driving her even higher.

Each smack on her bottom was like a hot wave of pleasure. Her clit was swelling, throbbing, and oh, she needed to come so badly that her body shook. "Pleeeeeze."

"All right, pet. I'll help you out since you asked so nicely." Chuckling, he gripped her hips, moving her...an inch.

The vibrator was suddenly buzzing on the other side of her clit—and the room flashed white. "Oh, oh, oh, ohhhhh." Not only her pussy but her entire body detonated, every cell and nerve shaking in pleasure, and the sensations surged through her until lights danced like stars in her head.

"Pretty Josie," he murmured.

He lifted her, twisted, and laid her on the bed, belly down.

Curling her fingers in the quilt, she lay there, shaking in the aftermath of her climax. Over the hammering of her pulse in her ears came the sound of his zipper and the crinkle of a condom wrapper.

She turned her head to watch.

Rising from a thatch of closely trimmed blond hair, his cock was straight and tall—and thick. A friend had a hypothesis that the thickness of a man's wrists indicated the girth of his shaft.

As Holt rolled on the condom, Josie studied his muscular forearms...and solid wrists. Her friend might be right.

The mattress compressed as Holt moved her legs apart and knelt between her thighs. "Up you come, pet." He gripped her waist firmly and lifted her onto her hands and knees.

When his cock pressed against her entrance, ferocious pleasure sizzled through the over-sensitive tissues. Oh God, her insides were still quivering from the last time she came.

He eased in an inch—and then penetrated her with one decisive thrust.

The sheer shock of his thick intrusion made her gasp. His size was almost unbearable, and her swollen pussy pulsed in protest... then growing pleasure.

"Easy, pet." Reaching around her, he slid his fingers over her puffy labia.

As his fingers tormented and teased her clit, everything inside her clamped down around his shaft, harder, harder, and suddenly, she came again in a rolling hard orgasm. "Oh, God."

Her arms gave out, dropping her onto her elbows. Her lungs burned as she gasped for air.

With an implacable grip, he held her there, impaled on his cock as pleasure simmered through her whole body. Through the surge of blood in her ears, she could hear his low, resonant laughter.

"You come so beautifully," he murmured. "It's a pleasure to watch." Leaning forward, he ran his hands over her back, around to fondle her breasts, and back down to take a new grip on her hips.

He pulled back, and she shuddered at the slick friction in her sensitized pussy. He pressed in and out a few times, the sensation growing more and more amazing. "Perfect. Brace yourself, pet."

Just the words in his smoky voice made her shiver...

He slowly increased to a hard hammering rhythm, and then his powerful hands were rocking her forward and yanking her back onto his shaft. The room filled with the slapping sounds of wet flesh. His grip was unbreakable, making her take what he gave her at a relentless, forceful pace.

He was using her for his own pleasure, and there was something so...satisfying about that.

"You feel incredible," he murmured. He slowed slightly, stroking his hands over her body again, up and down, and then over her well-spanked bottom.

Hissing, she flinched.

"A bit tender, pet?" He closed his big hands on her buttocks, squeezing the tender flesh.

The stinging, burning pain swept over her—and her pussy clenched his cock so hard that he laughed.

She loved making him laugh—his hands tightened on her, and he hammered into her, finally pressing deep, deeper—and she loved hearing him come with a throaty growl even more.

Josie was incredible. She'd given him her body, let him bind her, spank her, fuck her, let go of control, submitted. Her response to submitting to him was humbling. Gratifying. She trusted him.

Cared for him.

He pulled her into his arms, needing to hold her for a minute, to breathe her in. When she laid her head on his shoulder, contentment swept through him, and he rubbed his cheek against her hair.

God, she was amazing. And he loved her.

Jesus, he really did. This was what he'd wanted with others and never found—she not only cared for him, but she'd also given him this profound trust. He didn't feel deserving, but he'd protect her gift with everything in his power. His arms closed more forcefully around her, and rather than pulling away, she cuddled closer.

Yeah, he could stay right here with her in his arms...forever.

Unfortunately, eventually, he had to move. After disposing of the condom, he brought back a warm washcloth and ignored her objections as he cleaned her sensitive pussy and ass. Sure, she could do it—as she said—but why deny himself the pleasure?

He'd found a bruise ointment on her bathroom counter—probably for Carson. This time, it would be for her. "Hold still, sweetheart. This will help keep you from bruising." Sitting beside her, he rolled her toward him onto her face...and massaged the medication into her reddened ass.

"Hey! No, stop. Dammit." Her voice was so husky from multiple orgasms that even her outraged protests were sexy.

He grinned. Was it perverse to enjoy seeing the red hand-prints he'd left on her white skin?

Years ago, when he'd entered the BDSM lifestyle, leaving marks had made him feel like the biggest asshole in the world. Now, he'd learned the right amount of pain could open the way to a truly mind-blowing orgasm for a woman.

And the removal of a submissive's control over her own pain and pleasure could enhance the bond between them.

As it had tonight.

Did Josie realize trust went both ways?

Setting the ointment on the nightstand, he finished stripping and joined her on the bed. She was a soft bundle as he pulled her against him and put his arm under her head.

She blinked, her eyes slightly red from tears and sleepy with satisfaction. "You're an evil, mean person. I think you enjoyed applying that ointment far too much."

"I did." He kissed her lightly.

Her tiny snort of exasperation made him grin. As she looked up at him, her brows drew together, her gaze focusing on the rough scar-ring beneath his chin. With a light touch, she ran her fingers over it.

"Josie."

Not answering, she pushed herself up. Her face showed no

expression...at first...as she traced his scar from temple to jaw. Touched the burn scar on his neck. Bent to kiss the shiny burn scars on his shoulders.

His heart was melting inside his chest.

Exploring further, she found more burns. The still healing, slightly raised knife slices on his forearms. A few marks from his childhood when he hadn't dodged his aunt's boyfriend fast enough.

Her lip quivered when she touched the long knife wound on his belly. "Oh, God, Holt. You've had such a painful life."

Damn, she was killing him. "Sweetheart, they're just surface scars." He pulled her down on top of him, all soft tenderhearted woman. "You have just as many, but they're buried deep."

"I...probably. They might be healing up a bit, though."

"I'm pleased." That was what he hoped to achieve. He ran his fingers through her hair. "And I'm pleased with what we did tonight. You enjoyed yourself, it seemed."

"Mmm." Her lips curved slightly as she laid her hand on his cheek. "Honestly, I think I'm in shock."

"Well..." He put his hand on top of hers, holding her palm against his cheek. Would this make her retreat? Yet honesty and open communication were a Dom's duty. "I think *I'm* in love."

Joy. Yes, he could see happiness bloom in her eyes before she shut it all down. "No. No, you can't—"

"Mmm. I'm pretty sure I can."

Her eyes were huge. Appalled. "No, Sir."

Yes, he had more work in front of him. "Josie, I love you." Gently, he pushed her bangs out of her eyes. "Relax, pet. There's no hurry, no obligation."

"You don't understand."

"I have a fair notion of how you feel about me, Josie." If there hadn't been more than friendship between them, the little subbie would never have let him tie her up or spank her—and she sure wouldn't have come like that. Because for a woman, an orgasm was the most intimate gift she could give.

Josie might be submissive, but she was the kind of woman who needed to trust to let go truly. She had opened to him, given him her body and her climaxes.

More than that, she cared for him. Everything she did showed it.

But would it be enough to overcome the hurts in her past and her worry about Holt being in Carson's life?

Well, he was a patient man, and healing was what he loved to do.

CHAPTER EIGHTEEN

"Honestly, Laurent, get over it." On Friday afternoon, Josie glared at the words on her computer monitor. Redheaded Laurent should be acting like a heroine, working on her fire control. Not gazing into Tigre's eyes and getting all melty.

Damn that Tigre anyway. The inspiration she'd used for him was the muscular, blond Thor from the *Avengers* movies.

And now Josie had a walking, talking example of the sexy Thunder God living next door.

"Now, listen to me, girl," she ordered Laurent in her best authorial voice. "I totally know why you'd fall for Tigre but too bad. No romance. *Period.*" It didn't matter if the girl got flutters and weak legs whenever she saw the guy. And there would be no surging joy at words of love.

Words of love. Josie's heart did a slow somersault inside her chest. Holt *loved* her.

She gave her head a shake—something she'd done so often today that Oma had asked her if she had an earache.

Not an earache but a heartache. Because Holt was certifiably insane. Deranged. Loco. Crazy as a cuckoo. A few hoses short of a fire truck…oh, that was a good one. She needed to use that on him sometime.

Only…she shouldn't see him.

But she wanted to. Josie yanked at her hair in frustration. Maybe she was the one going insane.

Surely, his feelings of "love" merely meant he'd gotten caught up in the emotions of sex. And domination. Uzuri'd told her that submissives often got swayed by intense scenes and believed they felt more than a D/s connection.

Holt was a Dom, true, but…still…maybe he'd been affected by the stupendous sex.

Right?

Josie pressed her hand over the ache under her sternum. Hearing him say he loved her had been…staggering.

And then he hadn't left after they'd made love. He'd held her in his arms all night. Woke her at dawn with kisses and told her he loved her again, then took her in plain old vanilla missionary style and told her again.

She'd made him breakfast and…and it had felt so right, having him in the kitchen. Talking over their upcoming days, just acting normal. Teasing him, knowing she'd get pinned against the counter and kissed.

She pursed her lips, breathing out, and rubbed her chest. He loved her.

And…God help her, she loved *him*.

She bit her lip. If…he broke it off, it would hurt badly.

But maybe Holt was different. No, she *knew* Holt was different. He wasn't anything like her father or Everett. He'd never abandon someone because that person made a mistake. He wouldn't care more for his reputation than for a person.

Wouldn't betray her trust.

What about Carson? Holt was providing the guy-time her son needed. Her boy deserved to know someone as amazing as Holt.

Because Holt really was incredible.

But relationships went south sometimes, just because. For her boy's sake, she should be careful. Go slow.

She smiled slightly, feeling an upwelling of hope. She'd see Holt tonight at the Shadowlands and...and maybe afterward? Maybe he'd want to come home with her again?

Please, let it work out.

CHAPTER NINETEEN

Hearing doors slam across the street, Holt paused in the basketball game. Josie, Carson, and Stella got out of the car. Church must be over.

"Catch, Holt," Wedge called.

Brought back to reality, Holt caught the ball, took two steps, and did a nice layup.

Duke and Elijah groaned as the basketball ringed the hoop and dropped in. Holt exchanged fist-bumps with Wedge as Elijah rebounded and tossed the ball to his teammate.

While Duke dribbled in an erratic pattern, working his way toward the hoop, Holt asked, "You guys know I'm a firefighter, yeah?"

"Sure, man. We know." Duke dodged left.

Holt blocked. "You know about the middle school problems— some dumbass starting fires?"

"Heard that." Duke passed the ball to his teammate, barely getting by Holt's hand.

The kid zipped around Wedge and took a shot. Missed.

Holt rebounded and tossed the ball to Wedge who took a shot from where he stood. *Score.*

"Good shot!" Holt caught the ball on the way down. Instead of tossing the ball to Duke, he studied the three teens around him. They were uncomfortable, their gazes on the ball, rather than him. They knew something, dammit.

"Listen, guys. I've rescued children from burning buildings. And sometimes we arrive too fucking late." His jaw clenched at the memories. The sights, the scents, the sheer ghastliness of something that should never happen. "I know ratting out a friend is bad, but Jesus, don't put me through having to see a child burned to death again."

The boys were silent. He knew they'd heard him. Felt him. Because, contrary to belief, most kids were fucking openhearted and sensitive. A person just had to break through all the noise in their lives.

"Whoever's starting fires isn't one of us," Wedge said, finally. "I mean, not someone from the high school. Or a grownup. It's someone who goes to the middle school."

Holt felt his gut tighten. Young arsonists sometimes used fire as their way of coping...and could start hundreds of fires over a lifetime.

"Don't know more than that," Duke said.

Holt nodded. "Thanks." He tossed the ball to Elijah who spun, feinted, spun again, and shot the ball into Duke's hands. The teen dodged from the corner and scored.

"Nice job." Grinning, Holt heard his cell ring, glanced at the display, and backed away to answer it. "What's up, Jake?"

His friend sighed. "Problems. You know my vet clinic and the local animal shelter are co-hosting the adoption benefit today. The one at the local pet store?"

"Seems like you mentioned it. And?"

"And several of the shelter staff are home with the flu. I'm looking for warm bodies—no experience necessary—to help for three hours this afternoon."

"Sure, I'm in." Holt turned to look across the street at Josie's house. She'd invited him to the post-church dinner. Bet he could draft them into working. "I might manage to nab another one or two."

His woman wouldn't turn down a good cause.

As he hung up, he smiled. Fuck, he really did love her—although sometimes she looked at him as if she was thinking about fleeing the city, if not the state. Poor little subbie. She loved him. She might not say the words, but her body and emotions didn't lie.

On Friday and Saturday, he'd spent time with her at the Shadowlands, and after they returned home, he'd jumped the fence and used the sliding glass doors on her patio. He'd gone back home before Carson returned from Stella's place.

Someday, Josie would realize he was in her life to stay, and the sneaking around could end.

He could think of nothing finer than to wake with her in his arms every morning for the rest of their lives. When her worries weren't running through her head, she was funny, logical, caring, cute, smart, and strong enough to hold her own...or to let him take control.

However, when her past came to the forefront, she tried to pull away. Old hurts took time to heal.

When Beth and Nolan had adopted two abused boys, their social worker told them trust wouldn't happen completely until the children had lived with them for as many years as they'd been abused.

Holt shook his head. Just as well he was a patient Dom. Josie —and Carson—were worth waiting for.

Today, he'd go over and talk them into helping facilitate furball adoptions.

Followed by her son and great-aunt, Josie accompanied Holt through the pet store. Near the center, dogs in crates and on leashes filled the fenced-off area normally used for dog training. An eight-feet-high, transparent mesh tent held cats in carriers. At the opening in the fenced-off area, several people sat at a long table to handle with the pet adoption paperwork.

The adoption event appeared to be off to a fine start. Several potential adopters were already visiting with the animals. One young man was on his knees, crooning to a big mixed-breed dog. "Wanna go home with me, boy? I've got a big backyard and—"

"Holt, Josie, you came!" Hazel eyes bright with enthusiasm, Rainie motioned them into the fenced-off area. She was in jeans with a peasant shirt under a blue vest bearing the name of Jake's vet clinic and "ADOPTION STAFF". Her colorful brown hair was pulled back. "I'm sorry to mess up your Sunday. Whoever heard of everyone getting sick at once?"

"It happens during flu season. We had some firefighters out last week." Holt turned to Oma. "Stella, this is Rainie who manages a vet clinic near here. Rainie, this is Stella Avery, Josie's great-aunt, and this young man is Josie's son Carson."

"I'm delighted to meet you both." Rainie gave Oma an assessing look. "Mrs. Avery, how would you feel about helping with the screening paperwork and fee? Marcus can show you the ropes since he's handled the last three adoptions on his own."

Oma nodded. "I'm very good with paperwork. Lead me to it."

"Perfect." Rainie offered Oma her arm and called, "Gabi, can you put Holt and his crew to work?"

"You bet." Also in a blue vest, the strawberry blonde with a teal streak in her hair was easy to recognize. Gabi and her Dom, Marcus, had been the ones to stand up for Josie against Amber. "Welcome to insanity, you guys. I'm so glad you came."

Carson eyed Gabi's temp tattoos—orange kittens spiraled around her forearms—and grinned.

Josie put a hand on his shoulder. "Gabi, this is my son, Carson."

Gabi delighted Carson by shaking his hand. "It's good to meet you, Carson. You're going to have fun today. Our job is helping match people with pets, supervising the meetings, and escorting the new family to the front to get their paperwork done."

Carson stuck his hands in his pockets. "Sounds cool."

"It really is." Gabi dug into a box under the paperwork table and handed over blue vests. "Here, this makes you look official."

Josie pulled on the vest, saw Holt had moved to talk with Marcus, and Carson was...

Already in his blue vest, Carson was down on his knees in front of a cat carrier.

Josie, you idiot. Major parenting blunder. Their apartment hadn't allowed animals, but they lived in a house now, and her boy would spend the next few hours surrounded by adorable fur babies longing for a home.

Stepping back beside her, Holt followed her gaze. "You're so screwed."

"You *knew* this would happen, didn't you?"

"Sweetheart. A boy needs a pet." As he put an arm around her, and she saw the devilish quirk of his lips.

"You...evil person." She considered kicking him in the shin. No, that would set a bad example for her baby. "I'm going to add you into my book. As a villain. And have you dismembered. And de-dicked."

"Aren't you a vicious one? Ouch." Maybe Holt was evil, but his warm, masculine laughter could pull angels from the sky.

Gabi snickered. "I'm so going to read your books."

"You know I'm an author?"

"Holt told us how good your series is, and I love YA."

Holt told people about her writing? Boasted about her? Her next breath fought for room with the burgeoning happiness in her heart.

Gabi hooked her arm in Josie's. "If Carson is good with cats, how about you three help with the felines. Kim and Raoul and some of the others are handling the dogs."

"Lead the way." Josie realized Carson wasn't the only one suffering from a pet craving. "I'd love it."

The time passed swiftly. After perusing the history and personality information taped to each cat carrier, Josie used the knowledge to match adopters with adoptees. Each time someone chose a cat to adopt, she barely refrained from doing a happy dance.

Returning after another adoption, she glanced around the tent. The shelter staff had brought in more cats as carriers were emptied. On one side, Carson was teaching a youngster how to hold a kitten without getting scratched. A young couple was wandering from carrier to carrier.

An older, battle-scarred cat—the one no one wanted—was out of his cage. Rubbing his cheek against an elderly woman's chin, he was purring so hard his thin frame shook. Josie pulled in a breath and turned to wipe her eyes.

"Easy, pet." Holt moved to her side. The man—no, the Dom —saw everything. Wrapping a big hand around her nape, he tucked her head against his shoulder and let her blink away the tears. Sheltering her.

Pulling in his scent, she sighed, wishing she could stay, right there, forever. "Thank you," she whispered.

"Mmmhmm." He planted a kiss on top of her head and let her go.

"Sir, I'm taking this cat. What is the next step?" At the call from the elderly lady, Holt brushed his knuckles over Josie's cheek and went to assist.

As the time went on, she couldn't seem to stop watching him. Wanting to help. If he needed a hand with a cat, or a ribbon to mark an adoption, or...anything...she tried to be there for him.

When she'd fetched drinks for all of them, Holt had taken the can she handed him, seen it was Mountain Dew, and the smile he'd given her and his soft, "Thank you, sweetheart," had made her heart sing. She'd always liked to be helpful but doing something for Holt lit a glow in her heart.

As the time for closing neared, there was a lull in the visitors to the feline tent. Stepping out, Josie turned in a circle to see what to do next.

Raoul and Kim—the Shadowlands Master and his "slave"— were busy with the dogs. It was interesting to see Kim watching Raoul, giving him anything he needed before he needed to ask, and responding to the slightest motion on his part.

Josie snorted.

"What's funny?" Gabi walked over.

"I just realized that Master Raoul watches Kim as intently as she does him." Josie nodded to where the muscular Master wrapped his arm around Kim's waist, easing her away from a redneck who was trying to put the moves on her.

"I thought at first it was just me, then just the submissives— and it was overwhelming at first. But you're right, it's a two-way street." The redhead glanced at the table, and yes, Marcus's gaze was on Gabi. The exchange of looks held so much love and heat that Josie couldn't help but be envious.

Turning away, Josie looked for *her* two guys.

Holt stood outside the cat tent, looking in. Looking at...

Face filled with joy, Carson had a big black cat in his lap. Petting it. Talking to it.

Seeing Holt's tender expression as he watched her son twisted Josie's heart.

"So..." Gabi grinned and shoulder-bumped Josie. "Are you going to cave in and let Carson take the kitty home?"

Josie sighed. "I can't believe I didn't anticipate this." But she'd been too flustered when Holt had asked them to spend the afternoon with him. Honestly, her brain turned to total mush around the man.

"Holt!" A tall blonde called from outside the fencing. "Holt. Oh, it's you. Amazing. What are you doing here?" She dodged past two people walking dogs and grabbed Holt's hands. "I heard you broke up with Nadia. Oh, it's so good to see you again."

He smiled down at her. "Di, how are you?"

A bolt of sheer, green-eyed jealousy shot right into Josie's chest.

Gabi put an arm around her waist. "Go and shoo her off, girl-friend. Let her know he's not free."

Josie bit her lip. "But...he is. Really. We don't have—"

"You have something, Josie. You were talking about how Raoul watches Kim? Holt treats you like a girlfriend *and* watches you like a Dom with his submissive."

Josie's mouth dropped open. "He...what?"

"Would you like to go out for drinks after this event is over?" Still gripping Holt's hands, Di leaned forward and gazed up at him with big eyes. "I'm free this evening."

"Lord help us, she's going do the sexy hair flip any second now," Gabi muttered. "Go and save him."

"No." As Josie shook her head, she realized Holt was studying her.

He obviously knew she and Gabi were watching. He didn't answer the woman, and he didn't look away from Josie. When Josie didn't move, his eyes narrowed. Then he smiled down at the blonde.

Josie's heart sank. If he made a date with that woman, it would...hurt. But he had that right. She was the one who said she didn't date. Didn't do relationships. Hadn't said she loved him.

Di patted his chest. "We should—"

"I'm sorry, sweets, but I can't. I've fallen hard for a woman, and I'm not seeing anyone else." Smoothly disengaging, he nodded toward Josie. "There's my Josie."

My Josie. He'd *claimed* her. Even though Josie kept pulling away, Holt was claiming her in public. She didn't know what to say. Couldn't seem to breathe past the huge thickness in her throat.

"Oh." Di pouted. "I was sure you'd take longer to get over Nadia."

"I realized fast enough that everything worked out for the best." Holt grinned. "Since you can't have me, can I suggest a good-looking feline?" He motioned to a green-eyed cat in one of the show cages.

The blonde laughed. "Nice try. Unfortunately, my dog hates cats and so do I. I'd better get his dog treats and get back."

"It was good to see you. Stay safe."

As Di moved off, Josie let out a long breath. "I wish I could handle people as smoothly as he does," she muttered to Gabi.

Gabi laughed. "I've seen you working the bar, and you're... almost...as tactful as he is. Just almost—because I'm not sure anyone has skills quite up to his."

"Ladies, did you enjoy the show?" Holt was suddenly beside Josie and bent down to give her a firm kiss. "Were you taking bets on how quickly I could extract myself?"

Gabi laughed. "Actually, we were admiring your skill. Not even Marcus is as charming."

Holt glanced over to where Marcus was helping an older man fill out adoption papers. "That's because Marcus is a lawyer—they're all about the winning. I'm a firefighter, paramedic, and nurse. We're all about the helping."

"You really are." Josie stared at him. Her heart had that crazy overstuffed feeling again, like when she'd watched him during Anne's labor. He was just so...astonishing.

And as he looked down at her, his eyes were warm and tender and the most incredible blue-gray. Hearing Gabi give a small laugh, Josie realized she'd gotten trapped in his gaze. Again.

Forcing herself to look away, she noticed Carson was watch-

ing. From the sulky scowl aimed at Holt, her son had heard Holt
laying claim to Josie.

Closing her eyes, she pulled in a breath.

Every day, she fell harder for Holt. It was time to stop
pretending and have a talk with Carson about grownups and
dating and...and stuff.

Home from the adoption event, Carson set the cat carrier down
in his room and opened the door. "Hey, Poe. C'mon out."

Yellow-green eyes studied him, and Carson held completely
still. *Please like it here. Please like me.*

Slowly, Poe rose. Stopped at the door. Looked at the room.
Looked at Carson. Took two steps.

Carson held out his fingers.

Poe sniffed him and considered before butting his furry black
head against Carson's hand.

Tears prickled Carson's eyes. The cat still liked him. "I guess
we're gonna do okay." It was hard not to pull Poe into his lap for a
hug, for petting, but that would be like...like Holt yanking him
into a hug.

Maybe it'd be kind of nice, but it wouldn't be cool.

Carson growled under his breath. Not cool at all because the
guy was hitting on Mom. He was a neighbor and had the hots for
Mom. That wasn't right.

And Mom liked Holt back. She...watched him, and he
watched her. She leaned against him on the couch. And Holt
kissed her sometimes.

Carson's chest felt funny. She was *Mom*.

And then Poe ambled onto his lap, its tail brushing his chin.
Slowly, Carson stroked down the black fur. *I have a cat.*

Carson let out a breath. Holt'd been the one who took them
to the adoption event. And when Carson had asked Mom if he

could bring Poe home, Holt had winked at him and helped the lady Mom had been assisting. He'd given Carson a chance to talk Mom into adopting Poe.

And he'd helped Carson with the new phone and helped put cool stuff on it. He'd even added his phone number into the contacts list. Holt really was an okay guy.

Why couldn't he just stay a neighbor...and leave Mom alone?

A tap on the door sounded. "Permission to enter, captain?"

Carson rolled his eyes and half-grinned. Sometimes his mom was so weird. "Come."

Carrying a grocery sack, she walked in, saw Poe, and closed the door behind her. "I see he's found a good place to sit while he checks out the accommodations."

Poe had settled down, draped over Carson's lap.

Mom set the sack down. "Here's the litter box and litter, food and dishes. You can put the litter box in that empty spot in your bathroom. We'll keep Poe in your room for a couple of days so he knows that's his spot, then he can have the run of the house."

"Okay."

She took a step toward the door and hesitated. "About... Um..."

"What?"

"Carson, even mothers like to...well, have friends. Grown-up friends."

"You have friends."

"Mothers who aren't married also go out with men. Sometimes. Like dating."

His teeth made a funny grinding noise. "Yeah. So?"

"So, I know you like Holt. He's...well, we're seeing each other. He asked me to go out with him on New Year's Eve."

Shit-buckets. Carson scowled. They'd always spent New Year's Eve together and now Holt was ruining it. Ruining everything. "Uh-huh."

"Carson?"

Carson looked down at Poe. The cat's tail twitched. Up. Down. "Poe needs his food. I need to get him set up."

After a second, she sighed. "I hear you, honey. All right."

CHAPTER TWENTY

Following the hostess, Holt put his hand on Josie's lower back and guided her past the noisy, packed bar and into the restaurant section where only the clink of silverware and low hum of conversation broke the quiet. An upscale restaurant, Georgina's had become increasingly popular, and on New Year's Eve, there was a line out the door and a long, long waiting list. He was damn lucky Georgina had fit them in. Whatever he'd owe Clancy in favors would be worth it.

Holt smiled at the lovely woman at his side. Being a guy, he did adore having Josie completely naked, but he had to say, she was pretty damn gorgeous when she got dressed up. He'd almost swallowed his tongue when she'd opened the door tonight. Her deep green dress set off her beautiful eyes and dark red hair. Cut almost to her waist, the bodice revealed the inside curves of her breasts. Wonderfully snug to mid-thigh, the skirt section had a tantalizing slit in the front.

When he'd made a circle with his finger, and she dutifully twirled for him, he'd seen her entire back was bared except for the tiny straps. *Jesus.*

Although he'd figured she couldn't possibly be wearing underwear, he'd managed to wait until he got her outside before checking.

No underwear. He'd been half-erect ever since.

"Did I tell you how beautiful you look tonight?"

Her tiny snort made him grin. "You did. You know, in Texas, we'd say 'that girl cleans up well'".

"Baby, you clean up very, very, well." He kissed her lightly, then held her chair for her.

As he took his seat, the hostess handed them menus, introduced their server, and added, "Ms. Georgina wants you to have a wonderful evening—and says I'm to note your lady's dislikes. Otherwise, she's in charge of your meal."

Josie blinked, and then laughed. "You know the most interesting people, Holt." After a second's thought, she told the server, "I hate raw fish in any form. Otherwise, I like everything."

"Very good, miss."

The server left. The sommelier appeared, opened a bottle of wine, elicited Holt's approval, poured their glasses, and disappeared.

Josie was shaking her head. "I've never had service like this. Are you some billionaire and didn't tell me?"

"I do okay but no." Holt clinked his glass against hers. "Georgina is married to one of my firefighter crew—you'll meet them all one of these days—and she thinks I should get out more."

Josie's lips tipped up. "I take it she doesn't know about your Friday and Saturday nights at the den of kinky sin."

"Ah, no." Holt sipped the wine and smiled at the rich smoky flavor. "She does know Nadia and I aren't together any longer."

"Holt, I'm beginning to think the entire city knows about your ex."

He grinned. "Yeah, well, Nadia isn't one for keeping anything private." He reached across the table and squeezed Josie's hand. "You, however, are a whole different animal."

But he wasn't going to push. Not...yet. Instead, he turned to lighter subjects. "Is Carson going to fight with Stella over what to watch tonight?"

Josie relaxed, laughed, and started in on a Carson story.

Sometime later, Josie frowned as Holt poured the last of the wine into her glass. Not that she was complaining, but she had to admit her mind was a bit fuzzy. "You stopped at one, and I've had...a lot more."

"I'm driving," he said easily, then rose at the approach of a beautiful brunette in a black suit. "Georgina, you outdid yourself with the selection. Please give our compliments to your staff." He bent down to kiss her cheek.

She beamed at him. "I surely will, sugar." Turning she smiled at Josie. "I'm Georgina. It's wonderful to have you both here this evening." The sincerity in her Southern-accented voice couldn't be mistaken.

"Will you join us?" Holt asked.

Georgina looked delighted. "If I won't be intruding, I'd love to sit for a moment." Before she even turned, an attentive wait staff carried over another chair and seated her.

Josie almost laughed, thinking of the way the submissives hovered around all the Shadowlands Masters. "You have amazing people here."

"Oh, I do." Georgina smiled up at the young man. "Thank you, Manuel. Can you bring us a carafe of coffee, please?"

"Right away, ma'am."

The brunette settled into her chair with a comfortable wiggle and turned to look Holt over. "All recovered? Clancy said you're back at work." She added to Josie, "My Clancy works with him at the station." The wedding ring on her finger said her Clancy was probably a husband.

"I'm back to normal," Holt agreed.

"Good. Stupid nasty stalker." Georgina put a hand on Holt's face and frowned at the long scar. "That's healing, too. Good."

He laughed. "You have a soft heart, sweetie. By the way, Clancy told me the restaurant is delivering leftover food to the homeless shelter. Thank you."

"How could we not help after I saw what they were eating?" She turned to Josie. "The homeless shelter is one of Holt's pet projects. Everyone at the fire station has been dragged there to help with upgrading the building."

A homeless shelter? Josie glanced at Holt.

"It's a good place." His mouth tightened. "Living on the streets is...Well, sometimes people simply need a hand to get back on their feet."

Living on the streets. Those months had been the most terrifying, hopeless time of her life. Looking down, Josie swirled the wine in her glass. As she took a big swallow, she realized Holt's gaze was on her.

A waiter appeared and leaned down to whisper, "Georgina, the chef requests a word."

"Well, shoot. I didn't even get to hear how you two met." With a tiny pout, Georgina rose. "Josie, it was lovely to meet you. Holt, don't be a stranger."

Josie watched her sail away. "She's amazing."

"Yeah, she is. And under the southern charm is one sharp businesswoman. Clancy adores her." Holt leaned forward to take Josie's hand. "Why do I get the impression you were homeless for a while?"

Her mouth went dry. "It was a long time ago."

He rubbed the back of her hand with his thumb. "Guess that means we have something else in common, hmm?"

She stared at him. Not even the thin scar could detract from his gorgeous chiseled features. He wore the tailored black suit with the easy grace of someone who was to the manor born. "*You* were never homeless."

A corner of his mouth tipped up. "I'll share if you will."

"No." Talking about that time was something she never did.

He waited, the bastard.

She was dying to know why he'd been living on the streets. Stalling, she took another swallow of wine. *No, Josie.* His past wasn't important. She didn't need to know.

Dammit. "You first."

He turned her hand over and gave her a formal handshake. "We have a deal."

Leaning back, he drank his coffee. "My mother died of a brain tumor. A couple of years later—I was a bit older than Carson—my father was killed in a car accident, leaving a choice of foster care or my aunt. She took me in but her new boyfriend turned out to be a drug dealer. A violent, abusive drug dealer. He decided I'd make the perfect drug runner."

Josie stared and tried to imagine Carson being used to deliver drugs. "Your aunt let him?"

"She protested, and he beat the crap out of us both." Holt shook his head. "I'd been pretty sheltered, and the guy scared me to death. Between him and his customers, I got to be really fast on my feet."

"Oh my God."

"Unfortunately, he and his buyers noticed how fucking pretty I was." With a rueful smile, Holt ran a finger down his unscarred cheek. "The bastard tried to pimp me out. That's when my aunt and I stole his car and ran."

"Oh, thank God." Heart thudding hard, Josie took Holt's hand in both of hers.

He lifted her hands and kissed them. "That reaction there is why I love you," he said softly.

Oh. To hear him say that... Her voice came out husky. "Were you all right once you got away?"

"We lived in shelters until she found a job doing janitorial work. Tough work. But not long after that, my mom's agent saw me and—"

"Agent?" Josie interrupted.

"Mom was a model until she got sick. Her agent had adored her and hated what'd happened to me. So he found me jobs—catalogs, magazines, ads, commercials. We needed the money, especially when Aunt Rita's health started to fail."

How much loss could one child endure? Her heart ached for him. His voice was light, but the bottom line was he went to work when he was Carson's age. "I bet being a good-looking boy didn't help any in the shelters."

He gave a huff of agreement. "Some places were better than others...as you probably know." His thumb rubbed over the back of her hand. "Your turn, pet. Why'd you end up on the streets?"

"I grew up in a tiny Texas town. Mama took off when I was thirteen—ran away with a trucker. Pa was strict, being as he was a rancher and pillar of the church, and he turned bitter cold after Mama left. When I told him I was pregnant, he gave me an hour to get my stuff and all my whore's belongings—and told me never to return."

"But..." A muscle hardened in Holt's cheek. "You were sixteen."

"Yep." Her smile felt crooked. "A few months before, when I started an after-school job, he'd given me one of the ranch clunkers so I could drive to town. So, when I left, I had a vehicle and the money I'd saved up from working after school."

"I bet you drove from Texas to Florida, positive your good buddy Everett would help. The asshole."

A bubble of laughter rose at Holt's disdain. "You guessed it. Thus, I landed on the streets. It's tough to make enough money to survive, and shelters sure are scary. However, the staff at one place was amazing. They helped me find work and cheap housing."

He nodded. "They do try."

"Is that why you help out? Because you know what the streets are like?"

"That's why." He was still studying her. "Where was Stella when all this was going on?"

"Oh, her husband died before Pa threw me out, and since everything reminded her of him—they'd lived in New York—she took an overseas job. Pa didn't get along with her, and she didn't learn I'd been kicked out for years."

"How'd she find you?"

"When she retired and returned to the States, she visited the ranch. Apparently, after quite a shouting match, he handed over the letters I'd written to him." She breathed past the stab of pain. "He never opened even one."

"What a fucking bastard."

"Forgiveness wasn't in his vocabulary." How different her life might have been otherwise. "Anyway, Oma found me and was appalled—although I thought I was doing pretty well by then. She fell in love with Carson and decided to settle in Tampa."

"I'm surprised she didn't buy a house and move you in."

"She wanted to," Josie admitted, smiling at the memory. "But she was getting on in years, was used to living with only her quiet husband, and then by herself. Carson was a young, very energetic boy. Instead, we visited several times a week, and she insisted on babysitting him during my evening jobs." Josie took a sip of her wine. "Honestly, I was afraid if we overwhelmed her, she'd run back to Europe."

Holt grinned. "She's tougher than that."

"Yes, she really is. I'm so glad we're close enough to help when she needs a hand." She gave him a rueful smile. "This is the first time I won't see the New Year in with her and Carson."

Holt squeezed her fingers and glanced at his watch. "How about we join them for the countdown?"

"Really?"

"Sure. I can't think of anything I'd like better. Let's order up a dessert to treat everyone at home, and I'll ask Georgina for a bottle of champagne and something Carson would like."

Her eyes filled with unexpected tears as he turned to signal the waiter. Oh, she really did love him, so very much.

CHAPTER TWENTY-ONE

On Saturday, Carson walked out of his house in a filthy mood. Mom was cleaning and singing along with Huey Lewis and was all happy and everything.

Scowling, he pushed the garbage can down the driveway. Last night, he had sneaked into the kitchen for some cookies and on the way back, heard Holt talking. In Mom's room. In the effing middle of the *night*.

Were they doing, like...*sex*? Was Holt Mom's boyfriend?

Carson left the garbage can at the curb and wished he could dump it all over Holt's yard. Would Holt marry Mom? Be around all the time?

Jeez. Was everything going to change...again? He'd already dealt with a new house and neighbors and friends. And a new school.

His shoulders slumped. Break was over. He'd be back in school on Monday and have to see Jorgeson. Would the science teacher be able to figure out who'd burned his classroom?

"Morning, Carson. How's it going?" Holt came out of his duplex.

Carson smiled before remembering the guy'd been in Mom's room. "Hey."

"This is my day off, and I want to talk your mom into going out for pizza later. You in?"

Pizza, all *right*.

No.

Holt had the hots for his mom, and Mom was eating it up.

A sick feeling rolled over him until he wanted to run into his bedroom and slam the door so hard that his mom—and this *neighbor*—would know how he felt. "I...I'm hanging with friends today."

"Ah. Too bad." Holt stuck his hands in his shorts pockets. "You've probably noticed I like your mom, Carson. And you. I hope—"

"So, you go to work Monday, right? As a firefighter?"

The man blinked, then a corner of his mouth lifted.

Carson's face was hot; his hands, too cold.

"That's right. I actually do more of—"

"A big, hot firefighter." After a fire engine demo at school, Carson'd heard the girls talking weird about hot guys and muscles. Holt was a firefighter; no wonder Mom was stupid about him.

Carson curled his lip. "Girls like firefighters. Is that why you went for it? Instead of doing something normal like running a store?"

Holt tried to think what he'd done to piss Carson off. Nothing...except date his mother. It seemed he had a jealous boy on his hands. He should have anticipated this. The boy had shown flashes of possessive behavior previously. Since Josie's only dates had been when Carson was a toddler, the child hadn't been forced to deal with a man in his mother's life. Not until Holt.

Besides, Josie might not be the only one with trust issues. Everett had rejected Carson as well. "Actually, I was around your age when I decided to be a firefighter. Girls weren't even a blip on my horizon."

Probably braced for Holt's anger, the boy looked as if the mild answer had messed up his balance. "My age?"

That day...wasn't Holt's favorite. But Carson needed to see him as a person, not a rival for Josie's affection. "Yeah. My dad and I were on a mountain road. A drunk in a pickup took a curve too fast and smashed head-on into our car. Pinned my dad in the seat."

Holt's stomach twisted. He'd been knocked out. Woke to hear his dad groaning. Trying to talk. Struggling to breathe. He'd panicked, needing to help—only he couldn't even get his door open. "Other cars stopped, but the grass under the pickup caught fire. It was fall. Everything was bone dry. Within minutes, the fire was spreading to the trees."

Carson's eyes were huge. "What happened?"

"A fire truck showed up, sirens screaming." God, he still remembered the sense of awe when it appeared. The feeling of being rescued. He managed to smile. "They were amazing, and they got the fire out."

"What about the drunk? His truck was on fire?"

Not everyone could be saved. Holt looked away from the kid's big eyes. "Neither he nor his passenger made it. It wasn't good." The pickup's tank had blown, killing the drunk and the young daughter. The girl's voice was the first—and the most devastating —of the screams that haunted Holt's dreams. *Children and fire —dammit.*

"Jeez. Was your dad okay?"

"The firefighters cut the door off and got him out." Holt could still taste the smoke in the air, hear his dad's groans. Memories...sucked.

Carson stared up into his face, and his lip quivered. "But was he o-okay?"

Holt shook his head. "No. The crash messed him up, and he died a couple of days later. But without the firefighters, he'd have died there, choking on his own blood."

313

The boy turned pale.

Holt winced. *Too blunt, dumbass.* "Sorry, Carson. It's not a good memory. But, yeah, that's when I decided I wanted to be a firefighter." They'd known what to do, moved as a team, had been gentle with his dad—and Holt, too.

The kid swallowed. "You had your mom though. Your mom was okay, right?"

"She'd died a couple of years earlier from a brain tumor." During that last year, her ability to care for herself, to move, to eat had disappeared. Much of what he knew about compassion and caring for others had come from watching his father with her. The tenderness he had shown, the love.

An arm slipped around his waist, and Josie pressed against his side. When had she joined them?

She hugged him. "I'm so sorry, Holt. I know it was years ago—and I know it must still hurt."

"What-what happened to you? With no parents?" Carson looked like he wanted to hug Holt, too. Angry with Holt or not, the kid had a big heart.

"My aunt took me in."

Josie's face turned hard. "But his aunt's boyfriend beat him up. Made him run drugs."

Carson's mouth dropped open.

Josie growled. "You never said—is that jerk dead, or can I kill him?"

"I'll help," Carson muttered.

Their protectiveness sent warmth through Holt's heart. Reaching out, he pulled Carson into a one-armed hug—and the boy hugged him back. Hard. "Thanks, you two. No worries, though. One of the guy's rivals took him out."

"You told me your aunt's health failed." Josie frowned. "Were you an adult by then?"

"Ah, no, I spent a couple of years in foster care."

"Crap," Carson muttered.

"I survived. And I like where I'm at now." Especially with Josie against his side. He smiled at Carson who'd moved away and was trying to appear nonchalant. "Anyway, that's how I got into fire-fighting."

"Yeah. Uh, thanks." Carson rubbed his shoe into the grass before looking at his mom. "I'm gonna go to Brandon's now. Have a good time with pizza an' stuff."

As Carson headed for his bike, his mother gave a sigh.

"It'll take him a while, pet. Most kids love change...if they're the ones making it happen. Otherwise, not so much." Holt rubbed his cheek against her hair. "How about I bribe him with a ride on the Harley?"

Josie stiffened. "No."

"Even if I leave the drugs and loose biker chicks at home?"

Her frown remained...but he'd heard the laugh she'd tried to suppress.

Brandon's house was huge. He even had a whole "family room" just for him and his friends. Coming back from getting Cokes from the kitchen, Carson handed one to Juan and dropped down on the floor.

In the center of the room, Ryan and Yukio were battling it out in the new Xbox game Brandon had scored.

On the TV screen, blood was everywhere. They'd turned the sound up, and there was yelling and screaming.

His stomach feeling pukey, Carson took a sip of the Coke. Mom never let him play adult games. Maybe he was kinda glad.

Seated on the couch, Brandon nudged him with his foot. "Hey, I looked up your old man, Cars."

"Huh? How come?"

"Cuz it pisses me off the way the asshole dissed you. Like

you're nothing." Brandon leaned forward. "We should do something about him...and I got a plan."

Ol' Everett was a douche. He really was. But... Carson frowned. Brandon'd said the same thing about the science teacher and having a plan. Only the plan'd gone from dumping bagged shit in a classroom to starting a fire. Kinda a big difference. Carson shook his head. "I don't know, Brandon. It's—"

"Next Thursday." Brandon grinned and bounced on the couch. "I checked on Facebook. His bank's taking their employees and their kids to Disney World."

Carson blinked. To *Disney World?*

"Bet your daddy didn't invite *you* to go, did he?" Ryan said.

"No." Anger smoldered. Even though the amusement park was really close, Mom'd taken Carson there only twice cuz they couldn't afford it—or even do all the stuff there, either. Everett probably took his *real* kids to Disney World all the time.

Carson gulped more Coke. "Doesn't matter. He's an asshole. So what?"

"I saw his house, and I've seen your house. Not exactly the same, are they? He owes you." Brandon's face screwed into an ugly expression. "He treated you like you're a...a stray dog, not his son."

The knowledge hurt. It did.

Brandon opened his Coke, and it fizzed up. "No one'll be home. Just that big-ass house sitting there."

Carson hesitated. If no one was there, no one would get hurt. A room in the fancy house would get scorched. Maybe it would make ol' Everett feel a bit of pain. The dick deserved some pain.

Mom wouldn't be happy, but she'd never find out.

Frowning, Yukio paused the game and set down the controller.

Ryan snickered. "Yeah. Let's do it."

"It'd be funny. Sure," Juan said.

"I guess we..." Carson stopped at the memory of Holt's face as he talked about being a firefighter. Why he'd gotten into it.

A fire meant firefighters would show up. Everett wouldn't be home, but what if a firefighter or someone else got hurt? What if the fire spread to other houses?

"No," Carson said, and Brandon's grin disappeared.

So did Ryan's. "Why the fuck not?"

"It's fire. You can't control it. Like maybe somebody else'd get hurt. Firefighters or neighbors." Carson had a horrible thought. "What if they have dogs or cats?"

Juan's mouth dropped open. "*Dios*, if my dog got hurt, and I found out someone had set the fire, I'd kill 'em."

Yukio was still frowning.

"I think..." The ugly feeling inside Carson's stomach settled. "No. No fire."

Brandon's face darkened to the color of an afternoon thunderstorm. Dark and mean. "Jesus, I just wanted to help you out. Don't go acting all high-horse and shit."

Carson tried a smile. "Yeah, I appreciate it, bro."

"Right. Sure you do."

An hour later, when Carson said he had stuff to do and should go home, Brandon shrugged and didn't say a word.

CHAPTER TWENTY-TWO

J osie wasn't too bad at soccer. After all, she'd played in school, been to all of Carson's games, and practiced with him. She'd even watched YouTube videos to try to help him.

Compared to Holt's athletic grace, she moved like a spastic turtle. Even Carson was better.

Reluctantly, she motioned to where Oma sat on the back patio. "Listen, guys, I'm outclassed. I'm going to sit with Oma."

"No, you're not." Holt took her hand and moved her to stand beside Carson.

His big hand engulfed hers completely. How could just the touch of his callused hand make her want to sigh?

"You need to practice with us, not just for Carson's skills, but for your own." The afternoon sunlight lightened his eyes—and showed his confident determination. "Let's do some passing among the three of us. Remember to keep moving so you never kick to the same person or place."

She stared at him. "What?"

"Backyard play is more fun with more people," he said firmly.

"Yeah, Mom. I like when you play," Carson piped up.

When she was young, the guys had played yard soccer or football or baseball, and the women sat on the porch and cheered for their men. Josie'd never particularly wanted to be a cheerleader. She'd wanted to play...yet she'd been willing to go sit. Funny how childhood habits could blindside a girl.

And, damn, but she loved this man. She hugged him hard and kissed Carson's cheek. "Okay, then. Passing time." She glanced at Oma, and her great-aunt smiled and winked.

A while later, Josie slid the ball past Holt to score and got a whooping "Go, Josie!" cheers from Duke and Wedge. The two teens stood on the other side of the fence at Holt's place.

"Hey, Holt, you watching the game?" Duke asked. "It's starting in half an hour."

"Already? You bet. I need to shower, but the door's open." Holt glanced at Carson. "You up for a game, ace?"

Carson's face lit. "Sure. S'okay, Mom?"

"Of course." Josie turned to join Oma, and Holt tucked his fingers into her shorts, holding her back.

"Come over for a while," he said.

"I should work..."

He moved closer. His fingers under her chin angled her head up. Her breasts brushed his chest and sent a shiver through her.

"Subbie, you need a break from writing." His voice lowered. "I want you to come and watch the game for an hour."

The grass on which she stood sank a good three inches. "Yes, Sir." She blinked. "I mean—"

"Exactly that." He kissed her lightly. "I love you, sweetheart."

"I..." The words were there...blocked by her fears. Her past.

"Shhh. I'll have the words from you soon enough." His confidence underlaid his words and gleamed in his steady gaze. He ran his thumb over her lips, making her want more and more and more kisses.

He smiled and looked over at the patio. "Stella, want to watch football at my house?"

"No, thank you. But why don't you watch the game here? Josie's living room has more space."

"Woman, you know it's all about the size of the TV screen."

"Oh my, how could I forget?" Laughing, Oma rose. "You children have fun. I'm going to go get ready for evening church service."

"I'll walk you home." He gave Josie's waist a squeeze before striding onto the patio and holding the back door for Oma.

Oma gave an exasperated huff. "My legs still work, you know. I can walk myself home."

"I enjoy your company, Stella." Holt grinned, but his voice was firm. "And you don't mind mine, so stop it."

As they walked out the door, Josie grinned. Her great-aunt wasn't any more effective at dissuading the Dom than Josie was.

Wrapping her arms around herself, Josie stood in the center of her backyard.

Holt obviously liked Oma—really did like her. He openly enjoyed playing soccer in the backyard. His affection for Carson was clear—he wasn't putting on a show to win over Josie.

Whenever he saw something not working in the house, he'd fix it. The leaky faucet. A motion-detector light for the carport. Yesterday, they'd all painted the dining room with Carson on the roller, Holt handling the ladder, her doing the tricky areas around the trim. When she'd put on her chore playlist and started singing with the music, he'd joined in—and knew more of the lyrics than she did.

Over the years, when she occasionally met men who were interesting, she'd imagine bringing them home to Oma and Carson. And that would be the end of her attraction.

But there was no awkwardness with Holt. She grinned and shook her head. That Dom wouldn't allow awkwardness.

He...fit.

Fit so well that he'd already created a place for himself—not only in her life and her bed—but in her family as well.

"I love you, Sir," she whispered to herself. Now all she had to do was find the right time to say the words to him.

CHAPTER TWENTY-THREE

Monday night, it was Holt and Shoshana's turn to prepare supper for the firehouse crew. Neither of them being gourmet cooks, they'd fallen back on the old standby of spaghetti and meatballs. It'd turned out good, actually, and well-buttered, crusty garlic bread made everything better. Being vegetarian, Shoshana had insisted on a green salad, so they'd ended up with a balanced meal.

After parmesaning his spaghetti, Holt dug in as Clancy teased their probationary firefighter, Arlo, about mixing up the hoses on the last fire.

"I hear you have a pretty new girlfriend, mate." Across the table, Oz grinned at Holt.

"He does? Why haven't I heard?" Tank scowled.

"Come over sometime, and I'll introduce you," Holt said. "She lives next door."

"Georgina says Josie's nicer than Nadia." Clancy stroked his mustache. "She likes Josie. Wants her for you."

Holt grinned. "Your woman's a good judge of character. I want Josie for me, too."

"Ah, c'mon," Derek griped. "That Nadia was fucking hot."

"True enough." Holt eyed the young man who'd recently turned twenty-two. "Of course, that polished hotness took hours of work—and beneath it...I didn't find what I needed. With Josie... She doesn't need all that shit. In fact, in the mornings, when I see her without makeup or fancy clothing, I swear my heart stops. Because *who* she is shines through."

Clancy gave him a look of perfect understanding. The man adored his Georgina.

Derek was frowning. Not understanding.

Holt asked him, "Do you choose your friends by their appearance? Only have well-dressed friends?"

"Ah...no."

"You pick friends because of who they are. Because you like being with them. A wife—you'll be with her a lot more than your friends. Me, I want someone I can like, not only in the evenings, but every morning at breakfast, too."

Derek blinked.

"A nice rack is great"—and Holt had to admit Josie's breasts were fantastic—"but what's more important to me is someone who'll listen. Who's...kind. I should have looked closer at Nadia."

Tank considered. "Nadia seemed nice enough."

"Yeah, that's what I was thinking. How do you know your Josie is nicer?" Oz asked.

Holt leaned back in his chair. "You met the teens on my street —the ones who called 911 when I got knifed?"

Oz nodded.

"They adore Josie. She listens to them, whether they're complaining about school or wanting to share their new music discoveries. And she bakes cookies to treat them and her son's pals. She switched her life around, moved to my neighborhood to be close enough to care for an older relative. After I lost a patient, she insisted I come over and talk about it. Hell, everyone talks to her—mailmen, old ladies, kids. Because she listens...and she cares."

Derek's brows pulled together, and after a second, he nodded. Yeah, he was beginning to figure out the difference between internal and external beauty.

Taking advantage of the kid's distraction, Holt grabbed the last piece of garlic bread. Time to discuss something else. He and the ambulance crew hadn't had any interesting cases, just the usual heart attacks, strokes, older people who fell. He asked the engine crew, "You guys get anything interesting on your runs?"

"The funniest was the kitchen fire." Tank grinned slowly. "Newlyweds. She was cooking, but he wanted nookie and dragged her into the bedroom to have his evil way with her."

"Let me guess," Arlo said. "Grease fire?"

"You win the prize, probie." Oz laughed. "She was heating oil to fry potatoes. Neither of them turned off the stove."

Shoshana rolled her eyes. "As if a guy ever thinks about anything other than 'I'm gonna get some'."

"That's fucking cynical." Clancy tossed a carrot stick at her that she caught neatly. "True, but cynical."

"The not-so-funny call-out was for another arson near the middle school," Tank said. "The perp took the paper recyclables bin from the curb, dumped everything against a garage door, and poured on gasoline."

Holt's gut twisted, and he pushed his plate away. Children and fire. God fucking help him. "How close to the school?" *Carson's* school.

"A block down. Only the outside of the garage door was charred." Tank grinned. "The owner was damn relieved his vintage Mustang didn't get scorched."

"But his son was pretty hacked that his basketball hoop got crisped. The kid's on the basketball team." Oz chuckled.

"The Spartans?" Shoshana asked, naming the University of Tampa team.

"Nope. The boy's in middle school." Tank shook his head. "Sounded like his life was ruined if he couldn't practice."

"Tank, at that age, that's what they think. And, hey, if he's that passionate about the sport, he might well end up on the Spartans." Clancy smiled. One of his daughters had just turned thirteen.

"You figure the firebug is the same one who started the classroom and dumpster fires?" Arlo asked.

"I'm guessing yes," Oz said.

Holt frowned. "The middle school fires might've started out as pranks, but these last two are looking more like vindictive acts."

"Vindictive?" Shoshana dumped the last of the salad onto her plate.

"Yeah. I was wondering if our firebug might be a kid, so I talked to Cullen O'Keefe." The Shadowlands Dom was an experienced arson investigator and well known in the stations. "It seems classroom fires are usually about revenge. Tank, when you talked with the teacher of that room, what'd you think?"

"You're following my thoughts, man," Tank said. "The teacher's purely an asshole. I could almost understand someone wanting to light his shit up."

"But burning the outside of a garage?" Derek protested.

Holt's gut tightened. "The arsonist's willing to bust a window and toss in a Molotov cocktail...but he didn't. He deliberately started a fire outside a house."

Clancy's eyes widened. "If the arsonist is a kid, maybe the target *was* the basketball hoop. At that age, jocks can be obnoxious."

"At any age," Shoshana muttered and got grins from the guys.

Holt said, "I think our fire bug is escalating. Dumpsters to empty classroom...then a garage attached to an occupied house."

"I agree." Tank scowled. "Trouble is, we might have more than one offender."

"Yeah?" Arlo looked up from his plate. "How'd you figure that?"

Tank got a soda from the fridge. "When Clancy and I asked questions around the neighborhood, we talked with a guy who'd been jogging the track when the classroom was burned. He saw some boys hide their bikes in the bushes...and wondered why they didn't use the bike racks at the school."

"Interesting," Shoshana said. "Did he see them well enough to ID them?"

"Nope. He wasn't paying that much attention." Clancy rubbed his chin. "The bikes were normal. The kids wore baseball caps. Most wore daypacks. A black one. A red one. One pack had shiny lettering—fancy-like—on the back. Probably reflective stuff."

Holt rubbed the back of his neck, trying to think. He'd seen reflective lettering on a backpack recently. Somewhere. Wedge or Duke, maybe?

No, not them. His hand froze. *Carson*. Black material. Customized lettering—but not his name. Odd script.

Oh shit.

CHAPTER TWENTY-FOUR

I n her kitchen, Josie tried to settle. Holt was on his way over to talk with her—and Carson—he said.

When she'd heard his voice on the phone, her heart had leaped. She missed him last night when he'd been putting in his twenty-four hours at the fire station. She hoped he'd come over and spend the evening tonight.

On the phone, he'd sounded...off. Not happy. She'd almost asked him if Carson had pitched a ball through a window or said something rude. But she hadn't questioned him. If Carson had been rude, well... If she and Holt were going to be together—and, oh God, she wanted that—her two males needed to resolve their problems without her leaping in to help.

She snorted, because leaping in was exactly what she wanted to do.

Instead, she scooped ice cream into three dishes. Even males of the species could have their moods smoothed out with fat and sugar, right? And if not, at least *she'd* feel better.

As she set the dishes on the coffee table, a knock sounded from the front door. "It's open. Come on in."

Holt stepped in, and her heart once again gave a quivery leap like a drunken antelope. Was it because of the way his muscular chest and shoulders filled out a T-shirt? Or the shadow of stubble along his strong jaw. Or...that intimidating self-possession.

When his intent gaze trapped hers, her intoxicated heart did another bound.

"Hey," she said, brilliant conversationalist that she was.

Releasing her from his gaze, he shook his head as if trying to dismiss his thoughts. "Hey to you." Gripping her upper arms, he pulled her onto her tiptoes, and kissed her.

Oh, his lips were firm, velvety, demanding, and when he wrapped her in his iron-hard arms, every bone in her body turned to water. She put her arms around his neck—just to hold on, of course—and if that rubbed her breasts over his chest, well, she'd have to put up with the inconvenience.

God, he felt good. She ran her fingers through his thick, soft hair.

"Mmm. I missed you." He nuzzled her temple, and his hands curled under her ass cheeks, pulling her up against his thickening shaft.

Her thoughts scattered everywhere. Why did he have to be so...so devastating? Pulling in a breath, she stepped back.

With one finger, he traced a line down her cheek, and his masculine chuckle didn't help her rising lust at all. "When you look at me like that, I want to tie you to this coffee table and fuck you for a long...long time."

Every drop of moisture in her mouth disappeared.

His gaze focused on something behind her, and his smile disappeared. "Unfortunately, I'm here for something much less fun."

"What do you mean?"

He walked to the couch, bent to look at Carson's backpack, and traced the silver tape lettering. "Interesting script."

"It's Carson's name in Elvish—well, Tolkien's idea of Elvish. I wanted the backpack to have something reflective in case he was out at night."

"Beautiful work." Holt's jaw clenched. His tone darkened as he said, "Josie, I need to talk with Carson. With you present."

"What's wrong?"

He tilted his head toward the bedrooms. "Call him, please?"

Her stomach pitched. "Carson, can you come out? Holt is here."

"Coming!" Carson trotted out of his room, saw the coffee table, and grinned. "Ice cream! Awesome. You should come over more often, Holt." He grabbed a bowl and dropped into a chair.

Holt didn't answer. Or smile.

God, what was wrong? Unclenching her hands with an effort, Josie leaned her hip against Carson's chair.

Taking a seat on the couch, Holt scrubbed his hands over his face. Concern stabbed through Josie at the shadows under his eyes. "Carson, you know there've been fires at your middle school and around this area."

"Yeah, I'm aware."

Josie frowned at Carson's dismissive tone. "Around the area? What do you mean?"

"There was one at a student's home." The way Holt's gaze remained on Carson was starting to bother her. "Someone is deliberately setting those fires."

She straightened, anger joining the worry. "What does this have to do with Carson?"

"Just before the classroom fire—on a Sunday—a jogger saw boys hide their bikes in the bushes. One boy had reflective script on his backpack." Holt glanced at Carson's daypack.

"No." Outrage filled Josie so full that her voice rose. "You're not accusing Carson of being a...a...firebug. An arsonist."

Holt's mouth pressed flat. "Josie, starting a fire is more than a childish prank. People die. If Carson—"

"My son would never do anything like that." A hard knot

formed in her stomach. She thought Holt knew her, knew Carson —cared for Carson. How could he attack her baby?

Face white, Carson stood, his dish dropping from his lap. "I'm not any fire-starter."

"Listen, ace." Holt also rose. "I've heard the science teacher is a jerk, but starting a fire"—his voice grew rough and dark—"a fire in a school where there are children is—"

"I *said* I didn't do it." Carson glared at Holt. "You-you just want me in trouble, because you got the hots for Mom."

Josie shook her head. "Honey, that's not why—"

"It *is* why. He's an asshole, Mom." Tears were in her baby's eyes, running down his flushed cheeks. Hands in fists, he shouted at Holt at the top of his voice. "I hate you. Go *away*!"

Swiping at his face, Carson ran. The door of his room slammed shut.

Oh. My. God.

"Fuck. That could have gone better," Holt muttered.

Better? *Better?* He'd accused her baby of being a *criminal*. The betrayal ripped into her heart until the pain was unbearable. After Everett had thrown Carson away, her son found Holt. Was starting to love Holt like she was—and the bastard had stomped all over Carson's heart.

"Get out." If she held herself rigid enough, she wouldn't break into pieces. Not until he was gone.

"Josie." His voice was hard. Unrecognizable. "Someone is starting fires at the *school*...and, from Carson's reaction, he's involved."

"He is *not*. I can't believe you..." *I trusted you.* Choking back the words, she yanked open the door. "Get out. Get out now."

Anger simmered in his eyes, but his voice didn't rise. "Josie, I'll try to get you some time to talk with him, but sooner or later, Carson will have to talk to the authorities."

Authorities? He'd sic the police on her child? Her hands clenched.

As Holt walked out, she forced out the words through stiff lips. "We're done, Holt. Don't come back."

He started to turn around, shook his head, and kept going.

He kept going.

He didn't even protest.

The sound she heard as she closed the door wasn't footsteps, but her heart crumbling into pieces.

Shit-buckets. Holt *knew.*

Carson hunched on his bed, wanting nothing more than to crawl underneath it and hide.

Poe had already darted under there. The cat didn't like raised voices or slammed doors.

Carson was too old to hide under the bed, but...Holt *knew.* He was a firefighter. Of course, he'd figured it out. Would the police come?

Kids couldn't be arrested, could they?

His stomach twisted until he felt like he'd puke. Breathing hard, he slid down to the floor. It wasn't *fair.* He hadn't started any fires...only been there when Brandon surprised them all at the classroom. It was supposed to have just been poop. A bunch of shit in a bag. Not fire.

Holt called it arson. That was serious. And he'd said there'd been a fire at someone's house. What was with that?

Putting his arms around his knees, Carson shivered as his horror grew. Had Brandon, Ryan, or someone done...more? Had one of them started the dumpster fires? Everybody at school had laughed about those fires. So had Carson.

Shit-buckets, would Holt think Carson did those fires, too?

Should he have told someone about the classroom stuff? Told Mom?

No. The guys were his friends. Bros don't snitch on bros.

But *he* hadn't started any fires. Did being there count? His chin quivered, and tears burned his cheeks.

He sniffled, then listened. He didn't hear anyone talking. Had Holt left?

A tap came on his door, and he tensed. "Carson?"

Quickly, he rubbed the wetness from his face. "Yeah."

The door opened, but he couldn't look up. He stared at the floor.

Mom moved forward, and he saw her feet stop in the middle of the floor. She was barefoot. She liked being barefooted, she said. Because her heroine never wore shoes.

He sure wasn't like any of her heroes.

Would they take him to jail?

"Holt is gone...and he won't be back." Mom sat on the floor and tried to put her arm around him.

He wanted to climb onto her lap and cling, so he pulled back. Scooted away from her. "Good. He's an asshole."

She didn't say anything about his language and that...was weird. "Did you start those fires, Carson?"

"No!" His hands clenched tight. "I *said* that. I didn't start the effing fires." His tears dried as burning hurt his chest.

"I know you have the teacher whose—"

"Holt says I did something, and you believe him. Not me—because he's your boyfriend, right?"

"No, Carson, because—"

"I didn't do it, okay?" He jumped to his feet. His face was hot. His anger, hotter. His voice rose. "It wasn't *me*."

"Oh, honey." She shook her head and stood.

When she put her hand behind his neck, he yanked away. "Leave me *alone*. I don't want you in here." His voice cracked.

She looked at him for a long moment, then left. Walked out and closed the door, and he wanted to call her back. Say he was sorry.

Because she didn't look pissed off. Just...sad.

He stared at the door and started to cry.

Holt walked back to his duplex, thinking of all the things he might have said. Should have said.

Way to fuck things up, dumbass. He'd gotten...carried away. Because when it came to fire and children, his brain went dead, and diplomacy flew out the window.

Why the hell hadn't he talked to Josie first and led into the subject gradually? Maybe asked about Carson's pals. The kid had been trying to find new friends in middle school—a mom would understand how her boy could make bad choices in buddies. That they might have talked him into something stupid.

He sighed. Yeah, because every mother wants to hear that her son could be involved in arson.

Shit.

He walked into the duplex and kicked the door shut. Pulling out his cell, he considered it. Should he call her?

Would she even answer? Concern tightened his hand on the phone. Josie'd barely lowered her defenses to let him in, and now, she felt betrayed. After all, Carson was part of her heart.

Hell.

Once she had a chance to think, she'd see the truth...wouldn't she? She was a wise, smart, logical woman. Surely, she'd know Holt didn't mean to harm her son, and if the child was involved in any way, it was time to get him out.

He realized he was staring at his phone and slowly put it away.

Calling her now would be futile. Might make everything worse. She needed time to get over her anger, to slow down and think. To ask questions.

Carson was a good kid. He'd talk to his mom once they both calmed down. Holt pulled in an unhappy breath. Arson investiga-

CHERISE SINCLAIR

tions could get ugly. It would be best if the boy came forward on his own.

Unfortunately, Holt needed to turn this information over to someone else. He was too closely involved—look how he'd already fucked things up—and it wasn't his investigation anyway.

He had a cold lump in his gut as he pulled out his cell and dialed the fire department offices.

As the phone rang, a new icy worry slid between his ribs. Josie might well see his talking to the Captain as another type of betrayal.

If she did, would she abandon what was growing between them? Would she truly close the door and figure their relationship a lost cause?

His jaw locked.

If she did, she'd have a fight on her hands.

CHAPTER TWENTY-FIVE

After supper the next day, Josie washed dishes in Oma's small kitchen as her great-aunt grumbled about her reading club's next book selection.

"Literary fiction should come with black box warnings," Oma stated. "Something like: *Reading this book can lead to an increased risk of depression.*"

Josie managed to grin. Breaking up with a man should have the same warning. She rubbed her aching eyes, gritty from lack of sleep and crying. Her muscles and bones and everything ached.

Too many nightmares. Of Pa shouting she was a disgrace and a whore. *Get out, get out, get out.*

Or of a fire consuming Carson's middle school. She shuddered. Holt had been inside in yellow firefighter's gear, and she'd slammed the door, trapping him inside. The building collapsed on him, and she'd screamed as her heart ripped in two.

Or Carson being in a burning building, calling for her. She couldn't find him. Couldn't save him.

Waking, drenched in sweat and tears, she'd gone to Carson's room, to listen to him breathe. To see the cat curled in the curve of his body. She'd wanted to wake him and hug him and let him know whatever happened she'd be there.

She wanted to run next door to Holt and tell him the same thing. Oh, God, she missed him so much.

This morning, she'd automatically poured two cups of coffee... and fought tears as she dumped the second cup out.

Carson hadn't talked to her at breakfast, and she hadn't seen him since. He'd had afterschool soccer practice, then gone to Yukio's house to finish their co-written English project that was due tomorrow.

With a jolt, Josie realized Oma was frowning at her. "Did you ask me a question?"

"I asked if you were feeling all right, my girl," Oma said.

"I'm...a bit unhappy." Josie glanced at the clock. "But it's a long story, and your ride should be here in a minute. How about I catch you up tomorrow? Actually, I could use some advice."

"Of course." Oma gave her a wry smile. "Wisdom is gained from mistakes, and I've made my fair share of blunders, so I have plenty of insights to offer."

Josie laughed and heard the doorbell ring. "I'll get it, Oma."

Zuri was on the doorstep. "Hi, Josie. I got halfway here before remembering Mrs. Avery has church tonight. But I wanted to drop these off." She held up a batch of cuttings.

"Oh, I love geraniums." Oma took the cuttings.

Zuri beamed. "A friend of mine does landscaping design, and she was planting scented geraniums around our pond. When I told her about your garden, she snipped these for you."

"Please, thank her for me." Oma touched one of the leaves and sniffed her fingers. "Chocolate?"

"You have a chocolate mint, an apple, and a rose fragrance."

"Seriously? Chocolate?" Josie tested the same one. "That's amazing."

Oma gave Zuri a hug. "Thank you. I'll pot them for the patio so I'll have them close to enjoy."

A light beep at the curb made everyone turn. "There's my ride," Oma picked up her purse and a light wrap. "Josie, dear, will you put these in water and lock up for me?"

"Sure." Josie kissed her cheek. "Have fun." Catching Zuri's snicker, she amended, "Or pray hard or whatever."

"My young heretics." Oma was laughing as she strolled to her friend's car.

"She looks good," Zuri said. "She's abandoned her walker?"

Josie smiled. "She'd been using it for dizziness, but during rehab for her sprained ankle, her meds were adjusted. No more dizziness. No more walker."

"That's awesome. She hated that thing."

"Come in, if you have a minute," Josie motioned to Uzuri. "I see you at the Shadowlands, but we never have a chance to talk."

"You do stay awfully busy. But the members are happy you're there. Aside from Cullen, none of the Masters enjoy making fancy mixed drinks, which meant no one got mixed drinks because no submissive wants to annoy a Master. Especially Master Sam and Master Nolan."

Nolan was a bit scary. Master Sam? A lot scary. "It's nice to be wanted."

Thinking of the Shadowlands, she felt her heart start to ache. Holt was a member, and he was free now. He might—of course, he would—choose someone else to play with.

The stab of pain was so strong she almost folded. How could she bear it?

"Josie?" Zuri took her hand. "What's wrong?"

Zuri was Holt's friend. Mustn't put her in the middle. Josie pulled in a slow breath. "Nothing. It—"

"Oh, that's bull. Is Carson all right? Where is he, anyway?"

Josie glanced at the clock. "He went to a friend's to do homework. He's fine. It's just—"

Zuri set her hands on her hips. "I recognize that look. You've got man troubles, don't you?"

Josie huffed. "You're as perceptive as—" *Holt. Don't go there, Josie.* "Did you learn psychology from your Doms?"

"In a way." Zuri leaned against the counter. "I like making them happy, even before they ask for something, so I watch them, their expressions, everything. I guess I've gotten pretty good at it."

"I'll say."

"Did you and Holt break up?"

"Oh, Zuri." Josie sank into a chair. "It's such a mess. I'm so angry with him, and I miss him so much. If it was just the two of us, maybe we could work it out, only Carson's involved, and...I don't know what to do."

"And I thought two Doms were trouble. Adding a child into a squabble?" Zuri wrinkled her brow. "You need someone with kid experience. Let's go to your place and dig out some wine. I need to make a couple of calls."

A while later, Josie watched the scenery as Zuri whipped her small car through an open farm gate and up a long drive to a white, two-story farmhouse.

"Here we are," Zuri announced and parked the car beside the house.

Linda's ranch was lovely. The circular drive enclosed a pretty fountain and garden. Farther out were orange groves, the trees heavy with fruit. Barns sat off to one side, and horses grazed in white-fenced pastures. She caught a glimpse of a small pond with ducks on the grassy bank.

A *woof-woof-woof* came from a dog dashing toward them, followed by a man.

Josie froze. Wasn't that Master Sam? She turned a narrow gaze on Uzuri. "This isn't Linda's place, is it?"

"Well, technically, it's Master Sam's. But Linda lives with him, and she said to come here."

Master Sam looked even meaner in the full light of day. Lean rancher's muscles, weathered face, silvery hair, and pale, pale blue eyes that could freeze a person with one look.

Forcing herself to look away from him, Josie bent to greet the dog. It had reddish short hair, a stocky body, and cute ears that drooped at the tip. "Hey, guy."

After a glance back at his master to ascertain if she was a serial puppy killer, the dog wagged his tail, and she got a friendly sniff.

"Girls." Sam's rough voice could probably be used to sandpaper hardwood. "Go on up. Linda's inside."

"Yes, Sir," Uzuri said. "Come on, Josie."

Josie nodded politely to Sam and followed close after her friend.

Linda was coming out as they crossed the wide front porch. "Josie, Zuri." They each received a warm hug. "Gabi's already here and inside."

Gabi and Linda. Zuri hadn't said why she'd chosen them, and Josie felt at a loss. Really, if she was going to keep working at the Shadowlands, she needed to learn more about the members. She could start with the Masters and their women. Masters who liked whips should probably be at the top of the list.

But if Holt hated her, she might not be at the club long enough to bother. The hollow feeling in her chest increased.

Inside the house, the big living room was decorated in warm browns and creams with a faded Oriental carpet on the dark flooring. A small fire in the stone fireplace crackled pleasantly.

"Hey, you two." Gabi handed out hugs and settled back into a chair. "I'm a glass of wine ahead of you, so you'll have to catch up."

The coffee table held a bottle of wine and glasses, along with a cheese and cracker platter.

"This is lovely." Josie took the chair beside Gabi. "Thank you, Linda."

"You're welcome, honey." Settling on the couch beside Zuri, Linda started talking about the weather.

A while later, when the second bottle of wine had been opened, Zuri decided everyone was warmed up. She told the others that Josie was having Dom problems all made worse by her son. She talked a bit about Carson. Linda and Gabi already knew Holt lived next door.

"Tell the rest, Josie," Zuri said.

Sharing was...hard, but if Josie wanted advice, she needed to explain. She told them how Everett had rejected Carson, about Holt's arson accusations, and how her son said he hated Holt. And how she'd told Holt their relationship was over.

When she finished, there was silence.

Josie shook her head. "I know there's nothing you can do, but just sharing everything actually helped." She hesitated. "Speaking of sharing, you won't..." She glanced out the window toward the barn where Sam had gone.

Gabi smiled. "It's tough to keep things from our men, but Shadowkitten business is kept private. We need to be able to talk freely with our friends; it's part of being a woman. The Masters might not indulge in heart-to-hearts, but they understand we do."

When Josie relaxed, Gabi motioned to Linda.

Linda nodded. "Uzuri called me, because she knows I survived raising two children. They're in college now."

Josie grinned at the wry way she'd said "survived."

"When Sam and I first got together, my kids discovered I was seeing a sadist...because they showed up early one morning at my house. And then they threw one huge shouting tantrum in front of Sam."

Josie's mouth dropped open. "Oh. My. God. What did you do?"

"I was so mad that I kicked them all out. Including Sam since he really shouldn't have taken it upon himself to answer my door." Linda smiled. "And yet he went on to straighten everything out, although I'm not sure my children have ever recovered from his blunt honesty."

Josie almost cringed. Holt could be awfully direct, too.

"Now, let's look at your problems." Linda held up one finger. "First, you have your son's possible involvement in arson."

Josie stiffened for a second before she slumped. "I know what you're going to say. Yes, he's an honest kid and has always owned up to his mistakes, but saying '*I didn't do it*' isn't the same as '*I wasn't there*' or '*I don't know anything about it.*'"

Linda smiled in sympathy. "The thought of our babies doing something sketchy is painful, isn't it? But if you were positive he wasn't involved at all, you wouldn't be stewing."

"He was involved in some way or another," Josie said grimly. "He was too angry—and defensive. He's hiding something."

"Which means you have to pin him down and get answers. If you start with the fact that you *know* he's involved...sometimes that works." Linda huffed a laugh. "I'm pretty sure children never outgrow the belief that *Mom is all-knowing.*"

Gabi's mouth twisted. "I think only *good* mothers know every-thing. Mine never had a clue."

Josie reached over to squeeze the redhead's hand. If she ever met the woman who put that sad expression on Gabi's face, she'd rip her apart.

Gabi squeezed back.

Turning back to Linda, Josie straightened her shoulders. "Okay. One long, undoubtedly unhappy discussion with Carson coming up."

"Two discussions, I'm afraid. Not at the same time, of course." Linda gave her a wry smile. "Sometime soon, he needs to hear that you need other grownups in your life, including men. If you didn't date anyone until Holt, Carson's acceptance might take a while."

"I actually did try to have that talk with him. He totally shut down." Her heart ached. Her poor baby was so unhappy. "His father didn't want him—ever—and I don't want Carson to worry he could lose my love. But I guess I went overboard in tiptoeing around his sensibilities. He's old enough to understand I might want a male companion."

Zuri nodded. "Carson has a good heart. It'll take him a while, but he'll get it."

"That's it from me." Linda glanced at Gabi. "Your turn."

"You did good." Gabi grinned and turned to Josie. "My credentials don't include parenting, but I'm a social worker, and I do a lot of family counseling."

Josie bit her lip. "Okay."

"To begin, I'm rather surprised Holt hasn't tried to corner you again for a discussion."

"He hasn't." She'd told him they were done, and he wouldn't fight it. She'd sure proven to be more of a problem than an asset. At the chill emanating from deep inside her, Josie wrapped her arms around herself. "I'm sure he has better things to do."

"I didn't see his car at the duplex," Zuri said. "Isn't this his day to work at the hospital?"

Josie nodded. "7 am to 7 pm. He'd normally have returned before we left. He's staying away." *Because he doesn't want to see me.* Knowing that...hurt.

"Maybe or maybe not," Gabi said gently. "There are some questions I want you to think about before you two talk."

"He won't want to talk with me." Why didn't the woman get it?

"You two looked pretty tight at the pet adoption."

"And at the Saturnalia, too," Zuri said. "I'd say the man seemed to be heading straight into love."

The word, the dreadful four-letter "L" word slammed into Josie, stealing her breath.

"There it is," Linda murmured. "You love him. Does he love you?"

Josie's throat hurt as she fought back tears. "He said he did, but—"

"He did! I'm so stoked!" Zuri bounced on the couch.

"It was just in the heat of the moment." And a few other times, but—

"Oh, no, girlfriend." Zuri shook her head. "Holt's really careful about communicating with the women he dates. He tells them up front he only dates casually and isn't interested in a relationship. He wouldn't say he loved you if he didn't mean it."

Oh. There was no way she should be feeling joy. Not now. They weren't together. But to hear Uzuri say that Holt meant it? Yes, she totally felt joy.

And despair. Her shoulders slumped.

"Do you still think he won't show up at your door?" Gabi asked softly.

"I told him we were done."

"I bet you told him you didn't date, either." Zuri tilted her head. "Did he listen?"

"That's...different. Love sounds nice, but face it; I'm not a stress-free girlfriend. I have old baggage. My son might be involved with arson and says he hates Holt. I kicked the man out of my house and said we're done. Of course, he's going to cut his losses."

"Ah." Gabi reached over to rub Josie's shoulder. "Let's say Holt has a daughter, a handicapped one, who is annoying. Would you kick him to the curb?"

"Of course not."

"Okay." Gabi continued, "When you and Carson have a fight and he yells at you, do you boot him out?"

Josie glared. "No."

"I see. So...why do you feel Holt has less relationship stamina and loyalty than you do?"

Josie blinked. Because...because...he was male? Only that was totally sexist. She did know men who'd been married for decades, ones who were faithful. Loyal.

"Sooner or later, every relationship ends up stormy, but the good ones weather it." Gabi tilted her head. "Do you think you're not worthy of the effort to maintain a relationship?"

"I..." Josie pulled in a breath. Maybe? She...was worthy, wasn't she? Did she really have such poor self-esteem? No, sheesh, she liked herself. Was worthy of love. "Boy, you're really straightforward, aren't you?"

Gabi grinned. "Only with people who value honesty. I can tiptoe if I need to, but you're not fragile, Josie. You just have a blind spot, because you were hurt in the past. You need to think about it." She dusted her hands together. "Ladies, my work here is done, and it's getting late."

Josie glanced at the clock and nodded. "I need to fetch my son. Zuri, we should be getting back."

"Let's go." Zuri jumped to her feet.

On the way out, Josie gave Linda and Gabi hugs. "Thank you for the"—she smiled—"the *intervention*. And the advice and hand holding."

She bumped shoulders with Zuri on the way to the car. "Thank you, too. I needed this."

Zuri put an arm around her waist. "One of the nicest things I learned over the last year was that I could—and should—ask for help and that I would receive it."

"That's nice." If Josie went over to Holt's and asked for help and forgiveness, what would he do? Her heart gave a stutter of hope.

However, as they turned into Josie's drive, her fragile hope sank into a black abyss.

Holt's side of the duplex was dark and silent.

Carson closed the door behind him with a breath of relief. Homework and soccer practice had saved him.

Tryouts were coming up, and all the guys—the ones who really wanted to make the team—were practicing after school together. After soccer, he'd gone to Yukio's to work on their English project. When Mom'd picked him up, she'd wanted to talk, but he still had stuff to finish tonight. First time he'd ever been glad to have homework.

When Carson sat down at his desk, Poe jumped into his lap, pushy-pawing and purring. "I'm so glad you're here, cat," Carson whispered.

Mom'd said tomorrow they'd talk about the fire in Mr. Jorgeson's classroom...because she knew he'd been involved. She *knew*. And she looked disappointed...and sad.

His stomach ached, and his eyes burned. He didn't *need* his mother—it wasn't like he was a baby—but still...she was his mom and compared to other moms, she was really cool. She let him do a lot, because she trusted him not to screw up.

It felt shitty that he had.

He kinda hadn't realized how bad he'd messed up, not right away. If Brandon had told him first, he'd never have agreed to start a fire but, after it was too late, he'd figured it served Jorgeson right. Wasn't all that bad.

But when Holt'd asked Carson about the arson stuff, he'd been...not happy. At all. The way Holt'd talked, starting a fire really *was* bad.

If Carson'd broke the law by being there, what if they made him and Mom pay for what got burned?

He stared out his window at Holt's side of the duplex. All dark. At least, he wasn't here butting in and getting Mom upset.

Poe's tail started to lash, and Carson realized he was petting the cat awful hard and fast. "Sorry, Poe."

Poe was right—it wasn't Holt's fault. The guy was a firefighter. Guess that made fires his business.

"It's just...I liked him," Carson whispered to Poe. The times watching football and playing soccer had been awesome. And if not for Holt, Carson wouldn't have Poe. He was cool to talk with and didn't act like Carson was a stupid kid. And—Carson felt the ache in his belly increase—when those two muggers had attacked, Holt'd saved him.

Poe stared up at him, yellow-green eyes unblinking. *Well?*

"I messed up. Should've told him and Mom I was there. And I will." He didn't have to tell them who else had been at the school. Mom'd figure it out. She knew he'd gone to Brandon's that day.

The cat dug claws into his thighs, reminding him he had more to answer for.

"He's an asshole, Mom. I hate him!" The words he'd yelled made his stomach twist. He'd acted like...like the five-year-old brat across the street. Anytime she didn't get her own way, she'd be all *I hate you.*

Poe stared at him.

"I don't hate Holt. It's just..." Mom *liked* him. And knowing it made Carson feel weird.

Other kids' parents got divorced, and the moms sometimes got boyfriends. A couple of his classmates even got new fathers. Stepfathers.

Was Holt Mom's boyfriend now? He really *liked* Mom. Or he had. Only now...Mom'd been mad at Holt and kicked him out.

Carson's eyes started to burn. He woke up last night...and heard her crying. Because he'd been such a loser an' maybe because he'd screwed everything up with Holt, too.

Over at the duplex, Holt's side was still dark. The Harley was gone.

Maybe Holt hated both of them now.

And Mom had cried.

Tomorrow. Somehow, he'd make it all right tomorrow.

CHAPTER TWENTY-SIX

Holt rolled over in bed and yawned. He'd finished his usual twelve-hour ICU shift yesterday, and then, since the flu had left the unit short-staffed, he'd agreed to stay on and work the night shift, too. Because if he'd been home, he would've gone next door to have it out with Josie.

A glance at the clock said it was afternoon, so he'd gotten a few hours of sleep once he'd unwound enough to sack out. It'd been an ugly night. A head-on car crash had filled the last two ICU beds. With luck, the toddlers would stabilize. Thank fuck children were so resilient.

Damn vehicular accidents. Whoever'd invented cars should've been shot. Made a guy want to return to primitive times.

Rolling out of bed, Holt headed for the shower, even though he'd taken one last night. As he stepped under the hot water, he snorted. Primitive times would mean giving up hot water. No nurse in the world would go for that concept.

And four-legged transportation wasn't safer than cars. He smiled, remembering a western clothing ad he'd done as a kid. They'd tossed him onto a horse, and he'd been terrified. Eventually, he'd had fun...after getting past how far away the ground was.

Would Josie enjoy a western vacation? Maybe he could take her and Carson to a working ranch. It'd give him a chance to have some guy time with Carson.

Assuming the boy ever stopped hating him.

With a sigh, Holt finished his shower, pulled on a pair of jeans, and headed for the living room. His pretty redhead's time was up. They needed to talk. She'd overreacted...but he'd screwed up, too.

He picked up the package on his coffee table and headed to Josie's house. Using the bright gold ribbons, he hung the box on her front door handle. "Okay, subbie. The ball's in your court."

What would she do?

Fuck knew. She'd always admitted if she'd screwed up. But this time, it'd been Carson's screw-up.

Back in his duplex, Holt downed a quick sandwich, then grabbed a Dew and went out to his comfortable chair on the patio. Feet up, he drank the ice-cold liquid and tried to relax.

Josie's car was under the carport, but there was no noise from her house. No one in her backyard. He sighed, breathing in the sweet fragrance of Stella's blooming frangipani tree.

His Josie was sweet, too. And fucking stubborn. Was she still angry? Had she talked with Carson about the classroom fire?

His mouth tightened. His captain had agreed to give Josie time to get through to her son. After all, they had no real evidence aside from a vague description of reflective tape.

But Holt knew—and Josie knew—the boy was involved. Somehow. Dammit. He could help if she'd let him. If she'd trust him.

Was she going to give up on them and not even try? Holt scowled as the dismal thoughts circled his brain. She wanted him. Dammit, she loved him. But if there was a conflict between what she wanted and what her son wanted, she might just dump her relationship with Holt.

"There doesn't have to be a conflict," he muttered.

"What?"

Holt turned to see Josie on the other side of the fence, her forearms resting on the top of the wooden slats. She started to smile at him and faltered. "Um. You're home."

"That's right." Rising, he stalked toward her. His hands ached with the need to grab her. Hold her.

Her eyelids were swollen; her eyes, red. She'd been crying.

Hell. Remorse stabbed him. Maybe he shouldn't have given her so much time.

"I was fixin' to come over and apologize. To talk. To..." She bit her lip. "Um. I wasn't sure you'd want to see me, so if you don't, then...."

He curled his fingers around hers. She had a sturdy hand, yet it was so very fragile. Much like her. Tough on the outside, vulnerable on the inside. "Josie, I wanted to see you the second I walked out your door."

Her expression brightened in a slow sunrise of hope. "Really?"

"I figured you needed time but, sweetheart, your time is up. Have you opened your front door lately?"

Her confused frown said *no*.

"Go look."

A man shouldn't waste a perfectly good apology gift—and maybe she'd sample some of the contents and get those endorphins rolling around before they started talking about arson.

And relationships.

On an upwelling of hope, Josie opened the front door. A brightly wrapped box dangled from the outside door handle. The attached card said, *"I'm sorry. Let's talk. H."*

Oh. Oh, God. Her eyes misted. He hadn't given up.

Retreating to the living room, she tore the gold foil paper off. Chocolate. And not one of the generic standard boxes found in grocery stores. The man had visited the William Dean store and somehow handpicked her favorites.

He'd had an informant. *Oma.* No wonder her great-aunt hadn't been home.

All day long, Josie'd stewed and fumed and argued with herself. Whined. Cried. Oh, God, she'd cried. And then been so angry with herself—and Holt—that she'd written an entire battle scene in her book out of sequence so she could kill something, if only on paper. The reptilian race attacking the human village had died by the dozens.

It was good she hadn't seen Holt right then.

Shaking her head, she took a step toward the door, then turned, selected a pink-topped raspberry-brûlée, and popped it in her mouth. The explosion of chocolate and sweet-tart fruit was so intensely wonderful, her mind simply stopped.

He'd bought her chocolates. The time and trouble he'd taken was a revelation but not surprising at all. Not for him. No wonder she loved him so much.

She crossed the front lawn to his duplex and saw him. Leaning on the doorframe, arms crossed. Waiting for her.

When she neared, he curled his hand around her nape and kissed her gently. Sweetly. "Mmm. Chocolate tastes good on you. I bet it would taste good in a lot of places."

When he rubbed his knuckles over her breast, her blood heated.

No. She didn't realize she'd spoken until he moved her to his side and put his arm around her.

"You're right. We need to get this straightened out before we can indulge in makeup sex." He led her into the living room.

His casual assumption that they *could* work things out took her breath away. "But what if we can't? I...I haven't talked with Carson." Remorse stole through her. She should have pinned her boy down last night and to heck with his homework and sports. "I let him put me off with excuses last night."

"Babe." Holt tilted her chin up. "You know he's involved—if only peripherally—with whomever is starting the fires."

It wasn't an accusation as much as a statement of fact from a pediatric nurse who'd probably heard a lot of lies. His gaze was level.

"I know. And we'll talk as soon as he gets back from soccer." She set her jaw. "School night or not, we'll stay up as long as it takes."

"Poor kid. I wouldn't want to take you on when you get that look in your eyes."

The amusement in his low smoky voice was infinitely comforting, and she pressed her cheek against his muscular chest. "I missed you." The words slipped out past her control.

His iron-hard arm contracted around her, pulling her almost painfully against his solid frame. "I missed you, too, Josie. Why the fuck do you think I agreed to work an extra shift last night?"

She looked up at him quizzically.

"If I hadn't, I'd have been pounding on your door last night. I promised to give you time."

Like bubbles, her spirits rose to the surface. "Thank you."

"Tonight, if you need help talking to Carson, you can call me. But I figure you can get through to him better than anyone else."

She let out a breath of relief.

"Don't think you're off the hook, sweetheart. You and I still have things to discuss."

"We do?" Under his piercing gaze, her eyes dropped.

"You know what I'm talking about. The way you tried to end things with me—because your son was upset."

Carson had been more than upset. Guilt stabbed her chest. "He said he hates you," she whispered. The memory of his words still shook her.

"Josie, your son likes me. He was over here, hanging out, all the time until he realized you and I were serious. His behavior is simply how kids act when they're afraid their life might change."

Exactly what Linda had said last night. What Josie knew. "You're right. I'll talk with him. I tried after the pet adoption and...well, he pushed me away." She sighed. "He's always been upfront and easy to talk with, but he's changed. I need to learn to deal with this new adolescent behavior and not let him evade the hard discussions."

"Now you see what he's doing, you'll manage." Holt bent his head and kissed her...and deepened the kiss. He smiled down at her. "This is where the makeup sex ensues in case you were wondering."

With a jolt of surprise, she realized he'd moved them into his bedroom. Right into his bedroom.

"But—"

"No *buts*." He unbuttoned her shirt and slid it off. "Mmm, you have gorgeous shoulders. Probably from lifting all those bottles and trays." His lips were warm and velvety as he kissed her neck and nuzzled the curve where her neck met her shoulders.

A shiver ran through her. "Holt, we should...talk."

"We will. We'll have a serious discussion. Very soon." Her jeans dropped down around her ankles.

Shocked, she stared at him in the dim light of the bedroom. His eyes glinted with laughter and determination, a combination that put flutters inside her stomach.

Slowly, he ran his hands up and down her bare arms and waited, gaze on her face. Giving her a chance to protest. But oh, she'd missed him so badly, missed his hands on her, missed his...control.

After two days of worrying about how to please everyone, now, under his confident gaze, she knew she didn't have to think. At all. Silently, she leaned into his hands.

A corner of his mouth quirked upward...and he efficiently stripped off her bra and briefs, leaving her naked and him fully clothed.

She was exposed. Totally.

His gaze ran over her, and he cupped a breast. Weighed it. Caressed it.

She flushed from the heat in his eyes. "You're...still dressed," she said faintly.

"Noticed that, did you?" His smoky voice held a thread of amusement under the steely control. Setting his other hand on her stomach, he pushed her backward until her thighs bumped the bed—and didn't stop until she was on her back. He swung her legs up onto the mattress.

"Holt," she gasped, propping herself up on her elbows.

His raised eyebrow corrected her.

"Sir. You—"

"Shhh." He lifted her arm and lifted her right wrist over her head.

When he sat back, she couldn't lower her arm. *What?* Tilting her head back, she saw a Velcro cuff around her wrist, and even as she realized what he'd done, her left wrist was restrained. She tugged and couldn't get loose. "What are you *doing?*"

"Enjoying myself," he answered. "Pleasing my kinky nature. And yours, as well, I think." His gaze met hers. "The safewords are still red and yellow, pet."

Pet. Enjoying himself. Most of the time, his commanding personality was concealed by his easy-going air. But in bed, his true nature came forward—absolutely masculine, utterly self-confident, totally in charge.

When he ran his hands down her bound arms as if to emphasize her helplessness, the bed seemed to sink a foot.

She stared at him.

"I rather like that expression." Cupping the back of her head, he kissed her, possessing her mouth—not roughly, but with a controlled power that took everything she offered and more.

By the time he moved away, her every protest had vanished.

But when he gripped her left ankle and cuffed it to the bottom bedpost, all sorts of new worries rose. "Holt—uh, Sir. No."

"Yes." He walked to the other side of the bed and restrained her right ankle.

Oh, God. She'd seen this kind of bondage in pictures. She was *spread-eagled,* her arms secured over her head, legs spread widely. Her pussy was open and available for his use.

Her nerves were quaking, even as a disconcerting heat rose within her. Because she trusted him. Whatever he chose to do, he wouldn't hurt her. He'd not abandon her here or do anything she didn't enjoy.

Kneeling between her open legs, he leaned forward and brushed his fingertips over her very hard nipples. "I love how you get turned on by being tied down," he said softly. "Let's see how far I can go in keeping you this hot."

Bending down, he licked over one nipple, then the other, wetting them, blowing them to coolness, covering them with his callused hands. His caresses grew more demanding, harder. Bracing himself on an arm, he kissed her—and rolled her nipple between his fingers. Gently. Then more firmly.

She tried to gasp and found the sound blocked by his mouth, his tongue. Shivers ran over her skin as he switched to her other breast, still kissing her. She tried to pull away, to move her hands, but she was spread out like a banquet for him to sample as he chose.

He sucked on her throbbing nipples and laved them with a tender tongue, playing with her until heat suffused her every breath.

After kissing his way down her stomach, he settled between her open thighs. Pressing her labia open, he ran his finger up and down her pussy, coating the area with her own wetness.

Oh God. When she opened her eyes, she saw that even as he touched her, his gaze was on her face, her arms, her hands, her shoulders. Assessing her responses.

He smiled slowly, holding her gaze with his own as he deliberately slid his finger over her clit.

Excitement coursed into every cell of her body.

"Fuck, you're gorgeous," he said softly, his finger teasing her with circles and light touches.

Before she could start begging for more, he went down on his elbows and bent his head. Delicately, he took her clit between his lips.

The heat of his mouth almost sent her over, and he chuckled. With light pressure, he licked and flicked with his tongue, then sucked in tiny pulls.

Her clit and folds swelled, getting tight and tingling and urgent. Fighting the restraints on her ankles, she tried to raise her hips, to get more.

"Uh-uh, baby," he murmured. "You get what I want to give. When I want to give it. How I want to give it." He set his forearm over her pelvis and ruthlessly continued.

Oh, she was getting closer.

Two fingers slid inside her, stretching her, and the increased sensation buffeted her.

He continued, pumping lightly, until she hovered on the precipice of coming. The world narrowed to his fingers, his tongue, his lips. Couldn't he go just a bit faster? Harder?

Then he moved up her body. Kissing her stomach along the way.

"Holt," she whined.

"Who?" He nipped the side of her breast in reprimand.

"*Sir*. Please."

"Eventually." Holt took her mouth, hard and fast, silencing her completely. Then, with teeth and fingers and tongue, brought her nipples back to throbbing, aching peaks.

Her pussy was next. He used only his tongue this time, teasing and teasing, too lightly to get her off, touching her until she was again close and straining upward.

When he paused, she moaned a protest and yanked at her hands.

He sat back and watched her in silence. His lesson was clear. She had no power. No control. Couldn't even move. Something inside her seemed to fall, crumbling like concrete walls.

"Very nice." His touch was gentle as he stroked her open thighs.

Finally, he rose and stripped off his jeans.

His cock was perfectly straight, wonderfully thick in the middle, more than at the glans or base. Her fingers curled in a longing to touch. "It's so beautiful."

He followed her gaze and let out a huffed laugh before sheathing himself with a condom.

Back between her legs, he braced a hand next to her shoulder, rubbed his cock against her entrance to wet it, and pressed inside in one steady, ruthless thrust, making her struggle to accommodate him. She gasped for air, squirming beneath him.

He'd filled her completely, and her pussy burned with the intimate joining, the solid presence within her. Her clit was making urgent demands for more. "You feel so good."

"We fit well, don't we?" As he propped himself up on his forearms on each side of her head, his weight came down on her hips and belly.

All his weight. How was he going to be able to thrust?

Confused, she tilted her head back to look up at him. "Sir?"

"Now, let's talk."

Holt watched confusion fill Josie's lust-glazed eyes.

Her brows drew together. "Talk?" Her voice was husky from passion, strained from need.

She hadn't come.

Neither had he.

First, they'd talk.

"I love you, Josie."

Pleasure filled her gaze as she inhaled with a soft sound. "I wasn't sure you still..."

"Yes, I still love you. I want to be with you—in your life, yours and Carson's. When the time is right for you both, I want to marry you, be his father, and give him a brother or sister. And a dog. Definitely a dog."

"That's so..." Her voice trailed off, and slowly, her brows drew together. He saw her realize his cock wasn't moving. That he was settled in...to talk. She yanked at her wrists, glared at him. "You're fixin' to have a discussion *now*?" Her attempt to wiggle was frustrated by his weight on her torso, and she gave a frustrated shriek.

"Yes. Now while I'm deep inside you." As he slowly eased out and back in, then stopped, he had to exert all his control. "You need to understand what kind of a man I am. What kind of a Dom I am."

He pressed deeper, her cunt snug and hot around him. "If we're together, decisions will be made by us both—even if it takes hours of talking to reach agreement. I'll share in raising Carson. It'll no longer be you alone." He smiled slightly. "That's the good news and the bad news. You won't have to decide everything on your own, which can be a relief, but...you'll no longer *get* to decide everything, even if you want to."

Her mouth dropped open, and her body tensed as she grasped his meaning. If they were together, she would no longer have sole charge of her boy.

His chest felt tight, but...this was important. A make or break moment.

Her gaze took in his face, and her frown disappeared. As her lips tipped up, his heart did a slow somersault. She nodded. "I understand. That's how real families with two parents work. You might have to remind me now and then." Her eyes were still red from lack of sleep...and crying. He wasn't the only one who'd done a lot of thinking.

He nuzzled her temple, teasing the tiny hairs there before nipping the top of her ear. Her muscles contracted around his dick. *Mmm*. "I will."

Now, how to explain the next part.

"More?" She rubbed her breasts against him provocatively.

"You little brat," he muttered. "Yes, there's more." Tipping his weight to one arm, he slid his hand into her hair and fisted it.

Her pupils dilated with her pleasure.

"I like control, pet. Now, the only time where I *demand* control is in anything having to do with sex. However...if you want to relinquish more, I'll pick up the slack. Gladly."

"You're saying you want me to...lean on you?"

Her years of bartending had given her a wealth of knowledge about people. Yet, when it came right down to it, she'd never lived with a guy. Loved a guy. She was frighteningly inexperienced. "Sweetheart, in a healthy relationship, you lean on each other. Usually in different ways, but it's mutual leaning."

She gave a tiny spurt of laughter. "I like it. *Mutual leaning.*"

"My scholarly author." He had to kiss her. As he took her mouth, her cunt was a hot velvet sheath around his cock, her breasts soft under his chest. And her mouth was generous as he demanded a response.

She was going to kill him.

Pulling back, he cleared his throat. "As we talk, keep what I said in mind."

"Yes, Sir," she whispered.

Settling back into position, he kissed her forehead and got himself back under control. Time for her to talk. "I know you want me, Josie. You want what we can have together. But you're also damned uncertain. It's time to deal with your worries. Tell me what you're concerned about."

She bit her lower lip, nicely swollen from his kisses. "It's mostly about Carson. What if things don't work out between you and me? What if I bring you into our lives and then you leave, making Carson feel rejected by a father figure all over again?"

It was a legitimate concern. Her asshole father—and Everett —had done this damage. "You know what it feels like when a parent rejects you. I get it." Holt rubbed his cheek against hers.

"There are no guarantees in life. Circumstances change, people change. I can say I love you and want you and Carson as my own, but I can't make you an ironclad promise everything will work out forever."

Everything inside him wanted to do exactly that, to fix everything in the world for her.

"I know." She looked away. "I'm just not sure I should risk—"

He set his fingers under her chin. "Look at me, Josie."

Her eyes met his.

"Children learn by example. If you toss me aside to protect his heart—and yours—what are you teaching him? That he should flee every time his heart is at risk? That he should never fall in love because he might get hurt?"

Her eyes widened as his words struck home.

Life was full of lessons—and pain. After Nadia'd dumped him, he'd spent a fair amount of time thinking. Working through his reactions. It was instinctive to try to protect vulnerable bits. The balls, the throat...the heart.

"Oh, God. I've been teaching him to avoid love."

"And loving him at the same time." Holt stroked her soft cheek. "Truly living—and loving—is...risky, but isn't that what it's all about?"

When tears appeared in her eyes, his heart wanted to break. But the sweet acceptance was there also. She agreed.

He breathed out a relieved sigh. "Our relationship is going to take work, Josie. You, sweetheart, are a scrapper when it comes to everything else. Can you fight as hard to be with me?"

His muscles tensed as he waited.

"I love you," she whispered.

Yes, that was the answer he needed. *Thank-fucking-God.*

Josie rubbed her cheek against Holt's, breathing in his masculine scent. She loved him so much.

And she wanted him as a father for Carson. What finer gift could she give her son? Holt would show Carson everything a man could be. He'd fight for her boy. Comfort her boy. Love her boy.

He already did—she could tell.

She wanted Holt for her, too. She could think of nothing better than to spend her days with him, this man who would help her when she was weak, cheer her on when she was strong. He'd take charge if she wanted him to and wrap her in comfort and care.

And in turn, she'd be there for him. She remembered his grief that night after he'd lost a tiny patient. She had her own strengths to bring to the relationship, her own kind of comfort to give in return.

They were stronger together than they were apart.

Life wasn't easy, though. There would be struggles in their future. That's what he was concerned about. Whether she'd go the distance with him.

He'd taught her that he'd give his all to stay together. She smiled, thinking of the chocolates. He hadn't given up on her and Carson. He'd bided his time and paved the way with sweets. Then he'd tied her down until she had to talk with him. She looked up at the headboard and the wrist restraints. "You're pretty sneaky, aren't you?" she muttered.

His lips curved in a smile. "Sometimes."

"Yes."

"Yes, what, sweetheart?" he asked.

"Yes, I'll fight to keep us together. I won't cut and run. We'll work things out...together."

His eyes lit and the satisfaction in his expression silenced her completely.

At least until he started to move. Then the only thing she could do was moan as he took her...slow and gentle.

Hard and fast.

And very thoroughly.

CHAPTER TWENTY-SEVEN

Soccer practice finished, Carson sat on the grass and stuffed his soccer shoes and shin guards into his backpack. Around him, the rest of the kids were also packing up to go home. Muttering, Yukio was trying to unknot one of his shoelaces.

After zipping up his pack, Carson pulled his phone from the side pocket. A quick glance at the top of the display showed a tiny envelope. He'd gotten a text. He grinned. It still gave him a rush, having his own phone like everyone else.

"Yo, Cars, whatcha reading?" Yukio looked over.

"Got a message." Carson frowned, seeing the sender. "It's Brandon. Now what?" All week, Brandon had acted like Carson wasn't even in the room. So had Ryan. Made him feel like shit. At least, Yukio and Juan were still talking to him.

Carson read the message aloud. *"Cars, cuz yer my friend, your father is gonna pay for being an asshole and treating you like shit."*

"What?" Yukio said.

Carson read it again as fear grew in his belly. "Today's Thursday. Brandon'd said Everett and everybody would be at Disney World tonight."

"And he wanted to start a fire." Yukio scowled. "I thought you told him no. Did you change your—"

"No, I didn't change my mind. He's not even talking to me!" Carson's heart thumped inside his chest like he'd run a dozen laps. His thumbs felt fat and awkward as he texted back. *"Leave my father alone."*

Yukio beside him, he waited. A minute, then two ticked by.

He tried to make a regular phone call. Waited.

Yukio spoke first. "He's not answering. You suppose he really went to your dad's place?"

"Oh shit-buckets, what am I gonna do?"

"Call your mom?"

Carson shook his head. "What if Brandon's bullshitting, trying to piss me off or something?"

"Yeah, he does that a lot. But what if he's not?"

The other soccer players had left, and the field was quiet. The sports lights flickered and came on.

It was getting dark.

Carson swallowed. "I need to go check. Make sure." His voice came out thick. He'd told Brandon no. *Told* him. It'd take an hour to get to asshole Everett's house, and Mom expected him back when it got dark and that was like now. "Can you call, too? Keep calling? Tell him not to do anything? I mean..."

"Sure."

"I...I'll call the cops if I have to." The thought made Carson want to puke, but he hauled in a breath. He would.

Yukio grimaced. "Yeah, I hear you. Can you call me...whenever? Let me know if it's all okay?"

Nothing was going to be okay. He'd have to ride his bike in the dark past that street where he'd gotten attacked. What if those men were there? A shiver of fear went through Carson.

"Okay." After shoving his phone into his shorts pocket, he yanked his backpack on. "Thanks, Kio."

An hour later, Carson made it to his father's fancy house.

Near the place where he'd been attacked, the streets were filled with bumper-to-bumper cars. An accident had happened, and nothing was moving. Even the ambulances and fire trucks were stuck. *Jeez.* He'd only gotten through cuz he could take to the sidewalks.

Shaking inside, Carson steered into the driveway. He dropped his bike on the front lawn and spotted two others. Ryan's gold-striped bike lay in the shadows. *Shit-buckets.* This was crazy. After getting butt-hurt and ignoring Carson all week, why was Brandon acting like they were bros again? Saying he was gonna burn Everett's house *for* Carson?

Carson scowled.

Brandon's bike had a cloth cargo trailer hitched behind it. Carson walked over and pulled the covering off. The smell of gasoline wafted up.

The trailer was *filled* with red gas containers, glass bottles, and lots of other stuff. Carson's mouth dropped open, and he jerked back. Brandon was going to do more than toss one bottle into a room.

Carson shuddered, looking around desperately. Was anyone home he could tell? The sun was long gone, and most of the yard was dark. Only one dim light showed upstairs. The outside front door and garage lights were on, like people did when they left. Brandon had been right about Everett being gone.

Spotting movement at the corner of the house, Carson lifted his hand and hissed.

Brandon jogged over with Ryan trailing behind.

"I knew you'd show," Brandon whispered. His grin was big and happy and excited. He did a fancy victory shuffle. "This is gonna be epic."

Burning down a house was epic? "*No.*" Carson got up in his face, so mad he felt like his eyes would cross. "I told you *no.* Leave my father alone!"

"Oh, come on, Cars. It'll be fun," Ryan whined.

Brandon scowled. "You said you hated him. Now you're all loving to your asshole daddy?"

"I'm not. But setting a fire's wrong. Illegal."

"What a pussy. I thought you had a pair, but guess not. Wish I could burn *my* fucking father's place around his ears." Brandon unhitched the bike trailer and pulled it toward the house. "C'mon, Ryan."

Ryan hesitated.

Carson hauled in a breath. *Shit-buckets.* They weren't *listening*. His heart hammered crazy in his chest as he watched Brandon just...keep walking away. Toward the house.

Carson's hands clenched. He had to do *something*.

Putting his head down, he charged, tackling Brandon from the side. It was like hitting a wall—a mushy wall, but still.

Whipping around, Brandon punched him. Hard.

Carson landed on the ground, his shoulder hitting first. *Owwww.* Lying in the cold grass, he held his throbbing cheek. "You—"

"Stupid fucktard!" Brandon kicked him in the gut.

Pain roared through Carson as he grabbed his stomach, trying to breathe. Tears burned his eyes, making everything blurry. "Don't do it. Leave my fa—"

"I'm going to light this fucking place *up*." Brandon's lips pulled back so far his teeth showed like a dog's. "I'm gonna watch it *burn*."

As Brandon pulled the trailer around the side of the house, Ryan dropped down beside Carson, his eyes scared. "Jesus, Cars, he got you good."

Carson sucked in a breath. "Don't help him, Ryan. He's crazy."

"Yeah, kinda." Glancing at the house doubtfully, Ryan rose and pulled Carson to his feet. "I...I'm outta here. You better run, too."

"I will." Moving slower, Carson reached his bike and got on.

Ryan lifted his hand, bike almost flying as he sped toward the driveway. He got there and paused, looking back.

Rubbing his aching stomach, Carson waved him on, and Ryan pedaled into the street and away.

The yard felt awfully lonely. Slowly, Carson lowered his bike. He couldn't just...leave. It didn't matter who owned the house—burning it was wrong. He had to try to stop Brandon again.

But what if Brandon wouldn't stop?

Call 911? Jeez, he couldn't. They wouldn't believe him anyway —he was just a kid.

Call Mom? She'd come. She could do something. Only Brandon was awful big and strong and knew karate. He might hurt her.

Who could handle Brandon in a rage? *Handle*...the word brought back a memory. *"Just remember you can call me if you get into trouble you can't handle."*

He pulled out his phone, looked up the number, and touched the CALL button. Guilt swept through him. He'd sure been a stupid jerk.

"Yeah? Who's this?"

"Holt? I need help."

With Josie beside him, Holt parked at the curb outside Everett Lanning's house. He jumped out of the car, fuming with frustration. Detouring around a massive traffic jam at Dale Mabry intersection had delayed them.

What the fuck was going on? Why was Carson here? The kid hadn't explained, simply said he needed Holt *"right now"* and hung up. Jesus, he hoped the boy hadn't gotten caught sneaking around the asshole's house.

Josie'd been with Holt when the panicked call came, and she'd insisted on coming. Not that he'd argued. They needed to work as a team with Carson.

With Josie beside him, he jogged up the driveway, smelled fire, and stopped dead. White plumes of smoke rose from the house.

Through the busted-out front windows, he could see multiple fires consuming the walls and flickering over the ceiling. "Oh, *fuck*."

As fire alarms in the house blared, Holt yanked out his phone and punched 911. "Josie, do you see Carson?"

He heard the emergency dispatcher answer, didn't bother to listen, and snapped out, "House fire." How many of the normally answering units were stuck in the Dale Mabry traffic jam?

As he recited the address for the dispatcher, Josie headed to the left.

Spotting movement around the side, Holt ran toward the right.

Shovel raised over his head, a husky kid stood over a lump on the ground. Over *Carson*.

Holt roared, "Drop it!"

The boy—Brandon—spun, dropped the shovel, and ran.

"Carson." Holt sprinted forward.

Carson shoved to his feet and limped to Holt. "You came! He started a fire. We have to call 911."

"I called." After guiding him to the portico at the front of the house. The yard light revealed bruises and cuts on his face. What the fuck happened here?

Where had Josie gone?" Holt shouted, "I've got him, Josie."

Inside the house, the fire's roar was beginning to compete with the sirens and then something exploded with a loud bang inside. A new set of flames shot up. Had Carson's friend used Molotov cocktails here the way he had at the school? *Jesus.*

"Is anyone inside?" he asked Carson.

"No. Brandon said everyone was going to Disney World."

Relief rolled through Holt.

"Carson!" Josie ran toward them across the lawn.

"Mom." Breaking free, Carson met his mother in front of the broken out front window.

Above the portico where Holt stood, a window shrieked open.

"Help!" A dark-haired boy maybe a year or so older than Carson appeared in the window. "I can't get out—I'm locked in. Please, help my sister. Help Britney!"

Children. Holt's chest compressed as he moved to below the child. Dammit, what with that pileup, no telling how soon the firefighters would make it.

A terrified shriek came from inside the house.

"No!" Carson shouted, moving closer to the window. "The stairs are on fire. No, don't!" Evading his mother's grab, he vaulted into the house through the busted out window.

"Carson, no!" Josie screamed and followed.

And Holt went after them. As he reached the window, heat poured through it. *Fuck, no.* The room was reaching flashover when everything would ignite. Terror filled him.

A young girl stood frozen, as Carson charged up the burning stairs toward her.

Holt jumped through the window, seeing that Josie was half-way across the living room.

Bang! Something exploded. A sharp pain ripped through Holt's arm.

Fresh flames shot upward. Bottles were scattered here and there in the room—unexploded Molotov-cocktails—and Holt knew when the fire reached them...

Too close to the one that had exploded, Josie staggered. Blood poured from her shoulder and leg.

"Mom!" Carson reversed course to run down the stairs.

"Go up," Holt roared, running across the room. "I got her. *Go. Up.*"

Grabbing the girl's hand, Carson headed up the stairs.

Without slowing, Holt scooped Josie up and took the stairs, two at a time.

The children stood outside a room. Hammering came from inside. The girl—Britney—jiggled the handle, crying and yanking at it. "It's locked, it's *locked.* Timothy!"

"Put me down, Holt," Josie said. "We have to get that door open."

He glanced at her. Bleeding—but under control. His Josie was something special.

"Stand back, kids." He set Josie on her feet and yelled, "Timothy, get away from the door."

Carson dragged the girl away from the door.

Using the power in his hips and lower back, Holt kicked the door beside the lock. The piece-of-shit door cracked like an icicle and shot open. Holt shooed everyone inside.

With a *foomph*, the living room ignited. *Hell.* Shit would burn fast now—he needed to get everyone the hell out.

Josie dropped onto the bed, pulling a trembling Carson into her arms.

Grabbing a T-shirt off the floor, Holt yanked a big shard of glass from Josie's leg and made a hasty pressure dressing. "You with me, baby?"

"Yeah." She pressed her hand against the cut on her arm. "Can we get out of here?"

"I think we'd better." Holt saw the girl moving toward the door. "Stay here, sweetie."

She stopped, and when Josie held out her hand, edged toward the bed.

Timothy was at the window.

Holt joined him. "Is anyone else in the house?"

"Uh-uh. Just me and Britney."

Thank fuck. Holt leaned out the window, judging how far down the portico roof was, how far to the ground.

The boy looked up. "Are we stuck?"

"Nah, we can do this." Holt gripped his shoulder and told everyone, "I'm going to go out, stand on the portico roof, and help you guys out. You with me?"

The kid nodded. Carson nodded. Josie gave him a faint smile

and her "Yes, Sir," pleased the hell out of him. Beside Josie, Britney nodded.

Good enough. "After me, I want you, Josie."

"But—" she looked at Carson.

No time for explanations. "Trust me." He held her gaze.

She nodded.

"Then Britney, then Carson." He ruffled Timothy's hair. "You help the others out and come last. I'll be ready to catch you."

Timothy struggled to contain his fear. "Okay."

"Good boy." Holt didn't wait, but went out the window, feet-first, belly-down. He hung onto the windowsill until he'd calculated his angle, then swung slightly and dropped. The portico roof was almost directly under the window, and he only skidded slightly on landing.

He braced his feet, one on each side of the peaked roof. "Josie, stomach down, hang, and drop like I did. I'll catch you."

He could see her reluctance to leave Carson, but damn, she came anyway. A second later, he had her in his arms. He gave her a quick hug and pointed down. "I want you on the ground. I'll lower each child to you."

And looking at the concrete below the portico, she understood why she'd come second. "That'll work."

"Slide off the roof. I'll help lower you."

Without arguing, she turned over, eased herself off the edge, wincing as the gutter grated over the myriad of bloody cuts she'd gotten from the bomb. Holt flattened out, holding her wrists until she was completely off the roof. "You have a few feet of drop. I'm letting go now."

She fell the last few feet to the sidewalk beside the portico and gave a soft grunt of pain. Then was on her feet. "I'm ready." No tears, no hysterics.

"Fuck, I love you," he said.

She gave a tiny laugh. "Such language. There are children present."

CHERISE SINCLAIR

How could she make him smile at a time like this? Holt rose and called up to the window. "Help the girl out, guys. Hang onto her wrists until I tell you to let go."

The lights were gone. The second floor was dark with smoke billowing out and upward. The children must be half-blinded. But Timothy kept it together and guided his sister's feet out the window. He and Carson held her wrists as she slid downward.

Britney made panicking sounds as Holt reached up and grabbed her legs.

A siren sounded. About fucking time.

"Let go now," he directed, and the boys—one on each wrist—released. The girl slid down against him. Securing her, he turned, knelt, and lowered her over the edge of the portico to Josie in one smooth movement.

"Got her," Josie called.

"Carson. Out. Same way."

Carson did it on his own, while Timothy kept a hand on his wrist...just in case.

When Carson landed in his arms, Holt gave him a hard hug. "You kept your head better than a lot of adults. I'm very proud of you," he whispered, before handing him down to Josie. He noticed the little girl clinging to Josie's waist even as Carson was hugging his mother from the front.

One more. "I'm ready, Timothy. You know how to do it. Don't let go until I tell you."

The kid was already squirming out the window. He hung by his hands until Holt had a good grip. At least this one was tall. "Got you. Let go."

He pulled the trembling boy into his arms and held him a minute.

Sirens wailed as a fire engine hauled ass down the street and into the driveway. Lights flashed, reflecting off the building. "Let's get you down, or we'll both get wet."

The kid managed a small laugh.

When Holt lowered him to Josie, she staggered at his weight, and her leg almost buckled. Her arm, side, and thigh were covered in blood.

He needed to get her to an ER.

Holt slid off the portico, landed beside her, and tucked an arm around her waist. Britney wouldn't release her, and Timothy attached himself to his sister's side. Holt put an arm around Carson, and as a group, they headed down the driveway.

Josie could feel the young girl shaking. Actually, Josie was, too. Holt's arm around her waist was the only thing keeping her upright. Sweat was cold on her face, back, and neck. Her entire right side was a mass of burning pain and hot trickling blood.

Didn't matter. Her son was safe. The other two children were safe. She leaned her head for a second against Holt's hard upper arm and felt him kiss the top of her head. Holt was safe.

Oh, God, what a nightmare. Why, oh why, was Carson here?

Shouting to each other, the firefighters were running to the building with long hoses.

A short muscular firefighter ran up to Holt. "Is anyone else in the house?"

The children flinched at the loud voice, and Josie tucked the girl closer to her side.

"Timothy"—Holt motioned to Everett's boy—"said it was only him and his sister."

Timothy nodded. "Our parents are at a party. Only my sister and me were home."

"Good. That's good." The firefighter glanced at the upstairs window, then at Josie and Holt. "We saw you getting them out—nice job." And then he blinked. "Well, fuck me, it's Holt. Aren't you out of your territory?"

"Yeah. I'll need to talk with you—and the police. This was arson. I can ID the perp, but I need to get Josie to the ER."

"I'm fine." Josie pulled in a breath. "If you need to stay, we can get a taxi and head home."

"Baby, you're going to need stitches for some of those cuts."

Carson made a pained sound, and his eyes filled with tears.

Holt pulled him closer. "Josie, you're going to the ER." His gaze was level, his voice soft...and he wasn't giving her a choice.

The firefighter nodded. "Listen to Holt, ma'am." His gaze swept over the burning building, then narrowed on Holt. The black smudges on his clothing. "Tell me you didn't charge in there, gearless, like a probie."

"Yep." Holt ruffled Carson's hair. "My boy here charged in to save the girl. She froze halfway down the stairs—and would've been caught in the flashover."

Hearing the pride in Holt's voice, Josie almost smiled until she remembered that blast of sound and heat from the living room. Britney would have died—the fire truck wouldn't have arrived in time.

"And my woman went in after Carson," Holt continued. "You sure wouldn't have stood outside sucking your thumb if they were yours, Smitty."

"No, probably not." After a second, Smitty frowned at Carson. "Don't do that again." Then he grinned at Holt. "Gotta say, they got guts."

"I know," Holt said under his breath and squeezed Josie's waist. The pride in his voice made her eyes mist.

———

Josie wasn't sure how much time had passed as the E.R. nurses and doctor cleaned and stitched her up.

Earlier in the ER waiting room, Holt'd said she'd probably been cut by a bottle of gas exploding. His jaw had gone tight as he added that if she hadn't been turned half away from it, the glass could have hit her face and neck. Carson had burst into tears. With a wince, Holt had held him and told Josie, "Sorry," in a mutter. Angry at her injuries, he'd obviously forgotten Carson was listening.

Her right side and arm had a ton of small cuts as well as long slices where bigger glass fragments had carved through skin and flesh. By the time glass had been tweezered from every cut, and everything washed and stitched, glued, or bandaged, her whole side felt as if a thousand bees were stinging her. Thankfully, Holt kept workout clothes in his vehicle so she had his loose gray sweatpants and T-shirt to wear.

Following the nurse out of the cubicle, she found Holt in the waiting room with the children—all three of them. After hearing their parents were on the way back, the Lanning children had asked to wait with Holt.

Sitting in a corner chair, Holt looked like a hen with chicks. Britney had pulled her chair as close as possible to Holt and was nestled against him. Carson had done the same on the other side. Timothy was next to his sister and holding her hand. Obviously feeling safe with Holt, all three were half-asleep.

Earlier, Holt had mentioned maybe having a child. He'd make an awesome father—and, she smiled, Carson would make a wonderful big brother.

Carson looked up and saw her. "Mom!" He dashed over, skidding to a stop a second before he ran into her. "Are you okay? Are—"

Laughing, she pulled him into a hug and ignored the pain. "I'll be sore for a couple of days, but I'm fine."

He gave a huge sigh of relief.

She echoed it. Her son was alive and unharmed. But he sure had some explaining to do. She held him tighter...and felt him wince in pain.

What?

Releasing him, she stepped back and got a good look at him in the bright light. He had a black eye, a cut across his cheek, raw scraped knees. And his ribs were obviously sore. She touched his face. "Carson, what happened? With the fire? To you?"

"Brandon wouldn't listen to me, wouldn't stop. I tried, Mom. I tried to stop him. But he's bigger—and fights better."

"Fights?" Anger flared within her. *Brandon.*

Then Holt was there in front of her, the other two children beside him. Britney ran over to snuggle against Josie's side.

Holt put a hand on Carson's shoulder. "No worries, Josie. He's been putting ice on that black eye while we waited for you."

She caught the subtext. This wasn't the time or place to have a proper mommy meltdown.

"Timothy!"

At the woman's cry, Timothy turned, and relief filled his expression. "Mama!"

Coming in the ER door was a short, trim brunette around forty years old. Her expression frantic, she ran across the room.

Timothy met her with an audible thump and was buried in her arms. Her legs obviously failing, she went down on one knee, and Britney hit her a second later. All three were crying.

Josie pulled Carson close. When her independent boy actually clung to her, she felt like weeping, too. With an arm around him, she asked Holt, "What happens now?"

"Now we talk to the police. Probably the arson investigator." Holt scrubbed his face. "Brace yourselves. It'll be a long night."

"What the hell happened?" The shout of anger came from... Everett. Older, hair graying, beefier, but Everett.

Josie flinched, and so did Carson.

Everett stalked across the waiting room, two men trailing behind him.

Shoulders hunched, Timothy stepped away from his mother. "Dad."

"You started a fire, didn't you? Because I grounded your ass, you started a fucking fire."

Timothy cringed. "No. A boy started a fire. We heard glass

break and saw him. He ran around the house throwing stuff inside and then all of a sudden everything was on fire and—"

"You liar. What were you brats doing? My *house* is *burning*."

Even as Josie pulled in a breath to defend the boy, Holt asked, "Are you the one who left a child locked in his room with no way to get out?"

Everett took a step back at the sheer fury in Holt's voice.

The children's mother gasped and stared at Everett...who flushed a dark red.

"Yeah, you were. By the way," Holt said with a glance at the other two men. "Timothy is telling the truth. Neither of your children set the fire."

Everett glared at Holt before his gaze moved to Josie. His eyes widened. "You? Here?"

"Yes, Everett. There was a boy who—"

Seeing Carson, he darkened with fury. "You... Damn you, *you* burned my house, didn't you?" He took a step forward, hands clenched. "You're not my fucking son, you little bastard. I have a son. You're—"

"That's enough," Holt snapped, his hand on Carson's shoulder. "Carson didn't start the fire. He tried to stop the—"

Everett turned to Josie, and his rage was chilling. "You'll pay, you bitch. Pay for my house, for the trauma. I'm going to sue you until every dime you make comes to me."

"Doubtful," Holt said in a measured tone. "But a lawsuit will be an excellent way to open up a paternity suit and expose the bastard who committed statutory rape, got a sixteen-year-old girl pregnant, and dumped her without a backward look. You owe years of child support for your son here."

The blood drained from Everett's face, and he took a step back.

"Son?" Catching on faster than his sister, Timothy stared at his father, then Carson. "You're my brother?"

Carson's mouth dropped open. "I...I guess."

"No. No, he's not," Everett yelled. "She's a lying—"

"The boy looks like Britney." Everett's wife rose to her feet, arms still around her daughter. The woman's voice turned hard. "A sixteen-year-old, Everett?"

"Of course not, Pamela. She's lying. I would never—"

"You would." Pamela pulled her children closer and took a step away from her husband. Her face tightened. With betrayal. With disgust.

"Pamela, listen..."

"No, not any longer. I've tried to ignore your flings, but...to prey on a child?" The woman drew herself up straight. "And after grounding Timothy, you locked him in his room? With us gone? He was supposed to watch over Britney, and he was locked in his room? What kind of a father does that?"

She didn't wait for his answer. "No kind of a father. And you're no kind of a husband either." Arms around her children, she walked out the door.

Everett slowly turned to Josie, his anger so visible, she took a step back. "You—"

Without a word, Holt moved between them, pushing her behind his back.

The feeling of being protected was...indescribable, but she couldn't let him take on her problems. "Holt, no," she whispered.

One of the two men accompanying Everett heard her, and his eyes narrowed. "Holt? Yeah, I recognize you. Filled in for one of ours a couple of years ago."

"Yeah, Captain." Holt pulled Carson securely between him and Josie. "Carson here didn't start the fire. He tried to stop it. He can tell you what happened."

"Good. We'll need to—" The captain's cell phone rang, and he held up a finger to wait as he took the call. His brows drew together. "Hell, seriously? I'll be right there."

Scowling, he said, "Wind's picked up. Neighboring houses are at risk—we need to evacuate. I need to get back."

Josie's heart sank. More houses. This was a nightmare for everyone.

"Holt, ma'am, the police and arson investigation will take point on the interviews." The captain motioned to the other man who'd come in with him. "This is Detective Simonsen."

After nodding to Holt, the captain strode quickly out the hospital exit.

Badge on his belt, the stocky detective had dark hair and a beefy red face. He looked them over with a cold, hard expression. "We're going to the station."

To the police station. Josie suppressed a shiver and nodded calmly. "Of course."

Everett crossed his arms over his chest and he stared at her, then Carson, before turning to the detective. "Keith, make sure her lying bastard pays for what he's done."

Keith? They were friends?

When the police detective nodded, Josie felt her heart sink.

CHAPTER TWENTY-EIGHT

With his mom beside him, Carson waited for the detective to return.

The air in the ugly police station room was really cold, and he was sure that was why he couldn't stop trembling. They'd probably been in this cold awful room for hours.

It didn't even have any pictures or anything. The table was wood and old, and when Carson had given it a push, it hadn't moved.

At least Mom was here; the detective had kicked Holt out. Carson wanted Holt, too. Because... He looked up at Mom. "Detective Simonsen didn't believe me, did he?"

"No, he didn't." Mom's mouth twisted sideways. "I'd guess he and Everett are friends." Mom reached across the space between them and put her hand on his shoulder. "*I* believe you, honey. We'll get this worked out."

He could feel her fingers shaking. Mom was scared. Him, too, although his heart wasn't pounding like when the house was on fire. This felt more like he'd never get warm again.

The detective came back in. His face was mean in a way that

made Carson scrunch down in his chair. "The Lanning's house is pretty much destroyed. That make you feel good, boy?"

"Does it make you feel good picking on an eleven-year-old child, detective?" Mom's voice had the sharp edge that said she didn't like the man.

The detective's mouth twisted nasty-like, and he slapped the table, making Carson jump. "Since your mama can't keep you from breaking the law, you're gonna go to juvenile hall. It's where we send the—

"The children who are actually convicted of crimes." A really big guy walked into the room. He had an accent, like English only bouncier. He looked down at Detective Simonsen like the detective was a rat turd. "Carson hasn't been convicted of anything. In fact, he went to considerable effort and pain to try to stop the arsonist."

"Like you know anything about it, O'Keefe. The boy's been harassing Everett Lanning and showed up on his doorstep. He's admitted he was pissed off when Lanning told him to leave. What better way to get revenge than burning the house down?"

Holt quietly entered the room and walked around the table. He put his arm around Mom's shoulder and squeezed Carson's shoulder. His hand was warm and big, and Carson couldn't keep from reaching up and curling his fingers around it.

"What the fuck is *he* doing in here?" The detective glared at Holt.

Carson tightened his grip.

"Detective, a warning: The recorder is active, and your language is inappropriate." O'Keefe crossed his arms over his chest. "As to why Holt is in here? Any experienced interviewer would know a terrified child gives questionable answers. Since you were treating the boy's mother as abusively as you were the boy, I brought in someone he'd feel safe with."

Detective Simonsen looked as if he would choke. "You —you—"

"Yeah, me. As arson investigator—and this *was* arson—I'll be interviewing the boy, which we might have done together if you hadn't been a"—O'Keefe looked at Carson and winked—"an idiot. I suggest you talk with Yukio and Ryan. Ryan was there. If you check their phones, the timing and perpetrator are quite clear."

O'Keefe opened the door and waited.

The detective didn't move. "They're friends of the kid's. Of course, they'd back him up."

"Lanning's children aren't, and they're quite certain as to which boy was running around the house, throwing incendiary devices through the windows. They saw Carson tackle Brandon in an attempt to get him to stop."

"I'll see about that." With a disbelieving growl, the detective stalked out of the room and slammed the door.

Mom jerked at the noise, and her thigh thumped the table leg. She made a pained sound.

Carson's eyes filled with tears. She'd gotten all cut up because of him. Because he'd been stupid. "I'm s-sorry, Mom."

"Oh, hey, honey..." Face soft, she rubbed his arm. "...it's just tiny cuts. They'll heal."

She could have died. Carson's breath hitched.

Holt could've died. Carson looked up at him. "I'm s-sorry. I don't hate you, an' I shouldn't have yelled at you, an' you were right. I was there at the school. And that fireman yelled at you, cuz you went into the house. Cuz I called you, and you could've got killed. Because of me."

Carson tried not to cry, but the tears kept filling his eyes.

A corner of Holt's mouth tipped up. "Apology accepted for yelling at me, and I'm glad you don't hate me."

Carson held his breath.

"You made a mistake in your choice of a friend and in getting pulled into something wrong, but calling me was the right thing to do. You tried your best to keep Brandon from burning down a house—and I'm very proud of you, Carson."

Carson could only stare at him, holding the words as tightly as he held Holt's hand.

A chair squeaked over the floor as O'Keefe pulled it closer. When the big guy sat down, the chair made a groaning noise. "Carson, Josie, my job is to investigate fires. I have a nice long title, but how about you call me Cullen?"

Carson licked his lips. "Can Holt stay?"

"If you'd like." Cullen stretched his legs out, his hands clasped on his stomach. He looked comfortable, like he was going to watch a football game or something. "I've known Holt a while—firefighters and arson investigators run into each other a lot. If you want him to watch your back, I'm good with that."

With a relieved breath, Carson nodded and then had an awful thought. He'd been a real butthead to Holt. Biting his lip, he turned to look up at the man. "Will you?"

"Of course." Holt sounded like he still liked Carson. "I wouldn't have left you at all, but I wanted to get Cullen in here."

Carson's breath whuffed out. *Okay.* Feeling almost brave, he turned to Cullen. "What do you want to know?"

"You know what? Since you and Holt are buddies, I'll let him ask the questions—and I'll butt in if he misses something. How's that?"

Talk to Holt? Yes. "Good. That's good."

"First, let's get you two closer." Holt dragged Mom's chair closer to Carson's.

Right away, she put her arm around him...like the mean detective had told her not to.

Carson's eyes stung with tears again as he leaned into her.

Holt moved between Carson and the big guy. When he went down on one knee, something inside Carson loosened, because it was the position Holt used when he was showing Carson the cool stuff on a Harley, or when he was giving soccer pointers. His arms lay on his thigh; his hands were loose and relaxed. His gaze met Carson's, and yeah, this was Holt. All calm and easy.

"Ready?" He lifted an eyebrow and waited for Carson to nod, then half smiled. "Good boy. So I figure I want to hear about the classroom fire first. Why did you guys pick that room?"

Carson leaned his head against his mother's arm, took a breath, and told him.

He'd talked and talked and talked. Carson's mouth was dry, and his head buzzed like he had flies in his brain or something. He figured it must be awful late at night. But Holt and Cullen finally said they were done.

As Carson limped out of the ugly-ass room, Mom was holding his hand.

"This way." Holt put his arm around Carson's shoulders and guided him forward through the wide room filled with desks, computers, and detectives talking with people.

Shit-buckets. Carson stumbled...because Juan, Ryan, and Yukio were in the room.

Juan was talking to Detective Simonsen. Juan's tiny mama stood beside the desk, arms crossed over her chest. Her dark eyes looked angry as she stared at the detective.

A different guy detective was with Ryan. Ryan's mama held his hand. His father's arm lay along the back of Ryan's chair.

Carson gave a huff of relief. Ryan'd be okay.

At another desk, Yukio was showing his phone to a woman detective. His parents stood behind him, hands on his shoulders and nodding when he spoke.

As Carson crossed the room, his friends noticed. Guiltily, he cringed when they stared and stared, but then Yukio gestured to his eye. Oh. Right. Carson had a black eye and scrapes and stuff. After a second, his friends nodded to him.

Then, two cops in uniforms hauled in...Brandon. Brandon was fighting, kicking, and calling them ugly names.

Carson wanted to cry when they thumped Brandon roughly into a chair. If Carson hadn't told...

"Good. They caught him," Holt said. When he looked down at Carson, the hard look in his eyes went away. "Aw, hell, ace. You know, it's a tough place to be, torn between a friend and what you know is right. Remember though...starting fires was more important to Brandon than you guys were."

No, Brandon wasn't like that. Scowling, Carson started to pull away and winced, because his leg hurt. His shoulder hurt. Everything hurt. Brandon *was* like that. His "friend" had punched him, kicked him, and would've hit him with a shovel if Holt hadn't come.

Spotting Carson, Brandon half rose, his face filled with hatred. "You fucking pussy. I did it for you. To get back at your father and teach him a lesson. What was your fucking problem?"

"You didn't do it for me," Carson said slowly. "You did it because you wanted to set something on fire. And because you couldn't get to your own dad."

Brandon scowled. "Yours called you a *bastard*."

Everett had. And having his father be a total dick kinda hurt, but it didn't really matter. Carson shook his head. "I told you I didn't want you to do anything. Not for me."

"He's your father."

"Nah, he's just a"—what had Yukio said?—"a sperm donor."

At Holt's low laugh, Carson almost smiled. Because he had something Brandon didn't—something important. And hey, here was a way to make that clear to Holt and Mom without getting all mushy and stuff.

"Like anyone believes that," Brandon sneered.

"You're a moron. I don't need that asshole Everett." Carson lifted his chin, not daring to look up at the two adults beside him. "I'm getting a better dad."

This time it was his mother who made a sound—a big ol' gasp.

Grinning, Carson led his mom and *father-to-be* out of the room.

CHAPTER TWENTY-NINE

Her baby had a talent for soccer, Josie thought, as she sipped her Diet Coke and watched the middle school boys practicing for the upcoming tryouts.

It felt good to get back to doing normal activities after the horrible events of last Thursday. However, normal wouldn't last long. The principal had talked with the school board yesterday—Monday—and the administration wanted to play hard-ass.

Josie's mouth compressed. To protect her boy, she'd be a hard-ass right back. She might not be the only one, since Holt was as protective of Carson as she was. She felt a funny quiver in her belly. Every time a law enforcement person had shown up to talk with her son, Holt had been there. Guarding Carson.

He loved her, and he loved Carson. She'd begun to believe in romance and love the way she had when she was young. He was openly spending the nights with her. Last night, when he was working his 24 hours at the firehouse, the evening had felt wrong and flat without him there, discussing the day's events at supper, reading or watching TV, playing a game with Carson. During the night, she'd reached for him and ended up curled around his pillow. Yes, she missed him.

And loved him. Truly, nothing had been the same since he came into her life.

Wasn't it funny that, in the middle of winter, she felt as if spring had arrived?

She took another sip of Diet Coke and smiled as Carson took the ball down the field, feinted and dodged around a bigger boy, then shot the ball to Yukio. Her boy was amazing. "Woohoo!"

Recognizing her voice, Carson got a tiny smile, which he couldn't show, of course, because...hey, it was his mother.

Josie grinned, then frowned as someone crowded her on the bleachers. Without looking away from the field, she scooted over a few inches.

"I've heard that being ignored by a beautiful woman can destroy a man's tender psyche. You wouldn't want to inflict permanent damage, would you, pet?" A sexy, smooth murmur broke her focus on the game.

Her head snapped up, and she turned. "Holt? What are you doing here?" Every cell in her body began to dance and warble happy songs.

"I was checking Stella's blood pressure, and she said Carson had preseason practice. I wanted to see him when he has enough room to really run."

"Oh." The new net in the backyard had been getting a lot of use, but he was right. There wasn't much space.

"Besides, I missed you." The dark desire in his voice made her body hum.

"I missed you, too. I think you've ruined me for sleeping alone." Her voice came out grumpier than she wanted.

"I know the feeling. You..." His voice trailed off as his brows drew together. With his hand on the side of her face, he turned her toward him. "You have dark circles under your eyes. You really didn't sleep well."

No need to tell him about the nightmares. But the concern in his face said he'd probably already guessed.

She offered a smile. "I'll be fine."

"Yes, you will." His kiss was warm and possessive. "I'll be in your bed tonight. If nothing else, I can make sure you're fucked into exhaustion."

"Now that's romantic."

"No romance tonight, baby." He bent down and whispered against her lips. "Tonight, we'll go for raw and dirty."

A heated flush engulfed her. "Mmm. Okay." Her voice came out husky.

Smiling slightly, Holt settled closer, putting an arm behind her back as he studied the field. The young players had divided into two teams, some in dark T-shirts, and some in white to tell them apart. After watching a minute, he said, "Our boy's damn good."

Josie grinned at the pride in Holt's expression. "I worry a bit about that. He's a one-sport kid—he's not interested in playing anything else."

"But he loves books, video games, and motorcycles."

"You males and your bikes." Carson'd been even more enamored with motorcycles after Holt took him on the Harley.

At her dark look, Holt grinned and added, "And he's got a beloved cat and good friends. I wouldn't worry, Josie. He's amazingly well balanced."

She sighed. There it was. No great wisdom, nothing she didn't know, but having someone who loved Carson weigh in? It lightened her worries. "Thanks."

He must have heard the seriousness of her voice, since he turned to study her. Then, he pulled her against him and kissed the top of her head. "You're very welcome."

His voice deepened. "I do require payment for counseling services. Tonight, in fact."

Even though she elbowed him in the ribs, she knew he wasn't joking. He'd demand his "payment" in a fashion that'd leave her in a satisfied, near-comatose state in their bed. Of course, as he'd told her before, he was a Dom and he didn't need excuses to enjoy her whenever he wanted. Why that was so sexy, she didn't know.

"Did you two have your meeting with the principal?" he asked.

"We did," she said grimly. "He and the school board insist the boys pay for the broken classroom window. Brandon's mother will pay for the rest of the classroom since the actual fire was all Brandon's idea and doing."

"Sounds fair enough. Why don't you look happy?"

"The principal wants to suspend the boys, take away their extracurricular sports, and make them do a lot of so-called community service—which seems to amount to free janitorial service. And this will be part of their academic record."

Holt's mouth tightened. "That does seem excessive."

They both watched Carson do a smooth interception and pass to Yukio. Even as Josie cheered, Holt gave a pleased yell, "Way to move, ace!"

Carson turned, and a huge smile appeared on his face before he dashed back into the fray.

Josie's heart warmed. Oh, she did love this man. Both her men.

Leaning against Holt, she tried to remember what they'd been discussing. The school and Carson. "I agree with putting them to work. The rest—not so much. It's their first offense. But what really burns me is that the administration isn't admitting to any fault on their part. And the teacher is still working there."

Appropriating her diet soda, Holt took a sip before handing it back. "You lost me. What fault?"

She frowned, trying to remember what Carson had told Cullen and Holt in the police station. "Carson told you the science teacher was a jerk who picks on the students, right?"

"Right."

"Well, from what Carson said—and talking with the other parents—the science teacher, Jorgeson, is cruelly sarcastic, sexually inappropriate, and racist. He stands too close to the girls and touches them. He makes nasty jokes about girls, minorities, and the slower students. Being an intelligent white boy, Carson didn't have a problem with him—until now—but Juan's been harassed to the point of tears. Ryan, too, because he's mouthy."

Holt frowned. "Didn't the children complain to the authorities?"

"Oh, did they ever, as did their parents. Unfortunately, Jorgeson has been there a couple of decades and is a *respected* instructor. The principal didn't do anything, and since only Jorgeson teaches sixth grade science, the children couldn't transfer to another class."

Holt scrubbed his face. "I missed that, maybe because he didn't pick on Carson."

"Carson was sticking up for his new friends—and other class-mates—in the only way that lay open when the people who should have acted...didn't."

"In that light"—Holt's expression had turned hard—"pun-ishing the kids is wrong."

"That's how I feel. The other boys' parents and I explained it to the principal, but"—anger was a burning knot in her belly— "but he's not admitting he was wrong and that Jorgeson should be fired. I'm not sure what to do."

Holt was keeping an eye on the soccer action, and when Carson booted the ball almost to the other end of the field, he yelled, "Great kick!"

Josie hooted her agreement.

For a couple of minutes, Holt was silent. Then he glanced at Josie. "Kids are always recording stuff on their phones. What do you want to bet there are some videos of the teacher in action?"

Josie blinked. "Hmm. Let's ask Carson."

"We can have him put the word out that kids with recordings should email me a copy, that I'll keep the recording, but delete their email off my system. Also, we should have him tell the chil-dren not to boast about taking or sharing recordings."

"What?"

"Classroom recordings in Florida fall into a gray area of the law." He still looked angry about Jorgeson, but his eyes held a wicked spark. "One that would be difficult to punish."

"What are you thinking?" She poked a finger in his ribs. "Tell me, oh, Master Crusader."

"I'll explain tonight." He wrapped his hand around hers, removing her finger from his ribs, with an admonishing tsk-tsk. "You know, a naughty submissive might find herself strapped to the spanking bench next Friday."

Spanking...bench. At the thought, a wave of heat streaked right through her, and another followed when she saw the way he was watching her.

"Oh, yeah," he murmured. "We'll start with that."

CHAPTER THIRTY

On Wednesday evening, they'd eaten late because Josie and Carson apparently liked waiting for Holt to get home from the hospital. His sweet submissive was spoiling him.

Smiling, Holt wiped down the counters while Carson loaded the dishwasher. After a meal of Josie's shrimp fettuccini, Holt figured he'd better add extra time to his workouts and an extra mile to his morning run. The woman liked to cook—and he liked to eat. If he didn't take preventative action, he'd end up too fat to climb a ladder.

"Hey, Poe." He tossed the cat a piece of leftover shrimp.

As Poe did a perfect two-pawed pounce, Carson laughed—an open happy sound. Almost a week after the house fire, the boy was returning to normal. It helped that Brandon wouldn't be returning to their middle school.

Holt rinsed out the sponge. Since Josie'd cooked, she didn't pull cleanup duty and had gone to finish a scene she was working on. Stella'd bailed since she had her church group.

Good. He and Carson could talk without upsetting the ladies. "So, ace, how much grief are you getting in school these days?"

The boy grimaced as he racked plates in the dishwasher. "I guess Mr. Jorgeson knows who tried to burn his room. He marked all my essay answers way down on the last quiz. Yukio got a 60 percent, too. And we've always gotten As on our tests before."

That fucking teacher. Holt managed to smother a growl. "Are you doing okay with your classmates?"

"Kinda. Some of 'em act friendly, like weird friendly, cuz they like that I did illegal stuff, and..." The big brown eyes showed Carson's confusion.

"And that's not the kind of person you want for a friend?"

"Yeah." Carson brightened. "But Yukio wants me to come over on Friday, and his dad's taking us to that new horror movie. You like horror—you should come. Mom won't go, that's for sure."

Holt tilted his head, realizing he'd acquired a new movie buddy. This parenting job had some good perks. "I'd like that, thanks. Sounds like you haven't lost your friends over this."

"Guess not." Carson snorted. "Maybe. Might only be Ryan, Juan, and Yukio if they suspend us forever.

Damned if he'd let that happen. "Speaking of suspension, my email box is full. I bet I have a bunch of Jorgeson movies."

Carson grinned. "The guys and I spread the word, and everyone's sending you their recordings of him being a jerk. What're you going to do now?"

"First, I'll save everything without any identifying information. Then we'll snip the moments where Jorgeson is out of line and put everything together in a short video."

"We? I get to help?" Carson's face lit.

"Absolutely." He rested his hand on Carson's shoulder. "Fighting the bad guys doesn't always mean violence. This is another method."

"Awesome."

Later, Holt decided that "awesome" wasn't the right word. With each recording, his urge to go for a violent resolution grew. Jorgeson was past due for a beating.

Considering Josie's elevated color and tensed muscles, she was experiencing the same fury.

With an effort, Holt smoothed out his expression and looked at Carson. "You said you have a bit of homework left to do before bed?"

The boy's wrinkled nose was so much like Josie's expression that Holt laughed.

Josie smiled. "Off with you, then. We're done here."

Carson rose and hesitated. "I was mad at Mr. Jorgeson because he's mean and makes kids cry, but I didn't see the girl stuff. How they look when he gets too close or touches. It's kinda worse."

Holt looked at him and nodded. "It is, yes." The boy had a good heart—and the courage to stand up for what he believed.

Josie felt tears rising to the surface and breathed past them. Her son was growing up—and turning into a good man. "It is. Now you'll know when you see it again." She pulled in a breath and added the harder part. "Sometimes it's not only the girls who get targeted that way...so if it happens to you, you'll know to tell me?"

"Yeah, Holt warned me, too." Carson grinned. "I'll just tell him, and he can throw the guy over a car like he did that mugger."

Although Holt's lips quirked, his eyes held satisfaction. "It would be my pleasure. I'll even let you help."

As her boy giggled and trotted off to his room, Josie dropped into Holt's lap and wrapped her arms around his shoulders. Rather than push inconvenient children and women away, he would do anything he could to rescue them. "You are so amazing," she whispered, "and I love you so much."

His brows drew together. He had no clue what he'd done. His arms closed around her.

She leaned her head against his. "We've got enough on this video for any reasonable administration to fire Jorgeson, yet I'm not sure it's enough. The school board has already heard about his behavior from the students and parents."

"True. But physical evidence is more compelling."

"Maybe. Bigoted, white male dumbasses. They probably don't see anything wrong with his behavior."

"You know, you might be right." Holt frowned. "They might not be inclined to rock the boat—or admit they're at fault—without some incentive."

"Incentive? Hmm." She sat up straight. "What if we found a lawyer to educate them that they could be sued or liable or..."

Holt considered. "Yes, that'll work. It will be the perfect one-two punch."

"What will?"

"Threatening their reps and pocketbooks. You're brilliant." Holt kissed her.

She pulled back. "Good to hear, but, Holt, I don't know anyone the school board would listen to."

"You do. But leave it to me, pet. I got this." The lines around his eyes crinkled. "So, little girl, did you finish *your* homework? Is the scene in our book done?"

It wasn't. "You are being so..."

When he lifted his chin slightly, in what Gabi had titled "the Dom look", her stomach dropped.

Suddenly she could feel how her breasts rubbed on his hard chest, and the heat of his powerful hand on her waist. "I..."

"Go finish that chapter you're working on before you get in trouble with your editor. I'll make a few calls. Trust me, Josie."

When he gave her that level steady look, she knew she'd trust him wherever he led her. "I do trust you."

"Ah, for that you've earned a reward," he said softly. "I'll make sure you receive it tonight."

Now all her girl bits were tingling.

Leaning down, she brushed his lips and headed for her office. Her deadline was looming, and she had a chapter to finish.

And maybe when Tigre stepped in front of one of the

reptilian Grestors to save Laurent, she'd let the pretty fire-starter bind up his wound and give him that kiss the two had wanted since the beginning of the book. Josie knew Tigre would be there for Laurent no matter how bad things got.

Because Tigre was just like Holt.

CHAPTER THIRTY-ONE

The middle school's small conference room was air-conditioned to a polar ice cap's temperature. Between the chill and her nerves, Josie was shivering.

She wasn't the only one scared. In the rear of the room, Carson, Yukio, Juan, and Ryan sat in a fearful cluster. Josie and the other parents were seated around the rectangular table. Last night, they'd had a conference call about what recourse they had if the administration decided to be harsh.

Despite trying to look calm, Josie felt her teeth clenching with her frustration. Things were not going well. The science teacher was blatantly targeting Carson and his friends with his venom. Every time she'd talked with the principal about it, he'd blown her off. Sadly, the school board was listening to *him*.

The door opened. His face jowled like a bloodhound, the principal, Mr. Purcell, walked across the room and took a seat at the head of the rectangular table.

"Ladies and gentlemen." When he shook his head, her hand itched to slap the phony expression of concern off his face. "I'm afraid the school board has decided—"

The door opened again.

Josie stared as Master Z strolled in. He wore a white shirt and tie...and the materials and tailoring were as exquisite as that of his usual black club attire.

After him came Gabi in a conservative beige dress and dark brown blazer, then her husband, Marcus, in an impeccably tailored dark gray suit.

Entering last, Holt took a position against the wall, crossing his arms over his chest.

The principal rose to his feet. "Excuse me, but this is a private meeting. If you wish to speak with me, please talk with my secretary and—"

"I believe we have the correct room," Master Z said. "I'm Dr. Zachary Grayson, a psychologist...specializing in children."

Purcell shifted his weight uneasily. "Dr. Grayson, I know of you, of course. Your research is well respected in academic circles."

"That's good to hear," Z said smoothly and turned. "I'd like to introduce Gabrielle Renard, an FBI Victim Specialist, and Marcus Atherton, one of our state attorneys."

The principal's color faded slightly.

Carson slipped over to kneel beside Josie and surreptitiously slipped his hand into hers. "What's going on?" he whispered.

She bent and whispered with only a breath of sound, "Something Holt arranged to go with the video we made."

"Holt did this? Oh, man, the principal is screwed." The hope and confidence in Carson's voice lifted Josie's heart.

As her boy slipped back to his friends, Josie turned to Holt and mouthed *thank you*.

He winked.

Purcell resumed his seat as if establishing his territory. "Why are you here?"

Rather than taking a seat, Master Z leaned a hip against the low bookshelf to the right of Purcell. Josie almost laughed.

Owning his space—and standing. Had he learned the tricks of taking control from being a psychologist or being a Dom?

Master Z answered, his tone even. "The school has received numerous complaints about a teacher, Mr. Jorgeson, but ignored them with the excuse that the reports came from students."

Having taken a seat at the table, Gabi made a low sound of disgust. "When victims are dismissed as unimportant by those in authority, it can be very damaging."

Master Z continued, "Since their reasonable grievances were ignored, the children moved to another method to protest."

Purcell's face reddened with his indignation. "Vandalism isn't another method, it's—"

"Illegal," Z said. "I'm aware. Is ignoring severe, persistent abuse also illegal?"

Josie's eyes widened at the edge in his smooth voice. If she were the principal, she'd be crawling under the table. Around the table, the other parents had frozen.

Marcus's blue eyes were colder than ice, and anger hardened his slow drawl. "I do believe under federal civil rights laws, schools are obligated to address such conduct…as well as conduct that creates a hostile environment, which detrimentally impacts a student's ability to benefit from the opportunities offered by a school, as well as abusive conduct based on a student's race, color, sex, and/or disability."

The principal flinched. "There…there is no proof of that."

"It appears that the students, having been ignored over and over"—Z's grim tone was chilling—"took matters into their own hands. And phones." He glanced at Holt.

Holt placed a portable projector on the table and set his phone into it. Displayed on the blank white wall, the video opened with the teacher standing beside a seated blonde student, so close his groin was almost in her face.

"Invasion of personal space," Gabi murmured.

The clip changed to him, his finger belligerently pointing in a brown-skinned boy's face. "Can't figure out the carbon cycle? Maybe you should get your tail back to Me-hi-ko where you belong."

Another clip showed him fingering a girl's curly hair as she cringed away.

"How can you be so stupid?" This one showed Jorgeson leaning down, his glaring face no more than two inches from Juan's. The child looked terrified. "Can't be bothered to do your homework? Because you're stupid. Stupid and lazy."

Clip after clip flicked by. Different students. Different classes.

Purcell said faintly, "Recordings in the classroom aren't allowed. Florida has a wiretap law."

"Wiretap statutes apply when a person has a reasonable expectation of privacy, not in a classroom," Marcus said firmly. "But I can understand why you wouldn't want this video made available to the news media...or playing on Facebook."

The principal went totally white.

Master Z said, "I viewed this recording several times. The instructor's behavior is blatantly abusive. There is not only bullying, but also predatory sexual behavior, as well as racism and bigotry. You've opened your school to a wealth of civil suits."

Marcus crossed his arms over his chest. "Criminal ones as well. I can take this to a jury, sir, and I can win."

"The teacher has to go." Gabi gave the principal an icy stare. "The students in his classes are victims of abuse. You will see that they get counseling—at the school's cost."

"Yes." The principal's shoulders sagged. Then his mouth flattened. "But whoever took the recording is—"

With a laugh, Holt turned the projector off. "I think about half of Jorgeson's students recorded him at one time or another, especially after they and their parents were ignored because the school officials needed 'proof'. Since you asked for proof, a court might see your demand as giving permission to obtain it."

The principal's mouth closed. After a second, he pointed to the boys. "Nonetheless, they committed vandalism."

"They did." Josie squared her shoulders. She, Holt, and the other parents had discussed what would happen if they reached this point. The fight was in her corner now. "It's appalling that children in this school have learned that the authorities who should have been their advocates were, instead, their adversaries" —the principal winced—"still...we agree they're old enough to have considered the ramifications before acting. Doing the right thing can still come with consequences."

"Exactly." The principal started to look more cheerful. The *asshole*.

"So we think the children should work with the maintenance crew in washing windows since that was what they broke. At minimum wage. They will work until they've repaid their portion of the window's replacement."

Purcell nodded and then frowned. "And?"

"They broke it. They'll work to pay off the replacement cost," Josie said firmly. "Punishing them further because you and the school board failed to protect vulnerable minors from an abusive adult? Absolutely not."

A tiny whisper came from her son, "Go, *Mom*."

The principal looked at her, at the three "experts", and took in the resolute expressions of the other parents. After a long moment, he scowled. "All right."

He glanced at Holt. "The recordings...I don't suppose..."

Holt simply stared at him...and pocketed his phone.

Master Z looked at Josie and inclined his head an infinitesimal amount. Gabi winked, and Marcus gave her a small smile before they all headed for the door.

With a smile back, Josie felt her muscles start to relax.

Carson was whispering with his friends when one of the strangers stopped in front of them. The doctor one. The guy had black hair with gray at the sides. Gray eyes.

To Carson's surprise, the man crouched down. "You're Carson, I believe?"

Carson nodded.

When the guy had been talking to old Purcell, he'd looked really scary. Now, he smiled and looked different, almost as nice as Holt.

"Yukio, Juan, Ryan?"

His gaze showed he could tell them apart, and the others nodded.

"Sometimes when children go through tough times, it can be a struggle afterward. My job is helping kids work through what's happened. Help them figure out what they can do now, what they might have done better, and how to talk with parents or friends about it. Or anything."

Carson narrowed his eyes. One thing still bothered him more than the rest. "How 'bout figuring out when someone isn't really a friend."

"Ah." The gray eyes softened. "We all get played sometimes, Carson. However, I can show you a few things to watch for that will cut down on the chances."

"Yeah?" Ryan leaned forward. "Can I come, too?" Of them all, Ryan had felt the worst about Brandon's behavior and...betrayal. They'd been friends a long time.

"Yes, Ryan." The man tilted his head. "Since you all went through this together, I think it might go well if you all visited me together."

Yukio stilled. "You're a psychologist." He shook his head. "I don't think my parents can pay for something like—"

"Josie is a friend, and this is a way I can help," the man said gently. "There won't be a charge for any of you. I'll talk to your parents next, but I wanted to see how you were doing."

"See how screwed up we are," Ryan muttered.

The man's quick laugh was almost as good as Holt's.

Carson grinned.

"Are we screwed up?" Juan asked, almost in a whisper.

"Not even close." The psych person smiled slightly. "But you could be more comfortable about what's happened. I can help with that."

Comfortable. Carson nodded. When he thought about the fire and Brandon, it was like scraping his fingernail over a cut. "Yeah." He looked at the others. Would they call him a pussy like Brandon had? "I want to—if you guys will."

But they were all nodding. Ryan's eyes were red.

Carson let out the breath that he'd been holding. *All right.*

CHAPTER THIRTY-TWO

Freshly showered after a rousing backyard soccer game, Holt opened the dresser drawer for a clean T-shirt. Soon after the fire, Josie'd cleaned out half her dresser and closet space for him, because he'd pretty much ended up living over here. When his lease was up, he'd move in formally. When they'd discussed it with Carson and Stella, the boy had cheered. And Stella had made Holt a huge cake to take to the firehouse. It'd been her way of saying she approved. Damn, he loved this family.

"Mo-o-om, what're they going to do? Are they going to stick me?"

Pulling on his shirt, Holt chuckled at the question coming from Carson's bedroom. It was good the boy'd returned to being an exasperating pre-teen.

Sitting on their bed, Josie grinned at Holt and called to Carson, "The lab will swab the inside of your cheek. No needles."

"Holt says it's a syringe, not a needle." After the grumpy correction, Carson kept going. "Why are we doing this, anyway? I already know ol' Everett's my father, and he knows, too. He just doesn't wanna say so."

Josie closed her eyes. She was still sensitive about Everett and his rejection of Carson.

Holt wasn't sensitive at all. He gripped her nape and put their foreheads together. "I got this, pet."

Her relieved look was all the reward he needed. Holt headed down the hall, pleased he was here for this discussion. "You're right, ace. Everett doesn't want to admit the truth."

In his debris-strewn bedroom, Carson sat cross-legged on the floor. His mouth twisted into a lopsided frown. "Because he's a douche."

Smothering a grin at the word, Holt joined the cat on the bed. "Hey, Poe."

After a narrow-eyed stare, the cat stalked onto Holt's lap. Running his hand down Poe's soft fur, Holt turned to Carson. "You asked about the DNA test. It's like this: In the eyes of the law, each person must take responsibility for his actions, even if he didn't intend for something to happen. Like, if you break a window, you pay for the window."

Carson gave him a wry grin. "Guess I know that one."

"Yep. You had a nice straightforward consequence. Things can get complicated though." At breakfast, they'd discussed a Tampa news story about a drunk driving his pickup through a restaurant window. That'd be a good example. "If you run your car into a restaurant, you pay for the building as well as the hospital costs for whoever got hurt and their bills until they return to work."

Carson's eyes widened. "You mean that boozer'll have to take care of everybody he hurt."

"Exactly."

Josie stepped into the room, taking up a position against the wall. But she didn't jump into the discussion.

Still up to him, then. Holt stroked the cat. "Now, let's say sex is like driving a car."

Choking on a laugh, Josie murmured, "There's a unique comparison."

Carson's expression held puzzlement.

"Just go along with me, children." Holt hoped to hell he could say this right...without getting into a birds-and-the-bees lecture. "Sex is something you choose to do, and like with everything else, there can be consequences. One result can be a baby."

Brows together, Carson sat on the floor and pulled on a sock. "What's the consequence for making a baby?"

"The mother and father are responsible for the child until he reaches eighteen. Even if a parent isn't involved in the hands-on raising, well, a kid still eats food, needs clothes, all that stuff."

"Oh." Carson studied the other sock in his hands. "Everett should help, like, pay for my food?"

"He should have been doing that all along, yes."

Carson kept turning over the sock in his hands. Silently.

Not good. "Tell me what you're thinking, ace."

"I eat a lot. Maybe...firefighters probably don't make much money. I could... I don't need to eat as much."

Fuck. That sure as hell hadn't been his point. Holt held up his hand to let Josie know he was still at bat. She—bless her—let him take his swing.

"Money isn't a problem for me, Carson." Holt set the cat to one side and dropped to the floor beside the boy. "I earned a lot of money when I was modeling, chose good investments, and I make a good salary now."

Carson's head was still bowed.

Holt slung an arm over his shoulders and pulled him close. "You're my kid, dumbass," he said lightly. "Even if I didn't have money, I'd still share you with your mom. I'd just work harder to help support you."

"Then...why?" Carson had big eyes the color of chocolate. Puppy-dog-eyes that could turn a guy's heart inside out. Perhaps it was best Josie'd had him up to now. With Holt, the boy would've been spoiled rotten.

"We're not going after Everett for the money. It's because he should be held responsible for his actions." And it sucked that retroactive payments were capped at two years and the statute of limitations had passed for criminal charges. Holt would have preferred to send the asshole to jail. *Ah, well.* "We plan to dump whatever he coughs up into your college fund."

"Oh." After a second, Carson wrinkled his freckled nose. "College?"

"Yep. Call it a consequence for being so damn smart."

Carson started to grin. "Did you call me *dumbass* in front of Mom?"

A grumbling sound came from Josie. "He did."

"Just had to point that out, didn't you, brat?" Holt tipped Carson over on his back and dug his fingers into the kid's ribs until giggles filled the room.

Fuck, he loved this kid.

A few minutes later, they were heading out the door when the house phone rang. "Great timing." With a grunt of exasperation, Holt grabbed it. "Yes?"

A pause.

"Ah, do I have Josie Collier's home?" The woman's voice with a light Southern accent was familiar, but he couldn't quite recall whom it belonged to.

"That's correct. May I ask who's calling?" After the fire, they'd had more than a few calls from reporters, and Holt took point on those whenever possible.

"Of course. I'm Pamela, Everett Lanning's soon-to-be ex-wife." As Holt motioned Josie close enough to listen, the woman continued with a thread of cynical humor running through her tone. "I've spent the last couple weeks explaining to Timothy and Britney how their father could have a son we didn't know about."

Holt winced. "Ouch."

"Oh, yes. However, the children are thrilled they have a half-brother. As far as they—and I—are concerned, a sibling is a sibling. Would y'all be amenable to letting them get to know each other?"

With a wide grin, Josie nodded.

Holt looked down and saw Carson had moved close enough to hear as well. The kid looked as pleased as his mother—because his heart was just as big.

"We look forward to seeing you all." Holt ruffled his son's hair and smiled. It seemed his family was expanding again.

CHAPTER THIRTY-THREE

Two weeks later, Josie sat in the back seat of Max's car beside Rainie. Leaning forward, Josie tapped Zuri's shoulder. "You only said out for drinks. So where exactly are we going?"

"Oh, somewhere nice," Zuri said.

Max's smile flashed, but he didn't answer.

In the back seat, Rainie giggled and stayed silent.

Suspicious, Josie frowned at the streets going by and then straightened. She recognized this area. In fact...

Max pulled the car to the curb in front of The Highlands.

Josie stared. "You've got to be kidding. You do know I used to work here."

"We know—and it's a great place." Zuri slid out, not waiting for Max to open her door. "Won't it be fun to be a customer for a change?"

"Hmm. Maybe." Back at the Highlands. Where she'd been fired. Shaking her head, Josie followed.

Well, at least she was dressed to be a customer. And hey, she looked pretty damn good, too. Her faux black leather bralette pushed up her small breasts to create rather impressive cleavage. Her wide-legged black velvet pants and black stilettos added a

415

touch of sophistication. "You know, I wish Holt could have seen me. I look pretty sexy."

"You do." Rainie grinned. "Although, I've noticed two-thirds of our work is wasted on a guy. They get the overall impression —*oooo, cleavage. Oh, short skirts. Red lips.* But it takes another woman to notice things like the way your gold choker matches your earrings and your nail polish."

Zuri nodded a fashion-buyer's approval. "The gold and black combination is very classy."

"Holt gave me the choker and earrings last night." Josie ran her fingers over the necklace. "He said he wanted to remind me of who my Dom is." Then he'd reinforced his words in the most intimate way possible.

"Masters are so possessive. That's why my Dragon Doms gave me this bracelet." Zuri lifted her wrist. The diamond-studded cuff-style bracelet was shaped like a dragon.

"Yep, that's why." Max walked over, tilted Zuri's head up, and planted a kiss on her lips. "So remember that and behave yourself, princess. I'll be back for you later."

"Behave? Pffft." Laughing, Zuri linked her arm with Josie's, grabbed Rainie's hand, and pulled them toward the door.

As they walked in, Josie tried to view the place as a customer. The room felt like an old English library with dark wood tables and leather furniture. The left wall with the gas fireplace was aged red brick. Behind the bar, shelf after shelf of gleaming bottles climbed to the ceiling. A rolling ladder made it possible for bartenders to access the top shelves.

"They're here!"

At the cheering from the right, Josie stopped dead. She turned.

The round table held...women from the Shadowlands. Josie glanced at Zuri and Rainie. "Uh... Am I crashing a party or something?"

All Zuri'd said was that she and Rainie were taking Josie out on Thursday night. For drinks.

"It's not a party." Zuri tugged her forward. "The Shadowkittens try to go out every month or so for rowdy times."

Shadowkittens. The word referred to the submissives and slaves of the official Shadowland Masters. Josie blinked. Holt was a Master which meant...she was one of the Shadowkittens. Warmth spilled through her like the first sip of aged whisky.

The table held exactly three empty chairs. They'd been expected. Rainie and Zuri sat down on Josie's right beside brunette, bubbly Sally who'd been at Anne's barbecue with her two Doms.

Andrea, Cullen's submissive, was across the table. "We're so glad you could make it."

On Josie's left was redheaded Linda, Master Sam's woman. She patted Josie's hand. "You're looking much better. Did everything get resolved?"

"It did—thanks partly to your advice." Josie gave her a grateful smile. "You know, having trouble with a man is bad enough, but adding my son into the mix made it awful."

"You're right. A child can add a whole new level of distress to arguments." Across the table, Kari looked at Josie with obvious worry. "Two children would be even worse. Maybe Dan and I don't want another baby."

"You have a good point." It might make for a bumpy ride, but Josie still wanted to give Holt a baby or two. Smiling, she asked Jessica, "How about you? Are you and Master Z planning another child? Sophia's simply adorable."

"When did you meet Sophia?" Rainie asked Josie. "Wait, I know." She pointed at Jessica. "You're starting her out real early in the Shadowlands. Doing Domme training."

"Sophia has the Domme attitude already. No training needed." Jessica laughed. "Josie met our small bundle of trouble last weekend when Anne brought baby Wyatt to visit. Josie ran upstairs to see them before her shift."

Josie snorted. "And that was a mistake. When I was late getting back downstairs to the bar, Master Nolan had to fill in, and he wasn't pleased."

As the table of women made sympathetic sounds, Josie shook her head at the memory...

She had raised the pass-through and stopped just inside the bar space. Holt was pouring a beer for someone. She smiled. Would there ever come a time when her heart didn't do a happy spin at the sight of him?

Unfortunately, another Master was also behind the bar. Master Nolan. Doing her job. Because she hadn't been here. She felt a stab of guilt.

Nolan gave her a hard stare. "You're late, sugar."

"I'm so sorry." With a different Master, she'd have tried a funny rejoinder, but this Dom kind of scared her. Instead, she employed one of Carson's techniques—blame the authorities. "It's Mistress Anne's fault. She was in a bad mood and wanted advice on how to breast-feed when holding down a job. She wouldn't let me leave until I explained everything." Josie shook her head. "I've heard stories about her, and...I didn't want her annoyed with me."

Master Nolan's expression didn't change, but his black eyes lit with amusement. "Probably a wise choice, although now I'm annoyed with you."

Josie took a step back.

Laughing, Holt walked over. He ran his hands up and down her arms and gave her a swift kiss. "Relax, pet. Nolan has to ask my permission to beat on you."

"Really? You mean I can sass off to anyone and be safe?"

Even as she heard Nolan snort, Holt chuckled. "No. It means I get the pleasure of spanking your cute little ass."

And, later that night, he'd done exactly that. The brute.

Josie grinned at the women around the table. "I suffered for it, but at least, I got to meet Sophia—and Anne's baby. Wyatt looks as if he'll grow to be as big as Ben."

"And he has Anne's hair. He'll be tall, dark, and muscular." Sally tapped her chest. "Be still my heart."

Zuri giggled. "Ben'd wanted to name the baby *George*—for George Patton—but Anne talked him out of it, thank heavens. Wyatt George Haugen doesn't sound too bad."

"Did the Mistress *talk* him out of it or threaten his *manhood?*" Kari asked.

"Huh." Zuri looked intrigued. "I should have asked for more details."

"To Wyatt George Haugen." Sally raised her glass and stopped. "Wait. You guys don't have alcohol. How wrong is that?" She lifted her hand as Frederica, the head barmaid, approached.

"What can I get you ladies?" Frederica's eyes widened. "Josie? Josie, tell me you're coming back to us!" Setting her tray on the table, she hugged Josie hard.

Josie hugged her back. How had she not realized how much she missed the gang here? "Frederica, it's good to see you."

"You are returning, aren't you? Oh my heavenly stars, it's been horrible since you left. That girl can't pour a decent drink to save her life, and I'm the one who has to listen to the complaints."

Under the table, Zuri kicked Josie. "Told you."

Ouch. Josie started to answer, then stopped as the manager stopped at the table.

"Josie, great timing." His smile was big...and as fake as his look of regret had been when he fired her. "We'll soon have an open bartender position and would love to have you back. Our clientele has been asking where you went."

Grumbles came from the tables around them, along with a "demanding her return, more like" from one of the men.

She'd been missed. The knowledge was gratifying. "I—"

"Return here?" Andrea interrupted. "*Dios,* no. No way will you steal our bartender away."

A chorus of agreement came from the Shadowkittens.

Jessica lifted her chin and stared at the manager. "I'm afraid that Josie belongs to *us* now—and *we* know how to appreciate her."

Warmth swept through Josie.

The manager's shoulders slumped, but he knew better than to argue with the bar's clientele. "Of course." He gave her another false smile. "Good to see you."

As he walked away, Frederica heaved an unhappy sigh. "Damn. Still, I'm glad you landed on your feet, even if you're sorely missed here. Now, what can I get you?"

"Thank you, Frederica." Josie looked at the others. "What are y'all drinking?"

"Pitchers of Vieux Carre," Sally said blithely.

"Seriously?" Boy, the Shadowkittens didn't mess around. The New Orleans cocktail was seriously potent. "Ooookay, then." Josie looked at Frederica. "Can you start me a tab and..."

"No, Josie," Linda said. The other women were shaking their heads.

Jessica snorted. "We've tried to pay, but our Do—men always deal with the bill."

"That'd be nice, but Holt is working tonight, so I—"

"Doesn't matter," Zuri said. "None of them will let you pay."

"Bossy buggers," Josie muttered, making the group laugh.

"You have a man?" Frederica beamed as Josie nodded. "I can't wait to meet him. You deserve someone wonderful."

"She really does," Rainie said. "And he is."

"Will y'all be having the Vieux Carre then?" Frederica asked. When Josie, Rainie, and Zuri nodded, she said, "I'll bring more pitchers and glasses then."

"Perfect, thank you." Linda smiled at Frederica. "Could you also order us some stuffed mushrooms and a cheese platter, please?"

"Oh, also tater tots. Please," Andrea said. "I love them."

"A New Orleans drink—and tater tots. That's wonderfully

perverse." Rainie looked up at Frederica. "Can you make the tots a double order, please?"

"Got it." Frederica patted Josie's shoulder and headed for the bar.

When the barmaid handed in the order for more pitchers of the time-consuming drink, the manager's poor niece looked ready to cry.

Josie mentally sent her some calming thoughts, then settled back to enjoy being on the receiving end of food and drinks.

Alcohol and the Shadowkittens. Josie remembered being on the other side of the bar, watching the Shadowkittens partying, and envying them for their joyful comradeship. As the evening went on, she basked in being part of the group.

A long while later that night, she realized she was giggling. Giggling. *Her?* "Oh, God, I'm *drunk*."

Zuri busted out laughing.

"You really are." Jessica grinned. "We *have* been here a while, after all."

"But I almost never get toasted." Josie touched her lips. Definitely some numbness going on.

"Is Carson taken care of?" Linda asked.

"You're such a mom, but yes, he is. He's with my great-aunt tonight." She eyed the table of women. No one was sober. "I asked Holt if I was being over-cautious, and he laughed. He knew y'all would be here, didn't he?"

"Of course he did. And that we'd be drinking." Kari raised her glass in a toast. "Zane is with my mama."

"Sophia is with her grandmother." Jessica clinked her glass against Kari's.

"However, it *is* getting late, and I have to open the store tomorrow." Linda owned a small beachfront store. "It's probably time to call it quits."

"I suppose. We all have to work tomorrow." Rainie pointed a finger at Josie. "At least, you don't have to go in until evening."

"I'm spoiled that way." However, she planned to start her new book tomorrow. Stopping now would be wise. "I'm going to call for a taxi. Do any of y'all need a ride?"

Jessica looked around the room, and her gaze landed on something behind Josie. She lifted hand in a hail. "Nope, we're good. And if you call for a taxi, you might get in trouble."

Josie frowned. "You mean one of the Masters will give me a ride? That'd be—"

"*This* Master will give you a ride," Holt murmured, his resonant voice a heady caress along her nerve endings. His arms came around her from behind, and his warm cheek rubbed against hers.

"You're here!" She tipped her head back and got herself an upside-down kiss. When her head stopped spinning, she saw the rest of the Shadowlands Masters claiming their women. "I thought you were working late."

"I did. I think you lost track of time." Holt ran a finger down her cheek. "You're tipsy, pet." His wicked smile flashed. "Perhaps I'll take advantage of you while you are."

"Why...you...you..." *Uh-uh, don't call the Dom a pervert.* When his steely blue gaze met hers, she clamped her lips shut, remembering the last time she'd called him a name. How his callused hand had felt dealing out each stinging spank on her bare bottom...and afterward, how hard she'd come.

When she didn't finish her sentence, laughter lightened his eyes.

After helping her stand, he held her at arms-length. His gaze took her in, head to toes, and lingered on the bralette. "Jesus, if I'd seen you wearing this, you'd never have made it out of the house."

As his knuckles brushed the inside curves of her breasts, the heat in his gaze sent tingles through her everywhere.

"Get a room, you two." Arm around Sally, Vance grinned at them.

Holt chuckled and straightened.

As a group, everyone rose and started collecting jackets and purses.

And then she heard a phone ringing.

"It's your cell, pet." Holt picked up her purse.

She swiped the ANSWER button. "Hello?"

"Josie. I know it's late, but I just finished reading your new story. Let me tell you—" Sara continued to talk, her New York accent thick, her speech rapid-fire.

With Holt's hand on her shoulder, Josie listened, unable to get in more than a word or two. "Really? You did? Really?"

Tears filled her eyes, and despite her blurred vision, she could see that everyone in her group was frowning.

She shut off the call. "That—"

"Are you all right? What's wrong? Who made you cry?" Jessica looked ready to bitch-slap someone...if she could manage to aim. It looked as if Master Z was all that was keeping her upright.

Linda took Josie's hand. "Can we help?"

Beside her, Holt had his arm around her waist. "What's the matter?"

"I'm happy. These're happy tears." Josie swiped at her face. "That was my editor. She'd just finished reading my new manuscript and was so thrilled with the story that she didn't want to wait to tell me."

There was a second of surprise, and then everyone broke into cheers and congratulations.

Josie couldn't keep from beaming. She'd never had friends like these. Never felt so much a part of a group.

Smiling, Holt gave her a squeeze. "Of course she'd love it. You're an awesome author."

God, she loved this man.

"Did she say anything about those battle scenes we choreographed with the dolls?" Holt asked, shooting a grin at Zuri who'd made the costumes.

Josie laughed. "Actually, what she really liked was...the romance. Laurent and Tigre falling in love."

Holt tilted his head, brows together. "You added a romance?"

"I did." She put her arms around him. "It's your fault, Master Holt," she said, not even trying to lower her voice. "You made me believe in romance. In love."

And the story had changed and deepened when she'd learned to listen to her heart. When she—and her heroine—had opened up and trusted.

He stared at her for a moment and then rubbed his cheek against hers. His voice was smoother than any whisky in the bar as he murmured, "Do you have any idea how much I fucking love you?"

"Me too, you, Master Holt." As she went up on tiptoes to kiss him, she knew—totally knew—that their romance would end in a happy-ever-after.

ALSO BY CHERISE SINCLAIR

Edge of the Enforcer

Master of Freedom

Master of Solitude

I Will Not Beg

The Wild Hunt Legacy

Hour of the Lion

Winter of the Wolf

Eventide of the Bear

Leap of the Lion

Healing of the Wolf

Heart of the Wolf

Sons of the Survivalist Series

Not a Hero

Lethal Balance

What You See

Soar High

Standalone Books

The Dom's Dungeon

The Starlight Rite

ABOUT THE AUTHOR

Cherise Sinclair is a *New York Times* and *USA Today* bestselling author of emotional, suspenseful romance. She loves to match up devastatingly powerful males with heroines who can hold their own against the subtle—and not-so-subtle—alpha male pressure.

Fledglings having flown the nest, Cherise, her beloved husband, an eighty-pound lap-puppy, and one fussy feline live in the Pacific Northwest where nothing is cozier than a rainy day spent writing.